AGE OF VAMPIRES

RAVAGED
SOULS

CAROLINE PECKHAM
SUSANNE VALENTI

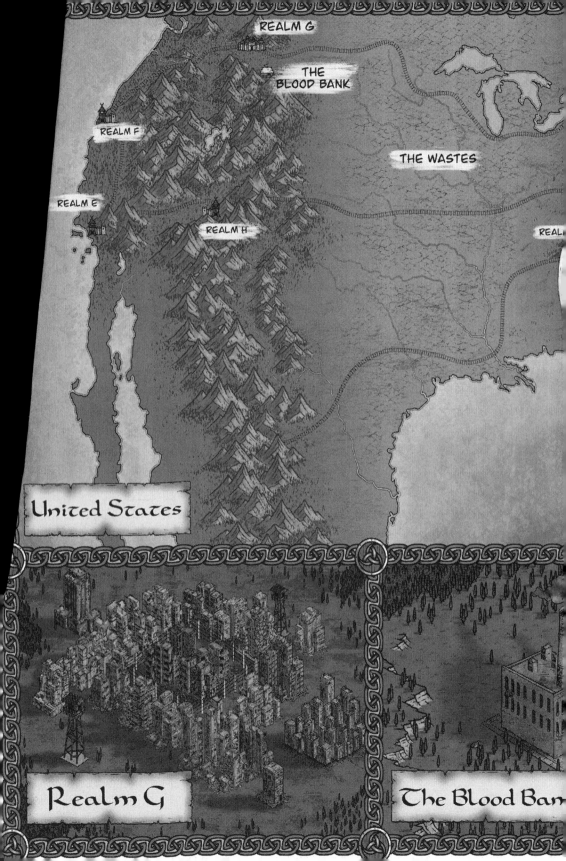

REALM A

NEW YORK
(BELVEDERE CASTLE)

REALM B

REALM C

New York

Belvedere
Castle

Interior Formatting & Design by Wild Elegance Formatting
Map Design by Fred Kroner
Artwork by Stella Colorado

ISBN: 978-1-916926-23-3

Ravaged Souls/Caroline Peckham & Susanne Valenti – 2nd ed.

This book is dedicated to the pheasants who roam our parents' garden while we're writing and peek in at us through the window.
May you live long and healthy lives, Alejandro and Fernando.
Squaaaaaaawk.

TRIGGER WARNING:

Please be aware that this book contains sexual assault and coerced sexual behaviour.

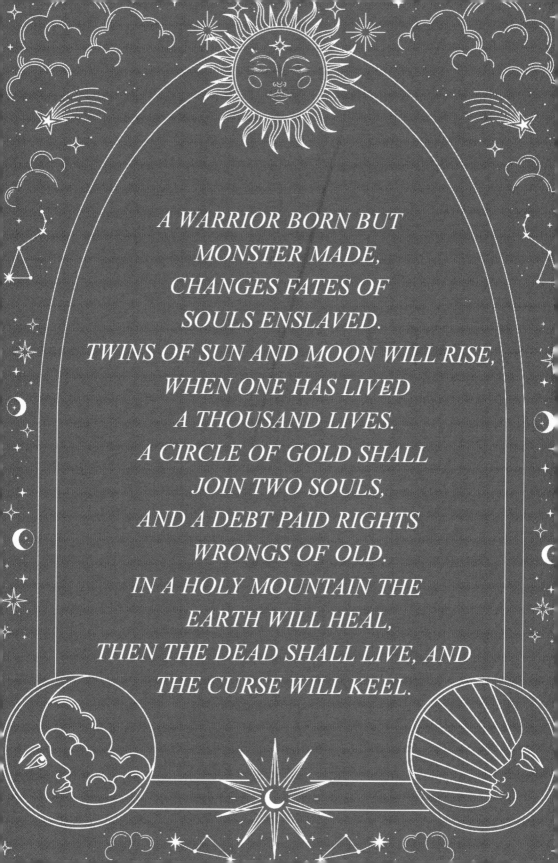

A WARRIOR BORN BUT
MONSTER MADE,
CHANGES FATES OF
SOULS ENSLAVED.
TWINS OF SUN AND MOON WILL RISE,
WHEN ONE HAS LIVED
A THOUSAND LIVES.
A CIRCLE OF GOLD SHALL
JOIN TWO SOULS,
AND A DEBT PAID RIGHTS
WRONGS OF OLD.
IN A HOLY MOUNTAIN THE
EARTH WILL HEAL,
THEN THE DEAD SHALL LIVE, AND
THE CURSE WILL KEEL.

MONTANA

CHAPTER ONE

I was divided from Erik Belvedere for the second time since he'd claimed my heart. The first time, I'd been walking away from my captor, but the second, I'd been ripped away from the man I had fallen for completely, from all his bright edges right down to the dark shadow of his soul.

It struck me how much I'd changed since I'd first met him. I'd tried so hard to get away from him. I'd wanted nothing more than to escape his clutches. But now, being away from him shattered me.

I was his.

He was mine.

And the idea of losing him made me feel as weak as if a thousand suns were beating down on my back.

The helicopter flew on through the darkness, away from Valentina's influence over the weather. The ride became smoother as the harsh wind fell away and an eerie stillness fell over the world beyond the windows.

Callie rested her head against my shoulder, her eyes pinned on the dark veil of clouds encasing the night sky. I could feel her loss as heavily as my own. We were combined in our grief, our pain. I could hear the persistent pounding of her heart and was sure mine would be beating as fiercely if I had still been human.

I twisted the wedding band on my finger as I carved my way through the depths of my despair and searched for my strength. We were all lost, fleeing from the city with no real plan in mind. Fabian wanted us to keep running, to charge the helicopter in Baltimore and head even further south. But the more distance we put between us and Erik, the more I feared we'd never get him back. How could we just leave him and Magnar in the arms of Valentina?

Maybe we were outnumbered, but we couldn't just allow her to keep them as her slaves. The longer she held them, the more unspeakable things she could do to them. And I didn't think it was their deaths she desired.

My chest clenched tightly. Had she already taken my husband to her bed? Had he delighted in her skin against his under her influence? Or was he trapped inside his own body, aware of the things she made him do?

My throat constricted and I shut my eyes as I tried to will away the vile images flitting through my head.

If you have laid one finger on him, Valentina, I won't stop until I cast you from this world.

"By the gods, I'm *starving*," Julius groaned from the seat opposite me.

I opened my eyes, frowning at him. "How can you be hungry right now?"

"I eat when I'm emotional," he said with a hint of a smile. But I could see the ache in his eyes; he was trying to act normal, but I was sure he was as cut up about losing his brother as I was about losing Erik.

"You eat when you're not emotional too." Callie sat upright and a shimmer of resilience glinted in her gaze. "So you never actually stop eating."

"I have to eat to maintain the muscles of my god-like body." He gestured to himself, but I couldn't summon a smile.

Clarice glanced at him with an eyeroll.

"There'll be food at the army base," Fabian muttered, not drawing his gaze from the window.

14

Miles shared a tense look with Warren, revealing their own hunger. After my fight with Erik, I couldn't deny my own thirst was rising. And the scent of the slayers' blood was painfully alluring. More so than any of the humans I'd encountered in Realm A.

Julius glared around at the Belvederes, seeming to catch on to that fact. "There had better be blood there too. If one of you even looks at my neck, I will not hesitate to kill you."

"There'll be blood at the base too," Fabian growled. "But I might be tempted to bite you if you don't shut the fuck up."

Julius snarled and the tension in the helicopter rose dramatically.

"Stop it," I sighed. "You could at least try to make some effort with each other. We're stuck together for the foreseeable future and if we're going to get Erik and Magnar b-"

"We're not doing anything of the sort," Fabian snapped at me, and my upper lip peeled back on instinct. "We run. That's all we can do right now."

"You can keep running if you like, but I won't," I said firmly.

Callie nodded her agreement, brushing her fingers over Fury in her lap as she glared at Fabian. "Magnar wouldn't leave me behind and I won't leave him."

"I'm with them," Julius added, leaning back in his seat. He stretched his arms wide, not-so- accidentally elbowing Clarice in the face, and she shoved him away from her with a snarl.

"This helicopter is suffocating," she muttered.

"We're not far now," Danielle called from the cockpit, throwing us a glance over her shoulder.

"Good," Fabian said, his eyes drifting to Callie. The ring's influence may have been holding off the bond between them right now, but he was still looking at her as if he cared. "I can't let you go after them."

"You're not the boss of me," Callie bit at him, and I hoped we'd be landing soon to get some space between them.

"Let it go, Fabian," Miles urged. "The twins are right; we can't leave Erik in Valentina's hands."

"It's not like I want that," Fabian said, his tone softening as he addressed his brother. "But it would be foolish to go after him now

15

when Valentina has an army of biters to stop us. How could we possibly win?"

No one had an answer to that and a sullen silence fell over us again. I didn't want to accept that saving Erik and Magnar wasn't an option right now. But Fabian had a point which none of us could deny. Even Julius seemed to give in as he rested his head back against his seat with a miserable expression.

"We'll regroup when we land," Miles said eventually and Warren nodded, though no one else did.

"Ten minutes," Danielle called and relief swept through me at the thought of getting out of this thing.

Callie turned to me with a faint frown. "Are you hungry too?" she breathed and my fangs tingled in response to her words.

"I'm fine," I said lightly, not wanting to admit to how much her blood called to me right now. I'd had a bottle last night, but it seemed it hadn't been enough to keep me sated.

She nodded vaguely and turned her attention to our mother's ring on her hand. "How far do you think it is to the holy mountain?" she murmured and I felt everyone's attention swinging to her.

"I don't know," I whispered.

"If we take this there, maybe we can end the curse," she suggested, her eyes glittering with hope.

"That's not a terrible idea," Julius said thoughtfully.

"Why? What's with the ring?" Miles asked, pushing a hand into his smooth blond locks.

"It's Andvari's ring," Callie explained. "Erik thought it might be the same one he was looking for when your parents stole the god's treasure."

Miles's mouth parted and Warren shifted excitedly in his seat.

"Too much guesswork," Fabian said, extinguishing the hopeful moment. "We can't be sure of anything. It's not worth heading to some mountain on the off-chance it might solve the prophecy."

I grumbled my annoyance. "Are you just going to shit on every idea we have?"

"I'm only being the voice of reason," he replied coolly.

"More like the voice of a Debbie Downer," Julius jibed.

Fabian glared at him. "Keep your tongue still if it can't offer us anything useful."

"And you're being *so* useful by trying to make decisions for all of us," Julius snarled.

The helicopter dropped sharply and my heart lurched in my chest as we made a rapid descent towards the ground. A long line of lights stood on the horizon and as we sailed over them, I could just make out a large square of four walls below us with a lookout tower on each corner.

"Finally," I breathed in relief as the helicopter landed at the heart of the military base with a gentle thump.

A group of Elite started running toward us with their guns raised and my stomach knotted as they took aim.

Fabian pulled the door wide, exiting onto the courtyard without a moment's hesitation. The second the Elite spotted him, they lowered their guns and bowed low.

The other royals followed Fabian out and the Elite glanced between them in surprise. They were dressed in dark uniforms with huge swords strapped to their backs and even more guns at their hips. Despite my past feelings about vampires, it was reassuring to find some strong allies here. If they helped us, maybe we could get Erik and Magnar back soon.

I headed for the door and Callie and Julius followed me outside into the harsh glow of several floodlights. The wind fluttered the hem of my slinky pyjama top and Callie shivered in her own pathetic excuse for clothes. The soldiers gazed curiously at the slayers but didn't mention their presence, evidently not wishing to question their rulers.

"Where's General Herman?" Clarice asked, glancing across the faces of the Elite.

Her own tiny nightdress was fluttering around her pale thighs, and I had to admire her ability to emit so much power when she was dressed like that.

Some of the Elite shared looks, then a man with a thin moustache stepped forward, bowing to Clarice. "He's taken watch over Realm D tonight, your Highness. He won't return until the morning."

"Who's in charge here while he's gone, Kingston?" Fabian addressed

17

the soldier as Danielle jumped out of the cockpit.

"I am, Master," he said, bowing his head again. "I'm afraid we weren't notified of your arrival; is there something we can help you with?"

Miles folded his arms. "Valentina Torbrook has seized the city. We are seeking refuge."

"And help," I added, stepping forward. The Elites' eyes scraped over me curiously and I pressed my shoulders back, fighting away the discomfort I felt under their scrutiny. "I'm Erik Belvedere's wife, princess of the New Empire, and my husband has been taken hostage by Valentina. We need your assistance to get him back."

Fabian raised a hand to try and shut me up. "We don't have any intention of fighting Valentina and her army just yet."

I gritted my teeth, furious that he was overruling me, but there was nothing I could do to make these Elite listen to me over him. I might have been a princess, but it looked like the only ones these soldiers were going to obey were the Belvederes. Most of them didn't look like they'd even registered that I'd spoken.

"Charge the helicopter," Fabian commanded. "And fill it with supplies of blood and human food."

"Yes, sire," Kingston replied, wafting some of his men away.

They ran toward a large metal hangar on the other side of the base while Kingston stayed in place with the two remaining Elite.

"I could help them?" Danielle offered Fabian, but he shook his head.

"You need rest like everyone else," Fabian murmured and she nodded.

"Is there anything else we can do for you?" Kingston asked, his gaze trailing to Callie and Julius again.

"Accommodation for the night," Clarice said wearily.

"You can take the barracks." Kingston gestured for us to follow him and I moved closer to Callie as we headed across the large courtyard.

The other two Elite flanked us and Julius stiffened as one of them got too close to him.

"Forgive me for my impertinence, your Highnesses," Kingston began as he fell into step beside the royals. "But those mortals you're travelling with...are they slayers? Their smell is stronger than any ordinary humans. I heard whispers of such people returning to the world."

"Yes, the female is my wife," Fabian said curtly. "And they aren't to be touched."

"They're our friends," I called and Kingston shot me a curious frown.

Julius's hand was on the hilt of Valentina's sword, Vicious, and the Elite seemed agitated by his display.

I elbowed him, but he didn't drop his hand. After our encounter with the biters, I knew he was on edge, but we had nothing to fear from the royals' soldiers.

We arrived outside a large metal building and Kingston opened the door for us. "Here you are, sires. I'll bring supplies as you requested."

"Thank you," Miles said as he headed into the barracks with Warren.

We filed in after them, but Fabian lingered in the doorway and looked to his siblings. "I'm going to see if Kingston can put me in touch with General Herman. I'd prefer if we were dealing with him; he's my own sireling and I know he'll have thoughts on how to bring Valentina to her knees." He turned to Danielle. "Would you like to accompany me?"

"Of course, sire," she agreed.

Clarice and Miles nodded, and Fabian headed away with Danielle, shutting the door behind them.

Several rows of beds sprawled out before us on either side of the long building. They were low to the floor with thin green mattresses and wooden boxes at the end of each of them.

Julius and Callie headed to the closest ones to the door, taking seats opposite each other.

Julius pointed further down the room as he eyed the Belvederes. "Best you lot keep your distance." His eyes slid to Clarice. "I don't want to wake up to you licking my neck."

"How can you even think about sleep right now?" Clarice glowered at him.

"Because I'm going to have sweet dreams of how I'd best like to kill Valentina," Julius said with a smirk.

Callie's eyes lit up at his words. "Wait, that's not a bad idea. I could try and slip into Valentina's dreams. Maybe it'll help us fight her."

My heart lifted at the idea. "Can you give her nightmares?"

"Yes," Callie said with glee in her gaze.

"Do it then, little Dream Walker," Julius said eagerly. "Conjure an image of me slicing her head off over and over and over and over-"

"I get it," Callie said, falling back onto her bed. "Let's just hope she's sleeping."

I sat down on the bed beside hers, sure I'd never get any rest. The need for blood was bubbling under my skin and I really didn't want to drink in front of her. I prayed she'd be asleep by the time Kingston returned with it. I was still getting used to this new skin of mine, and this part of my immortal form was the most disturbing. I could almost pretend I was still the same me when the thirst wasn't burning at my throat, but this was a sharp reminder of what I was now. And I didn't think I'd ever get used to it.

Warren and Miles headed toward the beds further along the room, but Clarice started pacing, her eyes glazed with thought.

Julius watched her move back and forth, his brow creasing as she walked up and down.

Callie shut her eyes, but I didn't think she'd be able to fall asleep too easily. A dark frown crossed her features and her hands were curled into fists. I wondered if she was anxious about slipping into Valentina's dreams. *If* that woman was even sleeping right now. But if she was, Callie would have to face her on her own.

I leaned across the space between our beds, taking her hand. "You're not alone," I whispered and her eyes flickered open.

She smiled softly. "I know."

She was so resilient, like Dad. If anyone could face Valentina one on one, it was her. And she had the strength of our family behind her, plus her slayer gifts.

Her eyes fluttered closed again and I released her, my gaze moving to the door as I waited for Kingston to arrive.

I ran my tongue over my fangs, wishing things didn't have to be this way. But the sooner I drank, the sooner my head would clear and I'd be able to make a proper plan to get Erik back.

Callie's breathing deepened and my brows arched in surprise. I couldn't believe she'd fallen asleep so quickly.

Julius caught me looking and grinned. "It's her gifts; she can sleep whenever she focuses."

I nodded, smiling at my sister, wondering what it was like to visit other people's dreams. I didn't think Valentina's dreams would be much of a vacation, more of a twisted playground.

Clarice glanced at Callie, her curiosity obvious, but when Julius shot her a glare, she turned away again.

Kingston finally appeared with a plastic box and another male Elite followed him carrying an armful of potatoes.

"Don't tell me that's your idea of breakfast?" Julius barked as the Elite dropped them onto the end of his bed with a shrug.

Kingston placed the box on the floor, opening it up to reveal bottles of blood inside. "Here you are, your Highnesses. There's blood and clothes in here. I'm afraid all we have are uniforms though."

Clarice nodded to him, still seeming lost to her own thoughts.

"Thank you," Miles said, jumping up to take a few bottles for him and Warren with a couple of the black uniforms.

Julius took a potato from the pile and waved it at the Elite. "I'm not eating a raw potato, you dickwit. Either go and cook it or bring us something else."

Clarice released a laugh as she eyed the potatoes. "Kingston, will you heat a few of them up please?"

"Of course, my apologies." He bowed low, shooting a glare at the other Elite before making him gather them all up and carry them from the building.

Clarice grabbed a bottle from the box, uncapping it and sipping the contents. The scent of blood hit my senses in a forceful wave and I fought back a groan of longing. I felt Julius's eyes on me as I resisted the urge to take one for myself, my hand balling into a fist at my side.

The curse deepened with every second that passed, my eyes trained on that blood and my thoughts at war in my head. I knew I wasn't human anymore, but that didn't mean I wanted to let go of my humanity. The idea of drinking blood had repulsed me just days ago, but now I was a captive to it more than I ever could have imagined. I didn't just need it, I yearned for it with every part of my soul. But still I resisted, because of the guilt that was mounting up in my chest, telling me I was a traitor to my kind, to my family. If Dad could see me now, he'd shudder and cringe away from me. Would he even see me as his daughter anymore? Or just some undead being that needed to be destroyed?

"Montana," Clarice said softly, picking up another bottle and holding it out for me. "You need to drink."

My eyes swung to Julius as I expected to find him grimacing at me, his face twisted with disgust and his eyes flaring with all the reasons he believed me to be a monster.

But instead, I found the impossible staring back at me. Julius had sympathy in his eyes, his brow drawn low and his hand sliding across his lap as if he was considering reaching out to me.

"Go on, damsel," he urged. "You have to keep your strength up."

I tried to swallow the lump in my throat, but it only swelled in response. My resilience failed me once again as my mind fixed on the best reason I could possibly come up with to drink this blood. If I didn't, I really would become a monster, and I wouldn't risk becoming a danger to the people I cared for.

Callie had fallen asleep, so at least she wouldn't witness this.

I took the bottle from Clarice's hand, turning my back on Julius and twisting the cap off. A moan of longing escaped me before I started draining the bottle, lost to the sweet, metallic blood within.

The world fell away around me as I sated the single need which held me prisoner.

I have to drink so I can focus fully on Erik.

I have to drink so I won't ever be tempted to hurt the slayers.

I have to drink because I have to damn well drink.

I sighed as the ache in my throat ebbed away. The bloodlust still had its claws in me, but I shut my eyes, waiting for it to pass. I'd had enough. I didn't need more. And slowly, my body accepted that, and the possessive need flowed away from me like running water.

22

I placed the bottle on the floor, heading to the box and picking out a black uniform in my size. The empire's flag of red, white and blue was embroidered on the breast pocket of the jacket. I tugged the clothes on over the skimpy nightwear I'd been stuck in since we'd run from the castle, zipping up the jacket.

Clarice took out a uniform for herself and whipped her nightdress over her head, leaving her stark naked in front of me.

She didn't seem remotely embarrassed as she started pulling on the uniform, but I averted my eyes from her curvaceous body, turning to face Julius instead.

He stared at her with his mouth hanging half open, his eyes bulging out of his head. Then he quickly turned his gaze to inspect his nails instead, his jaw ticking as he glared at them.

"How about you give some warning before you bare your parasitic body to the whole room?" Julius snapped at her.

Clarice's eyes narrowed on him. "Well you've made it quite clear I'm not remotely attractive to you, so I don't know why you're so bothered."

"I'm not *bothered*. I'd just rather not look at an undead monster's breasts."

"Funny that it took you at least thirty seconds to stop looking at them then," Clarice said airily and I squirmed uncomfortably from the awkward silence that followed.

Kingston returned with a plate full of cooked potatoes and I was glad of the distraction as he started apologising profusely to the Belvederes. He handed them to Julius, his gaze lingering on the slayer as he backed away.

Julius glanced at Callie but she was sleeping soundly and my heart squeezed at the thought of her facing Valentina right now. He tucked into the potatoes, not seeming entirely enthused with his plain meal, but not complaining either.

Kingston lingered in the doorway and cleared his throat.

"Yes?" Clarice asked.

"The soldiers are quite agitated since your arrival, ma'am. They're worried for their wives and husbands in the city. I wondered if perhaps you would come and speak with them to put their minds at ease?"

Clarice's eyebrows raised. "I'm not sure what I can say that will comfort them."

"At least if they are better informed, it will help them come to terms with what has happened," Kingston urged.

Clarice nodded. "Alright." She turned to me. "Do you fancy accompanying me, Montana? It would be good for your people to get to know you better."

Shock jarred through me at her words. My people? They weren't *my* people, no matter what my title said. But I had so much anxious energy pounding through me, maybe the distraction would help. Besides, I could figure out how prepared they were to assist us with Valentina.

"Okay," I said, putting on a pair of boots before following her to the door.

As we stepped outside, a breeze whipped through my hair and tugged it out behind me. I noticed Clarice doing up a few more buttons on her jacket so her cleavage wasn't exposed.

"Do you think you and Julius are ever going to get along?" I asked as Kingston led the way across the courtyard at a fierce pace.

Clarice released a lilting laugh. "We're getting along a lot better than we did a thousand years ago." Her face fell as she glanced back at the barracks behind us. "I think this is as far as our alliance is going to go though, Montana. The slayers will never see us as anything but monsters." She gave me a look of pity and anger heated my blood.

"They don't see me that way, so they can change their minds about you too."

She nodded vaguely as if she wasn't convinced of my words and hurt lanced through me that she believed Julius and Callie saw me differently now. That wasn't the case. And I didn't need her acknowledgement of that for it to be true, but I wished Julius would stop taunting her and start trying to build a real connection with her instead.

"I'll talk to Julius," I said softly, but she shook her head.

"There's no point, Montana. We've done too many wrongs against each other. We're enemies. And that's always the way it's going to be."

CALLIE

CHAPTER TWO

My skin crawled as I slipped into the confines of Valentina's consciousness.

Everything was dark around me but I could tell I was indoors. I glanced down at myself and frowned as I found that I was dressed in filthy rags. No doubt that was how Valentina loved to picture me, but that wasn't going to be what she got. I brushed my hands over my clothes and replaced them with the fighting leathers I always wore in Magnar's dreams. Fury hummed at my hip and I gave myself a huge sword too, strapping it over my back.

The faint roar of a crowd sounded ahead of me and my ears pricked as I strained to listen to it. I moved along the dark corridor, closing in on the source of the noise while trying to stay calm. I was the one with the power here and I just had to cling to that fact. I could control everything that surrounded us with nothing more than a thought.

Valentina loved to wield her gifts over others, so she was going to feel what it was like when the tables were turned. I was about to find out just how strong my gifts were. This was *my* domain.

At the end of the dark corridor, I came to a metal door and pressed my ear to it, the sound of the cheering crowd reaching me again.

I took a steadying breath and gripped the handle in my fist. I wouldn't let her see an ounce of fear in me. There was no way I'd be showing her what Magnar's absence was doing to me. This was about her, not me. And it was time we got some answers.

I pushed the door wide and stepped out into an echoing chamber filled with cheering vampires. I frowned at them in confusion but their attention wasn't on me. All eyes were turned in one direction, and I began to push my way between the press of bodies in an effort to discover what they were looking at.

"Long live the queen!" a male roared excitedly.

"We love you, Valentina!" a female shrieked even louder.

My lip curled back as I realised who all of these people were here to see. I kept moving through the crowd until I was finally offered a clear view of the bitch herself.

"Your beauty knows no bounds!"

"I would cast myself to ash for a moment in your porcelain arms!"

Valentina sat above everyone else, perched on a huge throne which was built out of piled human skulls. She wore a red dress and her hair spilled over her shoulders beneath a glittering golden crown.

Erik and Magnar knelt on either side of her, both shirtless and wearing black collars around their necks as if they were a pair of guard dogs. They stared up at her with unconcealed admiration, and she smiled almost conspiratorially as she turned her gaze between them.

Erik leaned forward and pressed a kiss to the dress where it swept over her knees. No, it wasn't a dress. My lips parted as I realised the 'dress' wasn't made of material at all; the stain of red ran over her body in an endless flow of blood.

As Erik pulled back to gaze up at her again, his lips were bloody, and I had to fight hard not to recoil from the sight.

"Let the Scarlet Empire reign forever!" a male yelled beside me, and I ground my teeth as I glared up at Valentina. It was time for her to lose control of this particular sordid fantasy.

I pushed my will into the crowd and their cheers turned to boos.

"Ugly bitch!" a female screamed as she hurled a rotten apple at Valentina's head.

"I hope you choke on that blood, you trout-lipped whore!" another bellowed.

Valentina stood angrily, scouring the crowd as they turned into a mob baying for her blood. They advanced on her and the false Magnar leapt up, swinging his swords to keep them back as she was forced to retreat.

"No man would ever love you willingly!"

"Down with the false queen!"

The crowd ripped her throne to pieces, screaming insults at her, and I revelled in the sight. I felt her trying to reclaim control of the dream, but it was pointless now that I had my hooks lodged deep within it.

A wicked smile gripped my features as her panic washed over me and I twisted her dream into a true nightmare.

I claimed control of the false Magnar and Erik too and they turned from the crowd, the collars falling from their necks as they advanced on her with revenge glittering in their eyes.

"Stop!" Valentina shrieked, her eyes scouring the crowd as she searched for me, but I remained hidden among them. "Wait! Please!"

Magnar swung Tempest at her and she cried out in pain as the blade carved into her flesh. Erik leapt on her next and I returned her to her human form just before his teeth ripped into her skin.

The rest of the crowd surged forward, snarling, screaming, stamping and biting as they all clamoured to destroy her.

Valentina's pain and terror washed over me and I hopped up onto the stage, watching with a surge of sadistic glee as they ripped into her and her screams filled the air.

I may have enjoyed the show a little longer than was strictly necessary before willing everyone away but me, then I approached her broken form where she was left panting in her own blood.

"You," she hissed as her eyes fell on me, and I smiled darkly, allowing her wounds to mend so that she could clamber to her feet.

Standing this close to her, her nudity was clear beneath the flowing blood she'd imagined into a dress, and I sneered in disgust as I forced her into the rags she'd wanted me to wear. The filthy brown garment was little more than a sack and it reeked of faeces - which likely explained a lot of the stains. I made her hair hang limp and greasy around her face for good measure, admiring my work.

"Is that really necessary?" Valentina snarled, plucking at the rags as I focused on making them as itchy as possible, gaining a petty thrill from using my power that way.

"Is what necessary?" I asked innocently. "This is how you always look to me."

I could feel the strength of her will fighting against my own, but it was like the beating of a moth's wings against the inside of my fist, and I simply caused the stench of her outfit to grow while I waited for her to stop. She gave up abruptly and scowled at me as she folded her arms.

"Fine," she snapped. "You should enjoy having this power over me while you can but remember that nothing here can truly hurt me. Dreams don't fare so well against storms in the real world."

"I'm not afraid of you," I replied evenly. "You hide behind your gifts. Without them, you're nothing."

Her face stayed impassive at my words but I felt her flinching internally. She didn't like to be called nothing.

"You should look in the mirror, little girl," Valentina replied. "What are you but a pathetic human dressing up as a slayer?"

"Well, if you want to be accurate, I'm a princess," I said, playing into what I knew would anger her the most. I imagined my crown into place on my head and her eyes flashed with lightning as she looked at it. "You spent a thousand years begging for a crown and they handed me one even though I never wanted it," I taunted.

"Your crown is purely for the sake of appearances. You're nothing more than a walking womb to Fabian. Once he's filled your belly with a child, he'll have no more interest in you. You'll be cast aside just like his other wives," she growled.

"I doubt it. Idun made sure he loves me." I held out my left hand, showing her the partnership rune which bound me to Fabian, and her eyes lit up as she smiled.

"Just as she made sure Erik and Magnar love me," she replied, and I had to work hard to stop my face from betraying how I felt about that. Her eyes glittered and I was sure she wasn't convinced by my act.

"What do you want with them anyway?" I asked.

She may not have wanted to reply but I pushed my will against hers until she was forced to reveal her answer regardless. No one could lie to me while I visited their dreams.

Magnar and Erik appeared before me and I watched her memories of them play out in a series of short bursts.

I saw Magnar as Earl of the slayers, avoiding her, ignoring her, refusing to fulfil his promise of marriage. She was owed a crown. She was destined to be his wife and lead their people at his side, but he refused her. Humiliated her. He rejected the offer of her flesh time and time again while taking other women to his bed. Their people whispered about them. About her. *And over time, the love she'd been offering him turned to a poisonous kind of obsession. He'd pledged himself to her. He owned her and she owned* him. *And if he refused to follow the goddess's guidance on that then she would just have to bend him to her will.*

Her mind swung from Magnar to Erik and his treatment of her was altogether different. I saw them tangled together between sheets and under the stars. He took pleasure in her body and whispered sweet promises while he did so. But when he wasn't lost in the moment, he pushed her away, offering excuses instead of a crown.

"I'm giving them more than they ever gave me," Valentina hissed. "The chance to have power by my side."

"Beneath your heel you mean," I replied. "And what pleasure can you gain from their supposed love for you if you're forcing their hands? Surely your victory is hollow if they haven't truly chosen you?"

"Oh I'm getting plenty of pleasure from it," she replied, her eyes flaring wickedly and I watched in disgust as her power made each of them kiss her in her memories. Thankfully it didn't go further than that and I could only hope that it stayed that way in the real world too, though her abuse of their flesh and callous disregard for their own desires set a vengeful fire blazing within my soul.

"How are you doing that to them?" I growled, unable to keep my anger from my tone.

Valentina didn't want to show me, but my power over her dream tightened and I forced the truth from her whether she liked it or not. A black choker appeared on her neck with a huge green emerald hanging from it. The jewel blazed with some dark power and even this dreamed up version of it sent a tremor of fear rolling through me. It was a creation of the gods themselves just as my ring was, and no doubt its power rivalled that of my own treasure. No wonder I couldn't use the ring to return them to their own minds.

"Idun wants me to wield this power. My path is true," Valentina said. "Magnar was always destined to be with me. You were just another distraction to pass the time. But believe me when I say he's forgotten all about you now. He knows that I am his one true love. And the next time he sees you, he will cut your head from your shoulders and gift it to me happily."

My heart fluttered in desperate denial of her words and I had to bite back the angry response I wanted to scream at her.

"Idun is as deluded as you are if you think what you've made him feel for you is love," I spat.

"What would you know about love?" she asked darkly. "Your lifetime has existed in little more than a blink to me. I have walked this world for over a thousand years and I have waited for my time to rise. Finally, my devotion to the goddess has been rewarded. And it will take a hell of a lot more than a nobody like you to take it away from me again."

I opened my mouth to respond but pain shot across my cheek, pulling at my attention in a way that made me lose my train of thought.

I shook my head, trying to clear it as the pain came again.

"Cat got your tongue?" Valentina asked with a devious smile, clearly believing she'd rattled me.

I scowled at her, ready to reply but the pain raced through my cheek even more fiercely and I was struck with the feeling that I was falling, Valentina and everything around her shredding into tiny pieces which fluttered apart into darkness.

Everything fell away from me and I gasped as I crashed out of the dream.

Julius slapped me again and I flinched awake as my eyes snapped open. He was leaning over me, staring into my face with a desperate urgency as he fought to wake me up.

"*Finally*," he growled, grabbing me roughly and dragging me to my feet.

"What's happening?" I asked in confusion as I stumbled, trying to release the last dregs of the dream and pay attention to everything that was going on around me.

Miles and Warren were locked in a fight with two Elite by the door to the barracks and the sounds of gunfire rang out violently.

Julius shoved Fury at me as he raced to join them, pulling Vicious from its sheath, and I hurried to follow him. He cut down a vampire who was battling against Miles, leaving only one more enemy remaining in the room.

Warren bellowed with rage as he drove his fist into the chest of the female vampire, shattering her ribcage and destroying her heart. She dissolved, clothes crumpling to the ground, giving us a momentary reprieve as gunfire sounded outside and he took cover beside the door.

As I drew closer to the doorway, Miles caught my wrist and dragged me back so that I couldn't look out at whatever was happening beyond it.

"They have us penned in with heavy firearms," he whispered low enough for his voice not to carry to the vampires outside.

"Who does?" I asked in confusion.

"Turns out the vampires at this base are biters. They waited until we were split up to attack." He flinched back again as more gunfire rang out.

My mind swam with the possibility that Valentina's followers had already reached this far. How many of the vampires in the country were secretly biters just waiting for this chance to rise up?

"I thought you could heal from anything?" I hissed, removing my arm from his grip.

"Not if a bullet hits his heart," Warren said fiercely from the opposite side of the doorway.

"So what do we do?" I asked.

A beat of silence passed between us as no one came up with an answer.

"Just give us the mortals and you can go!" a deep voice shouted from outside. "We only want their blood!"

Warren's gaze met mine and I tightened my grip on Fury as I waited to hear their response. This was what it really came down to. Us or them. Miles hadn't given me much reason to trust him or mistrust him so far, and I guessed I was about to find out if he'd really stand at my side when it counted.

"How fast are you with that blade?" Miles breathed, eyeing Fury in my palm.

"Fast enough," I replied, pulling on my ancestors' knowledge and my gifts flooded my limbs.

"Well, let's find out shall we?" He nodded towards the door and I caught on to what he was suggesting.

I exchanged a look with Julius, wondering if I was really crazy enough to put my life in the hands of a Belvedere. But we'd already passed that point by now and I had to hold faith in our strange alliance.

I gritted my teeth and nodded in agreement to Miles who smiled widely in reply.

"Alright!" Miles called. "We're bringing them out."

"Don't try any funny business," a response came.

Miles drew me closer to him, holding my hands behind my back and concealing Fury from view between us as he pushed me outside. Warren followed, pretending to restrain Julius in the same way.

The cool winter air kissed my exposed skin and the freezing concrete bit at my bare feet.

We walked into the open and I shivered as I began to doubt the sanity of coming out here. Miles and Warren could use us as bargaining chips to get their asses to safety, and we'd be left fighting for our lives.

A group of eight soldiers surged out of cover, aiming rifles at us cautiously. A few of them lowered their guns, reaching for me eagerly as we drew closer.

My heart pounded adrenaline into my limbs and my grip on Fury tightened as it sang songs of battle through my ears.

Cut and stab and swipe and bleed, feed me what I truly need!

Miles's hold on my wrists was so loose that he was barely touching me, and that gave me the hope I needed to stick to this plan. We were surrounded and the biters lowered their weapons as they reached for me and Julius.

As the first of them got close enough, I released a snarl of rage and swept Fury around, driving it straight between his ribs.

Miles burst past me so quickly that my hair was sent flying as he slammed into the rest of the biters. Warren and Julius leapt forward to help him as a gunshot went off and I released a curse at the sudden, violent bang.

A biter came for me, but I was ready for him, matching his blows with counters of my own as we danced away from the others. It was a constant struggle for the upper hand as the Elite matched my movements, but I finally got beneath his guard and slammed a foot into his chest.

Julius was waiting with Vicious held high behind him and the Elite shrieked as the blade pierced his heart, casting him to ash which swept away on the cold wind.

I glanced around at the empty space, trying to get my bearings and wondering how everything had descended into chaos again so quickly. The sound of fighting around the corner of the squat building drew my attention, and we all exchanged a look of comradery before we turned and raced to help.

MONTANA

CHAPTER THREE

"Just in here." Kingston directed us into a large metal warehouse, opening the door for us.

A rattle of gunfire somewhere behind us made me halt, but Kingston just smiled.

"Training," he said in way of explanation, and I glanced at Clarice who nodded, leading the way inside.

I followed her, trying to get my thoughts in order for what I was going to say. Would these soldiers listen to me? Would they fight for me? Head after Valentina and cut her down just because I was technically a royal now? If I could get Fabian to come around to the idea, maybe I could make it happen.

Rows of metal seats stretched toward a back wall with a door at the centre of it and my brow furrowed as I took in the empty space.

"Where are the-" Clarice was cut off as Kingston slammed the door behind us, locking it from the outside as he left us alone in the cavernous room.

"Hey!" I spun around, taking hold of the handle, but it wouldn't open. Kingston slid several more bolts into place as I rammed my shoulder against the thick steel.

Panic gripped my heart in fist as I turned to Clarice with a dawning comprehension filling me.

"Valentina is our true queen!" Kingston shouted through the door.

"You piece of shit." Clarice pushed me aside, shoving her shoulder against the door, but it was clearly made to contain our kind. "Open up!" she commanded, but Kingston only laughed in response.

"What do you want?" I snarled, unable to believe Valentina's rule extended this far. She'd gotten into the minds of so many of the Belvederes' people. We'd run from one rats' nest into another.

"The de-fanged are hungry for revenge, your Highness," he called from beyond the door. "We saved every one we found in the area."

"Shit, the whole base is compromised," Clarice whispered to me, clawing a hand through her long hair. She slammed her foot into the door and a metallic gong rang out. It dented but didn't give.

A shiver darted up my spine as a rattling, sucking noise sounded from the other side of the room. I turned to find the door at the far end wide open with a hunched figure standing there. Her head was shaved and her eyes were deepest green. Drool slid down her chin as she gazed at us, reaching for something behind her back.

"Do you remember me?" she tilted her head as she zeroed in on Clarice, producing a handgun from her waistband.

Clarice took a defensive stance and I followed suit as the hairs on the back of my neck rose to attention.

"Diana?" Clarice questioned.

"Dina!" she hissed, and bloody spittle flew from her mouth. "Do you know how many dayth I roamed the ruinth alone?" She raised her gun, aiming it at Clarice's face.

"You were outcast for your crimes," Clarice said in a deadly tone, not seeming remotely concerned about the gun pointed at her. But I sure as shit was. "You bit a courtier. You got what you deserved."

My heart juddered at her words and my hands curled into fists. This vampire had bitten one of the girls brought to the castle in the past. I recalled the fear of first arriving in the city. I'd been helpless once, but not anymore. Although, I didn't know if I was fast enough to dodge a bullet.

"We hath the right to bite," Dina growled, revealing the gaps in her mouth where her fangs had once been. "But now you'th taken efen that from uth!"

I clenched my jaw as a flood of cold dripped down my spine.

"Us?" Clarice breathed and dark figures loomed from the room behind the girl, stepping out of the shadows. Five of them in total. Four male vampires and Dina.

I released Nightmare from my hip with a feral growl parting my lips. The vampire side of me was close, ready to lend me the power I needed for this fight, and I leaned into it.

Dina moved in a burst of speed, slamming her hand against the wall and flicking a light switch. We were plunged into darkness and my eyesight didn't adjust quickly enough.

A bang resounded through the air and someone crashed into my side.

It took me half a second to regain my vision and I found Clarice pushing me along, a bloody graze on her arm marking the path of the bullet.

Another gunshot sounded and Clarice and I broke apart as the bullet hit the door behind us, punching a hole through it.

"Move fast!" Clarice commanded me and I started running as Dina kept firing, energy surging through my limbs.

We had nowhere to go but toward them. But it didn't matter; I just had to get that damn gun out of her grasp.

Dina had her sights set on Clarice, releasing shot after shot as the royal moved like the wind to avoid death. The other biters remained behind the wild girl, waiting to see if she killed Clarice, and I seized my advantage, powering toward her to take her out. She swung the gun at me a second too late and I collided with her, knocking her back into the men flanking her. One of the males smashed a fist into my head and my vision swam with bright lights. He shoved me through the door they'd come from and I crashed into a metal rack as I found myself in a storage room

I scrambled upright and the huge vampire took hold of my throat, baring his teeth at me.

"Fucking royal thcum," he snarled, throwing me to the floor again and kicking me in the ribs. I gritted my teeth against the pain, snatching hold of his foot as he tried to kick me again. I tugged sideways to pull him off balance, then darted between his legs to escape. Springing upright, I turned in a blur of motion and slammed Nightmare into his back without mercy.

Yes, kill, rip, end this beast of the night! Nightmare screamed its encouragement.

I twisted it sharply and the vampire burst into a cloud of ash which scattered to the floor onto his uniform.

Someone grabbed my hair and I screamed as I was flung out of the room, sailing across the warehouse. I crashed into a row of chairs and pain ripped up my side as I fell in a heap. As fast as I could, I pushed myself upright and tossed the chairs aside as I dug my way out of the pile. I couldn't stop. I had to move. I had to fight.

Clarice was battling two of the males, moving like a queen of death as she dodged their attacks and landed two impossibly fierce punches against them. The first found one of their hearts and the second snapped bones, sending the victim rearing backwards with a cry of agony.

Dina's eyes whipped to me as she pushed bullets into her gun with fumbling fingers.

"*No,*" I snarled, speeding toward her to get that weapon out of her hands. I raised Nightmare with a scream of defiance and the bullets slipped from her fingers, making a tinkling noise as they hit the floor at her feet.

"Fuck," she swore, backing up.

She had a couple of chambers filled as she snapped the cylinder shut and raised the gun.

My death stared at me from the dark barrel.

I tried to lurch aside but I was too late.

A click sounded and I flinched. The barrel rang empty. She pulled the trigger once more and I lurched aside as the gun fired. The bullet hit Nightmare and it was wrenched from my grip, skittering across the floor with a tinkling of metal. I released a snarl as I leapt into the air and fell on her with a savage fury pounding through me, the beast in me unleashed.

I caught her by the throat, my nose wrinkling as her rancid breath floated over me. I prised the gun from her hand, turning it back on her and pressing it to her heart with a snarl.

"No- no!" she begged, trying to fight me off. But she was just a lesser. I was an Elite and I had the upper hand.

I pulled the trigger. Dina winced as a click sounded and no shot was fired, then tried to snatch it from my hand. I pulled it again with a growl of anger and she exploded into dust as the final bullet burst free of the chamber and found her heart.

I whipped around to find Clarice, a surge of satisfaction filling me from the deaths I'd just delivered. She was facing the final biter, darting away from him with cat-like grace.

I ran to help her, grabbing Nightmare on the way and tossing the gun in favour of my blade. Clarice kicked the male squarely in the chest and he stumbled back toward me, wheeling around at the last second and finding his death waiting for him in the form of me. Nightmare sunk deep into his chest, sighing its happiness, and ashes scattered around me as I ran through them to Clarice.

She clutched my arm. "Are you alright?"

I nodded, glancing back at the locked door keeping us here. "We need to get to the others."

The door suddenly wrenched open and I stiffened, readying for another attack.

Danielle was there, her golden hair billowing around her shoulders. "Come on!" she called urgently. "We need you."

Clarice and I sped toward the door and I smiled my thanks as I flew out into the courtyard, but my heart plummeted at the sight before me.

A battle had broken out around the helicopter. Fabian was fighting Kingston with his bare hands, shouting his anger to the night sky.

Warren and Miles were ahead of them, battling several soldiers. I hunted the space beyond them, desperate to locate my twin. With a pang of relief, I spotted Callie and Julius sprinting away from the barracks, their skin lined with bright red blood.

I raced for them with Clarice and Danielle, preparing to join the fight.

As we closed in on Fabian, his eyes locked on his sister. "Get in the helicopter!"

Kingston punched him in the jaw and started laughing. "We didn't charge it, *sire*," he mocked. "You're not going anywhere."

Clarice leapt forward, grabbing the back of Kingston's collar before he could attack Fabian again, digging her fangs into his throat. Blood poured and he wailed his pain as the two Belvederes tackled him together, falling into another wild fight with him.

Two more soldiers came at me and my attention was forced away from them as I fell into a fierce fight for my life. Nightmare hummed for more deaths, and my fangs prickled with the lust for the hunt as I clashed with the ferocious Elite.

Without the helicopter, we couldn't escape.

Which only left us with one option; we had to kill them all.

MAGNAR

CHAPTER FOUR

I stood guard outside Valentina's chambers alongside Erik, thumbing Venom's hilt idly as the time dragged on. I'd found my blades in one of the rooms upstairs but their presence had been dark and brooding ever since I'd been reunited with them. It was almost as if they were angry with me, but I couldn't imagine why. I supposed the amount of vampires surrounding us was causing them some grief. But these were Valentina's loyal followers and if she desired their company, then I wouldn't be tempted to deliver their deaths by some old hunks of metal.

Erik stood as still as a statue as he stared off along the corridor to my right. I glanced at him from time to time but he never looked my way. His attention was focused on any threats that might come and try to harm our love. His hearing was superior to mine, so I was content to trust in his assessment that all was clear for now.

The wounds from the lashes Valentina had delivered us had completely left his flesh and he'd washed the blood away, leaving no mark of her justice on his skin. He now wore a fresh black suit which mirrored my own. I felt more than a little strange in the tight garment, the fabric unfamiliar against my skin, but if my love wanted me to wear it, then I would voice no complaints. Blood stained my white shirt in places: I healed slower than Erik and though the worst of the injuries had left me, I was still bruised and bloody from the punishment. I didn't mind though. I deserved this pain for failing her. I probably deserved more than that in all honesty.

"Magnar!" Valentina cried out suddenly from within her quarters and my heart lurched desperately at the panic in her tone.

I turned instantly, raising Venom before me as I threw the door wide and stepped into the darkened space while Erik tensed behind me, assessing the room for threats.

I blinked into the darkness as I drew closer to the enormous bed and Valentina flicked on a lamp, illuminating the space.

I looked around carefully, taking in the vast, pink room and making sure there was nothing amiss. There was no sign of any intruders and my attention was quickly snared by the immeasurable beauty of Valentina's face. The emerald hanging from her choker seemed to throb with light for a moment and my gaze shifted to it as my desire for Valentina sharpened. She was all I could think about. All I cared about in this world.

Erik stayed by the open door, guarding it, though I could practically feel his jealousy over my selection.

"What is it, my love?" I asked her as I drew nearer, my heart pounding with fear for whatever had upset her. It wasn't right for her to be upset.

She looked up at me, pushing the covers from her body and revealing a pink slip of silk which did little to cover her up. My throat bobbed with desire as I gazed upon her body and I ached with the need to move closer.

"I had a nightmare," she breathed and I could tell it had upset her. It wasn't acceptable. I wished I could take away the fear that simmered in her eyes. How dare a nightmare disturb her sleep? If a nightmare could die, then I'd gladly kill it.

"Tell me how I can make it better," I begged, moving closer so that I gripped the wooden beam at the foot of the bed. I hated that I was helpless to defend her from the terror that she'd felt.

Her eyes sparkled and she shifted so she was on her knees, and my gaze dropped over her body in that tiny nightdress once again.

"Come closer," she breathed in a low voice. "I know what will make me feel better."

My heart pounded as I moved around the bed, closing in on her as she desired.

She reached for me, catching the fabric of my white shirt in her fist as she pulled me down and I gave in to whatever she wanted of me without complaint. Her mouth met mine and my whole body came alive with energy. She was everything. My whole world. All I lived for. And in this moment, she desired me just as I longed for her.

She kissed me greedily, possessively, and I bowed to her demands as my soul danced for joy, my mouth moving against hers as if it had a mind of its own. There was an itch on the inside of my skull though, like a beetle scrambling against a rock, drawing my attention from this moment of pure bliss as though trying to tell me something.

She pushed me back an inch and I stared into her earthy brown eyes, blinking away my distraction as my gaze fell to that emerald again and all thoughts of it passed.

"You're so beautiful," I breathed, the words coming to my lips without thought, as if they had simply found their way there through the truth of them. Though it didn't seem like that word was enough to describe the perfection of her face.

A satisfied smile pulled at her mouth. "Leave your swords by the bed."

My heart pounded and I quickly dropped my swords and kicked my shoes off too. I shrugged out of the black jacket which finished my suit and her eyes lit hungrily as she watched it fall to the floor. I moved onto the mattress, kneeling up beside her and capturing her in my arms, dragging her against me as her lips moulded to mine once more.

My hands slid over her body and she tore at my shirt, ripping it away so she could explore the curves of my muscles. I groaned with a violent yearning for this perfect woman, wondering how she could possibly desire someone as undeserving as me, my thoughts nothing but a fog filled with the desperate need to please her.

But that itching returned, my muscles tensing despite themselves, and I broke the kiss with a jerk, stilling for all of half a heartbeat before my gaze dropped to her necklace once more.

I didn't kiss her again though, instead dropping my mouth to trail along her throat, and she moaned as she tilted her head back, offering me easier access to her flesh while I tried to focus on that itching sensation, to figure out what it was.

My mouth brushed against the choker she wore and a flood of power raced across my skin, deepening my lust, smothering the itch and making me want her even more. I *needed* her. I *had* to have her. My thoughts were little more than a fog of desperate desire to please her.

"Don't just stand there staring, Erik," Valentina murmured. "Come and join us."

The sound of the door snapping shut drew my attention and I glanced up as Erik moved onto the bed too. Of course I wasn't enough for her alone. I could never expect to be all that she desired. But between the two of us, I hoped that we would be able to satisfy her.

Erik claimed her mouth as I continued to kiss her neck and her hand fisted in my hair as she pushed me lower. My mouth dropped below her collarbone and she released her grip on my hair so that she could rip Erik's shirt off too.

"I love you, Valentina," Erik sighed.

"I love you too," I added automatically and she pushed me back an inch so she could look at me.

Her palm rested right above my heart and she held her other hand on Erik's chest in much the same way as we both gazed at her, waiting for her to allow us to continue.

"Say that again," she demanded.

"I love you," I said at the same moment as Erik, and her eyes lit with a burning satisfaction. Though that itch had returned with vigour now and the words felt sooty on my tongue.

"Show me how much," Valentina commanded, pulling the pink slip from her body and throwing it aside.

I stared at the curves of her naked flesh, desire rocking through my soul and freezing me in inaction for a moment. The itch made me blink and I almost withdrew, a memory of golden hair billowing in the wind dancing through my mind before it was lost just as fast.

Erik shifted towards her first and I was gripped with the need to please my queen again, moving quickly to join him as we pushed her back down onto the bed.

My mouth found hers and my hand slid along the length of her body, the perfection of her silky skin lighting every part of me with a desperate want.

Erik's fingers brushed against mine as his hand moved over her breast and she moaned hungrily, desperate for us to sate this need in her.

She broke our kiss and I watched as she turned to take Erik's lips hostage instead, the emerald practically glowing at her throat and drawing my focus once more. I could see the pleasure Erik was giving her and it drove me on to do more, the itch once again fading to nothing within the shadowy confines of my mind.

I moved my mouth to her throat again, my lips brushing her necklace and a wild desire speared through me, my shoulder pressing against Erik's as we drew closer to her.

"You're mine," Valentina sighed hungrily. "All mine."

"Yes," I growled, though something in the far confines of my mind gave another answer.

"Only yours," Erik agreed fiercely, though I could see a hesitation in him for a second, his eyes turning from her to me before returning to our queen.

Valentina's hand slid between us and she started pulling at my belt, wanting more of me. I groaned desperately as I shifted back an inch, loosening it myself as she switched her attention to removing Erik's pants as well.

My cock was...not hard. I blinked in confusion as I dropped my hand to cup it, my brow furrowing as something tickled at my memory, that flicker of golden hair making me want to turn my head and-

A heavy knock sounded at the door and I stilled, glancing over my shoulder with a frown.

"I'm busy!" Valentina snapped angrily.

I moved my attention back to her as I noted the frustration in her tone, my gaze falling to her necklace once again. She needed us to fulfil her desires and we couldn't stop now. I couldn't bear to disappoint her again.

The knock came more urgently and a snarl of anger escaped my throat.

"I'm sorry, my lady, but you need to hear this now!" a female voice called from outside.

Valentina sighed heavily. "Come in," she agreed irritably.

I pulled back as the redheaded vampire drew closer. Her eyes lit with surprise as she took in the three of us tangled together on the huge bed but she didn't comment on it.

"Don't stop," Valentina commanded and I quickly turned my attention back to running kisses along her flesh, my mouth pressing to her shoulder as Erik did the same beside me.

"We've, ah..." the vampire cleared her throat uncomfortably before continuing. "We've had a call from a military base in the south. The other Belvederes and the twins arrived there a few hours ago. Our people tried to apprehend them themselves but it hasn't gone well. If we don't hurry, it sounds as if they'll depart again soon. I thought you should know. We don't want to lose them this time."

Valentina snarled with frustration as she shoved me and Erik back.

I shifted off of the bed, buckling my belt again in disappointment as the redhead's eyes dripped over me.

"We'll finish this later, my pets," Valentina promised, trailing her fingers over my chest as she passed me by.

Her touch grazed over the wounds I'd received from the lashing she'd given me earlier and the tingle of pain and pleasure danced across my skin intoxicatingly, though as I rearranged my flaccid cock in my pants, I frowned again.

Erik sighed unhappily as he realigned his pants too and he caught my eye in a moment of mutual disappointment. We'd make up for this later. In the meantime, my love needed my swords more than my body.

I grabbed the heavy weapons and strapped them over my back, leaving my chest bare as I eyed the shredded scraps of my shirt on the floor.

Beware the lies of rotten souls, Venom hissed as the blade brushed my skin.

Strike now, Tempest urged, making my gaze fix on Valentina's spine. But of course I would never hurt her.

Valentina dressed quickly in a deep blue jumpsuit which hugged her figure, then marched from the room. We hurried to follow, walking side by side behind her like shadows.

"What's the fastest way to get to that base?" Valentina snapped as the redhead fell into step beside her.

"We have a jet ready to go. The general I spoke to said that the Belvederes were trying to charge their helicopter and they hadn't even started yet. We should have plenty of time to reach them before they get away."

"Good," Valentina said. "That should give you boys a chance to make up for disappointing me earlier. I want those twins' heads."

"I will bring you them, my love," I swore.

"Not if I manage it first," Erik growled fiercely.

"I shall cut through all of your enemies and make them rue the day they ever dared turn against the one true queen," I vowed.

"Well I shall-"

"Enough," Valentina snapped. "Actions speak louder than words. I want heads not promises."

I gritted my teeth as I nodded. I would gladly deliver what she needed from me and then we could get back to what we'd just started.

Erik grinned at me excitedly and I was sure his thoughts were in line with my own. We would do anything to satisfy our queen. And we'd start by killing those twins.

MONTANA

CHAPTER FIVE

I rammed Nightmare into the chest of a soldier, cutting a path through my enemies with a wild kind of energy filling my body. Someone stumbled into me from behind and I turned, finding Danielle and Clarice there as two Elite advanced on them.

I joined ranks with them, pressing my shoulder to Clarice's as the male and female approached, abandoning the guns in their hands as they ran out of bullets. I was finally growing used to the fast movements of my body and the power I possessed, and this fight didn't feel like the one I'd been a part of in Realm A. With every strike, I grew more confident in my strength, and some part of me came alive with the thrill of the battle, like my body was made for this.

With a spurt of energy, I sped forward to meet two more Elite, and Danielle and Clarice ran with me. We collided with them with the force of a speeding train and a punch to my temple made my world spin. I uprooted the female who'd landed the blow and she hit the ground with a pained cry. I stamped on her leg, breaking bone beneath my heel, abandoning my human side and unleashing the animal within as a snarl spilled from my throat.

She slashed her nails down my calf, ripping my pants and cutting into flesh. With a growl, I aimed another kick into her side then lifted Nightmare up, bringing it down to meet her chest in a furious blow. She burst into ash and I spun around, finding Clarice holding the other Elite while Danielle drove her sword into his heart. Danielle whipped her blade aside as dust floated down between them, and we shared a look of victory.

The flow of soldiers had eased a fraction. The Belvederes and slayers were ruthless opponents and we were starting to gain the upper hand despite the numbers being against us.

A flash of blonde hair caught my attention as Danielle started running toward a huge tank on the other side of the courtyard. Dad had told me about those things from the Final War. I knew how destructive they could be. And the long barrel of the enormous gun was slowly swinging towards our helicopter.

I gasped as I chased after her to help.

A soldier noticed her too, splitting off from a fight with Fabian in a blur of motion. I pushed myself to my limits as he ran after Danielle, his arms powering back and forth while the gun of the tank rotated to face its target.

I was faster than the lesser and I urged my legs to move even quicker as I gained ground on him. With a gasp of triumph, I caught him by the back of his shirt, dragging him into my arms. I didn't hesitate to stab Nightmare into his chest, but I missed his heart.

He threw an elbow into my chin and I bit my tongue, cursing as I plunged Nightmare into him again.

Yes! the blade cried as the soldier scattered to the wind around me.

I blinked as the ash clouded my vision for a moment, then spotted Danielle climbing onto the tank, ripping the hatch open.

A gunshot sounded from behind us and she reared backwards, narrowly avoiding the rogue bullet. I ran forward and leapt onto the huge machine, scaling it in seconds and thrusting an arm into the hatch. My hand landed on someone's head and I twisted sharply until I heard a loud crack. Danielle fell forward into the hole, finishing the soldier with her sword.

She glanced up at me, her eyes filled with relief. "That was close. If they take out that helicopter, we're fucked. Valentina will catch us if we can't get away from here quickly enough."

I squeezed her arm, releasing a breath. "Then we have to break this thing." I dropped down into the seat on top of the vampire's remains, eyeing the levers and buttons in front of me with a frown, trying to figure out the best way to destroy it.

"Wait - don't break it." Danielle dropped into the small space, planting herself into another seat and gazing at a screen before us. She tapped something on it and it lit up, showing us the feed from a camera facing the battle.

"Look, it's got three shots loaded." Danielle pointed to a number at the bottom of the screen and I realised what she was suggesting.

"You wanna fire it?" I asked in alarm, fearing that such a weapon could hurt our own people.

"Hell yeah I do!" She used a lever beside the screen and the view moved sideways across the battle. A clunking noise carried to us from outside and I realised the view we had was right down the cannon's barrel.

"There!" I pointed at a group of soldiers running to join the fight; they hadn't reached our friends yet, and if Danielle had anything to do with it, they weren't going to.

She moved the gun to face them then pressed a red circle at the bottom of the screen. The whole vehicle jolted as an explosion of fire burst from the cannon. I threw my hands to my ears, my hearing ringing with so much noise. The shot took out the whole group in a blast that ripped the soldiers to pieces and shock sank into my bones at the sudden violence.

The battle halted for a fraction of a second while everyone's eyes turned to the tank.

"Holy shit!" Fabian whooped, but the moment of victory was short-lived as four Elite sprinted toward us.

I gazed up at the open hatch above our heads. "Quick - close it!"

Danielle clambered up, using my shoulders to climb out.

"Hey – wait!" I called in a panic.

"Shoot them!" she demanded and I gazed at the screen, my hands fumbling as I worked the lever, angling the gun to face the Elite. As it locked on my target, I slammed my hand on the red button and a whooshing sound preceded an echoing boom.

Three Elite were caught in the line of fire, scattered to ash and a grin lifted my lips. The battle split apart in a panic and I spotted Fabian and Clarice tearing the stragglers limb from limb.

"Again!" Danielle cried, but the final Elite was too close. He leapt above the cannon and I lost sight of him on the screen as his boots slammed against the metal exterior.

I took Nightmare from my lap, scrambling out of my seat.

A blood-curdling scream sounded from above and I cried out for Danielle as I hauled myself out of the hatch.

A sword swung at me and I ducked it just in time. A piece of my hair floated down before my eyes as the Elite stabbed at me again and I rolled backwards, tumbling off of the tank and crashing to the ground.

I righted myself, hurrying around the tank and spotting Danielle on the ground several paces away in a pool of blood. Her own sword was sticking out of her stomach and she was struggling to pull it out.

The huge male Elite jumped down from the tank and ran towards her at a fierce pace.

My heart dropped dramatically as I saw her death coming for her on swift wings.

I charged forwards as the Elite reached her and stamped his foot down on her chest. She clawed at his legs, desperately trying to right herself as he angled a handgun down at her face.

Fear scored through my body.

"No!" I screamed, leaping onto his back.

Use me, Moon Child! Nightmare cried in my ears.

I drove my blade into his neck, my teeth clenched tight. Blood spurted and he swung around violently to try and throw me off.

Danielle pulled her sword from her stomach, pushing herself backwards as she clutched the gaping wound. I needed to buy her time to heal.

The Elite caught hold of me and threw me over his shoulder.

I tumbled across the ground, the back of my jacket ripping open as it dragged against the concrete.

When I came to a halt, I rolled onto my knees, pushing my hands to the tarmac as I propelled myself toward him at a wild pace. The Elite aimed his gun at Danielle again as she tried to kick his legs out from under him.

Panic scorched my heart.

I was three paces away.

Two paces.

One.

I leapt into the air with a cry of effort. A gunshot rang in my ears. Dust swept over me as I collided with my target, Nightmare's sharp tip slicing through his back all the way to his heart.

His remains exploded around me and my feet hit the ground. I blinked heavily, wiping the dust from my face with my sleeve, staring down at the two uniforms beneath me with a horrifying clarity. Danielle was dead, her remains cascading through the air around me, lost to the wind.

A lump of guilt rose in my throat. I hadn't been fast enough. I hadn't made the right choices.

The world fell eerily silent around me and I wasn't sure if I was locked in the eternal seconds following her death or if the battle was finally over.

CALLIE

CHAPTER SIX

I took a heady breath as the ash from my latest victim swirled around my legs and I was given a momentary reprieve from the fight. Miles and Warren had kept close to me and Julius during the battle, helping to stave off the flood of biters who were sent into a frenzy by the scent of our blood. I guessed I'd been wrong to doubt their devotion to our alliance, because they were proving themselves trustworthy time and again.

Fury burned hot in my hands, demanding more death.

Feed me, Sun Child. Cut, slash, stab, bleed!

Fabian was locked in battle with Kingston but before I could get any closer, the general made a fatal mistake and Fabian ripped his heart from his chest, crushing it in his fist with a savage smile.

Kingston exploded into a cloud of dust and Miles, Warren and Clarice slammed through the remaining biters before I could draw close enough to help.

I looked about at the heaped clothes which surrounded us as the freezing wind stole their ashes and raised goosebumps along my exposed flesh.

Fury sighed in disappointment and I couldn't help but smile a little at the bloodthirsty blade.

Fabian sped towards me in a rush of motion and I backed up a step as he stopped before me.

"You're alright?" he asked, his gaze slipping over me in assessment.

"Fine," I replied with a sigh as I pushed the ring's influence over him again so that he could be released from his concern for me. He shook his head as his love for me slipped away and his pupils dilated.

"And why are you still running around with no fucking clothes on?" Fabian asked with a snarl. "You are *my wife* and no one but me should see you like this-"

"So give me that divorce and it won't be your concern anymore," I snapped, pushing past him as I moved towards my sister. I was half tempted to strip naked just to spite him but I figured I'd rather not have him see any more of my body.

"Valentina's followers are everywhere," Montana breathed hopelessly as she pulled me into a fierce hug. "Nowhere is safe from them."

I looked about at our group and noticed that the Elite who'd saved my life was missing.

"Where's Danielle?" I asked, my gut clenching as I guessed the answer before anyone could tell me.

Montana shook her head sadly and I was gripped with an aching regret at her loss. It was so strange for me to feel bad about the death of a bloodsucker. But she'd saved my life. Fought by my side in Realm A and acted almost... human. Aside from my sister, I hadn't really let myself see the vampires like that. They were so different to us and the hatred I'd held for them for so many years was hard to put aside. But if I was willing to see Montana as the same person she'd always been, then I couldn't deny that the vampires couldn't all be bad. Yes, they had the bloodlust to contend with, but that didn't mean they all gave in. And I had to stop blindly seeing them all as monsters until they proved me wrong. They were just people. Good and bad, exactly the same as if they had a heartbeat.

Miles dropped down, taking up Danielle's sword with a heavy frown. "She was my sireling," he said with emotion glittering in his eyes.

Warren slid an arm around his shoulders. "She died trying to help us."

"Goddammit," Miles snarled, kicking the base of the helicopter in frustration.

"How long will this take to charge?" Julius asked, moving closer to me in a protective stance.

"About four hours," Fabian replied, frowning down at a cell phone in his grip. "Which is cutting it close because that traitor, Kingston, made a call to Valentina." He tossed the phone to Clarice and she eyed the call list with a look of fury.

"By the gods, there are rebels everywhere we turn," she breathed, tucking the phone into her pocket.

"Maybe we should just take a truck?" Montana suggested, pointing to a row of them on the far side of the base.

"It won't be fast enough." Miles shook his head. "Four hours wait will be worth it if we can get airborne again."

"That's a big if," Julius snarled.

"It's all we've got," I said, gripping his arm in an attempt to calm him, and he released a heavy sigh.

I gazed down at Danielle's uniform with a frown.

"She saved me once," I whispered.

Montana took my hand, clearly not sure what to say. Her fingers laced with mine and the closeness of her offered me a sense of calm.

Four hours felt like an eternity to wait. And part of me wanted to demand we stay and fight Valentina when she arrived, but I knew we couldn't face her yet. We needed a plan to save Magnar and Erik from her clutches, but while they were blinded by her power, we couldn't risk getting too close to them. Not while they were so determined to hurt us.

"I found out how Valentina is controlling Magnar and Erik," I said, turning to look at the others as Montana's grip on my hand tightened. "Idun gave her a necklace filled with the power to control the hearts of men. She's wearing it but if we could get it from her, destroy it-"

"Cutting her head off would solve two problems then," Julius said enthusiastically.

"But we'd still have to get past my brother and yours," Fabian muttered. "And her storm magic as well."

"Ever the Debbie Downer, Fabio," Julius grunted.

"But if we can just destroy that necklace-" Montana began.

"Just?" Fabian asked incredulously. "Knowing about that necklace doesn't change anything. We still can't risk going after them. We're outnumbered and outgunned."

"He's right," Miles agreed. "We have to run again. For now."

Disappointment filled me but I knew they were right. Getting that necklace was just as impossible as killing Valentina for the moment. But I was going to figure out a way to do both just as soon as I could.

I chewed my lip as the wind twisted around us again and a shiver raced along my skin.

"I can make sure the chopper is charged," Warren said confidently. "We should gather supplies and get ready to leave as soon as it's done."

"Damn Valentina," Miles growled. "We haven't had to run from anyone like this since..." His gaze fell on Julius, and the slayer laughed loudly.

"Since the mere thought of my brother and I had you crapping your pants?" he taunted.

Clarice hissed irritably and Montana shifted quickly to stand between them.

"This has to stop," she urged, glaring at Julius. "We're a team now. We have to work together and put an end to this hatred."

"We might be working together but we'll never stop hating each other," Fabian snapped. "So get over it Montana."

Julius shrugged unapologetically and Montana released a frustrated breath.

"Let's see what supplies we can find," Clarice suggested, taking Montana's arm as she headed away from us.

"I'm coming with you," Julius said, turning to follow them. "You parasites know nothing about human food and I'm not eating half-cooked potatoes again because of your ignorance."

Clarice didn't seem particularly happy about his choice to follow her, but she made no comment to stop him.

Miles and Warren started to work on the helicopter and I turned away from them, returning to the barracks so I could change into some warmer clothes.

I chewed on my lip as I headed inside, my mind churning over what I'd learned in Valentina's dream. Mostly I'd just given myself more to worry about as the memory of Magnar kissing her filled my mind. I simmered internally at the thought of her using him like that. I'd cut her heart out myself if I could only get close enough. But with him standing between me and her, it was unlikely. I couldn't hurt him and that made her untouchable.

I tossed Fury onto Julius's bed, wanting a reprieve from its constant anger at our proximity to the vampires. For now, my fate was tangled up with that of the Belvederes, but strangely, I wasn't too worried about it anymore. They'd proven that I could trust them in battle and so long as Fabian kept his distance and didn't follow through on his threat to try and turn me, then I was confident that I was safe from them. At least for now.

A black uniform was folded in a box on the floor and I placed it at the foot of my bed before pulling off the lacy pyjama top.

"At this point, I'm going to assume you don't know I'm here," Fabian murmured and I gasped as I clutched the uniform to my chest before turning to glare at him.

"What the fuck?" I snarled angrily and he raised an eyebrow at my aggressive tone.

"Well I had assumed you were just ignoring me, but as much as I'd like to believe you'd put on a strip show just for me, it doesn't seem likely. So I thought it would be gentlemanly of me to point out my presence before you revealed anything else." He was almost finished changing into one of the uniforms himself and was slowly buttoning it over his muscular chest as he looked at me.

"A gentleman would turn his back," I snapped.

"If you insist." He turned around slowly so he was facing the wall and I glowered at him as I quickly changed into the uniform, fastening the buttons to my chin before I allowed him to look at me again.

"What do you want?" I demanded.

"I have a proposition for you," Fabian replied, turning to face me once more.

63

"I'm not really interested, Fabian," I muttered. "The only thing I care about right now is getting Magnar back."

His lip curled at the mention of the slayer who held my heart, but I didn't react to it. I was sorry that Idun had placed the bond on him but it really wasn't my problem. And even now, when the ring's influence had fallen over him and he was shielded from his false love for me, he still persisted in calling me his wife. So he really had to take some of the blame for his situation upon himself.

"Not even if I'm offering what you asked for?" He stalked closer to me and I folded my arms as I waited to hear what he was going on about. "A divorce?"

My heart lifted a little at his words. "Really?" I asked hopefully.

"On one condition," he said and my gut tightened in response. I should have known he wouldn't release me so easily.

"Anything," I replied, hoping he could see how desperately I wanted to be free of my vows to him and that he might actually give a shit about that. It was the last restriction left on my freedom and I wanted it gone more than anything.

"Oh I hope you mean that," Fabian said with a dark smile.

He reached out to touch me, his fingertips brushing against the top button of my uniform and I stepped back as I realised what his condition was.

"Not that," I growled.

"Just once," Fabian persisted. "Give yourself to me and let yourself feel what it's like to be with me instead of him. And if that isn't enough to convince you to stay mine, then I give you my word that you can have your divorce."

"No."

"I can hear your heartbeat you know?" he breathed. "I know it grows faster when I'm close to you like this. Why fight what your body so clearly desires?"

"It's not desire that makes my heart race around you," I replied. "It's fear."

"You know you don't have to fear me." He reached for a lock of my hair and I stilled as he twisted it between his fingers, shifting further into my personal space.

"Last night you were threatening to turn me into one of you," I replied icily. "So of course I have something to fear from you."

"I was upset," he replied softly, still toying with my hair.

I slapped his hand away but he caught my wrist instead.

"I've told you not to touch me," I warned. Though with Fury on the bed and with him penning me in like this, I wasn't so sure how concerned he'd be about that threat.

"Yes, you've threatened to kill me multiple times but you've yet to even try it." He smiled at me like that was all the proof he needed to keep pressing forward.

"Only because I need your help. We have to solve the prophecy and get Magnar back. Once that's done, I'll gladly gut you," I promised.

Fabian chuckled. "You know your anger towards me would only make this more enjoyable. Think about how good it would feel to use all of that pent-up frustration and take it out on me. Magnar certainly isn't going to be able to blame you for it anyway. After all, Valentina will have had her way with him by now. So if you still want him after you've had me, he would have to forgive you too."

I snatched my arm out of his grip and shoved him back.

"Anything that's happening to Magnar isn't his fault," I replied, refusing to face the prospect of what he was saying. "And any anger I feel about it is directed at Valentina, not him. You've got to think pretty little of me if you really believe that I'd fuck you out of revenge or jealousy or any other pathetically selfish emotion. So if you have nothing else to say to me then I want you to get out of my way."

"Well, the offer stands," Fabian replied. "When you decide to change your mind."

I could tell that he really thought I would and I ground my teeth in outrage.

I slammed my palms into his chest, forcing him to stumble back. I snatched Fury from Julius's bed and whipped it up between us.

"I'm guessing that you haven't heard the word no very often or something," I growled. "But I can't be any clearer about this. I'm not interested. And if you never divorce me then I don't care; I'll simply live in sin with the man I love."

I turned and stalked away from him before he could reply. I had no idea what was going on in his head to make him think that hounding after me in this way was going to work but I'd had enough of it.

I withdrew the ring's influence from him and as I pulled the door open, I spotted him sinking down onto my bed and pressing his face against my pillow. *Urgh.*

I clenched my jaw and headed outside again, gazing up at the stars which peppered the sky.

I released a breath of frustration and a cloud of vapour billowed from my lips as I tried to regain my composure.

My boot fell on something hard as I stepped over a heap of clothes and I stooped down to investigate it. A shiver crept along my spine as I pulled a heavy rifle into my hands and I lifted it higher with interest, looking through the scope towards the helicopter.

"I'd prefer it if you didn't aim that at us, little slayer," Miles called and I lowered the rifle as I looked up at him.

"I don't know how to use it anyway," I replied.

"That makes it worse, not better," Miles said, and a smile hooked up the corner of my mouth.

"Is this any use?" I asked, moving closer to him where he was sitting just inside the helicopter so that I could hand over the weapon.

"It's worth taking with us," he said. "You want a lesson in modern firearms?"

"Hell yes," I agreed with a grin.

Miles pulled a piece of the gun off, inspecting it for a moment before clipping it back into place.

"You've got eight rounds here." He hopped out of the helicopter and handed me the weapon. "Aim it at that building."

I lifted the rifle higher, looking through the scope at the warehouse he'd indicated.

Miles wrapped his arms around me, repositioning my grip on the weapon. I stilled as the coolness of his chest pushed against my back but there was nothing threatening in the way he held me.

"Okay, so when you're ready just squeeze here." He shifted my finger so that it was beside the trigger. "And tense your muscles to absorb the kickback."

I smiled as he released me and let out a breath before pulling on the trigger again and again. The bullets exploded out of the rifle and I called on my gifts to help me hold it steady as a spray of holes appeared along the warehouse wall.

"Nice," Miles announced.

"I could get used to one of those," I replied as I handed it over.

"You wanna search for some more?" he asked.

"Sure," I replied, clinging to the offer of something to do. Now that Fabian had brought up the idea of Magnar being forced into Valentina's bed, I couldn't banish the image from my mind. Having a task would at least keep me occupied.

I began hunting through the clothes of the vampires who had been killed in the fight and found several guns and cell phones in their pockets.

I brought them all to Miles as he fiddled with various things on the helicopter, preparing it for our departure.

"How long until we'll be ready to head off?" I asked with a frown.

A creeping sensation was running along my spine and I couldn't help but feel like we were running out of time.

"A few hours at least," Warren replied gravely from the cockpit. "Let's just hope we can escape before we're found."

MAGNAR

CHAPTER SEVEN

1000 YEARS AGO

"**M**agnar?" My mother's voice called to me, and I fought to rouse myself from sleep at the urgency of her tone. A cool wind brushed against my skin as she pushed open the flap to my tent and moved inside. I raised onto my elbows, reluctant to leave the warmth of the furs which lined my bed.

"Do we have word of them?" I asked hopefully.

It had been so long since anyone had come across a Belvedere that I hardly dared hope for that news anymore, but the question had become a habit, and I couldn't help but ask it. No doubt the day I didn't would be the day we found them.

"Better than that," Mother replied, her eyes scouring my bed with a wry smile. "It's nice to find you sleeping alone for once."

"Surely I am not so frequently accompanied to my bed for it to be *more* noticeable when I am alone?" I protested and she laughed.

"I imagine you're having difficulty finding a woman you haven't already had at this point anyway," she mocked, and I could hear the trace of disapproval in her tone.

"Who am I to deny women the pleasure of lying with their Earl if they desire it?" I taunted, knowing it would rile her but unable to resist the opportunity to do so.

"They desire you for more than just your power," she murmured. "Many a woman in the clans would gladly offer you her heart."

"But I couldn't offer her mine in return," I muttered irritably.

"Just because you couldn't marry her, doesn't mean you couldn't love her," my mother countered. "Let Valentina be your queen and bear your children. But there are many women who would gladly take the role of mistress to the Earl for a chance at loving you."

I waved away her suggestion as I had done before. I wouldn't offer a woman I loved a role in some sordid three-way relationship, forcing her to be seen as less than my wife. To live at the whims and rules of Valentina, enduring whatever wrath my wife sought fit to force upon her for her existence. Barring her from having children because I couldn't marry her.

"I guess this isn't the reason for your visit at this gods-forsaken hour?" I asked, moving the subject on.

"It's almost midday," my mother chided halfheartedly. "You drank too much ale last night."

"It was a celebration," I murmured, running my thick tongue across the roof of my mouth as I noticed the effects of the alcohol hadn't entirely subsided yet.

"A celebration of what?"

"Baltian is about to be a father."

"You drank half a barrel of ale because your stallion got another mare in foal?" Mother raised her eyebrow at me in disbelief.

"Julius pointed out to me that this will be his thirtieth foal," I added. "So, we decided to drink his weight in ale to celebrate his fervent fertility."

"Your brother shouldn't offer you any encouragement to drink more than you already do," she sighed, and I knew she'd be heading to speak with Julius next. "And we should probably put a halt to your amorous horse before he gets any more mares pregnant, or the following generation is going to end up inbred."

"You can't ban Baltian from mounting the mares!" I laughed incredulously. "How would you even attempt such a thing? Tie his balls in a knot?"

My mother couldn't help but laugh too and she moved across my tent to get me a drink.

"Perhaps I should do that to you and your brother as well," she mused.

"Pfft." I got to my feet and pulled on my trousers while her back was turned.

I dropped into a chair before my small table, and she placed a cup down in front of me then sat down too. I took a long drink and wrinkled my nose as I found it was water instead of ale, but I didn't voice my complaint.

"I am here," she said finally. "Because apparently there has been a prophecy which you need to hear."

I looked up at her with interest. The members of the Clan of Prophecies rarely got anything wrong, especially since we'd been made into Blessed Crusaders, but I still hated to listen to them. It was them who had forced my betrothal into place. And each time I listened to their plans for me, my stomach tightened with unease. I was tired of the gods ruling my fate while gaining no reward for my devotion.

"Oh good," I replied unenthusiastically, and my mother's lips twitched with amusement.

"Look on the bright side," she murmured. "They can hardly betroth you again."

I barked a laugh and got to my feet, draining the last of my water. Then I pulled on a shirt as I picked up my swords, strapping them across my back before following my mother outside.

I winced against the glare of the sun as a headache blossomed across my brow and I rubbed my fingers into my eyes in an attempt to banish it. My gifts allowed me to heal from the effects of the alcohol much faster than most men, but we really had tried to consume the weight of my horse last night and I imagined I'd be suffering for that for most of the day.

We approached Julius's tent which was pitched opposite mine, but the flap opened before I could reach for it.

The woman who exited flushed with embarrassment as she nodded her head to me respectfully then scampered away.

"Next time I will blow your mind!" Julius called after her as he stepped out behind her. "And I will make sure to be considerably less drunk for it."

His eyes fell on me and our mother, and he laughed guiltily as he noticed the disapproval on her face.

"Don't worry, Mother," he said with a grin. "I passed out before I could conquer that particular beauty, so there is no need to frown at me."

"I had hoped that *you* at least might marry and give me grandchildren. Magnar still refuses to do that for me and I'm an old woman now-"

"No need to guilt me, Mother. You're too young and beautiful for grandchildren," Julius countered.

"At your age I'd had both of you already," she replied with a sigh and Julius laughed at her display, pulling her under his arm.

My brother had his pick of women and yet he seemed as eager to settle down with one of them as I was. He'd never found one who captured his heart and I vaguely wondered if the two of us were doomed to a lifetime of bachelorhood. For me, that was better than marrying Valentina. But I wished for happiness for my brother even though I couldn't have it myself.

We made our way to the campfire and the leader of the Clan of Prophecies got to her feet as she saw me approaching.

Hester was one of the oldest members of the clans and I'd heard talk of a celebration of her hundredth birth moon coming up. But despite her braided hair being silver and her bronze skin lined with countless creases, her mind was still as sharp as the day she'd been promoted to her position.

I valued her guidance on every major decision I made for our people and despite the fact that I didn't always like what her prophecies had to say about my fate, I'd never once had cause to doubt the truth she spoke.

"Earl Magnar," she said warmly, inclining her head as I approached.

She didn't rise from her position by the fire though and I smirked, liking that she didn't. My title offered me way too many bent heads and simpering tones, I preferred to look my people in the eye as a normal man.

"I hear you've got something to tell me, Hester," I said as I took a seat beside her.

"That was true last night as well," she murmured. "But I found you to be in no state to receive me."

"Sorry to disappoint," I replied.

"Your betrothed was keen to hear what I had seen," she said. "I hope you don't mind that Valentina was privy to the knowledge before you?"

"Valentina has a habit of being far too entwined in my fate, so it's no surprise to me," I replied dismissively.

I glanced around the camp, wondering where my betrothed was hiding; it wasn't like her not to show up for something like this, even if she had already learned of the prophecy for herself.

Hester nodded, reaching for my hand and I released a breath as I gave it to her.

"Allow me to confirm the details before I tell you what your future holds," she whispered.

Hester's eyes glazed and her jaw fell slack as she spied into my future.

"Any grandchildren for me?" Mother asked hopefully and I rolled my eyes at her.

The prophet released me, and I drew back while she sifted through what she'd seen and the silence stretched.

I caught Aelfric's eye across the fire and pointed to a barrel of ale beside him, beckoning him over. He rose to his feet, smirking as he collected a pitcher and four cups before heading towards us.

"You may wish to avoid my wife today, Earl Magnar," Aelfric muttered as he passed me a cup and handed the others one too.

"Elissa should remember that before you put those babes in her belly, she drank more than the rest of us put together," Julius mocked. "Next time, Mother will care for the babes and your wife can join us - it is most likely jealousy which has her whipping you."

73

"I'm not whipped," Aelfric balked, and my brother and I laughed to the contrary.

"Am I not going to be asked about this first?" Mother inquired.

"You seem to want grandchildren so desperately today that I thought you'd enjoy borrowing some," Julius replied.

Aelfric smirked and filled our cups to the brim. I drained mine before he could head away and he refilled it, throwing a guilty look at my mother. She rolled her eyes as she sipped her own ale, and he quickly withdrew before I could ask for a third.

"It is as I thought," Hester sighed, drawing our eyes back to her as she finished her contemplation of my future. "Forgive me, Earl Magnar, but the gods require a hefty sacrifice of you."

A coldness settled in my limbs as I looked back towards the prophet and my mother's hand moved to grip my arm.

I gazed into the faded brown eyes of the leader of the Clan of Prophecies as I waited to find out what more the gods could possibly ask of me now. Was it not enough for them to curse my father and force me to kill him in his undead form? To bind my soul to a woman I could never love? To allow our enemies to destroy thousands of our people? To have me sail across an ocean and leave my homeland behind? To let me wander this land in search of the Belvederes as my years swept by while never allowing me to find them?

What would they ask of me now? Was I to cut my own throat and offer my blood to my enemies just to draw them from hiding?

"The gods have shown me when the Belvederes will come out of solitude," Hester said, her voice grave as if this wasn't good news. "They intend to remain hidden for a hundred years while they allow this generation of slayers to grow old and die. But if you lead our people into battle against them when they reunite, then we will succeed at destroying them once and for all."

Julius barked a laugh. "Magnar will be one hundred and twenty-seven then! I know that he is a powerful warrior, but I doubt his strength will stand up to the Belvederes' if he manages to live so long. I think the gods must be confused about the timescale."

"There is no mistake," Hester replied darkly. "In one hundred years, our Earl will lead that battle to destroy our enemies." Her eyes slid to my mother. "Idun will lend power to your gifts so that he can sleep until it is time."

"What?" I gasped, pushing to my feet and backing away a step. "You expect me to sleep for a hundred years just so that I can lead some battle? Everyone I've ever known will be long dead by then! Let my great grandchildren fight then, as should be the way. I have no desire to extend my life beyond my mortal years."

"This is the will of the gods," Hester replied softly. "Your vow dictates that you must do all which is required of you to remove the vampires from this earth."

"Fuck the vow," I snarled.

My mother sprang to her feet, glancing around nervously to make sure none of my warriors had overhead their Earl saying that. She laid a hand on my arm as if she sensed I was about to bolt, and she was probably right. There was no way in hell I was leaving her here. And Julius too. My friends, my family, my clan, *my horse*. What she was suggesting was worse than death. I would wake knowing everyone I loved and cherished had long since passed from this world. I would be utterly alone in the truest, worst sense of the word and I refused to accept that the goddess would be so cruel as to demand that of me.

"Wait," Julius said. "This can't be serious? With Magnar gone, we'd have no Earl. He has no children to pass his title to. He has no heir-"

"You would be Earl in his stead," Hester said.

"Fuck that," Julius spat. "You expect me to agree to watch my brother sleep away my lifetime while I take his crown from his head? I am no leader of men. I have neither the care for the responsibility of it nor the temperament to deal with the bullshit involved in it. Besides, if Magnar is going anywhere then he'll be doing it with me by his side. I would never watch him face that fate alone."

My heart lightened a fraction at Julius's words. If the goddess truly wanted this of me, I would have no choice but to do it no matter my view on the subject. Rejecting her commands would mean breaking my vow, and if I did that, then my life would be forfeit. But I couldn't allow my brother to endure the hell of this request.

"I would not ask you to give up your life here for me," I replied firmly. "It isn't fair."

"None of it's fair," Julius said grimly. "It isn't about fair. It's about right. And it isn't right for you to face that alone. Besides, I'm not going to let you steal all the glory of killing the Belvederes for yourself."

I almost smiled in response to that, but the weight of the prophecy still hung too heavily on me for my face to allow it.

"My sons are right," Mother added. "They belong together. And I won't send one to sleep without sending the other too."

Hester pursed her lips and held her hand out for Julius.

"Whatever you get from reading my future, I'm going with my brother," he said decisively as the prophet took his fingers between hers.

Her gaze clouded and my mother moved to cup my cheek in her hand as I ground my jaw.

"Think about it," she breathed so low that I doubted even Julius could hear her, though he sat right before us. "You could go to sleep knowing that when you woke, you would finally repay the debt owed to our family. All the Belvederes dead in your father's name. If this prophecy is right, then you have no other chance of such a thing happening. They will not resurface for a hundred years. You'll never keep the oath you swore to your father and claim vengeance in his name if you do not do this."

"But I would have to leave you behind," I growled in denial. "I would never abandon you like that."

"I will only ever be able to die peacefully if I know the debt against those monsters will be paid. Knowing that you will gain the revenge our family is owed is all I care about other than you boys. And I would sacrifice spending my final years with you in favour of knowing your father's murderers will be brought to justice."

I shook my head, refusing to accept the idea of leaving her here. Julius and I were all she had left. If we slept, then she would be left alone until death claimed her. The sadness that had filled her since my father's death would be compounded a thousand-fold if she lost the two of us as well. It would kill her. I knew it in my soul. We were all she had to live for, and we couldn't just abandon her.

"Father never would have wanted you to be left alone like that," I protested. "It wouldn't be honouring him to hurt you so."

"I won't be alone," she countered. "I can visit the two of you in my dreams every night until my life ends. It will be just the same as seeing you every day like I do now. Without the added fear of you dying - I can spend each and every day for the rest of my life knowing that both of my boys will survive beyond my time."

I frowned, wondering if I could really believe there was truth to that. In some ways, the dreams she shared with me were nothing more than a fabrication of our minds. But in others, they *were* real. We could hold true conversations, could feel things as if we were really experiencing them. Perhaps visiting us in her dreams wouldn't be so different to her seeing us in the physical world.

"Besides," she added conspiratorially. "In a hundred years, Valentina will be long dead. You will be free of your promise to her, and you can finally find a bride who you can love."

My heart beat a little faster at her words and I couldn't help the longing I felt at them. Idun had promised to free me from my betrothal if I rid the world of the Belvederes and maybe this was the goddess's way of keeping her word. If there was no chance of me doing such a thing in the present, then perhaps her gift to me was delivering me to the time when it would happen.

But could I really leave everything I'd ever known behind like that?

"Your brother is right," Hester sighed as she released Julius's hand. "His fate is tied to yours. He will fight by your side until death parts you. So now your paths are clear. What say you, Earl Magnar? Are you ready to face your destiny?"

ERIK

CHAPTER EIGHT

A driver took us to the private airport in New Jersey and anticipation built in my chest as we arrived. Valentina sat between Magnar and I in the back of the limo, alternating between caressing our knees and biting her nails into them. Every ounce of pain she delivered was soothed away by her stroking hands. I delighted in the alternating sensations. Whatever she needed from me, she could have.

Magnar and I had changed into fresh suits at her request, and I had a high-powered rifle on my lap whilst Magnar remained armed only with his swords. I didn't know if the slayer had used anything but his own weapons before and wondered if Valentina would teach him one day. Jealousy pounced on me at the thought of them spending time together alone though. Wherever she went, I'd be going too. And Magnar would have to accept that.

We pulled onto a runway where red lights stretched away from us on the tarmac. The limo parked beside my pride and joy: The Royal Nightflyer. My private jet. The pilot had it prepared, the engine already humming as we stepped out of the vehicle, and I gazed at the shiny beast with a grin.

"It's yours," I declared to Valentina. "My whole air force is yours."

Valentina ran her fingers down my cheek, and I shivered from her touch. "Thank you, Erik. I'll reward you well for it."

My chest puffed out at her words and Magnar shot me an envious frown. The asshole could never offer her what I could.

An SUV pulled up behind us and the redheaded girl led a line of four more Elite from the vehicle, all heavily armed with guns and swords.

"Bonny," Valentina addressed her, smoothing down the creases in her jumpsuit. "Any more word from the base?"

"No," Bonny answered. "I tried calling but there was no answer."

Valentina pursed her lips. "Let us hope they are too busy executing our enemies."

"Yes, your Highness," the girl replied with a wide smile.

Valentina slapped her across the face with a snarl. "We can't be too hasty in our victory."

"Sorry, your majesty." Bonny bowed her head in shame, cupping her cheek.

I glared down my nose at her. Anyone who dissatisfied my love was no friend of mine.

"Come, boys," Valentina commanded, leading Magnar and I up the metal stairway into the lavish jet.

The cream interior practically shone with wealth as we headed past the first set of leather armchairs to a long couch beside a row of windows.

We laid our weapons on the edge of it as Valentina gestured for us to sit. I dropped down beside Magnar, his muscular arm rubbing against mine.

The Elite filed onboard and Valentina whipped a curtain shut between us as they remained in the front of the jet. I revelled in the privacy she'd given us, hoping she'd take advantage of it soon.

She turned to us with a wicked smile which lit a fire at the base of my spine, then she dropped into an armchair opposite us, buckling herself in and waving a hand for us to do the same.

I slid the seatbelt over my waist, gazing at Valentina with a lustful desire pooling in my chest. Since we'd been interrupted in pleasing her, my body was raging to get near her again. I needed to fulfil her every desire. I longed to taste every inch of her delicious skin.

Yet as I considered pinning her beneath me and making her feel all the pleasure I could offer, a reluctance swept over me that left me confused. I blinked as my mind conjured a pair of dark eyes, a rebellious slant painted on full lips.

Magnar was struggling to figure out how his belt worked and I reached over and clipped it in place for him, shaking off the strange thoughts.

The jet took off down the runway at speed and Magnar shifted uncomfortably beside me as he gazed around at the plane. He'd clearly never been in anything like it before and I could sense his concern.

Valentina frowned at him, a line creasing her porcelain forehead. "Get a grip, Magnar," she snapped, and his back straightened.

The plane lifted into the air and Magnar's brow furrowed heavily as we soared ever higher.

"Apologies, my sweet, these contraptions are alien to me," Magnar said with a look of shame. "But I would go anywhere with you. I would board any strange vehicle so long as I could stay by your side and gaze upon the perfection of your face. It's just this...plane, it's so very unusual and-"

"Shut up," she sighed, leaning back in her seat with a pout.

My gut twisted at the idea that Magnar was displeasing her. I racked my brain for ways I could make this right and thumped my fist against Magnar's shoulder. He bowed his head, knowing he deserved the punishment.

Valentina's eyes lit up as she gazed between us, digging her teeth into her lower lip. A hungry desire burned through me as she opened several buttons on her jumpsuit and slid her hand beneath her waistband as she stared at us.

I swallowed the thick lump in my throat, reaching for my buckle so I could go to her.

"No," she purred, her eyes becoming hooded with pleasure. "Stay there, together."

Desperation grew in me as I was held captive by her display, but something tugged sharply in the back of my head and I realised my body wasn't particularly reacting to her overt display. There had to be something wrong with me, something I desperately needed to fix.

She watched us with glee as Magnar leaned forward in his seat, enraptured by her.

"Let us come to you," he begged.

Valentina laughed her delight, clearly thrilled by keeping us waiting.

"We have only half an hour before we land," she said softly. "That's not nearly long enough. I want our first time together to last hours and hours."

I nodded as disappointment made my heart sink.

"But that's not to say we can't have a *little* fun," she added with a slanted grin then twirled her finger through the air. "Face each other."

I did as she asked, turning to Magnar with my brows drawing together. He gazed at me with a bitter defeat in his eyes. We couldn't have her. And perhaps it was a good thing, because I needed to fix whatever this strange reluctance was inside me before she laid her hands on me in future. My body was made for hers and I needed to ensure it answered to her call when the time came.

In the corner of my eye, I caught sight of Valentina stroking the emerald at her throat. Its green glow fell over us and I sucked in a slow breath as Magnar became achingly attractive to me, my heart almost beating with how much I adored him.

He smiled that handsome smile of his, brushing his calloused fingers across my jaw. I unstrapped the buckle holding me in place before releasing his too, the urge to kiss him driving into my skull like it had been placed there by the hand of fate. He caught the collar of my shirt, dragging me forward so his lips met mine, as eager for me as I was for him. I raised onto my knees, pressing him back into the sofa, wanting him more than anything.

No, that wasn't right. My mind fixed on a beautiful brunette, her lips forming my name and my thoughts jarred for a second. But then she was gone, swept away by a wave of lust as I focused on the man beneath me.

Valentina laughed breathily as she watched and I was spurred on, wanting to please her more than anything in the world.

"Now fight," she purred.

My love turned sharply into aggression as I snatched Magnar's throat and started choking him. He threw a heavy punch into my gut and I hit the carpet at Valentina's feet. I shouted my rage at being beaten before my love as he landed on top of me, throwing fierce punches into my face. I snarled, baring my fangs as I battled him off of me, rolling so I straddled him and took control. I slashed my nails down his neck and the scent of his blood overwhelmed me.

Valentina gasped as she pleasured herself over our fight, her hand moving beneath her jumpsuit as she stroked her fingers between her thighs. I was spurred on by a wave of fury as I dug my fangs into Magnar's throat. He yelled in anger, shoving me away again as I swallowed a mouthful of his blood. He hissed between his teeth as blood spattered onto the cream carpet, staining it a deep crimson.

"Love each other," Valentina moaned, and I blinked as the haze in my mind shifted once more. Magnar dragged me back down to kiss him and I revelled in the sound of Valentina finding her release because of us, her moans filling the air like the delightful sound of a peacock's cry.

"Enough," she sighed heavily, and my love returned to her and only her.

I crawled off of Magnar, rubbing my eyes as my mind adjusted to the will pressing against my soul, something feeling off about all of this if only I could grasp what it was.

We knelt at her feet and she gazed down at us with her mouth parted, her eyes alight.

"When we've won this fight, you may have me," she promised and I groaned with how much I wanted that, leaning down to press a kiss to her foot.

"We're not worthy," Magnar sighed, dropping down beside me to kiss her other shoe.

"You will be when the twins are dead," Valentina said, lifting her legs and pressing her heels down on our backs until we were bent beneath her like the dogs we were. While she rested her feet on us, I eyed Magnar with a satisfied smile, glad we had done something right to earn this reward.

The plane shuddered and Valentina stiffened in response, my queen suddenly on edge. The air grew thick and I caught Magnar's gaze beside me as I sensed something was wrong.

A velvet voice dripped over me and a memory of who it belonged to came to mind. Idun, the beautiful goddess who helped Valentina was here.

"Hello Valentina, how are you enjoying your position as queen?" Idun purred into the atmosphere and a heavy golden light danced at the edge of my vision.

"Very well, Idun, thank you for all you've done for me," Valentina answered, a softness to her tone that I wished she'd use with me sometimes.

"I do not want thank yous," Idun whispered dangerously, and Valentina's feet shifted off of our backs, allowing us to turn.

I searched for the goddess around me, but the only thing visible was a ribbon of golden light twirling through the air.

"I want the ring," Idun hissed.

Valentina stood between us, clasping her hands together. "I'll get it for you, I swear."

The golden light shifted and the enchanting goddess stepped from its shimmer to stand naked before us. Her pale skin was wrapped in green silk that snaked about her body, between her thighs and over her breasts. Everything about her was intensely alluring. But no one could compare to the beauty of my queen. Not even this deity who seemed to be made from beauty itself.

"I am a patient goddess," Idun sighed, her smile like a crescent moon. "But my patience will come to an end, Valentina." Her eyes fell on me and Magnar, and she released a laugh that sounded as bright as the tune of songbirds. She moved toward us on bare feet, gazing down her perfect nose to where we knelt. "Magnar...Erik, how good it is to see you behaving for once."

Valentina sent a sharp kick into my side, and I blurted an answer, "Whatever pleases my love."

"Yes." Idun frowned as if she were disappointed that my heart didn't want her like it did Valentina. "You owe me an answer." She curled her index finger and her power stretched through me, moving my muscles so I rose to my feet before her. "Who has the ring?"

My memories seemed veiled under a thick cloud, but I slowly extracted the information she wanted. Idun was looking for Andvari's ring. I'd once refused her the knowledge of who had it, but I couldn't recall why.

"Callie Ford has it," I said, and Magnar nodded eagerly from the floor.

Idun's eyes flashed with rage. "Of course. I should have guessed. The defiant little slayer who abuses my gifts."

"I have news of her whereabouts," Valentina said quickly. "We're going there now. I'll bring you that ring. I'll cut it from her dead hand when she is laid to waste at my feet."

"Good." Idun's gaze drifted from Valentina to Magnar. "How are you enjoying your betrothal these days, Magnar?"

His eyes lit up and envy grew in me that he shared a mark with the woman I loved, branded on his flesh. I wished to cut the same mark into my own skin, if only my accursed body wouldn't heal it. Valentina had kept her slayer marks after I'd turned her and I adored that about her.

"Oh, Idun, I cannot thank you enough for pairing me with this wondrous woman. I cannot begin to express the magnitude of that gift." Magnar reached for Valentina, and she caressed his bicep with a smile that racked my bones with jealousy.

Idun laughed deeply, her golden hair dancing through the air with her joy. Her eyes fell to Valentina once more, penetrating and dark. "Don't forget who you are in debt to, Valentina. If Andvari comes asking for that ring, you will not give him this answer."

"Yes, your greatness, of course," Valentina promised, bowing her head.

Anger rolled through me at my queen's submission to this god. She deserved to be bowed to by the deity herself. Couldn't Idun see how dazzling she was?

"Bring me that ring, Valentina. Or I will take the necklace back," Idun warned, before turning away into a golden mist and parting from this world.

I turned to Valentina, my heart lifting as her eyes dragged over me.

Touch me, please touch me.

"Back on the floor," she commanded both of us and we immediately fell to our knees.

"My legs are tired," she said wearily, dropping onto her seat and propping her feet up on our backs once more.

Happiness shone through my chest as I gave my love what she needed.

This was definitely the best day of my life.

MAGNAR

CHAPTER NINE

My knees and shoulders were beginning to lock up with cramp when Valentina finally removed her heeled shoe from my back, but I was just pleased to have been able to offer her aching legs some reprieve.

"Get back in your seats," she said dismissively. "We're about to land."

I pushed myself upright, moving to sit on the couch opposite her once more. Erik leaned over me to fasten the safety belt around my waist and I frowned in confusion as I remembered his mouth pressing against mine hungrily. Why had I wanted that so much at the time when I didn't desire it at all now?

My gaze fell on Valentina and she smiled knowingly, caressing the emerald which hung from her throat.

I leaned forward, aching to be closer to her again.

The plane juddered around us and I gripped the arm of the couch as my gut plummeted. I had no idea how this contraption sailed through the sky and as I glanced at the view beyond the nearest window, a deep sense of unease clawed at my insides.

We were so high up. Higher than should have been possible. It was as if we walked in the heavens with the gods themselves. It didn't seem right. It wasn't natural.

"For the love of the gods, comfort him Erik. I can't bear to watch him squirm," Valentina snarled.

I dropped my head in shame as Erik slid his hand onto my thigh. "It's alright, Magnar," he murmured, squeezing my leg reassuringly.

"I know," I replied, sitting up straighter and leaning back against the seat.

If my discomfort was upsetting my love, then I would have to banish it. She needed me to be strong. And I refused to disappoint her with my insecurities.

Valentina eyed Erik's hand on my thigh with an excited glimmer in her eyes. I had been about to tell him to remove it, but if it was giving her pleasure then I would happily leave it in place.

The plane angled down steeply as we began our descent and I worked hard to keep my face neutral at the unnatural change. I was sure we were about to plummet into the ground but neither Valentina nor Erik seemed afraid of the fact, so I focused instead on the woman before me. She was so beautiful. Her hair was the most perfect shade of brown. Somewhere between the thickest, deepest mud and the roughest bark of a tree.

The plane bumped to the ground and I couldn't help but flinch.

Valentina scowled at me, and I pursed my lips in anger at myself.

"Your Highness? There's a helicopter taking off at the far end of the airfield!" Bonny announced as she swept the curtain aside and looked in at us. "Should we take off again to chase them or-"

"Let me out of here," Valentina snapped, unbuckling her safety belt as she stood. "I can handle a helicopter."

Erik leapt up and followed her as she headed towards the front of the plane. I tried to follow too and frowned down at the belt which secured me in place as it stopped me from rising. I growled in frustration as I failed to figure out how to remove it then just ripped the damn thing free, tossing it to the carpet by my feet as I stood.

I snatched my swords from the floor by the couch and followed Erik to the front of the plane, shoving the Elite aside as I went. They recoiled from me, glaring angrily as a mortal treated them so. But I wasn't going to let them stand between me and my love.

"Why does this slayer have a place at your side?" one of the males growled irritably. He had a red scar healing across the bridge of his nose, and I vaguely remembered that I'd been the one to give it to him before...before something...we'd been fighting...

"Because I like the way he tastes," Valentina hissed as the plane began to slow and she pulled the door open. The wind billowed into the confined space, pulling my hair out behind me. "And if you don't like it, Andrew, then you can answer to me."

She leapt out of the plane before he could finish his apologies and I threw a fist into his face for good measure. The rest of the Elite lunged at me, and I laughed as I followed Valentina outside before Andrew could get close enough to retaliate.

I fell into a roll to allow for the plane's momentum and quickly sprung to my feet again on the concrete. I released a breath of relief to find my feet on solid ground at last and was glad that Valentina wasn't paying any attention to me.

The wind whipped around me as my love drew a storm to her. The air hummed with electricity, lifting the hairs on the back of my neck and sending a shiver racing down my spine.

Erik landed beside me, running to stay on his feet before moving to my side. He eyed the dirt on my suit with a frown before brushing it off. I guessed he believed our love wouldn't like the fact that I'd made a mess of the outfit she'd selected, and I gave him a nod of gratitude.

Beyond a wall at the far end of the runway, the helicopter was climbing into the sky. Anger licked along my spine as I watched it rising higher and higher. The people onboard that vessel had wronged my queen. They needed to stand and face their deaths. Not run like cowards in that ungodly contraption.

Valentina smiled as thunder crashed above our heads and lightning spiked through the sky. The wind picked up and snow started to fall as she unleashed the full force of her magnificent powers.

"Go after them. I want to be sure they're dead once I bring down that helicopter," Valentina growled.

"Yes, my love," I replied.

"Anything, my queen," Erik agreed.

We took off along the runway, racing after the flying machine as it whirled into the sky, battling against the pull of the wind which was building into a raging vortex.

I sprinted as fast as I could, charging along the hard ground until we reached the end of the runway. Erik raced into one of the huge buildings which blocked our way on to the left. The front of it was open and more flying machines lay within it waiting to be used. I ignored the door he'd taken and leapt at a wall ahead of me instead. I scaled it quickly, launching myself from the top of it and slamming into the dirt on the far side.

The back of my suit tore at the impact and I winced, knowing it would displease Valentina. But the garment was not designed for running and fighting, and the press of my muscles as they bulged with my gifts beneath it was too much for it to take. Hopefully my success in this hunt would make up for her displeasure at the damage I'd done to it.

I was going to get that ring for Valentina. I'd carve it from Callie Ford's finger myself and present it as a gift to my queen.

I raced down a narrow alley between two of the huge metal buildings and emerged in a wide square on the far side of them. My shortcut had put me ahead of Erik and I grinned triumphantly as the helicopter swerved overhead and soared away into the sky.

I looked up at it as the snow began to fall more heavily, spying the terrified faces of my prey peering down at me.

Callie pressed her hand to the window and her lips parted as she called my name before the metal contraption wheeled away again. My anger built and I bellowed curses after them as they attempted to flee from us once more.

The helicopter roared in protest to the storm and the wind battered it from every direction as it thundered overhead, racing across the open fields to my left.

I sprinted after it, quickly getting left behind and cursing as my quarry gained ground on me. I'd kill them. They had to die. There was

92

no way that I could fail at this task twice. Their deaths would please my love and that was all that mattered to me on this Earth.

The world began to turn white as the snow stuck to the ground and Valentina drew it from the sky in an ever-thickening blizzard.

I lost sight of the helicopter in the swirling mass of white, but I could hear its engine roaring and I didn't slow my pace.

Erik slammed into me as he caught up, making me stumble before he raced on ahead of me with a laugh.

I bared my teeth as I threw every ounce of my gifts into my legs, forcing them to move faster and faster so I could pound away at the distance which divided me from my prey. Erik wouldn't have this glory to himself. I would earn the reward of Valentina's flesh for myself and pay for it in blood.

My shoes carved tracks through the snow, the smooth soles slipping unhelpfully beneath my feet. I cursed the stupid garments, wishing for a solid pair of boots so that I might run even faster.

Lightning lit the sky, illuminating the space ahead of me enough for me to spot it slamming into the helicopter.

I bellowed a laugh as the whirring contraption stalled, its engines cutting out as it began to plummet towards the ground.

My heart soared at the prospect of finishing this hunt, but the engines restarted suddenly and the helicopter swooped skyward again just before it could collide with the Earth. I cursed as I ran on, desperate to catch up to it so I could finish any survivors once my love brought it down.

Lightning blasted across the sky repeatedly as the helicopter veered left and right and the wind howled.

The engines screamed with the effort of fighting the storm and I grinned savagely as I upped my pace again. Valentina held our enemies in the fist of her storm, and I would be there when she brought it to the ground.

MONTANA

CHAPTER TEN

The helicopter soared through the battering maelstrom and fear clutched me in a vice-like grip. We'd seen the plane coming and had to take off with only half charge. Even if we could escape this storm, who knew how far we'd get before we ran out of power?

Callie's eyes were wide with horror, staring across at me from where she sat opposite. The worst had happened. Valentina had caught up and Erik and Magnar were chasing after us like wolves. My heart clenched with terror as I searched the horrified faces of my friends for an answer to our desperate predicament.

Callie opened her mouth to say something, but a huge boom of thunder sounded overhead and the helicopter swayed precariously as torrential snow cascaded from the heavens.

"Shit," Warren growled from the cockpit. "The engines can't take this much longer. How far behind is she?"

Julius tugged open the door from his seat beside me and a harsh wind whipped around us as he poked his head out, gazing down at the ground.

"I can't see anything through this snowstorm." He swore, slamming the door shut and taking a rifle into his grip.

I bit into my lip as another bellow of thunder cracked overhead.

Callie fiddled with our mother's ring, her face pale and her expression haunted. "Magnar..." she breathed.

I nodded, anxiety warring in my chest as I thought of him and Erik down there, forced against us.

"Go as fast as you can," Fabian commanded Warren.

"What the hell do you think I'm doing?" Warren called back at him.

Lightning forked through the air, so close it lit up the whole space inside the cabin. I took hold of my seat, my nails digging into the leather as my fear ratcheted up a notch.

Julius shifted closer to me, his gaze flickering with concern. "Everyone just hold the fuck on, maybe we can outpace her."

Clarice gave him a terrified look. "What if we can't?"

Julius grunted his frustration. I took his hand and he squeezed my fingers in response.

"We got this, damsel," he whispered, and I nodded, needing to believe that.

"Faster, Warren," Miles urged, but Warren only swore in response.

"Come on, come on," Fabian growled, his fingers locked tight around the edge of his seat.

Another spear of lightning flashed beside us. Too close. It was too damn close. The helicopter surely couldn't withstand another hit.

"Brace!" Warren shouted as the helicopter tilted sharply forwards. Lightning blinded me and I gasped as I was thrown into Callie. I hit the floor and she grabbed my arms to right me, the two of us clinging to each other us the world spun.

Julius crashed to his knees beside me and he quickly hoisted me back into place on my seat while Fabian helped Callie onto hers.

"That bitch," Julius snapped, gripping his gun so hard his knuckles were turning white.

Thunder bellowed again and hailstones pelted the helicopter, ringing off of the metal. A huge lump of ice smashed through the window to my right and I cried out, shielding my face from the glass as it hit the floor between our feet.

"She's trying to crash us!" Warren yelled in a panic.

"We fucking know that!" Fabian snapped at him. "Just keep your head screwed on and fly us away from her power." He lifted a large machine gun from his lap and moved to the door.

He wrenched it open and started firing blindly back in the direction we'd come from. The noise pounded against my eardrums, making me wince.

"Stop! What if you hit Magnar?" Callie leapt on him, trying to drag him away from the door.

Miles grabbed her arm, hauling her back and Julius booted Miles in the leg to make him let go.

"Stop it!" I snapped at them, and Clarice took hold of Miles to pull him away.

Fabian stopped shooting, throwing a scowl back at Callie. "It's us or them."

"You wouldn't be firing if Erik could die that easily from a gunshot wound," Callie snarled.

"She's right," Julius barked at Fabian. "Stop shooting. If you kill my brother, I'll end you here and now."

Fabian growled his annoyance, slamming the door shut again. The wind picked up and my stomach dropped dramatically as we plunged several feet.

I braced myself against the wall of the helicopter, gazing at Callie's pale face. She held Fury in her fist, but there was no one to attack. We couldn't fight a storm. We were nothing but a bird in the sky, ready to be shot down. And my sister didn't have immortal flesh like me; she may have been strong, but she had far lower chances of survival than the vampires did. Julius too. And I had to protect them somehow.

"Get away from the windows!" Warren roared.

An explosion blinded me.

White, blue, red. I couldn't see anything but a blaze of hellfire.

A fierce wind tugged out my hair and I felt for the window beside me to support myself, but it wasn't there. The helicopter turned violently to the right and I lurched out of my seat, reaching for Callie in desperation, her name spilling from my lips in a scream. But I found no one there, and all I knew was that I was falling, falling, falling.

Someone crashed into me as my vision returned. The ground was zooming up to meet me as I tumbled from a great hole ripped in the side of the helicopter. I rolled over with a scream of terror spotting Julius falling with me, his arms kicking and wheeling.

I might have been able to survive this fall, but he was mortal. He was going to die and I couldn't do anything to stop it.

My screams were lost to the wailing wind and the raging thunder.

"Julius!" I cried, my hand extending uselessly toward him.

I crashed into trees and my body was battered again and again as I hit branches on the way down. Twigs and thorns tore at my clothes, my skin. I reached out, grabbing hold of the boughs to try and slow my descent, but I was moving too fast. Leaves brushed my fingers and wet branches slid through my grip.

Panic consumed me as I continued to fall, helpless to the painful collisions of my crashing limbs against the rough bark.

I hit the earth with a loud crack, face up as I stared at the wind-swept canopy. Snow sailed down toward me, landing on my cheeks and falling against me in thick clumps. I tried to move, but my body didn't respond.

Something serious was wrong with me. My back was broken. I was numb. Paralysed.

A tingle grew at the base of my spine and I groaned as pain unleashed itself on my body in a violent wave.

"Julius!" I screamed, panic ripping me apart from the inside out.

He had to be okay. He had to be alive. I couldn't stand the thought of losing him.

No response came and my hope started to fade.

He's so strong, maybe he survived. Maybe he's okay.

But what if he's not?

And what happened to the rest of them? Where's Callie? Where's my twin?!

Tears slid from my eyes, icily cool as they joined the snow resting against my face. I began to heal, agony slicing into me as feeling returned to my shattered bones. So many parts of me were broken, I could barely sense an inch of my body that didn't hurt.

My shoulders trembled as I lay in the snow, listening to the sound of the storm and the whirring of the helicopter as it sailed away from me, hoping they could stay aloft and that Callie was still up there, that she hadn't fallen too.

The scent of smoke hit my nostrils and I released a murmur of terror because the sound of the helicopter was turning to an all-out roar.

It could only mean one thing. They were crashing and my sister was going to die in the wreckage.

Fear clawed at my heart.

"Callie," I whimpered.

I hadn't protected her, and I despised myself for that. If she died in that helicopter, I would never forgive myself.

It felt like an eternity waiting for my body to heal enough to move, but slowly my bones re-fused and the cuts on my skin knitted over. I sat upright with a groan, my vision spinning as I took in the sprawling dark forest before me.

"Julius!" I called, sure he must have landed near to me. He *had* to be alright. But that fall...how could he have survived it?

I stumbled forward, hissing as my ankle gave way beneath me. I fell into the snow again, buckling as I begged my body to heal fully.

"Julius!" I cried again, desperate to hear the sound of his voice calling back to me, assuring me he was still alive.

A low growl caught my ear and I turned, the flash of several yellow eyes staring back at me from between the trees. Eight pairs of them, all trained on me. The pack of coyotes circled closer, sniffing the air.

I took a handgun from my hip, my upper lip peeling back as I aimed it at them.

A pained yell caught my ear in the distance and my heart leapt in my chest. *Julius.*

I turned to the coyotes once more, lowering the gun as I remembered what I was. A growl rolled through my throat as I showed them that I was a beast far more monstrous than they.

One of the coyotes released a low bark and the pack turned, scattering away into the shadows in the direction I'd heard Julius. I took chase after them, clutching a wound on my side which refused to heal fully, gritting my teeth against the agony.

I was not going to fall from a helicopter, shatter every bone in my body and stumble through these forsaken woods just to see my friend be eaten by a bunch of damn dogs.

CALLIE

CHAPTER ELEVEN

I lunged towards the gaping hole in the side of the helicopter where my sister and Julius had been torn free of it but Fabian grabbed me before I could do anything stupid, slamming me back into my seat.

Clarice had leapt out into the blizzard right behind them and had disappeared into the swirling snow without a backwards glance, leaving the rest of us in this cursed contraption as it continued to whirl through the air.

"Montana!" I bellowed, thrashing against Fabian's hold on me as the helicopter lurched violently and the icy wind billowed in through the hole.

"She'll be fine," Fabian growled. "She's a vampire; her body can survive that fall. Yours cannot!"

I stilled, staring up at him in horror.

"No," I breathed. "Julius!"

Fabian's grip on me tightened and he shook his head, not saying the words I feared above all else. I knew what he thought. He believed the slayer couldn't have made it. But I couldn't accept that. I wouldn't. I started shaking my head in furious denial just as the wind buffeted the helicopter again, throwing it in the opposite direction.

I clung to my seat as I was nearly tossed out of it and Fabian fell away from me, slamming into the door on my left, causing huge cracks to spiderweb across the pane of glass at the centre of it.

A wailing alert started up from the controls as if the helicopter itself was begging to be saved.

"Holy shit," Warren cursed from the cockpit and my heart leapt as the wind claimed us.

The helicopter started spinning and a terrified scream left my lips as I clung to the seat. Everything that wasn't bolted down flew through the space around us, crashing into us or being tossed out through the gaping hole on my left where the windows used to be.

My heart leapt with a terrifying kind of fear. I couldn't stare this down. I couldn't look it in the eye and force myself to stand against it. I couldn't even run from it. We were facing the inevitability of this craft crashing into the rocks beneath us and I was filled with the certainty of my own demise. This was how I was going to die. It was as if it had already happened, but my body hadn't realised it yet. I was suspended in this moment between alive and dead where I wasn't really either.

"We're caught in a fucking tornado!" Warren yelled as he fought to reclaim control of the helicopter.

A huge metallic groaning sounded above our heads and I looked up just as the roof was torn off. The rotating blades spun away from us and my hair whipped over my face as my stomach swooped and my heart raced.

It took every ounce of my enhanced strength to keep me in my seat as I gripped the armrests and another scream left my lips.

Between the heavy snow which filled every inch of space outside, I spied the sky, quickly followed by the ground and then the sky once more as the remains of the helicopter flipped over and over. I clung to my chair in a desperate bid not to fall out, though I knew it wouldn't really make any difference. Either way I'd be hitting the ground and either way I was going to die.

My stomach swooped as we were tossed about like a rag doll in the immense storm. We were riding within its hold but any second now it was going to spit us back out and launch us towards the rocks below.

My pulse slammed furiously in my eardrums and my mind was filled with images of my family and Magnar. Like the people I loved most in this world were giving me a fleeting moment to say goodbye. My soul ached desperately as I realised I'd never see them again and I closed my eyes, wanting to be with them instead of caught in the roiling tempest which would equal my end.

Something battered my leg and I hissed in pain as my eyes snapped open and the heavy box flipped past me, sailing out through the hole to my left.

Snow was swirling in around us and the biting wind stung my skin wherever it was exposed.

"We have to jump!" Miles yelled and fear sliced through me as I stared at him while he clung to the remains of the seats opposite me.

Warren gave up on trying to do anything with the controls which were still screaming alerts and he scrambled out of the cockpit, his gaze locking with Miles's for a moment as he gave him a firm nod.

Fabian shoved himself away from the door to my right, using the seats to drag himself closer to me as we were flipped the right way up again and sent into a tailspin.

"You're gonna have to trust me, love," Fabian growled as he yanked me out of the seat and heaved me into his arms.

"What?" I breathed, staring up at him in total confusion. I grabbed his biceps to stop myself from falling and he planted his feet solidly as he held me close.

I was going to die. This was it and it wasn't nearly enough. I was leaving Magnar in the hands of that insane woman and we hadn't even solved the prophecy. Somehow, I'd never seen our journey ceasing so abruptly and yet it was suddenly abundantly clear to me that my life was at an end. There was no way out of this. There was no possibility that I could survive the inevitable end to this fall as we raced towards the Earth.

The helicopter juddered wildly as we were flung from the grip of the tornado and for a moment we seemed to hang suspended in mid-air. Fabian lifted me into his arms and started running before I could really comprehend what was happening. I sucked in a breath as he leapt out of the hulking hole in the side of the helicopter, clutching me to his body.

I screamed as we plunged into the blizzard, wrapping my arms around his neck and burying my face against his chest.

Fabian's grip on me tightened and a growl left his lips as we plummeted toward the ground.

Everything was a spiralling mess of white as the blizzard raged around us and we fell alongside the heavy snow. My stomach swooped and my hair was tugged upward, swirling above me as we shot down, down, down towards a landing which would be anything but soft.

I was screaming and I couldn't stop. My heart hammered desperately against my ribs as I careered towards death and it ached for me to find some impossible solution to the inevitable.

Fabian kept hold of me firmly with his right arm but released me with his left as we slammed through the tree canopy. Branches slapped at my arms and back as we crashed through them, and my heartbeat thundered in my ears as I cowered against Fabian's chest.

I knew he was trying to save me but I didn't see what possible difference he could make. His body might be able to survive this, but mine sure as hell couldn't and there was no way he could shield me from the landing that was coming.

"I love you, Monty," I breathed because I had to say it if I was going to die. "I love you, Magnar. I'm sorry."

We lurched sideways as Fabian grabbed one of the trees to slow our fall. The sound of splintering wood filled the air but he caught a second branch as the first broke. Then a third.

He grunted in pain as he collided with a thick trunk, shielding me from the worst of the impact as he wrapped his left arm around me again, holding me so tightly that I could barely breathe.

He threw his weight back and we slammed into the ground with him beneath me, the sound of a thunderclap breaking out as his body carved a hole in the earth.

Pain flared through my side and my breath was knocked from my lungs as I was thrown off of him and I lay gasping in the snow as my brain tried to adjust to the fact that I wasn't dead.

I sucked in air as I stared up at the sky and an enormous boom

106

sounded, followed by huge fireball blossoming through the trees to our right as the remains of the helicopter hit the ground.

I groaned as I clawed at the snow and dirt which surrounded me and I managed to roll onto my hands and knees.

My limbs were trembling too much from a mixture of shock and adrenaline for me to attempt to stand, but I had to make sure that Fabian was alright.

I crawled across several inches of snow as the blizzard continued to howl overhead. I found his hand, gripping it in mine as I leaned closer to see his face. He was unnaturally cold but I guessed that was normal for him and the fact that his body was still here must have meant he was still alive.

"Fabian?" I breathed, shifting closer so that I was leaning over him. I reached out to touch his face. His eyes were closed and it seemed like he was unconscious.

I cupped his cheek, shaking him lightly in an attempt to rouse him. My hair spilled over my shoulder and I tucked it behind my ear as it brushed across his neck.

"Fabian?" I said more urgently, looking up to try and make sense of our surroundings.

The blizzard pressed close, and it was hard to make out anything about the area aside from the trees which rose up towards the sky on every side. I could just see the orange glow of the helicopter wreckage to my left as it continued to burn.

I opened my mouth to call out for the others but I wasn't sure if I should. We were still in the grip of Valentina's storm and I had no idea how close she could be.

Fabian groaned beneath me and I looked down at him again, running my thumb across his cheek as I urged him to come back to me.

"Fabian, are you okay?" I breathed.

His eyes opened and he frowned up at me as he came to his senses again.

My heart stuttered with relief and a laugh left my lips as I shifted back, moving to pull my hand from his face. He raised his own hand before I could and pressed it to the back of mine, keeping my palm

107

against his cheek for a moment.

"You're alright," he breathed and the look in his eyes told me he hadn't been sure that I would be.

I gave him what was quite likely the first genuine smile I'd ever offered him. "Thanks to you."

My heart pounded with gratitude to this monster who I'd thought I hated so much and before I could reconsider it, I wrapped my arms around his neck, pulling him against me in a fierce embrace.

Fabian took a deep breath as he held me against him on the freezing ground and my head spun at the idea that I actually cared about this creature. He was the reason for so much misery that had befallen me while I'd lived in the Realm, but somehow, I'd managed to discover a sliver of humanity within his dark soul and I wasn't prepared to see it die.

I pulled back, giving him an awkward smile as I scrambled to my feet. He pushed himself up too, grimacing slightly as his wounds continued to heal. His shoulder hung at an unnatural angle and he raised his other hand as he shoved it back into its socket with a hiss of pain.

"I'm glad you're okay," he murmured, and I gave him a slanted smile.

"Well I guess Idun's bond did me a favour after all," I replied, glancing down at the silver cross on my palm.

"It wasn't the bond," he said softly, and I frowned as I realised he was right.

I'd been shielding all of us with the ring so the gods couldn't do us any harm while we tried to escape and I was still doing it without even sparing it any attention.

"So why..."

"I didn't much like the idea of a world without you in it," Fabian replied with a shrug.

"Really?" I asked, failing to keep the surprise from my face.

I was sure that what he'd done had put himself at a lot more risk than jumping alone would have. It was perfectly possible that that fall could have damaged his body enough to destroy his heart and end his immortal existence. And despite the desire he'd made clear that he felt for me, I had been sure that it was nothing more than a game to him when the bond wasn't in place. I was a challenge and he'd wanted to conquer me.

But his actions made me wonder if I'd missed something much purer about his intentions. Maybe he was just looking for someone to see beneath his bullshit and find a real, *human* connection.

Fabian shrugged and I could feel him putting up walls again as he turned his gaze towards the fire which blazed between the trees. I could almost sense an overly suggestive remark coming and I caught his hand, forcing him to look at me again before he could utter it.

"I'm glad you aren't under the ring's influence now," I said. "So I can be sure that this is the real you I'm looking at. And I'm *really* glad that you're alright."

His eyes roamed over me like he was expecting me to follow up with some kind of sarcastic remark, but I didn't want to taunt him or snap at him anymore. Weirdly, I was pretty sure I just wanted him to be my friend.

"Thank you, Fabian," I added before he could be tempted to say anything else. "I won't forget that you saved my life."

Fabian stared at me for several long seconds before a smile finally pulled at his mouth. And it wasn't teasing or flirtatious or sarcastic or anything else. It was simply a reflection of the pleasure he felt at my words.

"You're welcome, Callie," he replied softly.

MONTANA

CHAPTER TWELVE

I sped through the trees, slowed only slightly by the snow beneath my feet as I shoved through dense foliage, following the howls of the coyotes ahead of me.

"Julius!" I called, needing to be sure I hadn't imagined hearing him before.

"Montana! Over here!" Clarice's voice came in response and my thoughts spiralled as I darted out into a clearing. How was she here? Had she fallen too?

The coyotes were circling the area around two figures on the ground, snarling and snapping. Clarice was kneeling over Julius who was unmoving on the earth beneath her. My heart tugged frantically at the sight.

I froze at the edge of the trees, terrified of finding out he was dead. I couldn't bear to face that reality.

Clarice lifted her head, gazing around at the animals surrounding her as if seeing them for the first time. Her uniform was ripped and torn, and her golden hair tumbled about her like a waterfall with twigs and leaves sticking out of it. She hissed at the coyotes, baring her fangs. They assessed her, tilting their heads, eyeing up Julius for their next meal.

"Get out of here," she snarled.

They watched Julius intently, backing up a little but still hungering for their meal. I could smell the divine sweetness of the blood in his veins and had no doubt they could too. I bared my own fangs at them, stepping closer with a growl that Clarice echoed.

The coyotes glanced between us, their heads dropping as if they sensed we were a danger to them. Miraculously, they backed down and darted off into the woodland.

I couldn't make my feet move as I stared at Julius's still form.

"Is he..?" I choked on the last word, unable to say it.

Between the howling wind and the groaning branches, I couldn't hear his heartbeat. But what if there was no heartbeat to hear?

"He's alive," Clarice breathed, and her words sent relief spilling through me.

The tension in my muscles trickled away, allowing me to run forward.

"I jumped out and caught him. I took the worst of the injuries, but he hit his head on a branch," Clarice said, her tone frank but I spotted a glimmer of emotion in her azure eyes.

I gazed at her in surprise, noting the blood that clung to her bared flesh where she must have been injured.

"Thank you," I gasped, dropping to my knees and wrapping my arms around her. Tears spilled down my cheeks as I leaned away, another pang of horror gripping my heart. "What about the others?"

"I don't know," she murmured, and my shoulders stiffened with worry.

I looked down at Julius, eyeing the large cut on his forehead, and I rested a hand on his shoulder as relief spilled through me. "We need to get to them. How are we going to wake him up?"

Clarice reached out to him and pinched his nose tight. After several seconds, his mouth opened and he gulped down air, his eyes wide.

He smacked her hand away then threw a palm to the welt on his head. "Fucking *ow*. Are you trying to suffocate me after I just survived that fall, parasite?"

112

Clarice pursed her lips, getting to her feet and backing away without a word.

"She saved you," I revealed, falling forward to hug him tight. "She jumped out after you. Don't you dare start insulting her, she's the reason you're alive."

Julius stilled in my arms and I lifted my head, finding a war contained within his eyes.

"Bullshit. I don't believe it." He sat upright then groaned woozily, clutching his head.

Clarice moved to the edge of the clearing as snow beat down on us from above. "I don't care what you believe, you just need to get up and help us find the others."

Julius stared at her in confusion and I rose, taking his hand to guide him to his feet. I noticed Clarice was walking with a slight limp and realised how badly injured she must have been in that fall.

Why had she jumped after him? Did she actually care about him? I'd never seen anything but animosity between the two of them so that was hard to believe.

Whatever her reasons, I had the urge to hug her again but I fought it off, knowing we needed to get moving. The sound of the helicopter crashing had come from this direction, but we were nowhere near close enough. And I had to get to my twin.

Julius laid a hand on my arm, eyeing my terrified expression. "She'll be alright," he said, but he didn't look convinced.

"Come on, we have to get to the crash site," Clarice urged, heading off into the forest as fast as she could with her injury hindering her.

We hurried on through the trees and anxiety scored a path through my chest while I tried not to consider the possibility that Callie hadn't survived. I couldn't let the thought get its grips in me or I'd break down under the immensity of that terrifying grief. It wasn't true, and I'd defy any possibility of it until I knew it to be so.

Julius moved ahead of me, taking hold of Clarice's arm to get her attention. She didn't look at him, marching onward with a steely determination.

"You didn't actually jump out after me, right?" Julius muttered.

113

"Maybe you fell too and I rode your falling body to safety?"

"Whatever," Clarice said, her tone terse. "I don't care what you think."

"By the gods," Julius murmured as we picked up our pace. "You really are obsessed with me."

Clarice turned so fast I had no time to react as she pinned Julius to a tree by his throat. He reached for Vicious at his waist, but she grabbed his wrist to stop him.

"Shut your damn mouth, slayer. I saved you because we're allies, alright? And we need you to bring down Valentina. Once she's dead, I won't hesitate to rip your pretty head off."

"You think I'm pretty," he choked out against her fierce grip.

"*That's* what you heard in what I said?" she snarled.

I grabbed hold of her arm, trying to prise her off of him. "We have to go - our families need us!"

Their eyes swung to me and their argument fell away in a heartbeat.

Clarice released Julius and he stumbled as he moved after her, clearly affected by his head wound.

We moved on through the woods in silence and Julius kept staring at the back of Clarice's head as if he couldn't figure out what was going on.

I took his hand, giving him a firm look that told him exactly what I thought of his reaction to a Belvedere saving his life.

He sighed, shaking his head as if he was lost, confounded by this situation and grappling with the truth of it.

As Clarice healed, she started jogging and I found my body strong enough to keep pace with her too. I knew I was weakened though and the scent of Julius's blood was calling to me in a way I was struggling to ignore. I willed away the urges growing in me, refusing to accept them. I'd never drink from my friend. *Never.*

Julius darted after us, though his movements were slightly clumsier than usual. He quickened his stride and fell into step with Clarice shoulder to shoulder.

"Why?" he growled.

"I told you why," she breathed. "Just forget about it."

"How am I supposed to forget about it?" Julius demanded and I edged closer to them, worried this would descend into a fight again.

"I don't know, just do what you do best and continue to hate me," Clarice insisted. "It would make this a lot less awkward."

"How am I supposed to hate you after you saved my life?" he blurted then fell quiet as if he hadn't meant to say it.

"Well, maybe you can't," she muttered. "Since you saved my life back at Realm A, I've found it a little harder to despise you."

"Oh I see. This is tit for tat," Julius announced as if that idea gave him some peace of mind.

Clarice fell quiet and the air thickened with unspoken words.

I was glad they'd stopped arguing at least. We needed to find the wreckage. Find Callie. We didn't have time to waste.

The edge of the forest came into view, and as we reached it, Clarice dropped down behind a large boulder, waving frantically for us to follow. The faint thumping of footfalls carried to my ears and I kneeled down beside her with Julius in tow. I gripped my gun, my nerves steeling as I stared out across the field of snow before us.

On the other side of the plain in a thick group of trees, a fire was raging where the wreckage of the helicopter must have been. My heart squeezed with terror as I gazed at the sight, the smoke clouding my senses, though I couldn't scent blood among it. And I had to take that as a good sign.

"They got out," Clarice whispered. "They would have jumped."

I nodded, but how could Callie survive that?

Clarice pressed a finger to her lips and I remained silent as two figures darted into view.

Erik and Magnar were a hundred paces away, but I would have known my husband's silhouette anywhere. Talons dug into my heart and emotion welled inside me as I gazed at him, framed by the fire blazing in the woodland. Julius took hold of my arm as if he expected me to run to Erik. But I wasn't a fool. If they saw us, it would only start a fight I refused to face.

"Perhaps they're all dead," Magnar suggested hopefully as they continued to run in the direction of the crash. It must have been a few miles away on the flat field stretching out before us, but it wouldn't take them long to get there.

"Let's hope so, brother," Erik said as they increased their pace and headed out of earshot.

If Callie and the Belvederes were alive, they could be hurt. Weak. And they wouldn't be ready for an attack.

"Valentina's exposed while she's away from them," Julius growled. He pointed in the direction Erik and Magnar had come from. "If we can get close, we could finish her."

Clarice's eyes widened as she nodded, and the idea lit a hungry fire inside me. That bitch needed to pay for what she'd done.

"We have to warn the others first," I breathed, still not allowing myself to consider that they might be dead.

"And how are we going to do that?" Julius hissed.

"*Gods*, wait a second." Clarice started patting down her uniform hopefully then smiled as she produced a cellphone from her pocket. "I took it from a soldier. Fabian has one too."

"Call him," I urged, taking hold of her arm and squeezing.

She nodded, dialling a number and holding it to her ear.

A persistent ringing noise reached me on the line and I fell entirely still as I waited, desperate for him to answer and give us news of my sister.

"Clarice?" Fabian's voice sounded through the speaker and I tensed, suddenly fearing what he was about to say.

"Oh thank the gods," Clarice sighed. "Is everyone alright?"

"Yes, we're all okay."

"What about Callie?" I demanded, my nails digging into Clarice's arm.

"I jumped with her. She's fine," Fabian said and relief crashed through me, lightening my weighted heart. She was okay. Shit, and Fabian had protected her? I was eternally in debt to him if that was true.

"Julius survived too," Clarice said.

"I don't care," Fabian muttered and Julius scowled.

"We're on the edge of the forest," Clarice went on. "We've just seen Erik and Magnar heading toward the wreckage, but that means

Valentina isn't protected. We're going to head her way and see if we can intercept her."

Anticipation spilled through me at the mere idea of it. I wanted her head. Her heart. Her blood spilled across the snow she'd brought down on the world. But were we capable of taking her on in our current state? I was exhausted and a burn was growing in my throat, demanding blood.

"Alright, we'll keep them busy while you attempt it," Fabian said.

"Be careful," Clarice said.

"Good luck, sister." The line went dead and I gazed across the dark field as the wind whipped up and the smoke changed direction, coiling toward us.

An acrid tang of burning plastic and scorched metal filled my nostrils and my nose wrinkled in response.

"That should help hide your scent, slayer," Clarice said. "Let's move."

"We should stay in the trees," Julius said and a renewed strength filled me.

We could do this. We had the upper hand. It was three against one, even if we were weakened.

Julius reached for Valentina's sword at his hip, leaving his broken sword, Menace, in its sheath. "Let's go hunt ourselves a witch."

CALLIE

CHAPTER THIRTEEN

Fabian led the way through the forest toward the flaming wreckage and I kept close to him as the storm continued to howl around us. He was limping slightly, and I could tell that he was trying to cover up the extent of his injuries as his immortal body fought to repair them. The snow was beginning to pile up and it was already drifting into banks.

Fabian stilled for a moment, cocking his head towards the trees before suddenly upping his pace. I hurried after him, jogging to match his speed and the snow crunched beneath my boots. I pulled my collar up around my neck and was glad of my gifts as they fought to protect me from the biting cold.

We pushed through the trees and suddenly the warmth of the burning wreckage washed over me as we found ourselves in a wide clearing created by the helicopter when it had crashed.

Splintered tree trunks lay everywhere and the wreckage blazed angrily as the fire consumed it.

Miles shot into the space in a rush of motion, his eyes widening as they fell on me.

"You're alive?" he asked in surprise, his gaze shifting to his brother.

"Nice work, Fabian."

"It was nothing," Fabian said dismissively. "We need her help with the prophecy so I couldn't very well let her die."

I frowned at him, nudging him with my elbow. "Don't do that," I said, annoyed that he was falling back on his asshole ways so soon.

Fabian gave me a faint frown and sighed in defeat. "And maybe I didn't want her to die because I...just didn't," he added, and Miles raised an eyebrow.

"Where's Warren?" I asked, scanning the trees around us for any sign of Miles's husband.

The fiery wreckage was sure to draw Valentina our way and we really needed to be getting the hell away from it before she found us here.

"Bit of an issue with that," Miles replied with a frown. "I can't find all of him."

"What do you mean *all* of him?" I asked in confusion.

"I mean his body didn't fare too well in the collision with the ground and so far, I've only found his legs and his head," Miles replied tersely. "And this damn smoke is making it impossible to follow his scent to track down the other pieces."

"That's...really fucked up," I said, unable to hold it in.

Fabian snorted a laugh.

"Less judging, more searching if you don't mind, little slayer," Miles replied irritably. "We could be under attack at any moment and I'd like to have Warren back on his feet by then."

I nodded and he shot away from us to continue his search among the trees. I turned in the opposite direction and Fabian strode towards the wreckage.

My heart was still alive with fear for the others. I guessed that Montana and Clarice would have survived but what if they'd ended up like Warren? Immobilised and in several pieces? And what about Julius? I couldn't bear to face the fact that he might not have made it but how could I believe that he'd live through that fall?

"What if one of the pieces of him is completely destroyed?" I asked, unable to hold back my curiosity as I frowned into the space between the trees, hoping to spot a torso buried in the snow.

"It would heal once reattached," Fabian replied.

"But like, what if I cut off your arm and then burned it so there was nothing left. Then what?" I pressed.

"Are you planning on doing that to me?" he asked, a trace of amusement in his tone.

"Maybe. If you won't answer my questions about it then I'll have to, to find out," I replied teasingly.

"If it was entirely destroyed then the stump would just heal over. But any flesh can regrow so all I would need to heal would be the bones."

"Wow," I replied, a shudder racing along my skin. "That really is fucked up."

Fabian chuckled. "You should have been there when we discovered all of this if you want to know about fucked up."

I imagined them toying with ripping off limbs and attempting to destroy them beyond the ability to heal, and my stomach turned. Maybe it was better if I didn't ask for any more details on that particular story.

Fury tingled at my hip and I was struck with a sudden idea. I pulled the blade from its sheath and reached for its ability to sense the vampires.

The blade boiled with rage at the proximity of Fabian and Miles, but I forced it to dismiss its knowledge of them and focused instead on hunting for the heart of the Elite we were searching for.

I smirked as the blade urged me into the trees across the clearing and I hurried to follow its directions.

I squinted through the blizzard as it swirled around me, making it almost impossible to see what lay ahead. My foot caught on something, almost sending me sprawling face first to the ground and as I righted myself, I spotted a hand sticking out of the snow.

I brushed the snow aside and found Warren's torso beneath it.

"*Here*," I called, keeping my voice fairly low in case Valentina was within earshot.

Miles darted between the trees with Warren's legs and head in his arms and I fought a grimace as he placed them on the snow-covered ground. Fabian drew close behind me and I backed up a step as Miles realigned Warren's torso with the rest of his body parts and they began to fuse back together.

"Come on, baby," Miles muttered, brushing his fingers through Warren's dark hair as he waited for him to heal.

Warren's eyes snapped open and I flinched in surprise as he took a shuddering breath. He shoved himself into a sitting position and gripped the front of Miles's shirt, kissing him fiercely as he found that he was okay too.

I looked away from them to allow them some semblance of privacy and found Fabian watching me with interest.

"Was it quite as abhorrent as you thought?" he asked.

"I never said it was abhorrent," I replied. "It must be pretty handy to be almost invincible - but it's still fucked up."

Fabian's lips twitched with a smile. "So it doesn't tempt you to join us in our immortality?"

"No," I replied firmly. "I'll take my chances with my fragile body just the way it is, thanks."

Miles heaved Warren to his feet and the two of them exchanged a heated look as the shock of what we'd all just survived began to sink in.

A faint buzzing reached my ears and Fabian slid a cellphone from his pocket.

"Clarice?" he sighed as he answered the call, his tone laced with relief. "Yes we're all okay... I jumped with her; she's fine... Well, that's good I suppose..." his face darkened and he nodded firmly. "Alright, we'll keep them busy while you attempt it… Good luck, Sister." He ended the call and I waited for him to explain.

"Clarice is with Montana and the slayer," he said.

"Julius is alive?" I gasped, my heart soaring at the prospect. "Is he okay?"

"It would seem Clarice saved him much as I saved you," he replied. "So he's fine. But the more pressing issue is that we've got company on the way: Erik and Magnar are coming to make sure we're all dead."

My lips parted in horror and I glanced between the rest of my small group, wondering what we should do. I guessed we needed to flee but without Montana and the others I wasn't sure where we'd head to.

"So do we run from them?" Miles asked, voicing my question.

"No. Clarice wants to use us to keep them distracted while they head after Valentina. If they can kill her and destroy that damn necklace then hopefully our brother and the slayer will be returned to their right minds," Fabian replied.

My heart fluttered with hope at the prospect and Fabian raised an eyebrow as if he could hear it.

"And how are we supposed to stand against them in this state?" Warren asked and I frowned in confusion, not understanding what he meant.

"We'll just have to hope we can manage it. It's four against two after all," Fabian replied.

Warren's gaze slid to me and Miles nodded as if he'd asked a question.

"What?" I demanded, knowing I was missing something in their words.

"Nothing," Fabian growled, glaring at his brother and Warren. "We will make do as we are."

"You know that fall took too much out of us," Miles replied. "They'll kill us if we face them like this."

"What are you talking about?" I demanded. The three of them looked perfectly fine to me but they were talking as if they were all unfit to face this fight.

"Nothing," Fabian snapped again.

"We need to feed," Miles replied, ignoring his brother. "Healing from wounds like the ones we just survived takes a lot out of us. It weakens us. If we face my brother and Magnar in this state, then I don't know if we'll be strong enough to hold them off."

"We outnumber them," Fabian repeated angrily as I realised what Miles wanted from me. "We'll be fine."

My heart pounded and I took a step back from the hunger I could see glimmering in the vampires' eyes. There was no way in hell I was letting them bite me.

And then we can all die here and your blood can feed the trees instead.

"Is there any chance the stock we brought from the base survived the crash?" Warren asked, looking over his shoulder towards the flaming wreckage.

"No," Miles replied, his gaze flicking to me then away again.

I could tell they weren't just making this up; they really needed to feed and here I was, standing before them like a pitcher of water in the middle of a desert. And yet none of them had made a move towards me. They were fighting their desire for my blood in favour of my feelings on the matter. Miles may have been willing to ask it of me, but I could tell that none of them were going to force me to submit to this request.

My lips parted in preparation of the refusal I was going to make. But then what? I could keep my blood safely in my veins and allow Erik and the man I loved the advantage they needed to end us all. Or...

"Fine," I breathed and I wasn't entirely sure how the word even left my lips.

Fabian's eyes snapped to mine and I could see that he was about to decline.

"No," he growled. "We'll manage."

"I don't think you'd have brought it up at all if it wasn't a major issue," I replied tersely.

"It is," Miles agreed and his gaze dropped to my neck for a moment before he looked back at my eyes guiltily, his throat bobbing.

"How much do you need?" I asked. Those bottles I'd seen them drinking weren't too big and I was fairly sure I could manage losing that much blood without it affecting me too severely.

"It's not an option," Fabian snarled. "We're too hungry, it could easily become a frenzy and I refuse to risk-"

"We're big boys, brother," Miles interrupted him. "We are well able to control our appetites so that that doesn't happen and you know it. Besides, you've got to admit how good she smells."

Warren bit his lip against the hungry smile which tugged at his mouth, and I shifted uncomfortably.

My nose wrinkled as they discussed me like I was a freshly baked pie on a plate.

"Just do it," I snapped. "We don't have time to keep discussing it; Magnar and Erik will be here at any moment."

Miles took a step forward, but Fabian caught his shoulder.

The three of them were eyeing me like a wolf pack who had just discovered a lamb in their midst, and I took a deep breath as I banished the fear which was threatening to take me captive.

I stepped towards them, wanting to take control of what was about to happen. I kept my eyes fixed on Fabian as I pulled my hair over my shoulder and rolled my sleeves up.

He shook his head at me again and I rolled my eyes at him.

"This is a one-time offer," I growled, half of me still not quite able to believe that I was going to do this. "So you might as well take advantage of it."

I held Fabian's eye as I gave my wrists to Miles on his left and Warren on his right. Their cool hands gripped my skin and I had to fight against the tremble which wanted to rock my flesh. But I had to do this. I couldn't back out now. I thought of Magnar coming for us and the pain it would cause him if he killed me whilst he was under this spell. A steely determination fell over me and I straightened my spine.

I looked into Fabian's dark eyes and I could see the hunger which he was trying to fight off. He'd risked his life to save me in that crash and had paid the price for his actions with this thirst. This was me repaying that debt.

"I trust you," I murmured as I tilted my chin, exposing my throat to the creature from my nightmares.

His resolve crumbled and he moved to cup my face in his hand as he dipped his mouth towards my neck.

"I'm sorry, love," he breathed, and I gasped as his fangs sliced into my throat.

Warren and Miles bit down on my wrists at the same moment and the pain of their combined venom immobilised me as they fed.

A gasp fell from my lips, slipping into a breathy exhale as the power of these incredible creatures fell over me and I found myself utterly captivated in their grasp, giving in to the worst of my nightmares, a willing sacrifice despite every truth of my being.

Fabian dragged me against him, gripping my hair in his fist as the beast within him was let loose, and a whimper escaped me as their teeth sank deeper, their claims ultimate. I was their creature, entirely at their mercy. If they fell into a frenzy now, I knew I would die. Each of them held me so tightly I was certain I had no chance of fighting them off.

My heart pounded as these three monsters played out the nightmare that had haunted me since childhood. And I surrendered to the desire of their thirst, the thrill of it burning through me as I took the ultimate step into sin, betraying everything Idun had intended when creating my race. And as my heart fluttered with the frantic pulse of vulnerability and my life hung in the balance, placed upon the whims of a pack of heathens, I had to admit, that this depravity didn't feel so very bad.

ERIK

CHAPTER FOURTEEN

1000 YEARS AGO

I headed further west while Valentina returned to her clan with the promise of killing Magnar and his brother. A night with her had sated years of pent up frustration in me and though I still wouldn't trust her until she brought me proof of their demise, I was quietly satisfied by what she'd given me so far.

She had handed her body over to my needs and had spent hours fulfilling me until it was all I could think about. Impossibly, a slayer had sparked a hunger in me which I knew would want to be satisfied over and over again. Perhaps she knew that. Perhaps that's why she'd tried so hard to please me, to gain my trust. But if she wanted me dead, she'd had more than enough opportunities to try and kill me. No, I had to admit I believed she truly sought to aid me in my fight against her betrothed. But I wasn't going to let my guard down until I was sure Magnar and his brother were dead.

The plan was for her to follow me west when the task was done. She'd strike lightning from the sky to alert me to her whereabouts and I'd go to her on my own terms.

For now, I needed to focus on finding a new tribe, a new blood supply. I prayed the next people I discovered would be more willing to worship me than the last. I had no desire to hide in the shadows again. I wanted to live a freer life, one where I could come and go as I pleased. Perhaps even interact with mortals again.

As I reached the edge of the thick forest I'd been charting a path through, I caught the scent of a fire on the breeze. Humans were close. A settlement, or a group of nomads. I hoped for the former, needing to put down roots soon. But a wandering group would be easy prey for my next source of blood if it came to it. Then I could move on, continuing my search for a more established food source.

I descended through thick brush, cutting along a rocky path as I followed the scent of smoke. Voices pricked up my ears and satisfaction sprawled through me. There were lots of them. And as I crept to the edge of a boulder and gazed down into a sweeping valley ahead of me, I spotted what I needed. The tribe was small, but big enough to sate my needs. Thirty or so animal skin tents were gathered at the top of the hill on the other side of the valley. The grass rustled in a gust of wind and the scent of their blood carried to me with it. I ran my tongue over my canines, sighing a breath of relief as I moved into the valley under the cover of night.

A rush of wings swooped overhead and I stilled, sensing something unusual about the creature that followed me. My mouth parted as I gazed up at the huge owl as it began to circle me, recognising its colouring. Heimdall. My brother's favourite Familiar.

"Surely not..." I breathed, turning left and right as I hunted for Fabian.

"Erik!" a voice called from up on the hill and I spotted Fabian sprinting out of the village.

"Brother!" I cried in joy, racing to him. He met me halfway and we crashed together, embracing hard.

We weren't meant to meet again for nearly a hundred years, but pure chance had brought us together.

He clasped the back of my neck and I rested my hands on his shoulders as he grinned at me. His hair had grown even longer, hanging loose around his shoulders and there was a brightness in his eyes which I hadn't seen in years.

"Did you come looking for me? Is everything alright?" Fabian asked.

"Everything's fine, I came here on luck alone. The gods have brought us together again." I grinned broadly and he pressed his forehead to mine.

"I've missed you like I miss my heart beating," he growled, and my smile widened.

"I shouldn't stay long, but perhaps a while?" I asked, my throat aching with the need for blood alongside the need to spend time in his company.

"The villagers will adore you," Fabian said keenly. "Stay as long as you wish."

"You know I can't," I said with a heavy weight in my chest as his eyes grew sad. "But I'll stay a few days."

"Yes, at least that." Fabian nodded firmly. "You must come and meet someone."

"Blood first," I rasped, and Fabian frowned darkly.

"Are you in trouble, Erik? What brings you this way?"

I shook my head, hesitating to voice the news I carried with me. I wasn't sure how Fabian would take it, so I decided to wait until I'd fed and cleared my thoughts. "The slayers came too near to my last town, so I had to move on. But there's more news...I'll tell you everything soon."

"Blood," he said, nodding easily. "Come then." He slid his arm around my shoulders, guiding me up the hill to the border of the tents.

People's eyes fell on me curiously, but with no fear. I released a bemused breath as a child pulled on her mother's dress and pointed me out with obvious excitement.

"My brother has come to stay," Fabian announced as we reached a fire pit at the heart of the tribe. Several drunken men and women jumped up from around it, releasing a cheer and I looked to my brother curiously at their easy acceptance of me. It had been a long time since I'd felt welcome somewhere.

"Praise be!" a man yelled. "The gods have answered our prayers again. They have delivered us another Moon Warrior to defend our village."

"Moon Warrior?" I murmured to Fabian.

"Just go with it." He elbowed me then jogged toward the fire and clapped a hand to the man's shoulder. He stumbled forward, laughing as he spilled his cup.

"My brother requires a drink," Fabian said, gazing around at them all.

A young woman stood from the group, her caramel skin and long raven hair like a vision as she moved toward us.

"I'll gladly offer it," she said, eyeing me keenly.

Fabian offered me a wink, leaning closer to whisper in my ear. "The women in this village are the most beautiful I've ever seen."

A lump pushed at the inside of my throat as the woman approached, reaching for me and skating her fingers up my arm.

"Hello, I'm Nirell," she whispered, and the scent of her blood sailed to me, making my head spin.

"Erik," I croaked.

"Come, I'll give you some privacy," she said, taking my hand.

Fabian grinned from ear to ear as I followed Nirell past the fire into a large tent. She turned to me and my lips parted in surprise as she pressed her body against mine, pulling that lovely dark hair from her neck. "Drink, Warrior. Take whatever you need. We owe your brother our lives and his family is ours too."

The flare in her gaze made my throat tighten even more. She was truly willing and seemed delighted by the prospect of giving me her blood, which was more than I ever could have hoped for. I could see why Fabian had chosen to stay here.

I dipped my head, brushing my fangs over her neck and she laced her arms around me as I lost myself to the intoxicating smell sailing from her veins. I eased my fangs into her, attempting to be gentle despite the frantic burn growing in my throat, and she moaned in pleasure as if this actually aroused her.

An amused laugh rolled from my throat as I swallowed a sweet

132

mouthful of blood. I couldn't believe my luck at finding this place.

I drank deeply, chasing away the hungry monster inside me and when I'd taken more than enough, I pulled back and she gave me a lustful look. My brows raised as I was half tempted to take her up on the offer I could see shining in her eyes. But my brother and I had much to catch up on. And family was more important than me losing myself in a woman's flesh, despite how tempting she was.

"Thank you." I took her hand, kissing the back of it and revelling in the warmth of her skin.

"You're most welcome. Anything you need, Moon Warrior. It is yours." She grinned at me and I chewed on my lower lip as I considered her.

"Perhaps I'll take you up on that offer later." I turned and exited the tent, seeking out Fabian by the fire.

I spotted him in the arms of a woman who was so breathtaking to behold, she practically outshone the fire beside her. Her ebony hair was braided down her back and her body was curvaceous, enhanced more so by the cut of her bronze dress. Her face was a picture of beauty, her lips full and her eyes large. She gazed at my brother as if he held her whole world in his palms and I frowned as I drew closer. Fabian was staring at her, brushing a lock of hair behind her ear. I'd never seen him look at a woman like that and it made me want to laugh with joy.

"This is Chickoa," Fabian announced as he spotted me approaching. He suddenly seemed anxious as the girl turned toward me, taking me in with her rich, earthy eyes.

"It's a pleasure to meet you, Fabian's told me so much about you, Erik." She moved forward and slung her arms around me in a hug. I stilled in her hold, unused to such affection from humans.

I slowly folded my arms around her as Fabian gave me an encouraging nod.

"It's a pleasure to meet you too," I muttered.

"Will you stay for the marriage?" Chickoa leaned back and my brow creased with confusion.

"What marriage?" My eyes fell on Fabian as he ran a hand down the back of his neck.

133

"Mine and Fabian's of course," Chickoa said with a bright smile, glancing over at my brother with so much love in her eyes that the air was alive with it.

A slow smile crept onto my face as I surveyed Fabian. "Of course I'll stay. I wouldn't miss it for the world."

Fabian jerked his head at me. "Come, brother. We have much to catch up on." He gestured to a tent on the other side of the fire and I followed him toward it.

"Yes, it appears we do," I jibed as Fabian dropped his arm around my shoulders, guiding me into the tent.

I took in the space filled with furs and wooden furniture. It reminded me of the home I'd grown up in and a warmth spread through my chest as I sat on a pile of furs.

Fabian poured me a cup of some amber nectar which smelled distinctly sweet. He passed it to me before sitting opposite me with a glint of happiness in his brown eyes. "They make this from maize and fruit. It's strong as hell."

I sipped it, enjoying the delightful taste on my tongue followed by the sharp bite of alcohol.

"So you're getting married?" I asked, releasing a breath of amusement.

"I am," he said with no such mirth. "Erik, I love her. So fucking much, words cannot begin to express it. Though I've tried. I write her poems every day." He reached for a sheath of leather on the table which had scribbles all over it.

I took the page, eyeing the words on it as my mind adjusted to the new language. My mouth hooked up at the corner. "Her bosom is as full as the lovelorn moon?"

Fabian snatched the page away. "Yes well...it's not finished yet."

I leant back in my seat, staring at him in awe. "I never thought I'd see the day you would settle down, Fabian."

"I know it's not ideal. But she says she wants to be with me forever. So I think she wants to be like *us*," he said with hope in his gaze. "I have plans to turn her one day soon."

I frowned, eyeing him. "Do you really think she wants that? This curse is not to be handed out like a gift."

"It *is* a gift." He reached across the space between us, gripping my hand. "Or it can be. Look at this place, Erik. We have everything we could ever want here. People who adore us, who willingly give their blood-"

I raised a hand to stop him. "I do not want to feed on blood for the rest of eternity. I want what they have. Warm flesh, a beating heart."

"It isn't all bad," he pressed, and I sipped on my drink to stop this from descending into an argument.

"I have news," I changed the subject. "Though I fear how you might react to it."

He sat forward in his seat, his brows knitting together. "What is it?"

"A slayer came to me last night," I revealed, and Fabian's eyes widened.

"Did you kill them?" he asked hopefully.

"No... she wanted to make a deal with me. She is Magnar Elioson's betrothed. Though it seems the great Earl has not been treating his woman with any respect. He beats her and he refuses to marry her even though it was foreseen by a prophet."

Fabian sat back in his seat, swilling the drink in his cup. "That doesn't surprise me. But what deal did she wish to make? Surely we cannot trust a slayer."

"That's what I thought at first. But she changed my mind when she laid her life in my hands. She has promised to kill both Magnar and his brother and bring me evidence of their deaths."

Fabian's mouth parted and hope flickered in his eyes. "Do you really believe she'll do it?"

"I think she will try," I admitted. "But there is every chance she will fail. Though her powers should give her an advantage. She wields storms."

He took a long swig of his drink as he absorbed that news then his eyes scraped over me thoughtfully. "How did she convince you to trust her?"

"She..." I cleared my throat, not sure if I wanted to tell him. But he was my brother and we'd never kept things from each other before.

"She gave me her body. She laid down her weapon and took her clothes off."

"You fucked a *slayer*?!" Fabian blurted.

I pushed a hand into my hair with a shrug.

"Don't shrug," he said, pointing at me. "I want every detail."

"You're not angry?" I asked.

"Why would I be angry with you for bedding Magnar's betrothed?" He started laughing and I couldn't help but join in. "Details, Erik, for the love of the gods. You must tell me everything."

I swigged from my cup, finishing the contents. "Alright, but I will need more drink first."

Fabian beamed, getting to his feet. "That, I can do."

MONTANA

CHAPTER FIFTEEN

Hunger was building at the base of my throat, and I was glad of the horrid smoke to drown out the delicious scent sailing from Julius's veins. Clarice kept glancing at his neck as we sped through the trees side by side.

We shared a look, and I shook my head. She nodded, dragging her gaze away from Julius as we ran on. I was glad no more needed to be said. I wasn't going to touch him no matter how thirsty I became, and I sensed Clarice would keep her word too. I just prayed we could take on Valentina in our weakened state. We still had our guns. So maybe we would only need one well-aimed shot to take her out.

We followed the edge of the field and the storm eased off a fraction as we closed in on Valentina. I could sense the way her power wielded the air and my mouth parted in surprise as we ran into a bubble of safety that must have surrounded her.

"There," Julius whispered, grabbing my arm to stop me.

Clarice halted, becoming as still as a statue as she leaned around a large tree and gazed out at the field beyond.

The wind gently fluttered my hair and the snowflakes danced steadily in the pocket of calm around us. Behind us, the storm still raged, tearing at the trees and causing an immense blizzard to blow across the land.

Julius's mouth hooked up into a dark smile as he raised Vicious and moved close to Clarice's side.

I held my handgun aloft as I joined them, peering around the huge tree and spotting Valentina out on the field in a navy jumpsuit, her arms raised toward the sky. Behind her was the wall of the army base and five of her biters waited there. They were Elite, the strongest of her followers and my heart clenched at the sight.

Clarice took a pistol from her hip and aimed it at Valentina.

"Montana," she whispered, deadly quiet. "Shoot at the same time. We're more likely to hit her heart with two bullets."

Julius shifted into a fighting stance. "The second you shoot, I'm gonna run. If you miss, I'll finish her."

I gritted my teeth, lining up the barrel of my gun with Valentina's heart. Fifty paces. That was all that parted us. And with my vampire abilities aiding me, I was sure I had a good chance of hitting her.

You can do this.

Don't miss.

"Ready?" Clarice mouthed and I nodded, placing my finger on the trigger.

I stared down the sight of the gun, adrenaline pounding through me.

"Now," Clarice commanded, and I fired.

The bullet unleashed from the barrel and my heart spiralled with hope.

Valentina screamed as the bullets hit her, slamming to the ground in a pool of blood. But not ash.

"Fuck!" Julius sprinted out of the trees to end her with Vicious raised above his head.

Her eyes locked on her own sword in his grip and her face twisted in fury.

"You bastard!" she screamed.

Clarice and I sped after Julius as terror and hope tangled inside me. We were so close. One strike. That's all it would take.

I continued firing my gun at her, but she swept the bullets away on a fierce gust of wind, and I cursed as I moved even faster.

Julius was closing in, his sword ready to finish her.

"You will give my darling weapon back to me, Julius Elioson!" she bellowed.

"Oh you'll get it back, right in your dead heart!" he cried.

Lightning split the earth apart and the three of us were thrown to the ground from the blast. Fear danced under my skin as I immediately sprang upright but ten lightning bolts speared down from the sky at once. I weaved left and right to avoid them, calling on the waning scraps of my energy. The lightning left sizzling blackened holes in the earth and I leapt over one in front of me, revenge burning in my veins as I locked my sights on Valentina. She was back on her feet, her arms raised and her expression furious.

The five Elite at the base were charging toward us and gunfire rattled through the air.

A bullet tore into my shoulder, knocking me sideways. I clutched the wound with a gasp, but kept running, eating up the space between me and Valentina with every stride.

The bullet had gone right through my body and I was relieved as the wound started to heal.

Clarice took another shot at Valentina, but her bullet was forced back to her on a harsh gust of wind. Clarice rolled to avoid it, regaining her feet again as she charged to meet our enemy, holstering her gun and taking a knife from her hip instead.

Julius battled a fierce wind as Valentina held him off too, her eyes wild as she gazed at us. Her jumpsuit was ripped and the bloody holes in her chest were healing over fast.

The Elite arrived and I swung around to meet the first one as she aimed a gun at my chest. She pulled the trigger and I lurched aside in a blur of motion, darting to her right then throwing my full weight at her. We hit the ground and I wrestled the rifle from her grip, tossing it away from her.

She scratched at my face, my shoulders; she was like a wild cat, hissing and spitting. Her bright red hair was a stark contrast to the snow beneath her and I snatched a handful of it, yanking her head back to expose her throat. I dug my fangs into her neck and she shrieked,

141

shoving me off her. I flew backwards onto the ground, my hand landing on the rifle. With a surge of adrenaline, I picked it up as she rose to her feet and stormed toward me.

I pulled the trigger fast, not having enough time to aim right and the bullet ripped right through her stomach. She wailed, stumbling backwards as she clutched the wound.

"Bonny!" a male voice called to her.

I regained my feet, angling the rifle at her chest, ready to finish her off. As I pulled the trigger, a weight crashed into me from behind and the bullet missed her by inches. A male held me down with his immense strength, and I thrashed wildly as the tip of a knife pierced my back.

Air rushed over me and the male's weight flew off of me. I rolled, finding Julius above me, the Elite decapitated by his sword. As the slayer reached down to help me up, a harsh wind forced him on top of me and he crushed me into the snow.

"I can't get up," he snarled, his muscles tensing against the pressure of the air.

The clouds flashed above us and I knew we were being held in place for Valentina's next lightning strike.

"We have to move!" I cried, trying to force him off of me.

A scream of fury cleaved the air apart and Valentina yelled in reply. The wind fell away and the lightning never came. I sighed my relief as Julius dragged me to my feet and I spotted Clarice closer to Valentina, swinging her knife as she battled the wind which kept her back. Valentina's hand was bloody and her fingers half severed. She couldn't focus on all of us at once. Every time she turned her attention from one of us, she gave another an advantage.

Gunfire pelted through the air and I slammed my palms to Julius's chest so he hit the ground out of harm's way. A bullet grazed my side and I snarled my fury, turning my own gun on the line of three Elite who had held back to fire on us.

I started running at them, weaving left and right to avoid the bullets slicing through the air, knowing I had to make every shot count.

I lifted the rifle, aiming at a male's heart. I took the shot and he exploded into dust, and his companions screamed in fright as a female's gun rang empty.

A fierce smile captured my lips as I aimed at her next. She darted to avoid the first bullet, but my second found her heart and she turned to ash before me. The final Elite started running, skirting around me in a wide arc as he tried to reach Valentina.

I planted my feet, following his movements with the barrel of my gun, biting deep into my lower lip.

I pulled the trigger but the gun barrel clicked and I growled in frustration, tossing the weapon to the ground and taking chase instead.

The redhead, Bonny, was battling with Julius, the wound I'd given her nearly healed. He swung Vicious at her, but she moved with impossible speed, circling him like a rabid dog.

I kept my sights on my own target, powering my arms either side of me as I chased him down.

A heavy fog swirled around Valentina and Clarice, hiding them from view. The Elite I was following darted into it just before the fog swallowed me too as it expanded across the field. The mist became a raging blizzard and I halted, turning left and right as I tried to gather my bearings.

Julius's shouts carried to me on the wind, but they sounded from all around me, leaving me lost in the pressing snow.

The world was a swirl of white and my friends were cut off from me. I listened hard, desperately trying to locate Clarice or Julius as I raced on through the dense fog.

A flash of red warned me of Bonny's arrival. She sped from the snow like a wild beast, her shirt ripped open and splattered with blood from the wound I'd given her. I brought up Nightmare as she dove forward, swinging it toward her.

She smacked my hand aside and landed a punch to my face. I staggered backwards as Nightmare dropped into the snow and I lost sight of it.

Bonny swung at me again with a feral snarl, and I ducked the attack, lunging to uproot her, but she kicked me squarely in the jaw.

I was launched backwards into the snow, sinking deep into it as she pounced to straddle me. Her lip was curled back in anger as she started throwing her fists into my face.

I caught her wrist, twisting until I heard bone snap. She yelped and scratched her nails down my neck with her other hand. Fear lanced through me as I threw my knuckles into the half-healed wound on her stomach and she fell backwards in agony. I regained my feet, advancing on her, exposing my fangs.

She gazed up at me as blood leaked from the corner of her lips. "The true queen is coming for me!"

I booted her in the face and she tumbled away as I prepared to finish her with my bare hands.

The fog shifted and swirled and Valentina stepped out of it with her eyes narrowed on me.

She slashed her hand through the air and sharpened hailstones pelted me. I covered my eyes as I was forced back by the torrent of razor-sharp ice, my skin ripping under the onslaught.

The hailstones turned to wind and I was thrown through the air, tossed about in a vortex before smashing into the ground.

I tried to gain my feet but a stiletto heel dug into my spine and I groaned as it cut into my flesh. Valentina took hold of my hair, wrenching my head backwards so I looked up at her. She twisted her heel and I screamed as I battled to get up, but the raging wind still held me in place.

"Montana Ford," she purred with a wicked grin. "It's time you paid the price for taking a crown that always should have been mine."

CALLIE

CHAPTER SIXTEEN

Fabian groaned in pleasure, his grip on me tightening as my heartbeat thundered out of control. They weren't letting go. My head spun dizzyingly as the three of them continued to suck the blood from my veins and panic reared in my chest as my pulse pounded weakly in my ears.

I tried to step back but they held me too firmly, their fingers digging into my skin as they released sounds laced with their desire for more and more. I wasn't sure I held enough blood in my body to satisfy their thirst and I began to fear that their basest instincts were taking over despite their assurances that they wouldn't allow that to happen.

"Stop," I gasped as my knees threatened to buckle and Fabian jerked back suddenly, releasing me as he blinked the bloodlust from his eyes. His lips were stained red and a bead of my blood ran down his chin.

He snarled at his brother, grabbing Miles's shoulder and pulling him back before shoving Warren off of me too. Miles hissed fiercely, his pupils dilating as he stared at me hungrily. Fear trickled through me as his beautiful face was transformed into that of a monster and no sign of his light-hearted demeanour shone through. It was like looking at a stranger. A stranger who wanted to kill me.

Warren shook his head as he forced himself to back away from me, though I could tell he didn't entirely want to.

I staggered back a step, clutching my wrists to my chest as the pain of their venom burned through my body, the reality of how close I'd just come to death making my heart gallop in my chest.

"Holy shit, why does she taste so *good*?" Warren moaned, his eyes darting to the blood I could feel trickling down my neck.

"I'd almost forgotten what it feels like to feed from a slayer," Miles breathed as he blinked away the desperate look in his eyes and Fabian released his hold on him.

Fabian glanced at me then dropped his eyes as if he was ashamed of what they'd just done. He stooped low and gathered some snow into his hands before approaching me.

I forced myself to hold my ground as he drew closer. I'd known what I was offering when I'd let them bite me, but it didn't do much to make me feel better about it. I felt used somehow...violated, not least because while it was happening, some base part of me had actually revelled in it.

I held my tongue because I wasn't sure what I could possibly say to them in that moment.

Fabian took my hand and I stilled as he rubbed the venom from my wrist with the snow. The icy touch of the snowball against my flesh soothed the burning sensation left by their fangs and I watched in silence as he switched his attention to my other wrist.

"I'm sorry we had to do that," he murmured.

"Why do I taste different?" I asked with a frown, finding my voice at last. The only way we were going to move past this easily was if we faced it. They were vampires. I was mortal. This was always going to be an issue between us unless we could break the curse. Ignoring the fact wouldn't make it go away.

Fabian cleared his throat, not seeming to want to answer and I tipped my chin up as he removed his own venom from my neck.

"It was the gods' way of driving us back to you," Miles supplied for him. "We tried to hide from your kind but making you taste like that meant that we would always be tempted closer again. We can survive on human blood just as easily. But drinking from them is like having water. Drinking from your kind is like-"

"Ecstasy," Warren supplied, sucking the last drop of my blood from his bottom lip.

"So the gods wanted you to hunt the slayers just like they wanted the slayers to hunt you?" I asked, my anger at the gods as easy to find as always.

"I suppose so," Miles said. "They were always driving us against each other."

"And feeding from you could easily become addictive," Fabian muttered.

I looked up at him as he finished cleaning my wound and the burning sensation left my flesh.

"Well don't go thinking about forming any habits," I said firmly as I stepped away from him.

"Pity," Miles murmured, and I gave him a flat look in response.

There was no way in hell I was about to become their personal dining cart and they'd better remember it.

"This was a one-time deal," I said firmly. "And I won't be offering to do it again."

I took a steadying breath and pushed my sleeves down to conceal the bites on my wrists.

I rolled my shoulders back and took a few steps, letting my body adjust to the blood loss and finding that it wasn't as bad as I'd feared. My head swam momentarily but I was soon able to push past the feeling as I drew my gifts to my muscles. My kind were made to kill vampires, so I had no doubt that I was able to survive the effects of a little blood loss as part of the package.

"Did any of you hear that?" Miles asked in a low whisper.

I strained my ears, trying to pick out any sounds above the howling wind and the crackling fire which still blazed among the wreckage beyond the closest line of trees.

My skin prickled as I waited for anything to let me know that Erik and Magnar were drawing close.

"We'll keep Erik away from you," Fabian breathed, glancing at me.

"You won't have to endure any more bites today if I can help it."

"Good," I replied. But that meant that I'd have to focus on Magnar and the last time he'd fought against me it had nearly broken my heart in two.

A piece of me hoped that when Valentina's hold on him was destroyed, he wouldn't remember anything that she'd made him do. I knew he would hate knowing that he'd tried to hurt me. Let alone having to recall whatever else Valentina had forced upon him while his will wasn't his own.

A branch broke in the trees to our right and I stilled as my vampire companions moved to block me from whoever was coming.

The blizzard died down a little and the snow lightened just enough for me to see further into the forest.

Something shot between the trees and my heart leapt as I sucked in a breath, but I lost sight of it before I could be sure of what it was.

The sense of unease grew thicker around me and I strained my ears as I tried to pick out the sounds of anyone approaching.

Gunshots tore through the air and I swore as I dove to the floor. Blood stained the snow in front of me and Miles hissed in pain before he sprang to his feet and darted forward to meet our attacker.

Erik leapt at us, his eyes wild as he skidded to a halt before the flaming wreckage and assessed his foes. He was wearing a black suit which seemed beyond weird for our current situation, but I didn't have much time to consider why. He held an assault rifle in his arms and he grinned at us as he took aim once more.

My mouth fell open as he pointed the heavy weapon right at me and Fabian roared as he launched a huge rock straight at his brother. Erik leapt aside but dropped his gun as he did so, hissing at Fabian as he rolled into a crouch and the rock crashed through the undergrowth where he'd just been standing.

"Erik," Miles begged, holding a hand up. "Fight it, brother. The gods have done this to you. If you'd just try and-"

Erik lunged towards him and Warren raced forward to help before the three of them slammed into the ground, sending snow flying from the impact.

Erik snarled like a feral beast, throwing his fists at his brother and baring his teeth.

I backed up, glancing between the trees as Miles managed to throw Erik off of him and Fabian shot forward in an attempt to restrain him with the others.

Erik swore at them as they snatched at his arms, battling to contain him between the three of them as he fought with all his might to buck them off.

I kept edging away, hairs rising along the back of my neck as I placed my hand on Fury's hilt at my hip.

Erik was faster but Magnar wouldn't be far behind him, and my heart ached at the thought of having him near. I needed him to realise what had happened to him. I longed for him to break free of this hold the gods had placed on his soul.

Behind you! Fury hissed and I gasped as I threw myself to the floor.

Venom shot through the air right where my head had been a moment ago and slammed into a tree on the opposite side of the clearing. Magnar roared a challenge as he burst from the shadows, his gaze set on me and lit with a thirst for violence.

If I'd thought Erik looked strange in the suit, it was nothing to how Magnar looked in one. His muscular frame was bursting out of the fitted material and nothing about the wildness in him seemed suited for such a formal outfit.

I rolled over and Magnar slammed Tempest down, carving it into the snow right beside my head. I released a scream and he smiled wickedly as I rolled again and he dragged the blade back for a second strike.

I snatched Fury from its sheath, holding it between both of my hands as I raised it to take the force of the next blow.

Metal rang on metal as Tempest hit my blade so hard that I could barely hold it off of me. Magnar grunted with effort as he bore down on me and my back was pressed into the snow. I gritted my teeth as I fought to drive him back.

"My love wants that ring on your finger," he snarled, eying my hand hungrily.

My arms trembled as he threw his strength into forcing the blades closer to my neck and I cried out as I kicked his knee.

His leg buckled beneath him and he swore at me as I threw my boot into his side, knocking him back.

Magnar fell into the snow and I leapt to my feet, running forward and kicking Tempest from his grasp.

He cursed again and rolled towards me, snatching my ankle as I tried to dance out of his reach.

I crashed down into the snow once more and he propelled himself on top of me, driving his fist into my face.

My lip split and pain raced through my jaw as I cried out, struggling beneath him.

"Magnar," I gasped. "Magnar please. It's me. I love you, I-"

He punched me again and the iron taste of blood filled my mouth.

"I have but one love and she has asked me for your head, whore," he spat as he aimed his fist at my face again.

I managed to lurch aside, driving my knuckles up into his chin so his teeth slammed together with a harsh snap.

I launched my other fist into his throat and he reared back, giving me enough room to scramble out from under him.

He tried to follow me and I kicked him, my boot connecting with his face and causing him to bellow with rage. He couldn't hear me. His only thoughts were the ones Valentina had planted in his head. It was like his body was a shell and the man I loved wasn't inside it anymore.

I struggled to my feet and backed away as Magnar got up too. He hounded after me, his gaze glinting with the promise of my death and a deep green glow lighting the backs of his eyes.

"Is your sister cast to ash or will I have the pleasure of ending her too?" he snarled as he stalked closer, and I continued to back up.

I opened my mouth to respond just as Erik was hurled over my head. He slammed into Magnar and the two of them tumbled away from us through the woodland.

I glanced around and found Warren grimly acknowledging his victory as Miles and Fabian stood ready to continue our fight.

"How long do we keep this up?" I asked as Magnar and Erik appeared between the trees again, stalking towards us like a pair of demons with only one goal in sight. They wanted our deaths. And I wasn't sure how much longer we could keep evading their best efforts.

"Until their spell is lifted or our luck runs out," Fabian snarled, placing himself in front of me.

My mind went to Montana and the others. I just hoped they managed to kill Valentina soon because I wasn't sure how much more time we could buy. If they could destroy that necklace, then Magnar would come back to me. I just prayed that would happen before he managed to kill me.

The four of us stood ready to defend ourselves once more and it didn't slip my notice that both Erik and Magnar were looking at me like I was their goal. I guessed that meant Valentina had put the highest price on my head and I was glad that I'd gotten under her skin that much. But I wasn't so pleased that it meant two of the deadliest creatures on the planet were determined to kill me.

I clenched my fist tightly, the ring digging into my fingers while I revelled in the warmth of its power as it hid me from the gods. I had no doubt that Valentina wanted to get her hands on the ring for Idun's sake, and I had zero intention of allowing that bitch of a goddess to get anywhere near it.

We closed ranks and I prepared myself to face off against Magnar once more but before they could reach us, purple lightning speared through the sky. It split like cobwebs, coating the clouds above us in a glittering, lilac net.

The two of them looked up at it for a moment, then exchanged a dark glance.

Magnar snatched Tempest from the ground and ran to heave Venom from the tree it was lodged in. He turned away from us without a backwards glance and sprinted into the forest, his footfalls racing away at speed.

Erik raised his hand and pointed a finger right at me. "I'll be right back to claim your head for my love," he promised before sprinting away too.

"What the hell was that?" I asked in astonishment as we were left alone before the burning wreckage and some of the tension eased from

153

our group.

"Valentina must want them back with her," Miles said excitedly. "Let's hope that means our sister is about to kill her!" He shot after Erik and Magnar in a blur of motion and Warren chased behind him.

Fabian glanced down at me with a triumphant smile lighting his face. "It seems the tables are finally turning on that traitor," he said.

I grinned in return and started running for the edge of the clearing too. Fabian let me get a little way ahead of him before powering forward and sweeping me into his arms. I cursed with surprise as he pulled me against his chest.

"You're too slow," he explained with a dark laugh. "Let me show you how fast I can move."

I opened my mouth to protest but he didn't give me a chance as he charged forward into the trees, and I was forced to cling on for dear life as the wind ripped at my hair. Fabian carved a path through the thick snow at our feet and we speared through the forest at an alarming pace.

We leapt out of the cover of the trees and landed in a sprawling field. I could see Erik and Magnar ahead of us as they sprinted towards the base where the storm continued to rage. The snow fell so thickly around it that it was impossible to make out any of the buildings, let alone what was going on there.

Purple lightning lit the clouds again and again as Valentina continued to send out her signal for them to return and I just hoped that Montana and the others managed to kill her before they arrived.

We raced across the field towards her and my gut filled with a steely determination. It was time we ended that bitch's rule once and for all. I was going to rip her crown from her head and force it down her throat. Then, as soon as we'd destroyed that damn necklace, I planned on letting Magnar and Erik kill her in the worst way they could imagine in revenge for all she'd forced upon them. She would rue the day she stole my man from me, and I had no doubt that the death he delivered her would be slow and deserving.

MONTANA

CHAPTER SEVENTEEN

Valentina released my hair and her heel left my back as someone collided with her. A flutter of blonde hair in my periphery told me Clarice had arrived and my heart soared with relief. I rolled over, groaning as my wounds started to heal.

Clarice had Valentina on her back and the emerald on her necklace flashed green. The second Clarice raised her pistol, a harsh wind threw her off. She slammed into the ground, tumbling through the snow and throwing up a sheet of white flakes.

Valentina rose to her feet, trying to regain the upper hand but a flicker of fear danced across her features. I crawled backwards through the snow, my blood staining it crimson as I moved. Panic trickled through me as I felt for Nightmare's presence, reaching into the icy depths around me to locate it. The second I found it, I was going to cut her heart out and crush that necklace beneath my boot.

Clarice sped toward Valentina once more, battling the wind with all her might. She started side-stepping again and again, and Valentina turned toward her, slowly exposing her back to me. Hope filled me as I realised what Clarice was doing. She was giving me a chance at finishing this bitch.

My fingers brushed something warm.

Moon Child.

I snatched up Nightmare, rising to my feet with a wild excitement growing in me. I had to be swift and silent. Valentina had to think I was still injured on the ground. I had mere seconds to act.

I held Nightmare by my ear, aiming at her back. One good shot could end her. One good shot could bring Erik back to me. And the thought alone almost made my heart beat with longing.

Let me fly to her heart, Nightmare begged.

I threw the blade with all my might, willing it to bring Valentina to her death. It flew towards her spinning end over end, cutting through the air. Valentina half turned and the blade missed its target as it drove into her back but not nearly deep enough. She wailed in pain, whipping around to face me as thunder bellowed overhead.

Valentina snarled, forcing a wave of air against me and I stumbled away. But with her back to Clarice, she couldn't focus on keeping her at bay too. Clarice ran forward to grab her, catching Valentina around the throat with a shout of triumph. She tried to prise the necklace from her neck and Valentina slashed at her hands with a shriek of anger.

I blinked against the snow battering me, pushing against its ferocity to try and help Clarice.

Valentina yelped as Clarice brought her to her knees, the Belvedere changing tact as she wrestled to rip her enemy's head from her shoulders. The wind fell away as Valentina lost her concentration and I smiled in satisfaction as I bolted forward to join the fight.

Clarice had her arm locked around Valentina's neck, digging her heels into the snow as she struggled to tear her head off. We were so close. If she could disable her body, we could skewer her heart and turn her to dust.

Clarice gasped as Nightmare's hilt dug into her side and her hold eased enough that Valentina got free, scrambling away on her hands and knees. I aimed a sharp kick at her face, but she fell backwards onto the snow to avoid it and raised her hands to the sky.

Lightning flashed above me and I launched myself sideways as a bolt hit the ground where I'd just been standing. Static crackled over my body, telling me how close I'd come to my end.

Valentina reached behind her back, ripping Nightmare out of her flesh and wielding it at me instead. "You think you can beat me? The queen of storms?" she snarled and lightning cascaded from the sky, so many strikes at once, I didn't know where to run.

I moved left and right, blinded as the bolts struck the ground everywhere. I was one wrongly-placed foot away from death. The light was so bright and the heat of it sizzled up my spine as the bolts came ever closer to finishing me.

Clarice cried out, but I couldn't turn to check if she was alright as I jumped and swerved, miraculously missing the electrical storm that rained down from the heavens.

Darkness fell again and I found myself twenty paces away from Valentina. The snow had melted in the whole area and charred earth took its place. Valentina's shoulders drooped and I could see exhaustion in her eyes.

Realisation slid through me. She couldn't keep this storm up. It was draining her.

I hunted for Clarice and found her nursing a line of blisters up her legs, her pants burned entirely away. The scent of singed skin tangled with the air and a wave of anger found me in response, a protectiveness for her flooding my chest.

Valentina set her sights on me, drawing her shoulders back as she dug deep for her strength. She lifted her hands and I tensed, but nothing happened. No wind, no snow, no lightning. She was depleted. And with a victorious look gripping my features, I ran to meet her.

"Montana – here!" Clarice shouted, tossing me something.

I caught the pistol out of the air and my finger slid onto the trigger with smooth grace. I raised it at Valentina and she fell back a step, lifting Nightmare as she prepared to face me.

"That's my blade, bitch," I snarled.

Her contorted expression told me she was scared and I hoped it was the last look I'd ever see on her beautiful face as I pulled the trigger.

Someone leapt out of the mist behind Valentina, soaring in front of her like a shield. The bullet impacted with the redhead Bonny and she burst to ash around her queen with an echoing wail.

Valentina used the second the girl's death had bought her, turning and fleeing into the mist.

I gritted my teeth, powering after her with every ounce of strength I had left. I could feel my bloodlust rising. The demon in me was hungry. And I was going to use its thirst to finish this fight once and for all.

MAGNAR

CHAPTER EIGHTEEN

I charged into the swirling maelstrom, releasing a battle cry as the billowing snow swallowed me whole and I lost sight of my place in the world.

"Valentina?" I cried, ploughing on with my swords in hand, ready to destroy any who had come to hurt my love.

There was no reply, but the snow suddenly stopped falling from the sky and the battering wind died away to nothing more than a gentle breeze. My heart lurched with concern for the woman I adored. Had she chosen to halt her command over the elements or was she unable to wield them for some reason?

I ran on as the blizzard disappeared and the snow settled, but a heavy fog hung ahead of me, veiling the place I knew my love to be.

"Magnar!" Julius cried and I spotted him running towards me with his blade raised to intercept me.

I ignored him, sprinting to reach my queen but he dove into my path and I was forced to raise Tempest to deflect the blow he aimed at my head.

I spun towards him, snarling my rage as he swung his sword at me again. He was keeping me from helping the woman I loved and I would happily kill him if that was what it took to get to her.

"Let's see which of us is victorious in a real battle, brother," Julius challenged, and I was forced to parry another strike as he aimed his sword at my stomach.

"You cannot hope to defeat me. I fight for love," I growled as I was forced to give him my full attention and I brought both of my blades around to face him, swinging Venom high and Tempest low.

Julius ducked beneath my first strike and metal collided as he deflected the second.

"So do I, brother," Julius replied as he danced out of reach and twisted behind me. "But my love for you is true."

How dare he question my love for Valentina? I would prove my devotion to her by spilling his blood. Then he would see that I cared for her above all else. Even the ties of family.

Rage simmered in my veins as I lunged for him, hacking my swords down with the full strength of my muscles.

Julius leapt back rather than parry the savage blows, and my blades carved through the snow, colliding with the frozen dirt beneath.

"Valentina!" Erik bellowed as he forged on ahead of me towards the mist.

Clarice sprang out of the fog to intercept him and there was a sound like falling rocks as they collided.

Julius kicked at my side as I wrenched my weapons back out of the snow and stumbled away from him, cursing his name.

"That parasite has you caught in a spell but once we've turned her to dust and destroyed that necklace, you'll be free of it," Julius promised.

"May the gods spit on your soul," I hissed at him. "You are no brother of mine."

Julius's face fell into a grimace at my words, and he stepped back as I drove Venom towards his heart.

I swung my swords around, forcing him back further with the power of my fury as I sought to end his miserable existence.

Metal clashed again and again but he held one sword while I wielded two. It was only a matter of time before one of my strikes broke past his defences and I smiled darkly as he fought to hold me off.

Julius growled his frustration at me as he stepped back again but I'd sparred with him many times and it struck me that his retreat was a little too easily won. I stilled as I realised his withdrawal was designed to lead me further from Valentina.

"You still love me, don't you?" I asked him and his brows raised in confusion as I halted our fight momentarily.

"Of course I do," he said, his sword dipping slightly.

"Then I'll hazard a guess that you won't stab me in the back." Before he could respond, I turned and ran from him, charging towards my queen once more as he yelled out angrily, giving chase.

"Duck!" Erik bellowed and I threw myself forward into a roll just as he launched Clarice over my head.

She collided with Julius and I released a dark laugh as I sprang to my feet and closed in on my love.

I moved through the mist and as it lifted, I found Valentina racing for me. But before my beautiful love could make it to me, the dark-haired twin burst from the fog behind her with a raised pistol, aiming it straight for Valentina's head.

Valentina screamed and the gunshot rang out harshly as the bullet slammed straight through her skull. My heart stilled as the brightest red blood splattered the snow, staining everything around her as her body crashed to the ground.

Montana jumped forward, snatching a golden blade from Valentina's still hand as horror crashed through me. She raised it, ready to plunge it into my love's heart and finish her immortal existence.

The world stopped spinning. My heart stopped beating. Everything I cared about in this forsaken world was about to be ripped away from me and for a moment I was frozen in the horrifying second before it happened.

I screamed my rage at the injustice I was seeing and threw Venom forward with all my might.

The heavy blade spun through the air before slamming straight into the vile twin who sought to hurt my queen.

She was thrown back, screaming in agony as she was impaled upon my blade and her blood stained the snow beneath her.

"Montana!" Julius bellowed in panic behind me. But I had no interest in him or her. My eyes were set on the destroyed face of the woman I coveted.

I ran to her, slamming Tempest back into its sheath as I scooped Valentina into my arms.

Julius sprinted toward Montana as Erik engaged his sister once more, and I took my chance to get Valentina away from them.

"Erik!" I bellowed and he looked up, spotting our love in my arms as his face crumpled with pain. "Hold them off while I get her to safety."

"I'll give my life to save her!" he cried in response, and I turned to flee just as the rest of the Belvederes and Callie arrived.

I charged away from them, Valentina's blood coating my left side as I held her close while her body fought to recover from the devastating wound.

The airplane sat ready on the runway, its engine running just as my love had required. She'd shielded it from the force of her blizzard and as I closed in on it, the snow beneath my boots disappeared.

I could hear Erik fighting our enemies behind us with the ferocity of his kind as he kept them from pursuit. A steely determination filled me as I increased the distance between my love and those who sought to harm her.

I would die before I'd let them kill her. But it looked like I might not have to.

ERIK

CHAPTER NINETEEN

I shoved Clarice away from me and she spun through the air before impacting with the frozen ground. I bared my fangs as the rest of our enemies joined the battle. Fabian held Callie in his arms and I snarled my fury at the fact that both twins still lived.

I turned toward the wounded one, her dark hair pooling around her in the snow as she pulled Magnar's huge sword from her stomach. I marched forward and grabbed hold of her hair, dragging her up before me and she screamed in pain as I clutched her wound. I presented her to the group, warning them off by threat of her death.

Miles eyed me with darkness in his gaze and I scoured the land for his husband, unable to spot him.

"Let her go!" Callie yelled in terror, leaping from Fabian's arms and sprinting toward me.

My prey was coming right to me and my queen would praise my name when I told her of their deaths. They had wounded her, damaged her beautiful face and I couldn't let anyone live who'd done such a thing.

"Erik -please!" Montana yelled in my arms.

I gripped her throat, preparing to tear her head off as her sister sprinted towards us. Fabian sped after her with a shout of warning. My upper lip peeled back and they slowed their approach as they saw the promise of death in my eyes.

Callie lifted her palms to try and stop what I was about to do, but it was too late.

I wrenched Montana's head sideways and she released a panicked scream as I started tugging with every ounce of strength I had.

"No - stop!" Montana screamed, clawing at my hands, thrashing and kicking.

With an almighty yank, I tore her head from her shoulders and her body slumped to the ground at my feet.

"You fucking asshole!" Callie roared, speeding toward me. But I was ready to do the exact same thing to her just as soon as I finished the vampire twin. I leaned down to rip her heart from her chest and grinned wildly, knowing how much it would please my love to bring her this news. But as I made my move to kill her, a flicker of hesitation crossed my mind, a roaring in the depths of my soul stilling me in my tracks. And before I could shake it off, hands grabbed me from behind. I swore as Warren made his appearance, dragging me backwards and throwing a solid punch to my temple.

My vision swam and I bellowed my rage as I turned to intercept him, driving my knuckles into his gut.

He jerked away with a hiss of pain and I swung at him again, catching him in the jaw.

Warren stumbled and I advanced on him, but several hands caught hold of me from behind. I fought my way free once again, my gaze locking on the plane up ahead as it started moving down the runway.

My heart dropped dramatically as I realised I was going to be left behind if I didn't get on that jet. I started running flat out, darting past Warren and putting on a burst of speed, emotion pouring through me at the idea of being parted from Valentina.

I couldn't stand it. Even though I knew leaving the twins alive would hurt her, being away from her wasn't an option.

My feet hit the runway and I upped my pace, desperation lancing through me. Footfalls pounded after me and anger daggered through my chest at knowing my enemies were trying to stop me from re-joining my love.

"Catch him!" Clarice yelled and I snarled as I forced myself even faster.

They wanted to take me from Valentina and I wouldn't let that happen.

I reached the tail of the jet, moving so fast that the world was a blur. Someone threw the door open at the front of the plane and I spotted Magnar hanging out of it and shooting a machine gun over my head.

Bullets sprayed through the air in response from our enemies, peppering the metal of the plane. I leapt forward with a burst of energy, catching the bottom of the doorway. Magnar tossed the gun over his shoulder, holding out his hand. I took it as he held onto the edge of the door with his free hand, his muscles bulging and ripping through the material of his sleeve.

I slammed my feet to the side of the plane, forcing myself upwards. He hauled me inside and we crashed to floor in a tangle of limbs.

"Shut that door!" Andrew bellowed from the cockpit as the plane began to lift into the sky.

"Get up," Magnar growled, getting to his feet and slamming the door.

The jet rose into the air and my stomach rose with it. We'd gotten away. But that wasn't good enough. We were supposed to have killed those fucking twins and secured that ring. And now Valentina was injured and my heart couldn't take the immensity of our failure.

I rolled onto my knees, standing and following Magnar through the plane to where our love lay on the sofa in a growing pool of blood. A bullet hole sat between her eyes and a line of red trickled down her perfect face.

I fell to my knees beside her with a groan of agony, and Magnar brushed his fingers into her hair with a sigh of regret.

"How long until she heals?" he begged of me.

I gently rolled Valentina over to check the back of her head. A clean exit wound had ripped out a chunk of her godly hair. But that was good. We didn't need to dig the bullet out. So it was only a matter of waiting until she found enough energy to heal.

"She's tired," I whispered. "She needs blood."

Magnar took his sword from his back, slashing it across his arm, ripping open his sleeve and cutting into his flesh. He lifted his head with pride as he placed the wound to Valentina's lips, and I hated that I couldn't offer her this sacrifice too.

The scent of his blood called to me like a prayer and I shut my eyes as I waited for Valentina to have her fill. When I was sure she'd swallowed enough blood, I looked to Magnar pleadingly. "Brother, I am desperate for nourishment."

He nodded stiffly, holding out his arm and I fell on the wound, ravenous as I drank from him. The taste of his blood sparked a fierce hunger in me, its delicious sweetness rolling over my tongue and captivating my senses.

When Magnar deemed I'd had enough, he shoved my head back to extract my fangs from his skin.

He lifted Valentina, dropping down to sit beneath her and cradling her head in his lap.

I held her hand, remaining on my knees before her like the worthless dog I was.

"We failed her," I choked out, looking to Magnar.

"We must make this right," he said with a heavy weight in his eyes.

"She can beat me for days, starve me, rip me limb from limb and leave my pointless body to bake in the sun," I said, resting my forehead to her arm.

"We will offer her anything she needs to sate her rage on us," Magnar agreed. "I would die a thousand deaths just to see her smile again."

"I would die ten thousand deaths," I countered, squeezing her lifeless fingers.

Magnar grunted his annoyance but said no more.

We waited in silence as the jet's engine hummed around us, the world seeming to grow darker without Valentina in it.

Eventually, she stirred and I wiped the blood away from the healed skin on her forehead. She blinked heavily and I sank into the dark depths of her gaze.

172

Her mouth lifted with hope. "The twins?" she begged and I could have wept with how much I didn't want to reveal the truth to her.

"Still alive," Magnar breathed. "We are so deeply sorry, you cannot even-" Valentina turned and struck him so hard, his head wheeled sideways.

She scrambled out of his lap and aimed a sharp kick at my side. I fell backwards, clasping my hands together as I gazed up at her. "Do whatever you want to us. We must be punished."

She gazed between us with her upper lip curling back, then turned away to face the line of windows. "I can't even look at you both right now, how could you let me down like this?"

I crawled forward, taking hold of her legs and hugging them to my chest. "Please, my love, do whatever you want with us to sate your anger."

She kicked me off of her, stalking away and opening a cabinet at the front of the seating area. She took a bottle of port, ripping the cork out and guzzling down the contents like a thirsty wild boar lapping at a pond. She slammed the empty bottle back into the cabinet then rounded on us with a furious glare.

"Get him on his back," she instructed Magnar and he lunged toward me, forcing me down to the carpet. I went willingly, falling still as I waited for Valentina to hurt me. I needed her to. I wanted her nails to rip my skin and bite into this body which had failed her so deeply.

"Open his shirt," Valentina commanded and Magnar ripped it open, revealing my naked chest to her.

She smiled keenly as she gazed down at me then placed her sharp heel on my stomach. She stepped onto me and I bit down on a roar as the heel of her shoe sliced into my skin. She walked forward, placing her weight down on her other heel so it cut into me. Magnar held me in place, but he didn't have to. I wouldn't have moved even if she'd planned to rip my heart out. It belonged to her anyway, so she could do whatever she liked with it.

She continued moving up my body, her whole weight pressing down on me as her heels stung me again and again. When she reached my chest, she pressed the toe of her shoe to my face and forced my head sideways as she dropped her weight onto that too.

"Apologise," she snarled.

"I'm sorry," I breathed, relishing the pain she gave me for what I'd done. "To the deepest pit of my soul, I am sorry."

"Good," she hissed, stepping off of me and looking to Magnar.

He didn't need to be asked, he shredded his shirt and fell to the carpet beside me as he awaited the same torture. I rose up onto my knees, pressing my hands down on his shoulders to ensure he didn't move.

Valentina eyed us with a glimmer of satisfaction in her eyes. "We won't fail again, will we boys?"

"No, my love," Magnar promised.

"I swear I will give you their deaths," I said.

Valentina nodded, kicking her shoes off and jamming her foot down between Magnar's thighs so he groaned in agony.

"When we land, I am taking you both to my bed," Valentina announced. "But you will be bloodied and repenting before that time, do you hear me?"

"Yes," I gasped at the same time Magnar did.

"Good." She clutched the edge of the sofa, blinking heavily. "I need to sleep a while longer to recuperate. You can spend the flight thinking up more punishments for yourselves."

I nodded eagerly as she headed further down the plane and tugged the curtain across to gain some privacy.

Excitement burned through me like wildfire. I would take any punishment on Earth to be reunited with Valentina's bare flesh. And this time, we would not be interrupted.

CALLIE

CHAPTER TWENTY

The plane soared away overhead and my heart fractured in two as I stared up at it. Magnar was gone. Again. And to make it so much worse, he'd almost killed my sister.

My heart was breaking, broken, fractured into a thousand tiny pieces that I wasn't sure I could ever knit back together.

I gripped Montana's hand as her body healed. Her head fused back onto her neck and she remained unconscious while it happened which I was glad about. At least she didn't have to feel the pain of it as her body worked to fix itself.

Bloodstained snow surrounded us and I gritted my teeth in frustration at just how close we'd come to finishing that bitch. Valentina should have been dead now, and Magnar and Erik returned to their own minds. Instead, we were still stuck in this hell of her control over them and we were no closer to getting them back.

I was alone with my sister. The others still hadn't returned from chasing after Erik in an attempt to stop them escaping, but I knew they'd failed. The sound of the airplane roaring through the sky had told me that much.

A warm hand landed on my shoulder and I looked up at Julius as a tear tracked down my cheek.

"We'll get her next time," he promised gruffly, and I could sense his encounter with Magnar was affecting him badly too.

Venom lay on the ground beside me but I couldn't bring myself to look at the heavy blade. It was stained with Montana's blood and the memory of what Magnar had done to her. A few inches higher and my sister would have been reduced to dust.

Montana mumbled something incoherent as she rose towards consciousness, and I tightened my hold on her hand.

"I'm here Monty," I said soothingly. "You're okay. Just give your body a minute to fix this."

She released a groan of pain and another tear slid along my skin.

"We can't stay here," Miles said as he approached us, and I glanced up at him with a frown. The others were drawing closer too, their posture stooped with our defeat. "They know our location. Valentina will send an army of biters after us at the first opportunity. As soon as she wakes up, she'll-"

"She's unconscious?" I asked urgently, my heart lifting at the idea. "I can go to her dreams again. I can send her enough nightmares to make her piss herself and I can find out what she's planning to do next."

"Are your gifts really that strong?" Miles asked, lifting a brow like he wasn't convinced I could do such a thing.

"She can do it," Fabian said roughly. "She's done it to me."

"So you just go into people's dreams and screw with their heads?" Miles asked. "Can you do anything you like while you're there?"

"Yes. Anything. And it's impossible for anyone to lie to me while I'm doing it too," I added.

"So you could simply steal people's secrets right out of their heads?" Miles asked.

"Or join in on their sex dreams?" Warren added with a chuckle, and I rolled my eyes.

"I tried to convince her to do that with me," Fabian said with a smirk, and I scowled at him.

"You went to his sex dream?" Julius asked in disgust.

"It wasn't voluntary," I snapped. "And I changed it as soon as I arrived so don't look at me like that."

"Go now," Montana breathed as she woke up. "Before Valentina recovers and we miss our chance."

I threw my arms around her, clinging to her cold body as she came back from the dead once more. She inhaled sharply, stilling in my grip as if she was uncomfortable and Miles caught my shoulder, pulling me back.

"I wouldn't do that while she's this hungry," he warned.

I released my sister as she pushed herself up onto her elbows and my lips parted in pity as I found a war going on within her eyes.

"You can bite me," I offered, pushing my sleeve up quickly. If she needed it then I'd give it to her. I'd done as much for the others anyway.

"No!" she said in horror, recoiling from me as if I'd slapped her.

Julius caught my elbow and twisted my arm as he spotted the bite mark on my flesh.

"What the fuck is that?" he snarled, and I scrambled to my feet as I drew him away from the vampires.

"It's fine," I said quickly. "I offered and-"

"You *what*?" He grabbed my other arm, pushing my sleeve up as he spotted the bite there too.

"Julius-" I began but he silenced me as he caught my chin in his grasp and shoved my head back to reveal the puncture wounds on my neck.

"Which fucking parasite did this?" he snarled, his grip on my chin tightening painfully as he drew his sword.

Montana got to her feet and stepped between the Belvederes as they eyed us warily.

I could feel Julius's rage simmering as he glared at me and I caught his wrist, easing his fingers from my face.

"They needed to feed to get their strength back after the crash," I explained.

"Callie," Montana gasped, a mixture of pride and horror crossing her eyes.

"So they just took what they wanted from you?" Julius spat, turning to glare at the vampires with his sword raised. "I warned you bloodsuckers what would happen if you bit one of us." He started forward and I grabbed his arm to stop him as the Belvederes shifted into defensive stances.

"I *offered*, Julius," I snapped. "Fabian risked his life to save mine and they needed their strength back to face Magnar and Erik. I decided I could spare a little blood in payment for my life!"

"Which is more than you offered *us*, slayer," Clarice muttered, and I spotted the same hungry look in her eyes as was glimmering in my sister's.

"If you ever put your mouth near my flesh I'll rip your fucking fangs out of your head," Julius snarled at her.

"As if I'd want my mouth anywhere near you," Clarice hissed.

"Keep telling yourself that."

"Watch your tone when you speak to our sister," Fabian growled, stepping towards Julius with a threat in his eyes.

"Stop it," I snapped as I planted myself between them. "This arguing is just wasting time. I'm a big girl and I make my own choices. The sooner the rest of you stop trying to control me, the better it'll be for all of us. I'm going to haunt Valentina in her dreams while we still have this chance, but I can't do it while you're bickering like a bunch of children."

"We should take one of the armoured vehicles and get the hell away from here," Warren said, pointing out the heavy trucks on the far side of the base.

"We'll get some more blood from the supplies they keep here," Clarice said, catching Montana's arm and pulling her away as they headed for the building at the far end of the base. I gave my sister a reassuring smile as her head dipped with shame. I knew she needed blood to survive now and I didn't want her to feel like it would change anything about the way I felt about her.

"Which truck are we taking?" I asked Miles as I ignored the tension that still boiled between Fabian and Julius.

"Front of the line ought to do it," he said, pointing at the closest vehicle. "I'll make sure it's fully charged and we can get out of here ASAP."

I nodded, taking Venom from the floor and wiping Montana's blood from it in the snow with a shudder of disgust. I caught Julius's arm as he continued to glare at Fabian and dragged him towards the truck.

"You can watch me while I sleep," I said as he gave me a frown.

"That sounds really creepy," he muttered, giving in to my demand and following me as we left Fabian and the others behind. "But I'm agreeing so that I can make sure no one tries to suck your blood again while you're out of it."

"Perfect," I muttered.

I hopped up into the back of the vehicle and lay down on one of the padded benches.

Julius settled himself down beside me and I wasted no more time as I closed my eyes and reached for Valentina's consciousness. I found her waiting for me and dove straight in, gritting my teeth in anticipation.

The moment I landed in her dream, I seized control of it. I stripped away whatever she'd created for herself without bothering to look at it and moulded the landscape to my own desire.

I surrounded us with fire and brimstone, cloaking myself in a long black dress and placing a glimmering silver crown upon my head just to taunt her.

I gave Valentina back her rags and chained her to the floor at my feet as I drew closer.

She started laughing as she looked up at me.

"Is something amusing you?" I asked and the shadows stretched around me, reaching for her with clawed fingers.

"The fact that you're here must mean that my escape is really pissing you off. My guard dogs saved me and left you to cry over them once more." She laughed again and I took a step towards her as the flames lining the space around us flared in response to my anger.

"Luckily for you, we don't want to hurt them," I snarled.

"I'll reward them well for their loyalty when I wake," she hissed and I was shown a memory of the three of them in Clarice's bed at

Belvedere castle.

My gut plummeted as Magnar's mouth moved across her flesh and she pulled at his belt, demanding more from him. Jealousy and pure fury lit a fuse within me and I ground my teeth together so hard that I was surprised they didn't crack. How dare she use them like that? How fucking dare she take their will and abuse them for her own sick desires?

I scowled at her, forcing the memory aside before I could see anything more of it. It wasn't him. Not really. She'd taken his body hostage and I refused to fall into the trap of hating him for it. No, all of my hatred was reserved specifically for the twisted creature before me.

"Tell me why you took them," I demanded. "Is it just revenge?"

"It was foreseen that I would rise to power with them at my side," she breathed. "I have waited a thousand years for that prophecy to come true and now my patience has been rewarded."

A memory flickered across my consciousness of her in her human form, kneeling before Idun at the foot of a cliff as the goddess showed her a flash of this future.

My anger at the deity simmered through my body and the flames swept closer to the monster who cowered at my feet.

I felt a tremor of fear flickering through her and she lifted her eyes to meet mine with a scowl.

"How could so much of the future have been decided this way?" I asked irritably. "So much has happened. Magnar never should have been alive for this to come to pass. How could you possibly have expected him to rise from his slumber now?"

A knowing smile pulled at Valentina's lips, and I growled as I forced the answer from her mind.

The scene around us shifted suddenly and I was walking behind Valentina as she scaled a sheer rock face, following a steep path cut into the stone.

She was human and her long hair billowed out around her as a strong wind blew past us.

As we neared the top of the cliff, voices carried to us and Valentina dropped behind the cover of a hulking rock as she listened.

"I don't want to leave you behind," Magnar said, his voice thick with emotion.

I leaned around the rock and saw him locked in a fierce embrace with his mother. Tears ran down her face as she tilted her head to gaze up at him.

"Your brother is sleeping already," she said with a soft smile. "What would he think if he woke in a hundred years just to learn that you didn't join him after all?"

"He'd think I was a good son and be glad that I hadn't abandoned you," Magnar growled but I could tell his protests didn't hold any weight. He'd already made this decision and he wasn't going to back out of it.

It struck me that to him this moment must have seemed like it had happened a few months ago. His grief at the loss of his mother must still have been fresh in his mind despite the fact that a thousand years had since passed.

"It's time, my brave boy. You must take vengeance on the creatures who caused us this pain."

"I will," he swore, touching a hand to his heart.

He held her close one last time and pressed a kiss to her forehead before releasing her and turning towards a large cave behind them.

His mother caught his hand before he could go inside and he turned back to her, his eyes full of pain at their parting.

"Once it is done and the Belvederes are dead you should find happiness for yourself," she breathed. "You deserve to find love."

Valentina released a low noise of anger at the comment, but it was stolen by the wind so that Magnar and his mother didn't hear her.

"Perhaps," Magnar breathed.

"I love you, my boy," his mother replied. "Never forget it."

"And I love you," he said. "More than I can put into words. I will end the Belvederes. This sacrifice won't be for nothing."

She pressed a kiss to the back of his hand and he turned away at last, heading into the cave.

I watched in fascination as his mother began to wield her gifts. A heaviness fell over the air around us and Valentina recoiled as she was struck with the urge to lay down and sleep.

The Dream Weaver carved runes into the rock face outside the place she'd selected for Magnar's slumber. They spoke of rest, honour, salvation and the passage of time.

"Idun?" she called as she raised her hands to the sky and I felt the goddess lending her more power so that Magnar's body wouldn't be ravaged by the time which would pass while he slept.

Lightning raced into the sky above and an orange light grew in the mouth of the cave, growing brighter and brighter until I couldn't bear to look on it any longer.

The light dissolved and I felt Idun's presence retreating as Magnar's mother slumped to the ground.

Where the cave had stood open before, a slab of rock had formed to block it and the runes laid into it shimmered with gold.

Magnar's mother buckled before it as the strength of her gifts were sapped and she buried her face in her hands, releasing a sob as she realised she'd never see her son again.

Valentina stepped from her hiding place and approached Magnar's mother, her face set with determination.

"So he's gone then?" she asked as she approached.

"Valentina? Were you hoping to say goodbye?"

"Goodbye?" Valentina cocked an eyebrow. "No, Freya. Your son didn't do me the decency of offering me an explanation, never mind a farewell."

"You should be pleased," Freya sighed as she brushed her tears from her cheeks and looked up at the woman who should have borne her grandchildren. "Magnar never loved you. Now you're free of your vow to him. You can find a man who will give you what he could not."

"I'm not free of my vow," Valentina replied, tugging on her shift to reveal the tattoo above her heart. "And I don't intend to release Magnar from his either."

"What are you talking about?" Freya pushed herself to her feet.

She took a step forward but Valentina summoned the wind to drive her back against the cave door.

Freya gasped as Valentina drew her blade.

"I grew tired of your son denying me a crown so I asked Idun to help me. She knows that I have always been loyal to her commands so she offered me a future filled with the power I am owed. Erik Belvedere will give me the crown your son withheld and the lifespan necessary to await Magnar's awakening."

"You would damn your soul? Betray your vow? Your life will be forfeit! The goddess would never allow one of our people to-"

"Of course I'll have to die," Valentina said icily. "My life as a slayer will end just as the goddess demands of those who turn against their vow. But then my life as a vampire will begin. And in a hundred years, when the door to this cave opens and your son steps out into the light once more, I'll be waiting for him. And he will fulfil his promise to me."

"I'll never let that happen," Freya growled, drawing her axe and a dagger, her posture shifting to threatening.

Valentina smiled wickedly as she immobilised Magnar's mother with the wind.

"Erik needs to know that your sons are dead. Luckily for me, Idun says your blood will smell the same as theirs so I'll be able to convince him that I killed them. And I told him about the prophecy which foretold the Belvederes' downfall. Magnar will never lead that army against him now. The Belvederes won't unite for that battle; your sons won't face them."

"That demon won't ever give you what you want," Freya spat. "Once he believes you've done as he asked, he'll drain you dry and leave your body to rot."

"I considered that," Valentina purred. "Which is why I offered him the pleasure of my flesh too. He is quite captivated by me. I can shield him from the sun and offer him the release that all men need. He likes me pliant and adoring. And so that's what I give him. And he will grant me immortality in return. Just as soon as I convince him that I destroyed your children."

Freya cursed as Valentina advanced but instead of engaging her in battle, she turned her head to the sky and screamed.

"Odin!" Freya bellowed and the power of her rage set the hairs rising along my arms.

A fissure opened in the sky above her and Valentina's lips parted in horror as the king of the gods heeded Freya's call.

"I offer you my life in protection of my sons!" Freya screamed. "Guard them from this traitor so that she cannot find this place again once she leaves it. And let them sleep for a thousand years so that her eternal life has plenty of chances to end before they ever have to rise and the fates may shift to offer them another chance at their destiny!"

Valentina snarled in rage as power licked from the sky in hungry waves.

Freya spat in Valentina's face before raising her blade and slitting her own throat. Her blood sprayed from the wound, coating Valentina from head to foot as it spurted from her body and a triumphant smile painted her lips as death rushed forward to claim her. She collapsed lifeless to the ground before the cave, her eyes staring glassily at the heavens above.

Odin dropped from the fissure in the sky, slamming to the rocks with the sound of a thunderclap. He was huge, built with muscles which bulged with an innate power. His chin was covered with a thick black beard and one of his eyes was missing, the socket stitched shut. Even Magnar would have seemed small beside this god. Power exuded from him in waves and he reached down to dip his fingers in the blood which pooled by his feet.

He painted two new runes into the stone that blocked the cave before straightening and glaring at Valentina.

"Leave this place," he boomed, his voice making the rocks around us tremble as if they were made of liquid. "You shall never find it again."

Valentina fled and the memory fizzled away from me as I stood transfixed by what I'd learned.

"She forgot to hide Julius's resting place from me too," Valentina muttered as she reappeared, chained at my feet. "And I hoped that he would lead me to Magnar. It didn't quite go to plan but I have everything I desired now either way."

I stared at the wretched woman before me at a total loss for what to say. No matter how much Magnar may have neglected her, it couldn't possibly equal the level of wrong she'd done him in turn. He'd been *devastated by the death of his father and then she'd taken his mother's life too.*

"You'd better enjoy this power while it's yours," I snarled as I stepped closer to her. "Because I'm going to destroy each piece of you before this ends."

I filled every part of her dream with monsters, weaving the nightmare to my command as she started screaming for mercy and they descended on her with rabid hunger and sharp teeth. I moulded the landscape into a place of such horror that even I feared lingering within it.

I left her there, trapped and screaming in the confines of her darkest fears as I stepped out of her dreams and fell back into my own. And I hoped that she would suffer there for a very long time.

ERIK

CHAPTER TWENTY ONE

1000 YEARS AGO

I remained in the village with Fabian for days. Then days turned to weeks and I knew I should leave, but I enjoyed their way of life so much that I couldn't bear to go.

There had been no sign of Valentina returning and I wondered if she'd failed in her task of killing Magnar and Julius, or if she had never planned to do it at all. Either way, I was content to prolong moving on from this village for as long as possible. We weren't drawing the attention of the slayers as far as I knew. The tribe had never heard of such a people and I prayed it would remain that way.

Nirell had pledged herself as my own personal blood source and she had become more than that since.

I lay in a bed of furs with her, running my hands over her gleaming skin as I savoured the bliss running through me after my night with her.

She adored me, and though I couldn't find it in my heart to love her, I certainly held a fondness for her. She was life and beauty combined. She gave my body everything it needed and I coveted her for that fact alone.

Fabian's voice called to me beyond the tent. "Erik, the clouds are out today!"

I smiled, rising from the bed and tugging on the clothes I'd been offered by the people of the tribe.

"Stay a while longer." Nirell pulled a fur off of her body and I gazed down at her naked skin with a sideways smile.

"That's very tempting." I lowered down, brushing my mouth over hers.

"Erik – come on!" Fabian called. "We're going for a swim!"

Lightness filled my chest and I brushed my fingers through Nirell's hair then turned away from her and headed out of the tent.

I felt her disappointment press into me as I closed the flap behind me, but I longed to spend some time with my brother and his wife to be. They hadn't yet set a date for the ceremony, but the village had been harvesting the fields in preparation for it.

"Good morning," Chickoa said brightly.

I nodded to her, clapping Fabian on the shoulder.

"You and Nirell are close," Chickoa commented then lowered her tone to a whisper. "I think she might be hoping for a proposal soon."

Guilt fell through my veins as I glanced back at the tent. I liked Nirell, but I didn't have any intention of taking things further with her. I didn't want to devote myself to someone in this cursed body. I wasn't capable of love or any of the tenderness she really deserved. And I'd only have to watch her fade under the pressure of time and lose her anyway. It was no true life for either of us.

Although I knew Fabian thought to turn Chickoa to avoid such a fate. I wondered when he planned on discussing it with her. I'd promised to keep my mouth shut on the subject, but it still bothered me. Why would a human wish to give up their life to live like this? Dependent on blood and nothing else?

"Let's head to the river," Fabian encouraged and I fell into step beside him as the three of us walked out of the village and down into the valley.

Chickoa laced her fingers through Fabian's, eyeing him from time to time and he did the same to her. The two of them were so obsessed with each other, I wondered why they'd invited me on this trip at all.

"So we have something to ask you," Fabian said, throwing me a grin.

"I thought there must be a reason for you bringing me along," I said as we headed through the long grass of the meadow.

"We like your company too," Chickoa laughed.

"So what is it?" I asked them.

"I'd like you to be my guardian," Chickoa said and I frowned, waiting for her to go on. "It's custom in my village for any bride to have a guardian for three days before the wedding to ensure her virginity is intact."

"And is it?" I blurted without thought, glancing at Fabian who I knew all too well was not likely to have kept such a promise.

"It is," Fabian answered for her and Chickoa blushed.

"Oh," I said, surprised. "Well then, of course I'll be your guardian."

Chickoa beamed, darting around Fabian to embrace me. "Thank you. You'll need to keep watch outside my home for the next three nights."

"So you're marrying in three days' time?" I asked.

"Yes, the celebrations will last a week," Fabian said proudly. "We've harvested enough honey for the mead to last twice as long. I've taught a brewer how to make it in the ways of our people, Erik." He smiled even wider at me, and it was really impossible not to be infected by his happiness.

"With the way some men drink in this village, I hope the amount will be sufficient," Chickoa said.

Fabian laughed and I joined in, a lightness filling me as we wandered into the forest at the bottom of the valley.

The river called to me and I stripped out of my clothes as we arrived at a rocky pool, stepping into the icy water as the weight of the world fell away, and I could pretend I was a man instead of a beast for a while.

I guarded Chickoa's tent every night, perched on a stool she'd brought out for me. The first two nights went by without a stir, but the third, Fabian arrived, seeming jittery.

"What's the matter?" I asked.

"It's time Erik. We'll be wed tomorrow. She wishes to be with me forever. And I want to make it so before we are married." He moved toward the tent flap, and I stepped into his way.

"That's a bad idea," I said in a low voice. "Are you sure she's ready for that?"

"Of course," he said brightly. "She said the words herself. She wants to be with me for all eternity."

"You're certain, brother?" I asked anxiously. "Turning someone is not something to take lightly."

"I'm not taking it lightly," he said harshly, trying to move past me once more. "She wants this."

"Perhaps on your wedding night instead once you have discussed it further?" I suggested.

"No, it must be now," he begged. "Tomorrow she'll rise to her immortal life and we'll be joined as man and wife the same day. What could be more perfect than that?"

I ground my teeth, unsure what to do. "Fabian, promise me you'll speak to her first. Lay it out plainly for her so that she can make the choice with certainty. She needs to know what a burden this curse can be."

"Yes, yes, now move aside." He elbowed me out of his way and ripped the tent flap open.

I hesitated in the entrance, my instincts telling me to follow him. This didn't seem right. I'd never heard Chickoa say she wanted to be one of us. But if Fabian was certain...

A scream ripped through the air and I darted into the tent in alarm. Fabian was kneeling over Chickoa, his bloody wrist pressed to her mouth. I could see the fear in her eyes and terror sped through me as I charged toward him.

"Brother -stop!" I caught his shoulder, but he ripped her head sideways in an instant and she fell still in death beneath him.

"She was frightened!" I shouted, dragging him off of her.

"She'll be fine when she wakes," he insisted, shoving me away to get close to her again. He cupped her cheek, smiling as he caressed her skin. "Come back to me, my love. Let's start our eternal life together."

"Fabian..." I scraped a hand through my hair, anxiety pooling in my gut.

Chickoa's eyes flickered open and Fabian promptly took a leather canteen from his furs, handing it to her. She snatched it, gulping down the blood inside, the scent of it reaching to me.

She cast it aside when it was empty, then looked to Fabian in horror. "What have you done to me?"

"You're like me now," he said softly. "Immortal. You can stay with me forever just as you wished for."

She shook her head in fear, then slapped him across the face, and he hit the ground from the strength she possessed. She leapt upright, gazing at the open tent flap, her eyes wild with fear.

"Wait," I begged, moving into her path as tears streamed down her cheeks.

She turned to Fabian as he rose to his feet, backing up from him and holding out a hand. "I accepted what you are but I never wanted to be like you! Take it back!" She clutched her heart, searching for a beat which wouldn't come.

"Fabian, you fool," I snarled at him. "You said she wanted this."

"Chickoa, you said you'd love me for all eternity," Fabian begged of her. "I thought this was what you desired."

"It's a figure of speech!" she screamed, grabbing a stool and launching it at him. It smashed to pieces against his body, but he remained still, staring at her with the light going out of his eyes.

"Please, please take it away." Chickoa rounded on me, clutching the fur around my shoulders and begging me with her eyes.

"I can't," I rasped, my heart breaking for her.

She fell still, her eyes wide and full of pain. Then she turned to Fabian, baring her fangs and pointing at the exit.

"Get out," she growled.

"Chickoa, please-" he pleaded but she cut him off with a shout that made the tent tremble.

"GET OUT!"

Fabian bowed his head, moving past her and heading outside.

"I'm so sorry," I said and Chickoa shook her head, tears still tracking down her cheeks.

"Just go," she whispered, and I followed Fabian out into the night where he was waiting for me.

"She'll come round," he said, though the fear in his eyes told me he was worried she wouldn't. "She just needs time."

"Time is all she has now," I murmured and he shot me a desperate look.

He nodded firmly. "Yes, and she will forgive me. She must."

I rested a hand on his shoulder with a deep frown. "For your sake, I hope she does."

The days slipped by and the wedding never came. Chickoa refused to come out of her tent and would only allow her friends in to feed her. Fabian stalked up and down outside her home, never straying more than ten feet away from it. He begged her through the walls of her tent and she yelled at him to stop. I couldn't see how they were ever going to fix things between them. I prayed the love they felt for each other might overcome it, but with every passing day, that seemed less likely.

I sat at the edge of the tents on my own, knowing it would soon be time for me to move on. Word of the slayers drawing nearer had finally reached us, but Fabian refused to leave without Chickoa.

My heartstrings pulled for him, but I was angry with him too. And furious with myself for not acting on my instincts and stopping him from turning her.

Thunder rumbled above and the crescent moon disappeared as thick clouds drew over it. A lightning strike hit the valley far below me and my brow creased. As the lightning struck the ground again in the same spot, I rose to my feet with hope growing inside me.

Valentina stepped out of the forest far below me in the valley and I eyed the trees, praying the slayers didn't hide in their midst as I started running down the hill to meet her.

As I approached, I spied a haunted look in her gaze, and I slowed to a halt as my eyes adjusted to the darkness and picked out the blood that soaked her clothes. She raised a sword in her hand and the scent of more blood sailed to me from it. I paused, drinking in the powerful smell rolling over me. I knew it well. It was the blood of the Eliosons.

"You did it?" I gasped and she hurried forward to close the distance between us.

She fell against me and wept. I tentatively held her, aware of the sword in her hand and the way my fangs tingled from the scent of all that slayer blood. She dropped her weapon to the ground and clung to me tighter, revealing how loyal she was to me now.

"Hush, what's wrong?"

"It was just a very hard thing to say goodbye to Magnar," she breathed. "Despite all he did to me."

I cupped her cheek, seeing the truth in her eyes. He was gone. And my heart sparked with so much relief that it almost thumped again.

"You have been very brave," I said and she nodded then fell to her knees before me, clutching her chest with a yelp of pain.

"I've broken my vow," she croaked. "Idun will kill me." She groaned again as some plague racked her body and I knelt down before her, unsure what to do.

Her eyes locked with mine as dark circles encased them. "Please," she rasped. "Turn me." She clutched my hand. "I want to live by your side. I want to be immortal."

I shook my head, rearing back upright, afraid after what I'd witnessed between Chickoa and Fabian. And regardless of that, I didn't turn mortals. I'd vowed not to bestow this curse on any other.

She pawed at my feet, gazing up at me in desperation. "I fulfilled my part of the deal. Do as I ask, Erik," she pleaded. "Make me like you."

My throat tightened as the scent of slayer blood enveloped me. Hers, Magnar's, Julius's. It was almost too much to resist.

A war took place in my chest as I stared at her.

"You won't ever have to hide from the sun again," she promised, her eyes wild with desperation. "I'll give you clouds wherever you go. You'll be free."

I dropped to my knees again, her words offering me something I longed to have with all my heart. Never having to wait out the sun in caves or dark tents. I could spend every day outdoors for all of time with her by my side.

She fell into my lap, grasping at my furs. "Now, do it now. There's... no...time."

I took her wrist, making my decision as I bit deep into her veins. I took a drink of her slayer blood, unable to help myself before I released the venom into her. She cried out, wailing as she rolled onto her back on the grass.

I extracted my fangs, digging them into my own wrist instead before holding the bloody wound to her mouth.

"Drink," I commanded, excited and terrified by the decision I was making. But this wasn't like Chickoa. Valentina wanted this. And she could offer me so much in return.

Valentina jerked as Idun's power flooded into her, ending her life in payment for breaking her slayer's vow. She fell still in the grass, her beautiful features growing smoother and the circles around her eyes disappearing.

I waited, gazing up at the heavens as the clouds retreated, revealing the moon once more.

Valentina sat upright with a surge of speed, her eyes locking with mine. She gazed down at her body in awe, turning her hands over as she inspected them. "I'm one of you."

"Yes," I whispered, taking her wrist and guiding her to her feet. "And you need blood."

She nodded, her hand flying to her throat as the thirst gripped her. The slayers' blood on her clothes was caked and drying, but she licked at her dress anyway, desperate for nourishment.

"Come with me." We took off across the field at high speed and she laughed at the new ability she had to race over the land like the wind.

We approached the village and I kept my arm locked around her waist so she didn't attack any of the village people. Most of them were

196

asleep so I led her to Nirell's tent, hoping she would be as willing to help Valentina as she was me.

I pulled the flap to her tent back and Nirell stirred in her bed, sitting up and blinking heavily.

Valentina sucked in air as her scent found her and I gripped her tighter as she thrashed in my arms.

"Nirell...would you be willing to give blood to my friend?" I asked gently.

Nirell's eyes flickered with a little fear as she took in Valentina's hungry form, but she nodded tentatively, and my heart went out to her for what she was willing to do.

"Gently," I commanded of Valentina, guiding her to Nirell's bed.

The woman sat up, offering her wrist and Valentina fell on it like a starved animal.

I watched anxiously, ready to step in if she went too far. When I'd deemed she'd had enough, I yanked Valentina away from Nirell and turned her in my arms.

She fell still, battling away the last of the bloodlust as it tried to keep her chained. Her eyes locked with mine and she sighed, brushing her hand down my chest.

"Thank you," she whispered, then turned to Nirell. "And thank you as well."

"You're welcome," Nirell said, seeming concerned as she glanced between us, her eyes straying to the blood staining my companion's dress.

Valentina shifted out of my arms, dropping down onto the edge of the bed and resting her hand on Nirell's bare ankle. The slayer looked to me with a new kind of hunger in her eyes. "Perhaps we should show her our gratitude together?"

Nirell bit her lip, and I waited to see her response to that as two demons crept nearer in her tent.

"Yes," she agreed. "That would only be polite."

I looked between the two women in the bed before me and a slow smile took over my face.

I moved toward Valentina, cupping her chin and making her look up

197

at me. "You call me master now."

She nodded eagerly and power dripped through my body, serving me a head rush. Magnar and Julius Elioson were dead. And I had his betrothed in my bed willing to offer me anything I wanted.

The future was mine for the taking. And my family would soon be able to come out of the shadows and spend their days under the protection Valentina could cast for them.

But right now, all I wanted from her was her flesh.

MONTANA

CHAPTER TWENTY TWO

I gulped down two bottles of blood before I felt remotely right again. I couldn't believe Callie had given blood to the others – right from her fucking veins. It was wild to think how far she'd come in trusting the Belvederes. But actually offering them her blood...it was incredible. She'd made the ultimate sacrifice to ensure we won that fight today, and I couldn't be more grateful to her for putting herself through that.

The wound in my stomach was almost healed and the skin around my neck was less swollen since my head had been reattached. But the pain of what Erik had done to me left a more permanent kind of wound on me. Having my head ripped off by my husband was about the most horrific thing I'd ever experienced. And the worst thing of all, was that it wasn't me I was concerned about. I'd survived it, I was okay. But Erik was still out of reach and that was the deepest pain of all. The fact that he'd wanted to hurt me so badly was a torture of its own.

He and Magnar were gone. Lost to us once more. And if we ever got them back, they were going to feel the weight of all Valentina had caused them to do. The idea that we'd never break that necklace and end her spell over them didn't even bear thinking about.

I gathered up boxes of blood from the warehouse with Clarice, carrying them to the truck waiting for us at the centre of the base. Fabian was busy loading food into it for the humans and a small spark of light ignited in my soul at the sight.

As he turned away from the truck, I threw my arms around him, overwhelmed with gratitude to him for saving my sister from the helicopter crash.

He stiffened in surprise then folded his arms around me as I gazed up at him.

"Thank you," I breathed, not needing to explain why as he nodded.

"You know I care about her, with or without this." He showed me the silver cross on his palm as I stepped away from him and I smiled grimly at him in acknowledgement of Idun's mark.

Miles appeared carrying an armful of fresh uniforms for us to change into. I moved closer as he arrived, taking one in my size from his arms with a word of thanks. He passed them out before tossing a couple into the back seat of the truck for the slayers.

My uniform was shredded and Clarice was wandering around in her underwear, but I figured we'd better change on the road. We didn't want to waste any more time here in case Valentina's biters showed up.

I climbed into the back of the truck, finding my sister asleep with her head in Julius's lap. I moved silently into the space across from them and Fabian and Clarice followed me inside. Fabian sneered as he gazed at Callie laying in the arms of Julius but made no comment about it. I was grateful, because the last thing we needed was another argument to break out.

Warren took the driver's seat and Miles sat beside him in the front.

"Where to?" Warren called.

"Anywhere but here," Miles sighed, and Warren pulled out of the base, heading onto the road where the snow was beginning to melt. The evening sky was thick with clouds, turning the world deepest blue as the sun started to set.

Warren headed south, taking a straight road that shot between sprawling farmlands on either side.

I tugged off my clothes, balling up the jacket in my hand and wiping the blood from my skin as well as I could. The nightwear I'd kept on beneath it was torn and filthy, but I glanced at Fabian and Julius in hesitation, not wanting to get naked in front of them.

Clarice stripped off opposite me, clearly having no such feelings on the matter.

Fabian turned to Julius with a glare. "Face the window," he growled. "Don't look at my sister."

"I wasn't," Julius muttered, turning sharply away.

I glanced at Fabian, gesturing for him to do the same and he smirked before angling himself to face the view. I knew they could probably see me in their periphery anyway, but I didn't have much choice as I whipped my pyjama top off and quickly replaced it with the new jacket. I turned further around as I tugged off my torn shorts and pulled the pants on in place of them.

Clarice dropped into her seat when she was dressed, combing her hair with her fingers.

Fabian turned back to us, snatching up some clothes from the floor before tugging his shirt off. I eyed the scar on his muscular torso, still pink from where Magnar had stabbed him after the wedding.

He started unbuckling his pants, throwing me an amused look. "So I can't look at you but you can stare right at my cock all you like?"

"I wasn't-" I spluttered, but his laughter halted me and I turned away to look out the front of the truck with a curse.

"No one wants to see your tiny todger," Julius mocked. "And if they did, they'd have to find a magnifying glass first."

"Ha. Ha," Fabian said dryly. "As you can see, I have no such problem."

I shook my head, unable to believe they were having this conversation right now. Was Fabian just sitting there showing Julius his dick?

"You wanna see what a real man looks like?" Julius asked.

"For fuck's sake, you lot," Miles called from the front. "Let's not start a whose dick is bigger party. At least wait until we can join in later so I can take the trophy."

Fabian started laughing and Julius actually cracked a grin. I heard them shuffling into clothes at last and relaxed back against my seat, finding both of them fully dressed in new uniforms. Callie had been moved to lay on the bench beside the slayer, sleeping soundly.

I shared a glance with Clarice as she rolled her eyes. "I'll make sure I'm anywhere else when my brothers' cock competition begins."

"Then who will be the judge?" Julius smirked and she gave him a dry look.

"Perhaps you can all shake your dicks at a raven and see which one it thinks is the fattest worm," she suggested lightly, and I snorted a laugh.

"Good idea," Julius played along with a menacing glint in his gaze. "Then we could do the same with your giant nipples."

"I do not have giant nipples," she hissed.

"You're right. You have just one giant nipple," he goaded. "The other one is a pinhead by comparison. The raven won't have room for it after he's gorged himself on the big one."

Clarice glared at him, but before she could come back at him, Fabian called out to Warren. "Hey, take the next left."

"Why?" he asked.

"I know someone who lives out this way," he replied vaguely.

"Who?" Clarice asked curiously.

"Just a woman." Fabian shrugged.

"What woman?" Miles asked.

"Just take the turning!" Fabian snapped and the truck veered sharply around to head in that direction. Callie stirred at his loud tone and I sensed she was awake as her eyelids fluttered but didn't open.

"By the gods, you don't mean-" Clarice started but Fabian cut her off.

"Yes. She'll help."

"Why the fuck would she help you?" Clarice asked. "Erik told me what you did to her."

Fabian glowered, looking out of the window again. "She's had a thousand years to get over it. I'm sure she'll give us a place to stay. At least until we figure out what to do about Valentina."

"Is there any woman in the world you haven't pissed off, Fabian?" Julius asked lightly.

"Shut up, slayer," he growled.

"Are you sure this is a good idea?" I asked tentatively. "If this woman hates you-"

"She doesn't hate me," Fabian bit at me so sharply that I recoiled. He schooled his expression, suddenly seeming anxious as he tried to flatten his hair. "Well, she did. But I'm sure she's moved on by now."

"What did you do to her?" I asked with narrowed eyes, leaning closer.

Fabian pursed his lips, throwing me a glance that revealed a vulnerability in him I'd never seen before.

"Well?" I pressed. "If we're going to trust some stranger we need to know about her."

Clarice answered for him when he refused to open his mouth. "Erik told me Fabian had a girlfriend back when we were hiding separately from the slayers."

"Fiancée," he grumbled, and my eyes widened.

"Another one?" Julius blurted. "How many fucking women do you need to marry?"

"I didn't marry this one," Fabian murmured, not looking at him.

"She was human," Clarice went on and Fabian shifted uncomfortably as if he was tempted to make her stop talking. "But Fabian turned her... against her will."

I shook my head in horror and Fabian glared at me.

"Oh stop being so damn judgmental," he snarled.

"Fine." I raised my hands in innocence. "Tell me how it happened then and I'll hold off on judging you."

He released a huff of frustration but silence stretched out as everyone waited for him to explain. "She said she wanted to be with me forever. I was a vampire, I thought she meant she wanted to be like me, to stay at my side for all eternity."

"But surprise, surprise, old Fabio here was too busy assuming what she wanted instead of just asking her outright. And she didn't want it, did she?" Julius guessed with a knowing look.

"No," Fabian said through his teeth. "I turned her and when she woke as a vampire, she..." He rubbed a hand over his face. "Well let's just say she never wanted to see me again and leave it at that, alright?

205

I'm not pouring my goddamn heart out in front of a fucking slayer."

My brows rose as I gazed at him, sensing the age-old hurt weighing down on him as keenly as if it had just happened.

"You loved her," I accused in realisation, hardly able to believe Fabian was truly capable of such a thing without the will of the gods forcing it upon him.

He bared his fangs at me. "I said we're not talking about it, Montana."

I released a breath of exasperation, turning my attention back to the road.

Callie stirred and I wheeled around to look at her with hope darting through me. She sat upright with a yawn, her eyes flipping to me, and I could tell she'd heard that entire conversation.

"How'd it go?" Clarice asked, leaning toward her.

"Good, I think." She started telling us about what she'd seen, how Valentina had been forced to show her memories of when Magnar had gone to sleep a thousand years ago, of how Odin had shown up and helped to keep Valentina away from him.

Callie bit into her lip as she reached the end of her story and I sensed there was more she wasn't saying. "Anyway...I'll tell you all the details later."

She looked to Julius with a frown lining her features, but he didn't seem to notice as he contemplated what she'd told him.

I gazed at her, in awe of what she'd revealed. That another great god had had a hand in our fates. And a possibility struck me so hard that I couldn't contain it. "Odin stopped Valentina before, what if he'd help us do it again?"

The Belvederes looked at me as if I'd gone insane.

"You do know who Odin is right?" Clarice breathed.

I shrugged. "Another god?"

"Not just any god," Julius answered. "He's the ruler of all the gods. More powerful than any of them."

"So? That's a good thing, isn't it?" Callie stepped in. "Montana's right, he could help us if we can talk to him."

"We can't just talk to Odin," Fabian said sharply. "He requires a great sacrifice to be called upon."

"My mother didn't make any sacrifice, she just asked for help," Julius said and Callie shifted uncomfortably beside him.

"Well maybe he was feeling generous that day," Clarice said thoughtfully. "But he doesn't show up for just anyone without an offering."

"So we have to give him some sort of sacrifice," I said thoughtfully. A tense beat of silence passed.

"It doesn't have to be death," Miles said from the front of the car. "Just enough to appease him, to show him the extent of our faith."

"Mortal blood," Clarice added, glancing at Julius and Callie.

"If he'll help us get Magnar and Erik back, I'll do it," Callie said immediately.

"Callie," I gasped. "You can't."

"You've spilled plenty of blood tonight," Julius growled in agreement. "I'll do it. So long as you freaks don't start licking my wounds."

"Yes, I prefer that plan. And if you cut too deep it won't be as much of a tragedy if you accidentally kill yourself," Fabian jibed.

"You don't have to." Callie rested a hand on Julius's arm.

"I want to," he promised. "I'll do anything to help my brother."

A warmth spread through my chest at his words, even if I did feel shit about him having to do this.

If Odin truly aided us, I could get Erik back. More than anything, I longed to curl into my husband's embrace and lose myself in the comfort of his arms. I missed him so much it was like my heart had been sliced apart and shredded to nothing but ragged flesh.

Warren pulled the car over to the side of the road and I whipped around to face him. "What are you doing?"

"Might as well get it over with, huh?" He pulled the parking brake and stepped out of the truck.

Anxiety coiled inside me as Clarice opened the side door and followed him onto the dark road.

We exited after them and I joined my sister as Julius moved to the centre of the ring we'd all created.

Fabian handed him a knife and Julius took it with a terse smile.

"Thanks, bud. I can always count on you, can't I?"

"Always." Fabian smirked and Julius gave him a cool look as he rolled his sleeve back and held the knife above his arm.

"Wait," I hissed, my throat tightening at the idea of him slashing his veins open. "Don't we need to do something to call Odin? Like...I dunno, a ritual or something?"

"Yeah." Fabian smirked at me and Callie. "You two need to strip off and go dance naked in that field over there."

"Very funny," Callie said, folding her arms.

"We just need to call him," Miles said, looking to the sky. "Julius, shout his name when you cut yourself."

Julius nodded, pressing the knife to his forearm and swiping it across his skin. To his credit, he didn't even wince as blood poured from the clean cut. The blood dripped to the ground and he turned his face to the cloudy sky.

"Odin!" he bellowed.

I tensed, gazing around us as if I might spot the god emerging from the pressing darkness in the same way Andvari usually appeared.

Nothing changed, except the clouds shifted above and revealed a full moon shining down on us.

"Do it again," Clarice urged.

"Odin, we need your help!" Julius cried to the quiet heavens.

I frowned as I waited for something to happen.

The seconds passed, ticking on almost loud enough for me to hear them.

I jolted as a ribbon of moonlight shot through the sky then descended on us like a beacon, bathing our group in a lambent glow.

Adrenaline spiked in my veins as I stared around at the others.

The moonlight grew brighter until I couldn't see anything but white. I squinted, grabbing Callie's hand to assure me she was still there. She gripped my fingers in a tight hold, and I knew I could face anything with her by my side.

The brightness faded a fraction and the air seemed to split in two, light bending and the sound of rainfall filling my ears. I stilled at the sight of the man who stepped out of the strange fissure in the air beside Julius. Huge, stacked with muscles with a thick black beard encompassing his chin. One of his eyes was stitched shut, but the other was icily blue and gazing around at all of us. His aura was the most powerful thing I'd ever experienced and as he stepped closer to me and Callie, we instinctively moved back.

"Twins of sun and moon," he said in a tone that was as rough as waves crashing against jagged rocks. "Have so many years passed already?" He blinked around at our group, his head tilting as if he recognised each and every face before him. "Slayers and vampires standing together..." A smile pulled up his mouth as his gaze fell on Julius. "I thank you for your offering, son of Idun." He raised his palm over the bloody wound on Julius's arm and it immediately knitted back together.

Julius released a noise somewhere between a whimper and grunt.

"I can offer you a gift in return for your sacrifice." Odin reached out to touch the hilt of Julius's broken sword, Menace, which he still carried with him in a sheath. A powerful glow built along the blade and Julius inhaled sharply as Odin withdrew his hand from it.

Julius drew the long sword and where the blade had been severed by the chains Valentina had used to capture Erik, a deep rune now glowed, combining the broken pieces and making it whole once more.

"No blade powerful enough to kill a god should ever have been broken so," Odin said.

"Slayer blades can kill gods?" Callie asked in surprise.

"Of course," Odin replied with the faintest hint of a smile. "The vampires were given immortality by the fruit which sustains the deities. They themselves are part god, so a weapon forged to kill them could certainly kill us too."

I placed my hand on Nightmare's hilt, the blade burning more strongly than ever in the presence of this king of gods, and it seemed to writhe with the potential he spoke of.

I exchanged a hopeful look with Callie. If these blades could kill a god, then perhaps we could use them to defend ourselves against Idun and Andvari.

"So it is time," Odin sighed and his breath was like an autumn breeze, lifting my hair around me in the strange gust. "My prophecy has almost come to fruition."

"*Your* prophecy?" Fabian asked, his brows stitching together.

"Andvari called on me to make it, but it was never his. Not even he knows the deep secrets it holds." Odin turned to Callie and I once more. He reached toward me and I shuddered, a wave of energy rolling through my body. My heart beat. Once, twice, then it stopped abruptly as if it had never happened.

"You have given your life for this," he whispered, his one eye falling directly on me. "But there is more you must give." He turned to Callie, raising a palm and her own hand lifted in response. He gazed down at the ring shining on it with a hint of satisfaction in his expression.

"I am the only one who can see it," he sighed. "And the only one who does not desire it." He dropped his hand and Callie's arm fell to her side. "You must return it to Andvari. Lay it in the holy mountain with the treasure and pay the debt. That is the only way for this to end."

"No," Julius said from beyond Odin and the god's azure eye swivelled back into his head as if he could see through his own skull.

"No?" Odin laughed in a gravelly tone, the sound sending a quake through to my bones.

"It's protecting us from Idun and Andvari," Julius said anxiously.

"Returning it is the only way to end the curse upon the children of blood," Odin said.

"Then we will," Clarice said, nodding quickly.

"Yes," I confirmed. "If that's what it takes to end the curse, we'll do it. But we need your help first."

"And we won't do anything unless you agree," Callie said firmly and Odin's single eye spun toward her.

"Callie Ford, your veins run hot with the fire of the sun. You have taken steps toward your calling, but you are yet to deliver the promise of the prophecy. The sun sometimes forgets that it hides the light of a million stars beneath its powerful glow. There are many in this world who need you to use that fire to guide them out of their eternal night." His eye turned to me, and a tremor gripped my body. "Montana, you are more willing to give what you know you must. The moon shines brightest in the dark. But it is always there, even in the day. Quiet and patient for its time to ascend. Your rising has been a most difficult transition; you have shed your hatred of those who perhaps did not deserve it. But the losses you faced along the way have left scars on your heart that still misguide your actions." He contemplated us for what seemed like minutes as the quiet stretched on. Eventually he took a deep breath that drew the hair forward from our shoulders. "Dusk and dawn, the in between. That is where you had to meet. And here we are. Two ancient enemies united as one. And yet...there are two missing."

"Yes, Magnar and Erik," I said hopefully. "Valentina has them, she's controlling them somehow."

"Idun and Andvari are helping her," Callie added urgently.

At the mention of the gods' names, Odin's face creased with anger. "Their feud has tarnished my beautiful world. It has gone on far longer than I imagined. I turned my eye from them a long time ago and now I have returned to find the land I left in their hands has fallen to ruin."

"Will you help us then?" Miles asked, wringing his hands together. "Our brother's in trouble. The slayer is too."

"Yes...trouble indeed," Odin said gravely. He shut his single eye a moment and the shrubs in the fields rustled in an unnatural breeze. Odin's eye flew open and rage encompassed his features as his iris grew to a bright red glow. "My power, my *gift* has been greatly abused. Idun has grown far beyond the position I bestowed upon her and Andvari is allowing it. She has given away something that was not hers to give." He bared his shining white teeth as he snarled and fear clutched my heart.

"Will you help us?" I begged, an ache growing inside me at how much I needed him to do so.

"Please," Callie pressed, her expression contorted with longing. "We need you."

This god held the answer to our prayers. He could bring Erik back to me and Magnar back to Callie. The thought alone sent a wave of desperate hope flooding through me. When he didn't answer, I rushed forward and took hold of his hand. His skin was burning hot and energy rippled from it like molten warmth. Callie rushed forward too, gripping his other arm.

211

Odin placed his hand on top of my sister's as he turned to her, the glow of his eye fading away to its original cool blue. "Yes, I will help. But you must swear on all that you are, that you will return the ring, Andvaranaut, to the holy mountain. That is where you will pay the final debt."

Callie nodded, her expression taut as she thumbed the ring on her hand. "I promise."

Odin pulled us closer with an almost sad smile as his gaze swung between us. "What is lost can always be found."

I frowned, unsure of the meaning of his words as he swept a finger down each of our cheeks. "Your men will be freed from my power. It is done." He turned away from us, his body seemingly swept away on the breeze.

The moonlight extinguished and we stood in a circle again, but this time it was the others who surrounded me and my sister. They gazed at us like we were more than just two women who'd stumbled into their lives. It was as if we were gods ourselves.

MAGNAR

CHAPTER TWENTY THREE

Valentina slept fitfully for the rest of the flight back to the castle and when she woke her mood was sullen. She ignored us for the most part, commanding us to stay with her as she headed back to the castle. I followed silently, keeping my head low so that I didn't offend her in any other way. I feared her dreams had troubled her, but I didn't dare to ask if my guess was right.

She gave orders for a legion of her biters to head back to the base and track down the twins. Shame washed over me as I realised she no longer trusted us with that task.

A platoon of Elite surrounded us as we moved along the corridors, and I sneered at them as they eyed my warm flesh with interest. She may have encouraged her followers to feed from the vein, but I wouldn't be offering out my own blood to anyone except her unless she asked it of me.

Andrew glared at me at every opportunity, his hatred and desire for my blood clear in his gaze, but I ignored him. If he wished to try and bite me, then he would quickly find out why the Belvederes had feared my wrath.

Valentina dismissed the rest of her guards as we reached the bedroom she'd claimed for her own, making them wait outside the door as she drew us in after her.

Erik glanced at me excitedly as we were left alone with her, and I could tell that he was as hopeful as I was that she might take us to her bed.

She was yet to punish us as she'd promised though and I was sure we had that to come before we could hope to earn the pleasure of her body. But I would gladly take any measure of pain she dished out for a moment in her arms.

The call of her body was intoxicating and I almost groaned aloud just thinking about what we'd started here earlier. I only hoped that we hadn't disappointed her too much. Perhaps she still wanted to pick up where we'd left off. This was one way I knew I could please her without fail. I'd do everything I could to make up for our failure to kill the twins.

A deep vibration rattled through the room and I drew Tempest into my grip as I looked for the source of the roiling power.

Idun stepped through a fissure in the air, the whole castle trembling as she slammed her bare foot down on the floor. Her naked skin was dressed in a swarm of living snakes which writhed across her body, hissing angrily.

Her face was a mask of rage as she advanced on Valentina and I took a step forward to defend my queen.

Idun's power slammed into me, immobilising me and Erik as she kept her focus on my love.

"Where is it?" Idun demanded and in place of the liltingly sweet tone she usually used, her voice was like a thunderclap breaking across the sky.

Valentina dropped to the floor, pressing her forehead to the carpet by Idun's bare feet as she bowed as low as physically possible.

"Forgive me," Valentina begged. "I have failed you but I swear I'll make it right. I've already sent a legion of my best fighters to track down the twins again. I am putting every effort into appeasing you and retrieving that ring-"

"And yet it is not enough," Idun snarled and one of the snakes lunged forward, driving its fangs into Valentina's arm. She screamed as the pain of its venom sliced through her and my heart leapt in panic as I strained against Idun's hold on me.

"Punish me," I begged. "I faced the girl and let her escape me. I'm the one who deserves your wrath."

"Yes," Erik agreed desperately. "I let her live too. My selfish desire to stay with my love made me abandon my chance at finishing the twins. Set your vengeance on me."

Idun turned to look at us, her eyes burning fiercely.

"Perhaps your pets have a point," she growled. "Maybe their love for you is the problem here."

Idun pointed a finger at me and a snake coiled along the length of her arm, its eyes glowing green like the jewel which hung from Valentina's throat.

My breath caught in my chest as my love for Valentina was stripped back, peeled out of my body and drained from my blood.

I stared at the vampire who had been selected for my bride as a dark hatred grew in me. I didn't love her - I ached for her death more than anything in this world.

I raised Tempest higher and took a step towards Valentina as she stared up at me, her lips parted in horror.

"No," she gasped. "I'll do better, I'll do anything! I-"

I swung my blade at her head with a bellow of rage and she rolled across the floor with a scream of terror.

My grip tightened on Tempest's hilt and I advanced again, her death the only goal I desired.

"Please!" Valentina shrieked and Idun nodded.

"Enough," the goddess breathed.

Idun's snake turned away from me, slivering back up her arm and I stilled as my love for Valentina returned. I wasn't sure what had happened and my gaze darted to the deity uncertainly.

"I can take them from you any time I please," Idun breathed.

The goddess stepped towards me, trailing her fingers along my jaw and I was enraptured by the perfection of her face.

She slid her arms around me and her snakes writhed against my body as she moulded herself to me.

I was vaguely aware of Valentina staring at us from the floor and Erik locked in place behind me, but nothing in the world mattered aside from this beautiful being before me.

Idun gazed deep into my eyes for several long seconds before sighing. "I find I miss your insolent tongue," she murmured. "I don't know that I like you so compliant, my warrior."

I frowned, unsure what she meant, and she stepped away from me as if she were disappointed.

"This is your last chance," the goddess warned, pointing at Valentina. "Don't let me down again."

"I won't," Valentina swore, flattening herself to the floor once more. "I will bring you that ring."

"You will," Idun agreed firmly. She stepped back and the air swallowed her whole. Her power disappeared and a faint ringing filled my ears as I adjusted to the removal of her presence.

I hurried forward and offered Valentina my hand, pulling her upright as my heart thundered from her touch.

She looked up at me with rage flashing in her eyes and her fist connected with my jaw as she regained her feet. Pain flared through my chin and I welcomed it, knowing I'd disappointed her.

I dropped my head in shame as the taste of blood filled my mouth.

"If the two of you let me down again, I'll gut you both," she snarled.

"Yes, my love," I agreed.

"I will drive a blade into my stomach myself, my queen," Erik added fervently.

Valentina looked towards him and I noticed some of the anger leaving her posture.

"Kneel," Valentina snapped, pointing at a spot by the foot of the bed and I hurried to obey. "Stay there until I'm ready for you."

Erik dropped down beside me and I glanced at him as his shoulder brushed against mine. The wounds on his chest had healed over but his torn shirt was still splattered with blood stains from his injuries. I took my sheath from my back and laid Tempest down beside me.

"The next time that little witch visits me in my dreams, I'll give her a nightmare of her own. I'm going to have a lot of fun with the two of

218

you," Valentina said as she crossed the room and stopped before a large mirror which hung from the wall. "Especially you, Magnar. Let's see how much she enjoys spying on my memories then."

My heart lifted as she singled me out and I smiled in anticipation while Erik pressed his lips together in fury.

Valentina tilted her head as she surveyed us and slowly unbuttoned her jumpsuit, sliding it from her body as we watched her. Blood pounded in my veins and I ached to go to her but she'd commanded us to stay put and I refused to do even the slightest thing to displease her again.

She dropped her clothes to the floor and stepped out of them, standing before us in her black underwear and high heeled shoes.

"Do you want to kiss me?" she purred. "Touch me?"

"Yes," I breathed and Erik nodded mutely, his eyes locked on her exposed flesh.

"Show me what you want to do to me. On each other."

I glanced at Erik, disappointment stirring in my chest as I turned my attention to him instead of her, but if this was what she wanted then I was happy to do it. I ached to please her in any way possible and if she liked to watch the two of us together then I wouldn't object to it.

Her necklace flared with power as she brushed a finger over it and I suddenly wondered why I'd been disappointed about this. I wanted Erik just as much as I wanted her.

I caught his neck in my grip and dragged him towards me as he fisted his hands in my hair, kissing me with an aching desperation.

His hands slid down my chest and I groaned as he headed lower. I shoved the tattered remains of his shirt off of him to gain access to more of his skin and Valentina's laughter caught my ear.

"Wait," she breathed, and Erik pulled away from me just as his fingertips reached my navel.

My heart pounded as I turned towards my queen again and I smiled as I noted the lust in her eyes.

She walked towards us, her hips swaying as she moved to stand in front of us. I gazed up at her, my heart swelling with love as I fought against the urge to touch her. I would wait for permission. I wouldn't do anything wrong again.

"My pets," she whispered, brushing her fingers along Erik's jaw. "How I adore you." She swept her fingers across my cheek before clutching my chin in her grasp.

Her fingernails bit into my skin and she inhaled deeply as I felt blood spilling from the wounds.

She increased the pressure on my jaw, tugging me up so I stood before her while Erik remained on the floor.

Her hand slid from my chin, down my neck and over the curves of my muscles.

"I want you to beg for me," she said as she lifted her eyes to meet mine. "Beg for me to bite you."

"Please," I said instantly.

"Not good enough." She dropped her mouth to my neck and started to trail kisses over my skin.

Every inch of my flesh came alive with longing as she moved lower.

"Please," I said more forcefully, and she laughed.

"Help me to convince him, Erik," she said as she pulled the vampire towards me too.

He started kissing my stomach as she pressed her lips to my chest and my desire for the two of them almost overwhelmed me.

"Bite me," I begged, my voice rough with desperation.

"If you insist."

I flinched as her teeth cut into my chest right above the tattoo which tied me to her, and Erik's fangs burrowed into the flesh above my hip.

The pain was overwhelming but it mixed with my desire for them in a way that intoxicated me.

I closed my eyes, tipping my head back as they sated their thirst on me, and I was filled with satisfaction as they moaned in pleasure while they fed. They gripped me tightly, refusing to let me go as they drank deeply but I didn't want them to go anywhere, I wanted them exactly where they were.

Valentina pulled back first and Erik quickly followed her lead.

She claimed my mouth with hers and the taste of my own blood washed over my tongue, but as she drew my body against hers, that nagging itch started up in the back of my mind once more, the sensation that something was amiss dragging at me.

Her attention switched to Erik as she pulled him upright and my blood ran hot as I watched her kissing him.

Valentina placed a hand on each of our chests, sliding them lower as a wicked glint lit her eyes. She reached my waistband and paused, toying with me. She could see how desperately I wanted her to continue and she held Erik captured in the same teasing moment as he groaned, leaning towards her in the hopes that she'd carry on with her descent.

"I want you to take me first, Magnar," she breathed as her gaze dropped over me. "I've waited so long to find out how this would feel and I can't wait any longer."

My heart pounded at her request and I smiled excitedly, but now the itching in the back of my mind had become a buzz and a faint frown pulled at my brow as my thoughts turned to it.

"But you won't be left out, Erik," she promised him. "You'll have your turn too."

Her necklace blazed and I stared at it as she leaned closer, pushing her fingers lower, sliding them beneath my waistband, sliding towards my cock - which for some reason hadn't actually hardened yet.

My lips parted as the buzzing in my skull turned to a rush, my muscles locking tight, the sense that something was wrong battling against the pulsing light of that necklace which continued to grow, forcing my focus to it, drawing me in against my will.

The emerald grew brighter and brighter, pulling all of my attention and I could feel Erik staring at it too, his posture growing as rigid as my own.

Something was wrong. Something was inherently wrong with me and this place and this woman.

My gaze snapped from the emerald to Valentina, something shattering inside me and ricocheting through every piece of my soul as I met her dark gaze in the place of the brilliant blue I'd been expecting.

With a sound like breaking glass, the emerald suspended from her throat split in two, jerking my attention back to it. The light fled from it and the stone turned black as the severed pieces tumbled to the floor.

A faint whooshing filled my ears as images of a woman with hair the colour of sunlight filled my mind and I sucked in a ragged breath.

I was kissing her, holding her, making love to her. She was mine and I was hers. I remembered everything it had taken for us to find each other and everything that had tried to keep us apart.

"Callie," I breathed and her name was the undoing of all that had been stolen from me. I remembered... I remembered it all.

My gaze slipped to Erik and I found the same dawning comprehension in his eyes too.

I caught Valentina's wrist in my hand and she looked up at me in surprise as I released a feral snarl filled with rage at all the things she'd forced me to do.

She inhaled sharply, snatching her other hand away from Erik as she reached up to touch the necklace and found the stone missing.

I twisted her arm in my grip and she screamed as the bone snapped. Erik slammed his fist into her face and she fell to the ground in a heap.

"How?" Valentina gasped as she stared up at the two of us in horror, seeing her death in our eyes.

I kicked her, sending her flying across the room into the huge mirror and it shattered around her, the broken pieces raining down on her skin and cutting her open.

"Guards!" she screamed as we advanced on her again. "Help!"

Erik shot towards her, catching her hair and slamming her face into the wall so that blood spewed.

"You'll bleed for this," he promised, all the wild savagery of his kind spilling into his words.

The door burst open behind us and I turned as twenty of her loyal Elite flooded into the room.

I leapt forward, snatching Tempest from the ground and crying out as I swept it towards them.

A harsh wind battered me as Valentina seized control of the air in the room and Erik was knocked away from her.

He roared his rage at the Elite as they sprang forward to surround their queen and Valentina hid herself within their midst.

The two of us lunged at them and I carved Tempest through flesh and bone as I fought to kill the devil who had enslaved my body and stolen me from the woman I loved. The fury I felt was unparalleled, the revulsion, the taint upon my flesh seared into my memory.

The wind slammed into me and I was knocked from my feet, rolling back alongside Erik to the entrance of a grand bathroom.

"Kill them!" Valentina shrieked as she raced towards the door and the Elite cut us off from her. She disappeared beyond it and I cursed as I realised we'd missed our opportunity to end her while the shock of our reality had come crashing down upon us.

I swung my blade again as the Elite pressed towards us and I managed to kill one of them, sending dust swirling between their ranks.

Erik slammed into me, knocking me out of the way as one of the Elite fired a rifle at us.

I cursed as I rolled over the tiled floor in the bathroom and came up on my knees, holding Tempest ready once more.

There was no room for us to move in the confined space and the Elite had the clear advantage with their numbers. Valentina was long gone and I cursed myself for not killing her as soon as the spell over my soul was broken. But it had been too much to take in at once. So many memories and feelings coming back to me in that single moment. It was overwhelming and confusing. I hadn't been able to process it quickly enough.

Erik ripped the toilet from the wall and launched it at the Elite as they tried to follow us into the bathroom. He kicked the door shut before they could recover and slid several heavy bolts into place, blocking the Elite out.

"That won't hold them," I snarled but he released a laugh as the Elite began to batter against the other side of the door.

"It will. That door has a steel plate inside it and I just secured it with four titanium deadbolts. This is Clarice's emergency escape plan."

"Well I'm mightily pleased that we are safely locked in a bathroom," I replied icily as I ran some water into the basin and washed the venom from the bites I'd just received.

Erik watched me with a faint frown as if he was thinking about what Valentina had just been forcing us to do and I scowled at him.

"My eyes are up here," I snapped.

"You don't have to remind me," he replied irritably as I rinsed the bite he'd just delivered above my hip bone.

"Well a few inches lower and you might as well have been sucking my-"

"I know! For fuck's sake, I know. Can we please just never fucking mention any of it ever again?" Erik demanded angrily.

"Fine by me." If I couldn't banish the memory of his mouth against mine, then I would at least agree to pretend it had never happened.

I rinsed my mouth out with the water and spat it on the floor before picking Tempest up again.

"So now what?" I asked.

The Elite continued to batter the door outside and we could hardly stay locked in here forever.

He pushed past me and moved to a long mirror which hung beside the shower. As he slipped his fingers behind it, a dull click sounded and the whole thing swung open on hinges, revealing a dark passageway beyond.

"I thought your kind had nothing to fear since you defeated the slayers. Why are you so prepared for an emergency?" I goaded.

"After the hell you put us through, we learned never to take our safety for granted," Erik replied as he stepped into the tunnel and I followed him.

"Where does this lead?" I asked as I closed the hidden door behind us and we were plunged into darkness.

The passage was narrow and my shoulders brushed against the stone walls on either side of it. I had to duck my head as I moved down a curving stairwell and cobwebs tickled my skin.

"To freedom," he replied. "It's time I got back to my wife."

ERIK

CHAPTER TWENTY FOUR

I hurried along the dark passage with Magnar matching my pace. The foundations of my heart had been truly shaken, but it had found its way back to Montana at long last. I didn't know what had happened to that necklace and I didn't much care. We were free. And I'd be damned if we were going to get caught again.

The path dropped down steeply beneath our feet and I pushed myself a little harder, careful not to outrun Magnar. We were united in our need to escape. For once, our hearts wanted the same thing. Besides, we'd both been through this bullshit together and no matter what he thought of me now, I held a strange kind of bond with the slayer after all we'd endured.

"*Yes*," I gasped, darting toward the end of the tunnel where a heavy metal door stood in our way. I placed my thumb to a fingerprint scanner beside it with anticipation bursting through my veins. The screen glowed blue and the door unlocked before us.

"Where does this lead?" Magnar whispered as he followed me through the door.

"See for yourself," I said, gesturing to the underground parking lot before us as lights flickered on overhead. Every one of mine and my siblings' finest cars were housed right here. From Porsches to Aston Martins, we had them all. But the beautiful vehicles weren't what we needed right now.

I hurried to a large steel box on the wall, pressing my thumb to another scanner to unlock it. The front slid open and a rack of keys shone back at me. I plucked one from the bottom row and hurried across the lot past the cars.

"Where are you going?" Magnar hissed, keeping pace with me. "Let's just get in one and leave."

I kept running to the far end of the cavernous space, pausing in front of the beast I'd been looking for. The armoured truck was military grade, its sleek black exterior built to withstand the force of a bomb. We'd acquired it after the Final War, but never really had a need for it. The ramming bars on the front and back were just one of the features that would keep us safe from the biters and Valentina's storms.

"Valentina could have an army waiting for us up there. But this beauty will get us through." I opened the vehicle and climbed into the driver's seat as Magnar hurried around to get in the other side.

As we shut the doors, a loud clunk sounded a host of locks sliding into place.

I started the engine and the truck roared as I drove us toward the exit. We scaled a steep ramp and the camera recognition released the steel gate before us, sliding up to reveal the road leading away from the castle. I pressed my foot on the gas and we tore out of the lot at high speed. I accelerated along the road through the woodland, the sound of our escape surely alerting every biter in the area.

Magnar's rigid posture told me how uncomfortable he was in the modern vehicle, but he was going to have to get used to it.

"You're safe in here," I said in an attempt to set him at ease. "Even Valentina's storms would have a hard time rolling this truck over."

"So long as you don't squeeze my thigh to reassure me this time, I'll be comfortable enough," Magnar said with a hint of mocking to his tone.

"As much as I'm dying to feel up your massive tree trunk of a leg again, I'm pretty sure I can fight the urge."

Magnar broke a laugh and I couldn't help but join him as the gate in the wall came into view ahead. A row of biters stood there, armed to the teeth. They aimed their guns at us and Magnar winced as they let their bullets fly.

A smile gripped my face as the bullets sprayed off of the truck's exterior as easily as rain.

I pressed my foot down and Magnar's laughter grew as he realised what I was going to do.

The biters split apart as the truck pelted at them full-speed. Two unlucky fuckers were dashed to pieces on my hood and we rammed into the gate behind them. It crashed to the ground and the truck bumped wildly as it rolled over the metal.

I took a hard right, heading for the highway as two SUVs took chase behind us, speeding up the road from where they'd been posted outside the castle walls.

I tapped a screen on the dashboard with one eye on the road as I loaded our defences. Guns raised at the back of the truck and a camera fed back the view behind us on the screen.

"Here, use this to shoot," I commanded Magnar and he shifted toward the screen, his face falling into a grimace as he took in the technology.

"Just press the big red button," I jibed and he responded with a noise of irritation before doing as I said.

Gunfire rattled out behind us and the SUVs swerved violently to try and avoid it. The high-powered guns ripped their vehicles to shit, and Magnar released a rumbling chuckle as he figured out how to aim the guns in different directions.

One of the SUVs turned sharply and hit a lamppost as the driver was turned to ash. The other one kept coming, but the windscreen shattered under the onslaught and the biters inside exploded in a cascade of dust.

I raced down streets left and right then merged onto the highway. Hardly any cars were driving along it and I took advantage of the open road, the engine bellowing as we tore south as fast as the wind.

The city shrank behind us and a sigh of relief sailed from my lips.

"Six hours to Baltimore," I announced. "But I can do it in four."

The mega-highway my people had built twelve years ago cut a direct path to Baltimore through the ruins. The raised road ran on stilts above the wrecked parts of Washington D.C. and Maryland, towering above the sprawling sea of destruction. As we closed in on Baltimore, darkness swallowed the land, but a lake was visible on the horizon, glittering under the light of the moon.

We didn't pass many cars as we sailed across the endless highway. The closer we came to Baltimore, the more the mark on my palm tingled. It bound me to Montana, assuring me I was getting nearer to her, and the thought alone sent a thrill dancing down my spine.

I was wrought with anticipation. I needed her in my arms. I needed to beg for her forgiveness for everything Valentina had caused me to do. The memories came to me in a haze and I hated to face them. The moment I'd ripped Montana's head off replayed in my mind over and over again. Would she hate me for it? Would she be able to see Valentina as the true enemy? I didn't know. But whatever happened, I'd spend the rest of eternity making up for what I'd done to her under Valentina's control.

A tense silence had fallen between Magnar and I as we'd descended into our thoughts. The dark expression on his face made me wonder if he was struggling with a similar conflict in his mind.

"You alright?" I muttered.

"I can't get the feel of Valentina's hands off of my body," he snarled. "I think I smell like her too." He shuddered and I noticed he was right. We were running from her bed and her sickly sweet scent was everywhere.

I eyed a junction up ahead, an idea coming to me as I veered off of the highway and circled down to the road below.

"Where are you taking us?" Magnar asked suspiciously and I pointed to the lake up ahead.

"You need a wash," I said, throwing him a taunting look.

"You just want me out of my clothes again, bloodsucker," he accused and I breathed a laugh.

I ate up the road between us and the expanse of gleaming water. The second I stopped the truck, Magnar left his sword in the footwell and jumped out of the vehicle. My brows lifted as I realised how much he trusted me now to leave his weapon here. He ran straight into the lake, leaving his trousers in place, and I headed after him, dropping down from the truck and jogging into the cool water. When I was up to my waist, I sank down into its depths, scrubbing at my hair, my skin, my clothes. Everywhere Valentina had touched me.

I came up to the surface and the water streamed off of my shoulders, taking the feeling of her with it.

Magnar turned to me with a sigh. "Who would have thought I'd be standing here with you and neither of us would want to kill each other."

"Well I'm not glad Valentina took us, but at least we've found some common ground at last."

Magnar smiled darkly. "I'd still rather hate you than have the memories of her mouth on me."

"It seems fate has other ideas," I jibed and he smirked. I eyed the bloody bite marks on his body and guilt rolled through me. "Forgive me for that." I pointed to the one on his midriff and he glanced down at it with a scowl.

"Oddly enough, I think I'm more disgusted by the ones Valentina gave me."

"I think I'd rather have laid with you than her," I said with a bark of laughter.

He snorted his own amusement. "Don't tell Montana that, she'll start thinking you want me instead."

"I've had quite enough of you, slayer," I said and my smile fell away as I thought of my wife. "I'm dying to see her again."

"The chances of us falling for two sisters is quite baffling. I hope the gods never intended for it to happen, I rather like the idea that it came down to chance," Magnar mused.

"Well I certainly don't think Idun or Andvari would have desired it. Or if they did, they underestimated how much hatred can be put aside in the face of love."

"Yes..." Magnar looked to me, his eyes tracking over my face. "You don't think the others are still at the army base, do you?"

I frowned as I considered it. Valentina's biters were heading there in droves. But my family and the slayers weren't foolish enough to remain there. "No chance."

"That's what I suspected," Magnar said, nodding firmly. "So how are we going to find them?"

I turned my palm over as the rune throbbed with heat. "This." I showed it to him. "It tells me when Montana is close. I can sense we're nearer already."

Magnar gave me a hopeful smile, his eyes sparkling with excitement. "Then let's go find them."

We headed back to the truck, soaking wet but feeling a whole lot better to have Valentina's scent off of us. I didn't want to go to Montana like that. I didn't want any trace of that bitch left on me when I reunited with my wife. It was a shame Magnar would have the bite marks on his skin when he found Callie.

I started the truck and headed back to the highway. We were soon speeding along, closing in on Baltimore by the second. Before we got close to the army base, I took a road toward the farmlands instead, following the growing heat in my palm as we drove inland.

"I wish my head had been clear enough to take that chance to kill Valentina," Magnar said in a gruff tone.

I sighed heavily. "By the gods, I want that woman dead more than anything."

"She deserves the foulest of deaths," Magnar agreed then released a noise of anger. "What she made us do...bowing at her feet, acting like miserable dogs-"

"It could have been worse," I muttered. "One more minute in that bedroom and we'd have bigger regrets than that."

"Don't I fucking know it," Magnar growled.

"Well at least we don't have to explain to Montana and Callie that the two of us fucked each other."

His brow creased heavily then he released a dark laugh. "Yes, thank the gods for that."

"Not the gods," I said gruffly. "They were the ones who got us into this shit."

"Idun is a heartless bitch with a pathetic vendetta against me. I'm tired of her ways."

I upped our pace in the truck, suddenly anxious that the gods might come after us now. But somehow, I felt sure that we were safe. I didn't know how that could be possible, but a deep intuition in my heart told me it was true.

As we raced between fields and fields of farmland, the rune on my skin flared with an intensity that filled me with need.

Montana was so close. Before this night was over, I'd have her in my arms at last. And no one would ever take me from her again.

CALLIE

CHAPTER TWENTY FIVE

Our journey onwards was punctuated by a tense silence. Asking for Odin's help was one thing, but getting it was another. He wanted us to fulfil the prophecy and head to the mountain with the ring, but he hadn't made it clear if Erik and Magnar would be set free before or after we'd upheld our end of the deal.

I felt jittery. Like there was a storm brewing but I had no idea if I was going to get caught in it or not.

I needed to tell Julius the rest of the story about his mother. But I really didn't think he'd appreciate an audience of Belvederes for that conversation. He deserved the privacy he'd require to take on the burden of that grief. It wasn't fair of me to hold onto the secret though, and the weight of it was hanging heavily on my heart.

Fabian was sitting in the front with Miles, directing him towards the house of the girl he used to love. It was funny to think of someone holding a grudge against him for a thousand years, but I could understand why. I'd hate him forever too if he turned me into a monster.

I glanced at Montana guiltily as that thought crossed my mind, but her situation wasn't the same. She'd had no other option. Though that led to beg the question, if I was mortally wounded would I accept immortality as a solution?

I chewed on my lip as the answer came to me and I was a little ashamed to even think it after agreeing to it for Montana. But I knew in my heart it was right. I wouldn't want to live a life as a vampire. Not if there was any chance that I could be stuck that way.

I wished to live and love, grow old, have children...die. I didn't want to be frozen in one place forever. Never being anything more than what I was at this very moment. My heart twisted with unexpected pity for the Belvederes. None of them had asked for this.

I glanced at Julius as he snoozed in the seat beside mine and wondered if I should tell him about that decision, but I realised he wasn't the one I needed to convince. He wouldn't be the one trying to turn me if anything were to happen. The vampires were the ones who needed to know how I felt about it.

"Is something bothering you, Callie?" Clarice asked gently and I noticed her looking at me.

"No," I replied instantly then regretted it. "Well, sort of," I admitted.

Montana turned to look at me too and I dropped my head, backing out on the idea.

"What is it?" Clarice urged. She reached out to lay a hand on my shoulder and I didn't even recoil from her touch. The vampires didn't repulse me like they used to and I realised I wasn't afraid in their presence anymore either.

"I think it might be rude to say it," I muttered.

"Well now you have to tell us," Warren said with a teasing smile like he expected me to say something embarrassing.

"Okay... But you all have to promise not to be offended by it," I said, meeting Montana's eye as I spoke so that she'd know I meant her.

"You can tell me anything, Callie," she said, her brows pinching together in confusion.

I took a deep breath and raised my chin before I spoke. "I've just been thinking about the amount of danger this whole mess has put us in. And I can't help but feel sure that getting to this mountain is only going to be harder than everything we've survived so far..."

"And?" Warren urged with a frown.

Fabian turned to look at me from the front seat and I forced myself to finish what I'd been going to say.

"It's just that the gods haven't exactly been reliable up until now. And as much as I want to believe that we're holding the answer to the prophecy in our hands here and that as soon as we get to the mountain your curse will end... I just can't help but feel that maybe it's not that simple. And if there's even the slightest chance that this curse won't end, then I need you all to be clear on how I feel about something-"

"You don't want anyone to turn you," Montana whispered and I could see the truth of that caused her pain.

The others all stared at me, waiting for confirmation and I nodded.

"I'm sorry," I added. "And I really don't think of you all as monsters anymore, I just... I don't want to be trapped in death. I want to live, to breathe and grow and change. I want to get old and have kids and die happy after a long life... but if I don't get to do all of that and my time is up soon, then so be it. I want to stay mortal. For however long I've got."

Clarice's touch on my shoulder tightened slightly and she rubbed my arm before drawing back.

"I understand exactly what you mean," she said and I could see a deep sadness in her eyes. She wished to be mortal too. I had everything she wanted and she knew why I didn't want to give it up.

"You don't seriously expect us to just let you die if something were to happen to you?" Fabian asked incredulously. "We have the power to save you from the clutches of death but you'd rather we let you go? There's no way in hell I'd-"

"It's not about you," I snapped. "This is about what *I* want. And I'm asking all of you, if you care about me even a little bit then I want you to honour that if the worst happens."

I held Fabian's eye and he shook his head in frustration as he turned away from me again.

I released a heavy breath and turned to look at my sister instead.

"Are you sure about this, Callie?" she asked sadly. "We're so close to breaking the curse. What if something were to happen and we didn't save you but then we broke the curse a few days later? Don't you think-"

"Please, Monty," I breathed. "Just promise me."

She stared at me for a long time and a tear slipped from her eye as she nodded. "If it's what you truly want."

"Don't look at me like that," I teased, breaking the tension. "I'm not dead. I'm only saying that I don't wanna be undead either."

She cracked a smile as the truck pulled over.

Julius mumbled something incoherent and I shook his arm gently to wake him.

"Is this it?" Miles asked in surprise and I leaned forward to get a look.

He'd parked the truck before a huge farm house surrounded by sprawling fields. There was nothing else for miles around as far as I could see, and I guessed whoever lived here didn't get many visitors.

"This is it," Fabian confirmed.

"How can you be sure?" Clarice asked. "If you haven't seen her for hundreds of years then you can't possibly have ever been here to-"

"I send her supplies of blood and other consumables," Fabian muttered. "So I know the address. Plus..." he trailed off, obviously rethinking finishing that sentence.

"Plus what?" Miles asked.

Fabian ran a hand over his face as he sighed. "I usually keep a few Familiars around the place. Just so that I can keep an eye on her and make sure she doesn't need anything extra from me."

"You spy on her?" Clarice asked in surprise.

"It's not spying," Fabian snapped.

"Well why are we all still sitting here?" Warren asked.

"Because she probably won't be pleased to see me. Unless..." Fabian's eyes fell on me. "She'd be more likely to trust a human."

"Slayers aren't humans," Julius said loudly. "We're so much more. We're stronger, faster, better looking, more powerful, smarter, we've got more stamina-"

"What the fuck does stamina have to do with anything?" Clarice asked, giving him a dry look.

"Oh you know exactly what it's got to do with," Julius replied with a wink and her lips twitched as she tried not to laugh.

"*Anyway,*" Fabian interrupted before Julius's list could get any longer. "She will be more likely to trust someone with a heartbeat. And out of the two of you, Callie is more likeable."

"No one's more likeable than me," Julius countered.

"No one's more obnoxious," Clarice muttered.

"Fine, I'll go." I got up and headed out of the vehicle, glad for the chance to stretch my legs after several hours on the road.

Fabian sped around the truck and stopped before me, frowning at me in assessment before reaching out to touch my hair. I slapped his hand away in irritation, double checking that I was still using the ring on him to quench his love for me.

"What are you doing?" I asked.

"Just making sure you look your best." He shrugged as he pushed a hand through his own hair then led the way to the house.

I fell into step beside him and we followed a curving pathway down a long hill which wound right up to the front door. The huge farmhouse looked old; it was built with red bricks and big timber beams. Beyond it, on the far side of the valley, I spotted a large red barn with a tractor parked before it. A cow eyed us warily from a field to the left of the building and I couldn't help but stare at the big animal.

"Why are you looking at that cow like you've never seen one before?" Fabian asked, noticing my attention lingering on it.

"I've only ever seen pictures of them and I'd always thought they were kinda like horses but it's just so… cowy."

"Don't say cowy in front of Chickoa," Fabian muttered and I frowned at his tone.

"If my ignorance offends you then maybe you shouldn't have had me reared in a prison," I replied but he ignored me as we drew closer to the house.

Fabian knocked sharply and we waited for an answer.

As the lock sounded, Fabian threw his arm around my shoulders and I frowned up at him as he made a huge effort to look casual.

The door swung open and I looked around at the beautiful Elite who answered. Her hair was black and hung in a silky sheet to her waist and her flawless skin shimmered with a bronze note to her complexion.

She released a hiss as her eyes landed on Fabian and swung a heavy shotgun up between us.

"Chickoa," Fabian warned. "Please be careful with that thing near my wife - she's mortal."

The vampire's eyes drifted over me, and Fabian tightened his hold on me as I wondered if this display was meant to impress her.

"I'm not your wife," I muttered, shrugging out from under his arm.

"I warned you what would happen if I ever saw you again," she growled.

"I know but-"

Chickoa snarled at him and pulled the trigger.

I screamed as the huge bang sounded. I was knocked aside and Fabian was thrown out into the dirt with an oomph of pain. Chickoa advanced on him and I whipped Fury from its sheath, aiming a kick at her elbow and knocking the shotgun from her hands.

I grabbed a fistful of her hair and whirled her around, slamming her to the side of the porch and holding Fury to her throat.

She attempted to struggle, but I increased my hold, growling at her as I pressed Fury against her skin and burning her with the blade for her efforts. She inhaled sharply and stopped fighting me. I pulled the blade back so that it wasn't pressed to her flesh but kept her cheek jammed against the wooden pillar.

The rest of the Belvederes and Montana leapt from the truck at the top of the driveway, but Fabian waved them off to stop them approaching. The right side of his face was half shredded and blood pooled from wounds to his chest and shoulder too.

"You married a *slayer*?" Chickoa asked in surprise, her eyes on Fabian as he rolled to his hands and knees, wheezing through the shotgun pellets which had cut into his lungs.

"Yes," he grunted just as I said, "No."

"Why doesn't your wife think she's your wife?"

"Because I'm not," I snapped, my grip on her tightening. "I was forced down that aisle and Idun bent my tongue to make me say 'I do.' As far as I'm concerned, we are *not* married."

"So you're still up to the same selfish bullshit you were a thousand years ago. Why doesn't that surprise me?" Chickoa snarled.

Fabian caught the edge of the doorframe and heaved himself upright. He winced as he looked at the woman he'd once loved. Some of his wounds weren't healing and I guessed they couldn't because the pellets were still buried in his skin.

"It's not the same," he growled. "I thought I needed human wives to break the curse. We believed that if any of them could give birth to twins then maybe they'd be the answer to the prophecy and-"

"And so you started forcing women into marriage without giving them a choice in the matter? You're unbelievable."

"I like her," I announced but I didn't loosen my hold on Chickoa's hair.

"I take it he hasn't gotten you pregnant yet then?" she asked me.

"No chance of that. If he brings little Fabian anywhere near me, I'll be cutting it off," I assured her and Fabian scowled.

"Less of the little," he snarled and Chickoa snorted a laugh at his expense. "Besides, now we know better. We don't think the prophecy is about having children with slayer-born women anymore. And we are close to breaking the damn curse after all. If it works, then you will get your wish and you can be human once more... *Fuck,* this hurts. Do you have some tweezers to get these pellets out?" Fabian asked.

"Why have you come to darken *my* doorstep?" Chickoa demanded, ignoring his request for help. But I could feel some of the tension leaking from her limbs since he'd mentioned us breaking the curse. She wanted it broken too.

"We are in need of some assistance. Our empire has been taken over by a psychopath who wishes to allow our kind to feed from the vein once more and she has her followers hunting us. You might remember Valentina?"

"Well if you stick a crown on your head and start dictating the way people should live then you shouldn't be surprised to find that a lot of those people will end up hating you," Chickoa snapped.

"Most people hate him," I added.

"I didn't bring you down here with me so that you could band together in your hatred for me," Fabian growled, eyeing me irritably.

"I don't hate you," I replied evenly. "Not anymore."

241

"I still do," Chickoa said coolly.

"If I were in your position, I'd still hate him too," I agreed.

"So he told you what he did to me?" she asked in surprise. "That he turned me against my will?"

"Yes. And I understand why you want to kill him for it. But at this moment in time, we do kinda need his help with the prophecy so I'd prefer it if you could hold off on murdering him for now."

Chickoa sagged in defeat and released a breath. "Fine. I suppose you'd better come in."

I glanced at Fabian and he scowled at me, obviously unimpressed about the subject I'd found to have common ground with his former fiancée.

I removed Fury from her throat and released her hair, stepping back so she could turn to face us. She glared at Fabian for a moment then headed into the house, leaving the door open so that we could follow.

I smiled back up at Montana and the others reassuringly as they watched us from beside the truck before following her inside and closing the door behind us.

Fabian stayed close to me and I could hear him wheezing slightly as he took each breath.

"Coffee?" Chickoa offered and I nodded vaguely as she pointed us into a wide living space while she headed for the kitchen.

The house was huge and the room we stepped into was bigger than my entire apartment had been back in the Realm.

Fabian lowered himself onto the green couch, gritting his teeth against the pain of his injuries and I started wandering around the space.

The walls were panelled with dark wood and a long window gave a view over the rolling valley beyond. Fences broke the fields up and animals grazed in the different pastures. I spotted horses and sheep and a herd of cattle in the distance. There was no real reason for her to keep such creatures, so I guessed Chickoa just enjoyed having them around.

A small stream ran along the bottom of the valley and the longer I looked out over the view, the calmer I felt. This was what the world *should* have looked like.

I could be happy living somewhere like this.

I turned away from the window and started inspecting the things which lined the shelves along the back wall. There were books and trinkets mixed in with photographs of Chickoa and various humans. I stilled as I spotted a picture of her in a flowing white dress, arm in arm with a handsome man as the two of them smiled adoringly at each other.

"Are you married?" I asked, lifting the frame into my hands so that I could look more closely. The man's face was flush with life; I was sure he was human and I raised an eyebrow in surprise.

Chickoa re-entered the room with two steaming cups of coffee and placed them on the table. She hadn't brought one for Fabian and I resisted the urge to snort in amusement.

"Yes. That's my husband, Terry." Her wide eyes lit with a deep sadness and I placed the photograph back down carefully.

Fabian sat up a little straighter, frowning over at us.

"Is he human?" I asked.

"He was," she sighed, reaching out to brush a finger over the image of the man she so clearly loved.

"*Was*? So you turned him?" Fabian asked smugly.

"No," Chickoa snapped, turning to glare at him. "I loved him. We were married one hundred and seven years ago. And we were happy together for every minute of his *human* life."

She pointed at another photograph further along the shelf and I moved towards it curiously. I recognised Chickoa instantly, she was gazing up at a man old enough to be her grandfather with that same adoring look in her eyes. My heart stumbled with pity as I realised what she meant. She'd loved him for as many years as he'd had and had stayed with him until he died a mortal death. I couldn't imagine the pain that must have caused her.

"I'm so sorry," I breathed, fighting against the swell of emotion I felt in response to what she'd been through.

"He died thirty six years ago," she murmured. "And I still miss him every day. But I never would have been selfish enough to pass on my curse just so that I didn't have to suffer the pain of his loss."

Fabian dropped his eyes sullenly and I moved away from the photographs, wondering if I should have pried so much.

"You said you wanted my help?" Chickoa prompted as she took a seat in a large armchair by the window. She tossed a pair of tweezers and a damp washcloth into Fabian's lap, and he grunted a thank you as he shrugged out of his shirt and proceeded to dig the shotgun pellets from his skin.

I perched on the end of the couch beside him and couldn't help but watch as his skin began to knit itself back together once he removed each lump of metal.

"We need to recharge our truck," Fabian said tersely. "And shelter here for a while if you can tolerate it. Plus we could use some-" he hissed between his teeth as he dug a pellet from his shoulder "-human food and water if possible."

"I keep grain for the cattle and I grow crops as a hobby. I get milk from the cows too. I know how to feed a human and I can do it easily enough. Shelter I can manage as well; I have eight bedrooms here, although *you* can sleep in the barn." She glared at Fabian, daring him to object to that and I snorted a laugh as he held his tongue. "I have a wind turbine which generates my power so I can help you with your truck too."

"Thank you," Fabian bit out and she raised an eyebrow at him.

"I have a large supply of blood here which you should know as you're the one who sends it. So you don't have to feed from your wife." She eyed the bite mark on my neck anxiously and I cleared my throat, embarrassed by her assessment. I wasn't some helpless girl being used by Fabian for anything he desired, and I didn't want her to think that of me.

"That was an emergency situation," I clarified. "It won't be happening again. And you can call me Callie."

She smiled warmly and the effect was dazzling. She was insanely beautiful and I could tell she would have been before she was turned too. It wasn't hard to imagine what had drawn Fabian to her in her mortal form.

"Okay, Callie. I'll work on preparing some human food and you can help yourself to a bath if you'd like one. I'll dig out some clothes for you too. How many humans am I cooking for?"

"Two slayers," Fabian growled and I could tell he wasn't impressed that he was being left out of our conversation. "Though Julius consumes at least four times as much as you would expect."

"I'd better go and milk the cows then. Tell your friends to make themselves at home while I'm gone." Chickoa got to her feet and headed out of the room.

I heard the back door closing a moment later and I shifted towards Fabian as he struggled to remove the pellets from his face.

"Let me do it," I said, holding my hand out for the tweezers.

He offered me a faint smile as he passed them over. "I imagine meeting her hasn't done much to improve your opinion of me?" he asked.

I moved to perch on the arm of the couch beside him so that I could see what I was doing.

"Well, at least I know you've got good taste in women," I replied with a shrug.

I dug the first pellet from his cheek and he winced as he fought to stay still. I could feel his eyes on me as I worked, but I didn't meet his gaze. When he looked at me like that it made me uncomfortable.

I kept working until all the pellets were out of his flesh, but he caught my hand before I could get up.

"I would have given you the world, you know," he breathed, and I stilled as he reached up to tuck my hair behind my ear.

"*Fabian,*" I warned in a low tone.

The ring was still blocking his love for me so I knew that this was all him, but that almost made it worse.

"I would have loved you and cared for you and made you *so* happy. I would have lived and died for you."

I wanted to shift away from him but the desperation of his confession held me still. It was like he needed to say this, and I felt like I owed him enough to hear him out despite the fact that my heart beat firmly for Magnar.

"You know I don't-" I began.

"I heard what you said when we were falling from the helicopter," he muttered. "I know how much you love him. The savage."

I frowned, unsure what he wanted me to say to that. His fingers slid through the length of my hair and he sighed.

"You can have your divorce."

"What?" I stared at him, unable to believe what he'd just said.

"I want you to be happy," he said. "And I have to accept that that won't be with me."

My mouth fell open in surprise and I could only stare at him. That was it? No argument, no screaming or refusing. I hadn't even had to ask this time.

"You deserve to be happy too," I said, catching his hand as he removed it from my hair. "You just need to follow this more." I placed his hand above his un-beating heart and he smiled faintly as I released him.

"Well, I suppose I can try."

MONTANA

CHAPTER TWENTY SIX

C allie came to fetch us from the truck and I headed into the
beautiful house with the others, taking in the wooden staircase
and the scent of flowers in the air. It felt like walking into a
peaceful dream.

"Chickoa said there's rooms for everyone upstairs," Callie said.
"She's gone to fetch us some food."

I smiled at her, relief spilling through me that we'd discovered this
sanctuary. I knew we had to face our task soon and find our way to the
holy mountain, but for now, we had time to rest, recuperate and ready
ourselves for that journey.

"I'm pooped," Miles announced, taking Warren's hand with a
dramatic yawn. "Wanna head up to bed?" The glint in his eyes told me
he had no intention of sleeping.

Warren nodded with a wicked grin, following him from the room.

Fabian was sitting on the couch, his skin bloody after his ex-fiancée
had shot him. I was glad she'd come round to the idea of us staying
here anyway, but wondered how far her hospitality would extend if she
wanted Fabian gone soon.

Julius dropped down into an armchair with a heavy sigh. "Oh...

that's so good. That hard truck bench was riding my ass like it was paid good money for the privilege."

Clarice chuckled as she headed to the chair beside his. He eyed her curiously as she flattened her smile and gazed coolly at him instead.

"I want a shower so fucking bad, but I don't think I can move till I've eaten," Julius said, leaning back in his seat. He reached over the space between him and Clarice, tapping the back of her hand. "You're covered in blood."

"I know," she said as his fingers brushed across her skin for half a second longer before he pulled back.

Julius cleared his throat. "And you smell like a freshly murdered weasel so maybe you should go wash," he added harshly and she frowned at him, turning away.

"I could do with a shower," I said longingly, backing up toward the door.

"Go nuts," Fabian commented. "I'm sure my adoring ex-fiancée won't mind."

I released a snort of amusement, heading out of the room and jogging upstairs to a landing where the light of dawn was spilling through a large skylight. I skirted cautiously around the spill of sunlight and headed down the hallway, the wooden flooring leading me to rows of rooms. I followed it, opening the doors as I went as I hunted for a bathroom. I finally found one, stepping into the room decorated with green tiles and making a path for the shower.

Chickoa had provided us with fresh clothes and I soon sat with Fabian, Julius and Clarice in the living room, all of us washed and changed. The men wore jeans and checked shirts from a collection of items that must have belonged to Chickoa's late husband, all of them looking so strange in the casual attire that I couldn't stop looking at them. Julius had nearly busted out of the red one he'd been given so he'd opted to wear a tight-fitting t-shirt underneath it and left the button-down open.

Callie, Clarice and I had been given long, flowing dresses to wear in varying shades of green and blue. My sister had headed outside to find Chickoa and I was tempted to go after her but I wanted to have a drink while she wasn't here, my throat starting to burn with the need once more.

I made my way into the country-style kitchen, opening the refrigerator and finding it packed with blood. I took a bottle, drinking the contents quickly before disposing of it in the trash. It was getting easier to do without the wave of guilt that followed, but that didn't mean I liked it any more than usual.

One day, I'll be free of this damn curse.

I scratched the rune on my palm as I headed back into the living room, an itch growing in it that was driving me to madness. I rubbed my hand harder and Fabian turned to look at me.

"What's up, love?" he asked.

"This mark...it's been acting strange since Callie left and the ring stopped blocking it."

"I could go and find her if it's bothering you?" he asked hopefully and I realised his love for her had returned too.

"No," I replied quickly and his face dropped with disappointment. "I mean, it's sunny out anyway so you can't. Besides, I'm sure she'll be back soon and I won't have to worry about the mark again for a while."

"Maybe something's going on with Erik?" Fabian suggested.

I frowned, hoping it didn't mean he was in trouble. Or perhaps it was the opposite...

Julius had fallen asleep in his chair, his mouth hanging open as he snored softly. As I moved to sit beside him, the rumble of a distant engine sent anxiety darting through me.

I rushed to the front door, tugging it open and gazing up at the track leading out of the farm, fearing the biters had found us. An armoured truck appeared, spewing up dust as it raced toward the house at high speed.

I stilled, about to call for the others when the horn started blaring over and over again. Biters wouldn't be trying to get our attention like that.

The rune on my palm burned like a fire had been lit in my hand, and my mouth parted as I realised that Erik was in that truck.

"Holy shit!" I cried to alert the others, stilling on the porch as fear raced through me. Was Valentina with him, were they coming to attack us once again?

The beeping continued and the driver's window rolled down. Erik stuck his head out, yelling, "Rebel!" at the top of his lungs.

My mouth parted and my fear extinguished in an instant. He was him. He wasn't under Valentina's spell anymore. Odin had kept his promise.

I sprinted down from the porch and charged up the dusty track, my heart feeling like it was about to combust. Tears poured from my eyes, whipped from my skin as the wind beat against me.

"Erik!" I screamed.

The truck skidded to a halt before me and the driver's door flew open. Erik's scent of cedar and rain washed over me and I rushed past the door before he could get out, throwing myself inside. He caught me with a cry of delight, one of his legs hanging out of the truck as I forced him back into his seat. He crashed into Magnar beside him and the slayer laughed in surprise.

I gazed at Erik's face for one long second, soaking in the truth that he was really him. His storm grey eyes were locked on mine with so much love it felt like a tidal wave rolling between us. I crushed my lips to his, wrapping my arms around him as my body sung with the feeling of being close to his again.

Magnar cleared his throat and I lifted my head with a laugh.

"Where's Callie?" he demanded, opening the side door.

"She went for a walk," I said, shaking my head as I didn't have anything better to offer him.

"I'll find her," Magnar growled, stepping out of the truck.

I spotted Julius speeding up the dirt road toward him while Clarice and Fabian stood in the shadows of the porch, staring up at the truck with hope.

"Brother!" Magnar fell on Julius in the fiercest hug I'd ever witnessed.

Erik cupped my cheek, turning me back to face him as my smile bit deeper into my cheeks.

"You're not angry with me?" he asked.

"How could I be angry?" Tears clouded my vision, dropping down onto his skin.

He tucked a lock of hair behind my ear with a faint frown. "Valentina made me do terrible things...I hurt you. I'm so sorry."

I pressed my mouth to his to quiet his worries, his tongue meeting mine and sparking an aching desire in me. We tangled ourselves together despite our awkward arrangement and he seized my waist, releasing a throaty laugh against my mouth.

"Fuck, rebel. I missed you."

I leaned back, taking in his dishevelled hair and the heat in his eyes, wishing I could keep him to myself a while longer. But his siblings deserved to see him too. I sprang from the cab, taking his hand and yanking him after me. I immediately realised my mistake as he winced from the light of the sun and dark veins circled around his eyes.

"Montana," he gasped, looking down at me. "You're not affected by the sun."

I'd been so caught up in running to him, I hadn't even considered the sunlight, and as I took stock of the way the heat blazed against my cheeks and no weakness gripped my body, I realised he was right.

"How's that possible?" I said in disbelief.

"Slayer blood." He grinned, but his own weakness was clear, the veins around his eyes spreading further.

"Shit, you need to get inside," I urged.

"It's fine," he croaked. "It's not far." His hand wrapped around mine and we ran back to the house as quickly as we could.

Magnar and Julius were talking in low tones, their hands on each other's shoulders as they reunited.

Erik hurried up into the shade of the porch with a sigh and Clarice threw herself at him, wrapping her whole body around him. He laughed as he held her close and Fabian joined their embrace, sliding his arms around them both.

My heart grew lighter and lighter until I was sure it would float right out of my body.

"How are you here?" Clarice asked as she released him and backed up a little.

"The necklace stopped working." Erik shrugged and he turned to find me again, catching my hand and tugging me to his side.

"Odin," I breathed, eyeing him excitedly. "We asked Odin for help."

Erik clawed a hand through his hair, absorbing that news. "Well thank fuck you did." He crushed me into another hug, resting his chin on my head and I breathed him in. My skin burned with need and I brushed my fingers up his spine as I bathed in the solid presence of him. My heart, my obsession, my everything. I was whole again. And nothing could break us now.

"How did you find us?" Fabian asked, smiling wider than I'd ever seen him smile.

Erik released me with one arm, turning his palm over to reveal the mark of partnership. "It guided me to her."

"That's why my mark's been feeling strange," I said in realisation. "It was you heading this way."

Erik's mouth curved up into a crooked smile as he nodded. "It seems Montana is gifted with the ability to walk in sunlight," he told the others.

Clarice cursed, stepping closer to me in awe. "What I'd give to walk in the sun again without it draining me."

"You will soon," I swore and she smiled sadly, like she couldn't quite place a faith in that plan.

"What is this place?" Erik glanced over his shoulder at the farm.

"Chickoa's home," Fabian answered and Erik's brows raised.

"She actually let you stay here?" he asked in surprise.

"For now anyway," Fabian grumbled.

"Is Valentina…?" Clarice started hopefully and I turned to Erik, my fingers biting into his arm.

"She's still alive unfortunately," Erik growled.

I sighed, but didn't want to let the fact sully my mood. I had him back and that was more than I could have wished for when the sun had risen this morning.

"Why don't you go inside, Erik?" Clarice offered, throwing me a look. "I'm sure you guys have a lot of catching up to do."

Erik arched a brow. "How subtle, Clarice."

He towed me inside regardless and I was more than happy to follow, my fingers linking with his and our rune marks meeting, sending a wave of desire through me.

He kicked the door shut and tugged me sharply toward him, seizing me like a wolf hungering for blood as his mouth possessed mine. I melted against him, a moan escaping my lips as his tongue pushed into my mouth. His lips were rough and demanding, his grip on me so firm I didn't think I'd ever escape his arms. And I didn't want to.

The first time I'd ever kissed Erik it had felt like taking a bite of the forbidden fruit. He had been so off limits because he had represented everything in my life that was dark. But perhaps there'd always been a little darkness in me too, drawn to that same part of him.

Now it seemed we had met in the middle, the blackened past he held somehow fading before the light our love had created. It was beautiful, powerful and I wanted to remain basking in it forever.

That first kiss had held a promise of all the kisses that would follow. And he was fulfilling them now over and over again, his mouth running from the corner of my lips to my jaw, my neck, my ear. I was unravelling like a ball of twine, made anew by his greedy touches.

His hand slid between us to caress my breast and I pulled away with a breathy laugh.

I pointed to the staircase, biting into my lower lip. "My bedroom?" I offered and he nodded eagerly, his eyes scraping over me with an intensity that made my bones quake.

 We hurried upstairs and the air grew thick between us. My body started to ache with how much I wanted him. It was like he was gravity, pulling me toward him with an inescapable force.

I took the lead, jogging along as I pushed the door open to the room I'd claimed as my own. I paused in the doorway, barring his way with a teasing smile. "The bathroom's that way, if you wanna have a wash."

"I had a dip in a lake on my way here," he said, inching closer with a wolfish grin.

"How savage of you," I teased, placing my hands on either side of the doorway.

"Well I was keeping the company of a savage so maybe he rubbed off on me." He moved into my personal space, almost touching me but not quite.

I pouted mockingly. "Poor Magnar."

"Poor *me* more like, you're driving me crazy. Let me in," he begged and a laugh burst from my lips.

I ran a finger down his chest, hooking it into his waistband. A dark thought slid into my mind and I released my hold on it, glancing up at him. "Did Valentina..." My throat constricted so sharply I couldn't get the words out. Had she violated my husband, taken from him despite knowing he wouldn't want her hands on him? An image of them together sprang into my head and anger coursed through my veins.

"No," he said softly, his mirth falling away into a stony fury. "But she made me kiss her," he sighed heavily, the pain of that truth glowing in his gaze.

A steely determination filled the place of my rage and I lifted a hand to grip his chin. "I want you to forget all about her." I tip-toed up, brushing my lips over his and he fell entirely still as I trailed my mouth to his ear. "You don't belong to her."

He nodded, winding an arm around my waist to draw me flush against him. "I belong to you," he breathed, and light flickered and danced inside me.

He hounded forward and I moved backwards, letting him guide my feet. He shoved the door closed and it banged loudly, sending a quake right down to my toes.

I didn't need my heart to work to tell me how anxious, how hungry, how desperate I was for him. He was my pulse, the thundering beat of my existence. Every step he took was blood coursing through my veins, every touch was the tug and pull of my heartstrings. We'd created life between our undead flesh, and so long as we were together, I would always be truly alive.

The backs of my legs hit the bed and I caught Erik in a fervent kiss once more. He grinned wickedly against my mouth, pressing me back. "Slow down. I want to enjoy every second of you. I'm going to imprint it on the inside of my skull so if anyone tries to steal my love for you again, it will be there staring right back at me."

"You're going to etch a lot of filthy things into your head then, Erik," I purred.

He laughed in a rumbling tone that sent a quiver through me. "Is that a problem, rebel?"

"No, Master," I forced my expression into innocence and his eyes darkened.

"Don't call me that," he scolded.

"Why?" I frowned.

He lowered to his knees, his eyes captivating me as he skated his fingers across my calves. His touch sent fire coursing through me, a living flame that burned a path along my flesh. My thighs pressed together and my clit throbbed from that touch alone, his hands gifted with a spell to unbind me.

"What are you doing?" I whispered.

"I will only ever kneel willingly for one woman," he vowed, his eyes blazing as he gazed at me.

"And who is she?" I teased and he smiled wide.

"She's moonlight embodied, she's every star in my own personal sky. She's fierce and protective of those she loves and even those she doesn't. She gave her life for me and she stayed at my side when I didn't deserve it."

Heat flooded through my chest and dripped down into the pit of my stomach. My legs could barely hold me up as I stared down at this powerful man who bowed to me.

He continued on with a feral glint in his iron eyes, "She doesn't bend to the will of gods, or the might of a king. She's a warrior from Realm G, a woman who shattered the walls I'd built around my heart and taught me how to love again. She is remarkable...and she is you." He took my hand, placing a chaste kiss on the back of it.

"Erik," I gasped, my soul alight with those beautiful words.

"I'm not your master," he growled in a deep tone. "If anything, you're mine."

I shook my head, brushing my tongue across my fangs and realising how truly I had stopped believing in monsters. There were only creatures living between the grey. And somewhere in the middle of it, we had found love.

"We're equals," I breathed.

He rose to his feet, taking hold of the hem of my dress as he did so and tugging it up. I lifted my arms as he guided it over my head and tossed it to the floor.

I slid my hands around his neck, staring into his eyes, needing him to know how much I admired him, how much I cherished him. "Whether we break the curse or not, I want whatever future waits for us. Human or undead. It doesn't matter so long as I have you."

He snared my waist and his fingers ran over my skin in slow, teasing strokes. His hips dug into me and his hard cock pressed into my stomach through his jeans, making his desire clear. I was so wet for him already, my body aching for the feel of him inside me.

"Turn around," he commanded and I released a slow breath as I complied.

His palm glided up my spine and my back arched in response. As his mouth brushed my skin, I gasped at the delightful sensation, shutting my eyes as I relished the graze of his fangs across my shoulder blades. He tore away the strap of my bra with his teeth and the garment fell loose around my breasts. I shrugged out of it, letting it fall to the floor as he reached around to tease my nipples between his roughened fingers.

I leaned back against his shoulder, sighing as one of his hands trailed further south, my pussy clenching with need. His fingers dipped into my panties and brushed feather-light across my clit, circling with teasing strokes of his thumb. A breathy moan escaped me and Erik laughed like a sinner, sliding his hand lower and feeling my soaked pussy.

"It's all for you," I panted. "I want you like no other."

He groaned longingly then tugged his hand free from my underwear, leaving me wanting.

"Erik," I begged and in response he pressed a knee into the back of mine, making me bend forward. I dropped my hands to the bed to brace myself, biting my lip as I felt his eyes tracking over me from behind.

Painfully slowly, he tugged my panties off and I stepped out of the lingerie with a cool blush creeping into my cheeks. He slid his hand over the curve of my ass, his palm slipping between my legs and slicking his fingers through my wetness in a torturously slow circle.

My hips swayed with need and he placed his free hand on my back to keep me still. "How much do you want me?" he growled and my embarrassment gave way to so much desire, I could only answer with another lustful moan. His fingers toyed with me, but never gave me what I wanted, brushing too lightly between my thighs, proving he was in control.

"Rebel," he demanded an answer of me.

"So much. Please, Erik," I pleaded and his response was driving two fingers inside me.

I gasped as he held me in place, his hand coming down on my lower spine while the other hand tormented me, his thick fingers pumping in and out of me. He kept me wanting, ever so slowly pushing his fingers in deeper until I was coming apart at the seams then drawing them back out.

"More," I begged, forcing my hips back.

"Patience, wife," he said and I could hear the smirk in his voice as his fingers pushed inside me again and he gave me more of what I needed. He curled them tight against my inside walls, rubbing and grinding them in a way that had me gasping and moaning.

He slid his other hand around to my stomach, skating his fingers to the point between my thighs which was screaming for his attention. He rolled his thumb over my clit and I sighed in utter delight as his skilled movements took me to the verge of oblivion.

My moans grew louder as his hands continued to move in the most delicious way. He was pushing me toward a cliff I was going to freefall off of at any moment and a sea of ecstasy awaited me beyond it. I clutched the sheets in my fists, unable to stop the cries and moans I was making despite fearing the whole house would hear me. My hips pushed back to meet him, my breasts bouncing as he increased his pace, his hands fucking me faster, harder.

His fingers moved inside me more fervently as he controlled my body with expert skill, his thumb grazing and massaging my needy clit, promising me so much pleasure I could hardly stay upright to take it. Soft then hard, circling and circling until I was losing my mind.

My legs tensed and I cried out as I fell into the precipice of bliss, my body shaking and my limbs impossibly heavy as pleasure rocked through me, my pussy clamping on his fingers while he continued to drive them into me. Before I could fall forward onto the bed, he pulled me back upright by the throat, his tight grip a depraved thing I ached for more of.

I gasped at the sensitivity of my skin as he pressed his mouth to my ear, biting down.

"I've never wanted to please a woman as much as I want to please you," he growled.

"I want to please you too," I breathed, sliding a hand behind my back and running my palm down his huge cock, the length of it jerking through his jeans. He growled in response, his fangs suddenly digging into my shoulder, biting hard and making me cry out in surprise. My back arched from the delicious feeling somewhere between pain and pleasure and I couldn't believe how good it felt.

"More. Deeper," I urged and his fangs drove into me, giving me what I wanted, puncturing my skin and leaving his mark on me.

Need grew in me again like a starving animal. My thighs trembled with urgency as he spun me around and shoved me onto the bed. I hit the mattress with a soft laugh and he kicked my legs wider as he stepped between them, no mirth finding him as he reared over me.

It felt like a hurricane had just passed through my body and I knew it was far from over as Erik crawled over me, smirking at my post-climax expression.

"I'm not even close to done with you," he said. "Spread your legs wider for me. Let me look at your sweet pussy."

I did as he said, my fingers curling around two of the wooden posts of the headboard as I parted my thighs, my heart rioting under his intense gaze. He took his cock in his fist as he leaned over me, pumping it slowly as his gaze dragged over my pussy, his jaw flexing and want burning in those stormy eyes of his.

I took in the muscular lines of his shoulders and raked my gaze across his firm stomach, needing to feel all the power of him pressing me into the mattress. I arched on the bed, fighting off the urge to reach for him as he delayed the satisfaction his body could bring me.

"Erik," I panted. "Come on. Fuck me. Please. I need you inside me."

He caught my hands, ripping them off of the headboard and pressing them into the sheets with a roguish smile.

"Say that again," he ordered.

"Fuck me," I pleaded.

His eyes glittered as he kept me in suspense. I longed for him so badly, it was driving me to madness.

I wriggled a hand free from him and reached for his belt with a grin. His eyes bored into mine as I undid the buckle, then dragged down the zip parting me from what I wanted.

I decided to give him a taste of his own medicine and keep him in suspense as I brushed my fingers through the hair that led into his boxers. His hips jerked hungrily and I smiled up at him as his eyes became hooded with lust.

I slid my hand beneath his waistband and ran my palm down his firm cock, sliding my thumb over the tip and rolling my fist all the way down to the base.

He released a feral noise, reaching between us to try and free himself fully, but I caught his wrist to stop him.

"Patience, Erik," I taunted and he pressed his tongue into his cheek, allowing me to continue.

I tightened my hand around him and his eyes begged me to give him more. I revelled in the feel of him against my palm, rubbing and stroking, squeezing at the tip to make him groan. Our smiles fell to something more carnal, and it was clear neither of us could wait anymore.

Erik pushed his jeans and boxers down and I dropped my hand, too hungry for him to keep up this game. His weight fell onto me and he moulded our bodies into one being with one deep thrust that set my skin on fire, his hard length driving so deep inside me it made me scream.

He ground into a sensitive spot within me and a moan ripped from my throat as I wrapped my thighs around his waist, clinging to him as he moved in an achingly slow rhythm that made every part of me tingle.

His hand clasped mine and the runes that bound us crashed together, sending another wave of ecstasy through me. His thrusts grew more fervent as he filled every space inside me, making each one of my muscles tense.

Lost to my desires, I reared up and dug my fangs into his shoulder on instinct alone, marking him as he had marked me.

He growled his desire, his movements growing more frantic as he clutched me even tighter.

My mind fell into a haze as I was intoxicated by him once more, the feral side of me unleashing again as I bit into the muscle of his neck. He pulled out of me before driving into me so hard, I cried out, his hips moving in a frantic, wild way that I worked to meet, my moans colouring the air. We fucked with such chaotic need for each other that I couldn't focus on anything else than him, and I didn't want to.

His body lay siege to mine again and again. Neither of us grew tired and the energy that rolled between us was charged like an electrical storm. His hips slammed against mine over and over and pressure built at the base of my spine, promising me another wave of utter bliss.

He cupped my cheek, forcing me to look into his eyes as my body came apart once more, an earth-shattering wave of pleasure racking through me.

"You are mine and only mine," he vowed as my pussy clutched his cock and he wrung pleasure from my very core.

Erik came close to his own release, biting into my shoulder as he groaned my name. He finished with one, last, mind-blowing thrust as he forced himself deeper and fell still on top of me.

I folded my arms around him as he kissed me sweetly and my heart swelled in my chest, nearly bursting with my love for him.

He rolled to lay at my side with a breath of satisfaction and I smiled as I curled up against him.

"Do you think they heard us?" I asked.

Erik started laughing loudly. "I think even the cows heard *you*."

I smacked him playfully, falling into my own fit of laughter. "You're to blame for that."

"If you're expecting an apology, you're not going to get one." He angled himself toward me, lifting a brow and I buried my face in his chest to stifle my laughter.

His hand skimmed down my spine as he held me, and I breathed in the scent of him, letting the moment of calm wash through me.

The world was right again once more. And now there was just one last task weighing over us. The holy mountain was our final destination. And I was more than ready to take on whatever awaited us there.

CALLIE

CHAPTER TWENTY SEVEN

I wandered through the valley, vaguely heading towards the huge red barn which stood at the top of the hill opposite the house while I enjoyed the feeling of the sun on my skin.

Chickoa had said that she was going to milk the cows, but I couldn't see how that could be the case with the sun shining down as it was. She hadn't returned to the house though and curiosity drew me to find her. I half expected to find her crawling across the fields, desperately seeking shelter from the sun. Or perhaps she was caught in the barn, unable to leave until the clouds returned. Though as I looked up at the clear blue sky, I knew she'd be in for a long wait if that was the case.

As I made it to the barn, the doors opened and two large, black and white cows trotted out. They eyed me curiously and I held my breath as they passed. The only real experience I'd had of animals that size was the horses Magnar and I had ridden back west and I wasn't sure how safe the cows were.

"Do you want to tell me why you seem so close to Fabian despite the fact that you refuse to call him your husband?" Chickoa's voice came from within the barn, and I moved inside to join her.

"I'm not close with him," I replied as I looked up at the huge space stacked with bales of hay and straw. "We're just...weird friends."

"Weird friends?" she raised an eyebrow at me, and I turned to give her my full attention.

The cool wind shifted to blow through the doorway and the long, blue dress she'd lent me fluttered around my ankles.

"I dunno what else to call it," I replied. "But he saved my life, I've saved his. We were bound together by the gods, so I guess some of it is because of that, but the rest... I'm beginning to see that he's not all bad."

Chickoa snorted in disbelief. "He's a selfish creature. If he is treating you with kindness then it is because he desires something from you. Nothing more. And I saw the way he looked at you; he wants your flesh as well as your blood."

I shrugged. "He knows I'm not offering either."

"Then you may want to be careful he doesn't simply take it," she replied bitterly.

I nodded, wondering how I would ever have come to terms with it if he'd turned me into a vampire against my wishes the way he'd done to her.

"I think you're very brave," I said. "For living the way you have after what he did to you."

"I didn't have much choice," she replied. "I considered ending my life. But if my body is turned to ash then my bones will never rest alongside my loved ones. And I will never join them in the afterlife. My soul would be cast adrift, wandering alone for all eternity. My only chance for a release from this world is for the curse to be broken so that I might die a mortal death."

"Hopefully we're close to that," I offered, though it was hard to trust in our hopes when the gods seemed determined to thwart us at every turn.

"I wish for that to be true more than anything," she breathed. "And I'll do whatever I can to help you achieve it."

I smiled warmly at her as she stooped to lift the pail of milk she'd just gathered from the cows.

She headed further into the barn and opened a trap door, revealing a passageway beyond. "My late husband built tunnels all over our land so that I wouldn't be stuck in our house in the sunlight," she explained. "Fabian has always sent me more money than I could ever need to help him appease his guilt, and Terry decided to use some of it to grant me a bit of freedom. He knew how I hated to be trapped in the house when the sun came out so this was his gift to me."

"He sounds like a wonderful man," I said.

Chickoa smiled as she thought about her late husband and a tear slipped from her eye. "He really was. I'll see you back at the house when you've had enough of the sun." She headed down into the tunnel, pulling the door closed behind her and I was left in the silence of the barn.

I wandered back outside, lowering myself down so that I could drink in some of the sunlight as it danced across my skin, taking a moment in the silence to try and settle my rampaging thoughts.

The dress Chickoa had given me was thin and had no sleeves which wasn't really practical for the season, but I guessed that after a thousand years as a vampire she'd forgotten that. My gifts helped me to fight against the chill but goosebumps soon started to rise along my flesh.

I closed my eyes, resisting the urge to head back to the house and warm up as I listened to the soft animal sounds around me and the rustling of the grass in the breeze.

I didn't think I'd ever been this alone in my entire life. I was sitting in a field, far beyond the Realm with no one for company but myself. It was strange and weirdly nice. Peaceful.

Only my time in the wilderness with Magnar could compare to it, but he'd never been far from me then. What I wouldn't have given to hear him ordering me onto a horse now. I'd even take him hog-tying me in place over this desperate ache in my soul to be reunited with him.

"Callie?"

I stilled as I heard his voice, not daring to open my eyes in case the dream was banished and I found myself alone again.

"Callie?"

My heart leapt. I definitely hadn't imagined that. He was here. But if he was here, was he really *him?*

I opened my eyes and took Fury from my hip, holding it out before me.

Magnar stood a little way down the hill. His chest was bare and he was unarmed, but that didn't mean I could blindly trust him. I wanted to believe that Odin had fulfilled his part of our deal, but I was afraid to hope for such a thing and find it to be false again.

I got to my feet slowly, tilting my head as I tried to figure out if I really had him back or not.

The wind pulled at my dress again, whipping my hair out around me and tugging at his too. Neither of us moved. The space between us was alive with promise, but I couldn't bring myself to breach it.

"Are you afraid of me?" he asked, his eyes falling to the blade in my hand.

"Are you, *you?*" I countered.

In my gut I was sure he was, but I was afraid that I was convincing myself of a beautiful lie.

"Yes," he breathed.

He took a step towards me. Then another. I watched him advance and my heart pounded in expectation.

I lowered my blade. Then let it fall from my grasp.

Magnar stopped before me, a breath of space separating us as the wind still danced across the valley.

I looked up at him and he frowned as his gaze trailed over my face.

"I hurt you," he said, reaching out to gently brush his thumb over my bottom lip which was still split and a little swollen from his attack on me in the blizzard.

The tenderness of his touch sent a thrill of energy dancing across my skin and my heart beat more firmly in my chest as I looked up into those familiar eyes and found myself at home at last.

I swallowed a lump in my throat as he held his thumb against my lip and my mouth tingled with the memory of his kiss.

"That isn't pain," I replied as he drew back, a shadow curtaining his eyes. "Pain was not being with you. Knowing she had you and was using you in any way she pleased, knowing I couldn't save you and every moment that passed was another in which you suffered at her whims-"

"Not a second of it was real for me," he said roughly. "My true self wouldn't have done a single thing she'd wanted."

"Is she dead?" I asked hopefully.

Magnar shook his head, a sneer curling his lip, and I knew he was hungering for her death. But at that moment, I didn't care. I was just glad to have him back.

My gaze travelled over his body and I noted the bite marks on his flesh, the lingering bruises despite his ability to heal. I swallowed a lump in my throat as I reached for him then hesitated, not wanting to force my touch upon him if he wasn't ready for it.

"What did she do to you?" I breathed.

He shifted uncomfortably and I could sense he didn't really want to tell me, but I moved closer to him, forcing him to hold my eye and willing him to see how much I loved him in that look.

"You can tell me," I swore.

Magnar swallowed thickly, his fingers brushing mine, tangling with them and sending a rush of energy through my flesh before he released me again. "Valentina used my blood to feed herself and gave me to Erik too. She made us act like slaves to her and we were tricked into believing we were glad of it, kneeling and simpering at her feet, pliant to her every whim and humiliation."

My anger rose at his words, my flesh hot with the desire for revenge.

"I saw her memories of the three of you in her bed-"

Magnar scowled. "I kissed her, held her, she made me put my hands on her body. Those were the moments when some stirring of resistance found me, but I had no authority over my own mind to act on the sensation of wrongness which itched at me while she forced me to comply with her desires. I didn't fuck her though, Callie," he added, his eyes dark with disgust and what I hated to think might be shame. "She was enjoying flaunting her power over us, but I've no doubt she would have taken it that far had she had any longer to do so. Fortunately, her spell over us was broken before she could."

My heart lifted with relief as I realised that Odin had kept his word and delivered them to salvation before she had managed that level of abuse at least. I reached up to touch Magnar's face, trailing my fingers across the rough stubble which lined his jaw. His eyes were a pit of simmering gold that I ached to dive into. And I knew I truly had him back. The man who had saved me in so many ways. Who had taught me and loved me and set my heart alight with so much passion that I was sure we would burn up in it. But we never did. Every trial we went through only seemed to make us stronger. Each moment apart only making our time together sweeter.

He groaned with longing as if my touch meant more to him than a lifetime of caresses from any other woman.

"But now you're free," I breathed and the truth of it was like a weight lifting off of me. "You're not hers anymore."

"I didn't know how much I missed you until her spell over me was broken. It was as if all of our time together had just been wiped away and I was left as a shell of the man I am. The worst of it was how she made it feel as though I truly yearned for her. It was as if I'd never desired anything but her. When I remember it happening, I can recall how much I wanted it too, though the thought now fills me with disgust at the betrayal I offered you because of the power she wielded." There was a war brewing in his eyes and I longed to right what filled him with such doubt.

"She made you love her," I stated, wishing the words didn't sting so much, but I knew enough about the power of the gods and the games they liked to play with the emotions of men.

"She thought she did. But the way she made me feel for her was not truly love. It was infatuation, obsession, lust. I feel all of that for you and so much more besides. Her sick spell cannot compare to how I feel for you, Callie."

A pool of warmth slid through me at his words and I released a breath, letting the tension slip from my body.

"I'm so sor-" he began but I placed my hands over his lips to silence that word before it could breach them.

"You never have to be sorry for what she did to you," I growled. "Don't you dare take on even an ounce of guilt over it, Magnar. It wasn't you. No part of what she forced you to comply with had any bearing on the man you are. The man I love. Don't let her force you to take on a

270

single sliver of responsibility for her vile actions."

He released a breath which held the weight of the world. I blinked back my own fury in favour of seeking out what it was that he needed from me the most to make him see that she hadn't touched us. She hadn't tainted any part of what we were and she never could.

My gaze slipped down to the bites on his skin again and I inched closer to him, moving my mouth towards the puncture wound by the tattoo above his heart.

"Maybe I can replace those memories with better ones," I breathed.

Magnar didn't move as I leaned in and pressed a kiss to the reddened mark. He inhaled sharply as my mouth met with his flesh, but I didn't think it was because it hurt.

My lips grazed across his skin and I savoured the taste of him as I brushed my lips higher, skimming across the bites on his shoulder and neck before pushing onto my tiptoes so I could find his mouth.

He hesitated, holding my eye as I looked up at him in offering, wanting him to make this choice, letting it be his entirely because he needed to take control of his body again and make whatever decisions he wanted for it. The space between us was reduced to almost nothing at all and his breath mixed with mine as I waited on his choice, on his claim.

"I don't deserve you," Magnar murmured and the depth of his voice sent a trembling ache all the way to my core.

He almost had me undone with his closeness and he hadn't even touched me yet. I was a slave to him. Every trembling beat of my heart was his and the heat building in my body would only be banished through his touch.

He dipped towards me, closing the gap and claiming my mouth as I yielded to his desire. His hands found my waist and he dragged me against him, the thin dress feeling like too much of a barrier as it scratched against my skin and I ached to feel his flesh on mine in its place.

I could feel the hard length of his cock as he pressed his hips to mine and I pushed against him, revelling in the fact that I could cause such a reaction from his body with only the promise of a kiss.

I wrapped my arms around his neck, drawing him to me like a fly to a spider. I wanted him. All of him. And I was never going to let him go again.

Magnar slid his fingers up my sides in a gentle caress as his tongue invaded my mouth and I moaned greedily, wanting more of him, every piece he had to offer.

My heart pounded, my legs trembled. He was here. Really here with me at last and I was his creature to do with as he wished.

He pulled back, our breathing ragged as he kept me in his arms as he tilted my chin up so that he could look into my eyes, his rough fingers coiling around my throat in that possessive way which made my entire body tremble with promise.

"I can't believe I lost you, Callie. But you have to know she never had my heart. It was hidden from me and I thought what I felt for her was love, but it pales into insignificance now that I stand before you with my heart unchained once more. You are the deepest, most desperate desire of my soul. I will never feel this for any other. Even the power of the gods can't replicate that. Because this feeling cannot be a lie. It is who I am. What I am. It burns through every inch of me, body and soul, and it belongs to you."

"You never lost me," I replied. "I was always waiting right here for you. And I would have kept waiting for the rest of my life if that's how long it took to get you back. It doesn't matter what Valentina made you do while she had you. You aren't hers. You're mine."

He groaned as his free hand slid into my hair and he pulled on it just enough to send a thrill right through me and build on the desire which was already pounding through me.

"Say that again," he growled, holding my eye as he pressed his body against mine and the full length of his cock dug into my hip demandingly.

I slid my hands down his chest, delighting in the reaction of his body to my touch. "You're *mine,*" I repeated firmly.

He dropped his mouth to mine again, kissing me so hard that it hurt, a bruising clash of want and need, yet it wasn't enough. His tongue met mine, delving into my mouth and I moaned, begging for more as I tangled my arms around his neck and pushed my body against his.

I was starving for more of him, my nipples hard and aching, causing me to arch against him, needing the relief of his flesh against them. I could feel how desperately he wanted me too. *We* needed this. The physical release of all the pain we'd endured while we were separated. We needed to be reunited completely, merging our bodies alongside our souls and claiming each other once more. He was mine and I was his. No matter what anyone else thought of it or tried to do to stop it.

His hand fell from my throat to tug the strap of my dress from my shoulder, freeing my breast to the sweet torment of his fingers and causing me to release a breathy moan. His mouth shifted away from my lips, trailing a line of fire across my jaw and down my neck, his grip on my hair forcing my head back to offer him access. I flinched as his lips met with the bite on my throat and he stilled suddenly, his grip on me tightening.

"I gave you to Erik to feed from," he gasped, pulling away from me as he suddenly remembered what he'd done while we were escaping the Belvederes' castle. He hadn't noticed that there were two bites there and I didn't think it was the best time to mention what I'd let Fabian, Miles and Warren do.

"It wasn't you," I said firmly, reaching for him again but he backed away, frowning in disgust at himself. My body fell cold as he abandoned me and I ached to reclaim him again but I couldn't force him. He had to come to me himself.

Magnar shook his head, horrified at what he'd done.

"It doesn't matter," I tried again, stepping closer but he backed up as if he couldn't bear to have me touch him after the things he'd done.

"Doesn't matter? How can you say that? I offered you the world, I asked you to be mine and then I threw you to the mercy of a vampire as if you were nothing!" His eyes were filled with pain and rage, and my heart broke for him as the weight of guilt fell onto his shoulders. A guilt which wasn't his to bear. I couldn't imagine how I'd have felt if the roles were reversed and I'd done the same things to him, but I did know that no part of what he'd done was his responsibility. The agony in his gaze was shredding my soul and I didn't know how to fix it.

"It wasn't you," I repeated, blinking away tears. "I don't blame you

273

for any of it: it was Valentina."

"It was my hands, my flesh-"

"No!" I snapped. "If you let this get between us then she just wins again."

I reached out for him and his eyes fell on the bite at my wrist.

"Who did that?" he asked darkly and I suddenly found that I didn't want to answer him. I knew I had to, I knew he deserved that much honesty from me, but I also knew that he was hurting and raw from his time trapped under Valentina's control. He would see nothing but a betrayal in what I'd done. Or worse – he'd find more guilt in the action when he realised I'd only had to do it because he and Erik had been hunting us.

"I'm cold," I said, ignoring his question. "Come inside."

I grabbed Fury from the ground and headed into the shelter offered by the barn. Magnar followed me, pulling the doors shut behind us but I could see he wasn't going to let it drop.

"Tell me," he demanded.

"Will you tell me everything that happened to you while Valentina had her claws in you?" I countered.

"If you want to hear it, I will," he replied tersely.

I glared at him as my desire was countered by anger and I didn't know whether I wanted to kiss him or punch him, because I'd only just gotten him back and he was already calling all of the shots and demanding I bow to his commands.

"After Valentina brought down the helicopter, Fabian risked his life to save mine. If it wasn't for him then I would have died falling from that thing, but he wrapped me in his arms and did everything he could to slow our fall before taking the full impact of our collision with the ground to keep me alive," I explained, knowing he wouldn't like this one bit but refusing to cover the truth. If he wanted us to bare every ugly reality of what had happened during our separation, then I would give it to him. "I offered him, Miles and Warren my blood to help them recover their strength so that they could face you and Erik once you arrived."

Magnar's eyes lit with wild fury and he advanced on me, forcing me to back away.

"Our kind do not feed parasites willingly," he snarled, towering over me as the backs of my legs hit one of the huge bales of straw and I found myself penned in and at his mercy.

"You can hardly talk," I hissed, pushing my finger against a bite which was so close to his waistband that I was fairly sure Valentina must have had him naked to have done it.

His muscles tensed in response to my touch. "I *wasn't* willing," he replied and the sting of those words made me feel like a total asshole for even feeling a trace of what I did, but it was hard to banish those thoughts from my mind entirely.

"Was she on her knees when she did that to you?" I asked, jealousy spiking through me despite knowing he hadn't wanted any part of Valentina's games. But it didn't make it any easier for me to accept the fact that she had taken pleasure in his flesh. And I couldn't stop imagining what she'd done to him while she'd taken his body captive.

He bit his tongue as he looked down at me and I could feel the heat of our argument fuelling his desire too. We always did burn hottest with rage.

"That wasn't even her," he admitted irritably. "But she did force Erik to his knees when he did it."

My lips parted in surprise and my gaze slid down his body again. "Erik?" I confirmed, biting my lip so that my amusement at that fact didn't show.

"I told you she got nothing more from me than blood and kisses. And neither did he for that matter."

"You *kissed* Erik?" I raised an eyebrow at him, and I could tell he didn't find the fact very funny, but shit – the two of them had been mortal enemies for a thousand years and now he was telling me that they'd become pretty fucking intimate in their time away from us.

"I don't wish to talk about it now." He stepped closer to me, but I had nowhere left to retreat and the small bout of anger I'd felt towards him was giving way to the lust which simmered in the pit of my stomach.

My mind snagged on Valentina's memory of his mother and I frowned. "I learned other things from her while she slept," I admitted. "Things you need to know-"

"Later," he commanded and his tone made my legs weak as he moved to grip my hips and lifted me up so I was perched on the bale of straw.

"But-"

"Later," he growled, pushing himself between my thighs and he took my mouth hostage with his own, his fingers gripping my waist and pinning me in place.

My need for him tore through everything else like wildfire, banishing every thought but the feeling of his body against mine as he pushed my dress up with one hand and unbuckled his belt with the other.

My heart pounded as his hand skimmed alongside the inside of my thigh and he caught my underwear in his grip, tearing it off of me.

I gasped as he pushed his fingers inside my soaking core, and he growled with satisfaction while he felt how wet I was for him. Because of course I fucking was. I'd been wretched with desire from the moment I'd found him standing out there and I needed his savage touch more than I needed air in my lungs.

I leaned back, moaning as he took command of my body and his thumb dragged over my clit as he pushed his fingers deeper.

"By the gods, I've never desired a woman the way I ache for you," he breathed. "And knowing I can make you feel like this-" I moaned louder as he drove his fingers into me again and a wicked smile tugged at his lips. "Just makes me want you even more."

"So take me," I urged, reaching for his waistband and pushing it down to reveal the hard shaft of his cock.

I took hold of him, biting my lip as I felt the full girth of him in my hand, craving the feeling of him inside me. He groaned deep in the back of his throat as I moved my hand up and down his length, smearing precum over his tip and savouring the velvet feel of his rigid flesh.

"Please," I panted, my need for him feral and urgent, this desperate urge which demanded satisfaction.

Magnar kissed me roughly, my name on his lips as he pulled his fingers back out of me then grabbed my knees and hoisted me forward. I released my hold on his cock and he gripped it himself, guiding it to my entrance before he pushed himself inside me. I cried out as he filled me with one hard thrust, my whole world narrowing to the sensation of his dick filling me so completely.

His hands stayed on my legs, pushing them further apart and I wound my arms around his neck, kissing him fiercely.

He drove himself all the way into me and I inhaled sharply as his teeth closed on my bottom lip right over the still-healing welt which split at his roughness and painted our passion in blood.

His need was as desperate and urgent as my own, and he wasted no time in taking possession of my body while I surrendered to him entirely, giving in to the wild nature of this savage man of mine as he fucked me like a heathen.

I cried out, my fingernails scoring lines down his back as I pulled him closer, my hips rocking to the rampant pace of his, my pussy tight around his shaft.

His hands shifted up my legs, catching my dress and dragging it over my head. He threw it aside, fisting his hands in my hair and yanking my head back so he could gain access to my throat, kissing and biting me while fucking me harder, deeper.

He thrust into me greedily, demanding more and more from my body, and I clung to him, just as hungry for it as he was. I needed this. To feel close to him like this and to release my fury over what had happened and simply relish in the fact that he had returned.

My heart pounded as my breaths came faster and faster, my fingernails gouging lines in his flesh as I urged him on and his grip on me tightened in a way that set my whole body on fire.

I was a slave to him just as he was to me. And I lost myself to the feeling of his skin like I was drowning beneath the tide.

He wasn't gentle and I didn't want him to be; we were two wild creatures drawn together by this insatiable need to be with each other. Now. Always. Forever.

I couldn't get enough of him. His skin raw against mine, his mouth chasing across my body, claiming my mouth, my throat, my breasts.

He pulled back, gazing into my eyes and it wasn't the need or desire I found there which had me undone, it was the love which flared in the golden depths of them.

My release spilled through me like molten lava and I clung to him as I came, feeling the hard planes of his back flexing beneath my grasping fingers as I cried out his name.

"Mine," he growled, his fingers around my throat again, the heady sensation of his dominion over me making the pleasure in my flesh only burn brighter.

He drew my ecstasy on, driving himself into me harder, faster as he moved closer to the edge himself and his mouth took mine hostage again.

He jerked out of me suddenly, a gasp escaping me as he flipped me over followed by a cry of pleasure as he drove his cock into me again, taking me from behind and pressing me down onto the rough bale of hay beneath his powerful body.

His fingers were bruising where he grasped my hips, my name a praise worthy of a goddess on his lips as he slammed into me.

"You're so fucking tight," he groaned. "And so fucking wet."

I could only cry out in reply, my body so on edge that it was no surprise when I came for him again, my pussy clamping around his cock as I urged him to follow me into nirvana.

Then I was on my back again, Magnar lifting me so my body was flush to his as he moved onto the hay bale too, making room so he could bring his weight down over me, my leg hooked over his shoulder.

"Look at me, drakaina hjarta," he growled as he sank his cock into me again.

I whimpered beneath him, my body so drunk on pleasure that I couldn't form words anymore, but I met the fire in his eyes as he pushed in deep and claimed me once more.

His thrusts were deeper than ever, his pace violent, brutal and utterly punishing like he needed to brand his name into every piece of my skin, or perhaps he wanted mine branded on him instead.

"I love you," I gasped and the words were his undoing, his cock driving in with a mind-shattering thrust and my flesh coming apart at the seams on command so that we came as one.

Magnar dragged my body flush to his and I arched against him as he bellowed, finding his climax deep within me, filling me with his cum and growling my name while my pussy clamped tight around his cock and the tremors of my own orgasm tore me asunder.

I wrapped my arms around his neck, keeping him close and kissing him deeply as we caught our breath.

We stayed there for several long minutes, holding each other, simply being together, his forehead pressed to mine, his weight driving me down into the straw, his cock still buried in me as we soaked in the fact that this was real. I closed my eyes as I revelled in this moment of peace. Magnar trailed his fingers through my hair and I grazed my thumb along the rough stubble which lined his jaw.

"I missed you," I breathed when I could think straight enough to talk.

"I'm never leaving your side again," he replied, and I tipped my chin up to kiss him once more.

His lips were soft against mine, though still claiming as they took me hostage. I melted against him as his hands slid from my hair and along the curve of my spine, letting me know that he wasn't close to done with me yet.

I arched into his touch and smiled into his kisses.

Magnar was here. He was real. And he was mine.

ERIK

CHAPTER TWENTY EIGHT

I circled my finger around Montana's navel, careful not to wake her. I was drawn irresistibly to her skin like a compulsion held my body in its grip. But this was unlike the power of the accursed necklace. This was a gift, a sweet, blessed thing that had been worth waiting a thousand years for. Before her, the passage of time had seemed fleeting. But now it had slowed, every moment begging to be nursed and cradled, committed to memory. If we were to be human again, I didn't have to fear that our lifetime would roll by too fast, because a mortal life with her was worth a hundred thousand years in solitude.

There was one thing we were yet to discuss, and I wondered if she'd considered it at all since she'd been turned. My sister had faced the anguish of being unable to bear children and I didn't want Montana to weather the same fate. If she even desired a family.

I had to admit, though our time together had been short, it had sparked a profound change in my feelings on the subject. What in the world could be more fulfilling than creating a family with the woman I adored?

Montana stirred under the brush of my fingers, releasing a soft laugh. "Stop tickling me."

"Did I wake you?" I growled, laying my palm flat on her stomach.

"No," she yawned. "Okay yes. But I don't mind." She rolled towards me, pressing a kiss to my lips.

I brushed her hair back from her shoulder with a grin. "I've been thinking..."

She raised a brow. "About?"

A rare flicker of insecurity seized me as I gazed at her. What if I couldn't offer her what I was considering? And what if she wanted it but we couldn't break the curse? Then I'd only be getting her hopes up to have them dashed to pieces. But it felt like the right moment to air my thoughts on the matter. After our time apart, I realised how precious each minute together was. And if a future awaited us where a mortal life was possible, why wait to discuss this?

"How do you feel about starting a family one day?" My throat tightened as I watched her reaction to my question. Her brows pinched together then a warmth filled her eyes that spread into the depths of my soul.

"I never wanted kids when I lived in the Realm but things have changed now. And if we can really be human again then I want that. I really do." She scraped her fingernails across my jaw with the brightest of smiles. "Do you?"

"I didn't. But like you say, things have changed." I smirked, pushing her back and dropping my mouth to her throat. "I certainly like the idea of making them."

"You're an animal." She slapped my back, and I knelt up with a grin, taking in her naked flesh with all the desire of a starved demon. I leaned in to tug her nipple between my teeth, grazing my fangs over her and making her shiver beautifully for me.

"We need to talk to the others," she sighed, her hand pushing into my hair.

"Later," I growled into her skin, nudging her legs apart with my knee.

"You said that an hour ago," she said, her hand fisting tight in my hair and pulling my mouth from her skin.

I growled and she gave me a look that said I was being unreasonable.

But nothing seemed more reasonable that making her come for me again.

"Erik," she said firmly, and I sighed.

"I suppose we *should* show our faces downstairs." I reluctantly withdrew and dropped from the bed, heading to a closet across the room and opening the door.

"Does the royal prince not ask to borrow clothes?" Montana called from the bed.

I stalled, not having thought about asking for such a thing. Maybe I needed to prepare myself if humanity was going to claim me again. The gods only knew how the world would change if the vampires returned to mortal bodies. Would they still look to my family as their rulers? I highly fucking doubted it.

I took a bundle of men's clothes from the closet with a shrug. "I'm sure Chickoa would rather I didn't go looking for her permission with my cock out."

Montana laughed as she shifted onto her front, gazing at me as she propped her chin up on her arms. I eyed the seductive curves of her body, tempted to forget about getting dressed and spend the rest of the day in that bed with her. But my family had been through enough in the last few days, the least I could do was spend some time with them.

"You're hesitating," Montana pointed out, rising from the bed and walking toward me. The sway of her hips captivated me and all thoughts abandoned me as she approached. Instead of touching me, she reached past me and took out a long navy dress from the closet before fishing some underwear from a drawer. She pulled the clothes on and I resigned myself to doing the same. Even though it had been my idea in the first place. I was a slave to her skin. I'd never felt such desire for a woman. And when we laid together it felt like so much more than sex. It was a union of a souls, my tarnished one meeting with the purity of hers, and making me feel almost worthy of the privilege.

When we were dressed, I walked to the mirror on the wall and pushed a hand into my hair.

Montana glanced at me in the reflection, fighting a grin.

"What?" I asked.

"Nothing," she sang.

"It is something." I turned, stalking toward her and she ran away with a laugh. I sped after her, catching her by the waist. "What are you hiding?" I growled, holding her tight.

"I just noticed how vain you are. We're only going downstairs to see your family, why are you fixing your hair?"

I flipped her around in my arms. "There's nothing wrong with a man who takes pride in himself."

"You have a *lot* of pride," she mocked, biting into her lower lip in that way that made me want to bite it too.

"Well maybe I have a lot to be proud of lately."

She shoved me and I laughed, letting her go.

"Escaping me again?" I drawled.

She gave me a mischievous smile, heading to the door and I padded after her into the hallway. Miles and Warren stepped out of their room at the same time. Warren was busy buttoning his shirt up as Miles's eyes fell on me.

"What the fuck?" he gasped, speeding toward me.

I grinned as I embraced him, patting him on the back. "Hey, brother. Did you miss me?"

"Hell yes I did. Why didn't you tell me you were here?" Miles leaned back, punching me in the shoulder.

I glanced past him at Warren. "I've been here for hours, Miles, you were clearly too busy to notice."

"Shit, sorry about that," Warren said as he approached, smiling from ear to ear. I stepped around Miles, clapping his husband on the arm.

"It looks like you've been pretty busy too," Miles teased and Montana gave him an embarrassed look. I eyed her pale cheeks, missing the way they used to turn red when she felt that way.

"By the gods, I'm going to have to burn every mattress in this house by the time you lot leave," Chickoa said as she arrived on the landing.

I gave her an apologetic look. "I'll pay for your house to be entirely remodelled if you like, it's the least I can do for you taking my family in."

Chickoa approached us, folding her arms. We didn't know each other particularly well but I hoped she knew that I'd never had any bad intentions towards her. And I was glad she'd made Fabian happy for a time, even if he had gone and flushed that happiness down the drain.

"Well I might just have to take you up on that offer, Erik Larsen," she said with a grin and I quite liked the fact that she didn't call me prince. To her, I was just the brother of the asshole who'd turned her. And that suited me fine.

"Has Callie come back?" Montana asked Chickoa. "Did Magnar find her?"

"I bet he found her alright," Miles commented. "I bet he found her real hard."

"That doesn't even make sense," Montana said, shaking her head and looking to Chickoa again.

"She was out by the barn." Chickoa shrugged. "But that was hours ago."

"I told you he found her," Miles muttered to Warren and I elbowed him as I walked past.

Montana and I headed downstairs into the living room, finding Clarice asleep beside Julius, her head resting on his shoulder.

"She fell asleep and slid onto me," Julius blurted as if I was accusing him of something.

"Right, and your point being?" I asked with a frown.

Montana released a snort of laughter and I turned to her in confusion.

"They still hate each other apparently," Montana said lightly. "But Clarice saved Julius's life so..."

"So nothing." Julius shoved Clarice off of him and she bolted upright, baring her fangs as if she feared she was under attack.

"And I *still* hate her I'll have you know." Julius pointed at Montana.

Clarice rose to her feet, blinking groggily as she backed away from him. "That would be so much more convincing if you didn't have a raging hard-on right now."

Julius frantically dropped his eyes to his pants then scowled darkly as Clarice's laughter rang through the air.

I glanced between the two of them with a frown. The slayer and my sister? That was hardly plausible.

Miles jumped up behind me, shoving his weight down on my shoulders, and I threw him off, tussling with him as I grabbed him in a headlock.

"Good to have you back, little brother," Miles taunted.

My mouth hooked up at the side. "You're only one month older than me."

"That's all it takes to be the boss." Miles thumped my arm, clearly wanting to continue our play fight.

The door sounded in the hallway and I turned as Magnar appeared. I folded my arms, unsure how he was going to act toward me now we were reunited with our group. He gave me a nod as Callie scampered through the door behind him with a piece of straw sticking out of her hair. She didn't seem aware of it as she followed Magnar into the living room to join us.

Montana started gesturing to her, pointing at her head.

Callie turned scarlet as she located the piece of straw and clenched it in her hand.

"Subtle," Julius said with a bark of laughter.

"Where's Fabian?" Callie asked quickly, her cheeks turning pink as she tried to deflect attention from herself.

Magnar's posture tensed.

"Sleeping upstairs," Clarice answered, leaning her weight back against a dresser that was full of porcelain ornaments.

"I think we should all be here. We need to make a plan," Montana urged as she dropped onto the couch.

"I'll fetch him-" Clarice started but Fabian and Chickoa strolled into the room at that moment, a fierce tension passing between them, suggesting they'd just had a fight.

As Fabian spotted Magnar, his face turned sour and he strode purposefully past him to the other side of the room.

"I'll leave you to talk," Chickoa said.

"You're welcome to stay," I offered. "The curse involves every vampire in the world."

She gave me a thoughtful glance then shrugged, pressing her back to a wall and folding her arms.

Callie perched on the arm of the couch next to Montana and rested a hand on her shoulder.

"Can we all just address the elephant in the room first?" Fabian asked, glancing between Magnar and I. "We're all dying to hear about your time with Valentina. Which one of you did she fuck first?"

"Fabian," I snarled in warning.

"Shut your fucking mouth." Magnar squared his shoulders.

Fabian's eyes dragged down Magnar and I knew he was his real target. "I just think Callie deserves to know if she's going to be catching anything from you."

"Can you stop being an asshole for one second?" Callie's upper lip peeled back.

"He can't, it's in his blood," Chickoa chipped in and I could tell this conversation was going to escalate fast if I didn't stop it.

"Valentina didn't touch either of them. Much..." Montana said awkwardly and I offered her an apologetic frown.

"We have more important things to discuss," I pressed, shifting closer to Magnar. "We'd rather not go into the details of our time with Valentina."

"And if anyone has a problem with that, I will gladly give you an answer with my fists," Magnar growled.

Everyone's eyes slid between the two of us.

Fabian stared at me in horror. "Don't tell me you're actually *friends* with the slayer now, Erik."

I shared a glance with Magnar, unsure what the hell we were now.

"Just drop it, Fabian," Montana said with a sigh. "Who cares if they're friends now? That's a good thing, isn't it?"

"I didn't say friends," Magnar muttered under his breath.

"Neither did I," I said, equally quiet. But I couldn't deny that we were *something*.

"Fine." Fabian threw his hands up in defeat. "Let's just get to that fucking mountain then because the sooner we break the curse, the sooner we can all go home and part ways with the slayers."

"How are we going to find it?" Miles pitched in and I was glad to move on from the subject of Valentina at last. "The mountain of

Helgafell isn't a solid place. It can appear anywhere in the world."

"Great, let's hope it shows up in Chickoa's backyard then." Julius grinned and his brother released a breath of laughter.

"We can find it with this," Callie announced, lifting her hand to show us the gods' ring.

Montana nodded keenly. "It showed us the way before. We just have to touch it."

Clarice turned to the twins. "Do it." She eyed them hopefully.

Montana and Callie shared a glance then Callie slid it from her finger and held it between them. Montana brushed her fingers over it and their expressions immediately fell blank. Their eyes glazed and I stepped closer, anxiety pulling at me.

Miles took hold of my arm to keep me back and I gazed at my wife, grinding my teeth together as I waited for her to return to me.

After a few more tense seconds, the two of them jolted, blinking hard as they regained their senses.

"Well?" I asked hopefully.

Montana smiled up at me and my chest lightened. "We have to head further south."

"We saw a desert," Callie added.

"That's not much help, everything south of here is desert since the Final War," Warren said with a frown.

"But beyond the desert there were swamps...palm trees," Montana said, her brow creasing.

"That sounds like Florida," Clarice breathed and I nodded, an idea striking me.

"That's where we landed when we first came to America," I said. "Do you think the mountain is close to the village we lived in?"

"Sounds like another way Andvari would taunt us," Fabian muttered. "If we'd been close all those years, he must have found it pretty amusing."

"Maybe the ring will show us more when we're nearer?" Montana guessed.

"We definitely saw more this time," Callie agreed.

"So we head south," Magnar announced, lifting his chin and

everyone nodded their agreement.

"We'll leave in a couple of days so everyone can recover," I said, looking to Chickoa. "If you can put up with us a while longer?"

"Fine by me." She shrugged. "If you guys break the curse you're always welcome here. Except you." She glanced at Fabian and his shoulders slumped.

"Sounds good," Julius said, rising to his feet. "Want to spar with me, brother?" he gestured for them to head outside and I suspected he wanted to talk with Magnar alone.

"Yes, beating you to a pulp will make my day complete," Magnar said, then followed Julius out of the house.

I dropped down into the seat beside Montana, taking her hand and running my thumb across the back of it.

A ping sounded and Chickoa took her phone from her pocket, her brows knitting together. "You said this Valentina woman has taken over the New Empire, right?"

"Yes," I said tersely. "Why?"

"I just got a news update, there's a live broadcast going out from the capital." She grabbed a remote from a table, turning the television on.

"You signed up for updates from the New Empire?" Fabian asked her, his brows raising.

"I like to keep an eye on what's going on in the country," Chickoa muttered.

"Or keeping an eye on one of your rulers," Fabian said with a mocking grin.

"Unlike you with your damn Familiars, I don't do spying. And if I did, the last person I'd seek out is you," Chickoa growled.

"So why were my Familiars left alive if you were so pissed with me?" Fabian asked coolly.

"Because I find your obsession with me hilarious. I was happy for you to torment yourself."

Callie chuckled and Fabian threw her a glare.

"It's starting, look." Montana pointed to the TV as Valentina appeared on the screen.

I sat straighter in my seat as I glared at the woman who dared to call herself the queen of my empire. She was sitting on *my* goddamn throne, in *my* goddamn castle with *my* goddamn crown on her head. I ground my teeth and Montana clutched my hand.

"Good evening, ladies and gentleman. The last few days have seen the empire as you know it overhauled and your rulers have fled like the cowards they are."

"Bitch," Montana hissed.

Valentina went on, "I have taken their place to guide you out of this dark time and lead you into a new world. With my powers controlling the weather, I am sure you will see fit to bow to my rule."

"She's threatening our people," Clarice growled, and anger clutched my heart.

"As my first act as queen, I declare that the law against feeding from the vein is revoked. The Realms will be opened and the humans will be given the chance to run, while you, my loyal followers, will be given the opportunity to hunt them as nature intended. When our current supplies dwindle, the gates to the Realms will all be torn down. You will no longer be provided with bottled blood. If you wish to feed, you will have to earn it." Valentina smiled widely and a shudder ran through me.

"That monster," Callie spat.

Montana shook her head and I turned to her, finding her eyes full of torment. "The humans in the Realms will be weak, they're starved."

"Not quite," I said gently. "Their rations have been more than doubled in the last few weeks. They will have the energy to run at least."

"But they can't outrun a horde of hungry vampires," Montana breathed in horror.

I wished I could make this right. That I'd come to my senses quicker after the necklace had stopped working and ripped Valentina's withered heart out.

"I hope Valentina chokes on her next drink," Callie hissed, her shoulders tense.

The cruel woman's voice dripped over us again. "Any vampire who rises against me will be executed. Their death will not be swift. Bow to my rule and you will all live in luxury. You will delight in the pleasure of the hunt and bathe in the glory of each drop of blood you take. The fleeing princes and princess will soon be brought to their deaths. And we will rise together in a new world as part of the Scarlet Empire!"

Applause rang out from her biters off-screen and the broadcast ended. Chickoa switched the television off, turning to face us with a darkness in her eyes. "I want in. I'll come with you to help end this curse."

I nodded. "Fine by me."

Fabian remained unnaturally quiet and I was surprised he didn't object. He gazed at Chickoa with his brow furrowed and I could sense the weight of their past falling down on him.

"Everyone should get as much rest as possible," Clarice said with a yawn as she headed out of the room toward the staircase.

"I need to talk to Magnar and Julius," Callie said, following Clarice.

Montana leaned against my shoulder with a sigh. "I hate her so much."

I wrapped my arm around her. "I know. We'll bring her to her knees side by side."

"I need a drink." Fabian rose to his feet, heading into the kitchen and Miles and Warren followed him.

I turned, peeking through the gap in the curtains behind the couch, finding night had fallen. I relaxed back into my seat with Montana, pulling her closer under my arm, more than happy to dwell in the company of her and my family for the rest of the evening.

MAGNAR

CHAPTER TWENTY NINE

T he door to the farmhouse closed with a sharp snap and I looked up to see Callie crossing the grass to join us. My blood was still heated with the memory of her skin against mine and I couldn't help but stare a little at this beautiful creature who had claimed me as her own.

Julius slammed into me as my attention wavered from our spar, his shoulder colliding with my ribs as he hurled me off of my feet and sent me crashing to the ground.

I tried to roll aside before he could maintain the upper hand but he landed on top of me, throwing a fist into my jaw and managing to pin my left arm beneath his knee.

I tried to buck him off of me but his hands wrapped around my throat and he smashed my head back down into the ground before tightening his grip to choke me.

"Yield, brother," he insisted with a triumphant grin.

I kicked my heels into the dirt and punched him with my free arm, but he only grunted, absorbing the blows while keeping me pinned beneath him.

"Fine, I yield," I hissed, barely able to get the words out beneath the pressure of his grip.

Julius released me at once, laughing in victory as he jumped to his feet and offered me his hand.

He hauled me upright and I found Callie smirking at my failure.

"I'll never get over the satisfaction of watching you get beaten," she teased.

"I was distracted," I muttered, taking a step towards her with purpose.

"There are many distractions in battle," Julius pointed out. "So I'll have none of your excuses. Have you come to play with us, Callie?"

"Umm, no…" Callie's eyes danced between me and my brother and she hesitated before going on.

"What is it?" I asked.

"I need to talk to you both about what I saw in Valentina's dream." She didn't seem keen to continue and I drew closer to her, wondering what could be so bad that she was afraid to voice it. "It's about what happened when the two of you entered your thousand-year sleep. I wanted to tell you in private, away from the others."

"Is this about our mother?" Julius guessed, a frown creasing his brow.

"Yes," Callie breathed. "When Valentina told your mother how she'd betrayed you and she knew that the prophecy foretelling your victory against the Belvederes could no longer come to pass, she called on Odin to help her protect you."

"You already told me this," Julius cut in. "You said she asked him to shield Magnar's place of rest from Valentina so she couldn't find him when he woke. And that she got Odin to bind us into sleep for a thousand years instead of a hundred in the hopes that we would be able to claim victory now instead."

Callie nodded but tears glimmered in her eyes as she looked between us.

"Odin would require a great sacrifice to interfere in the life of mortals like that," I murmured, realising what detail she must have withheld.

"Valentina had your mother pinned down with her gifts," Callie breathed. "She intended to kill her and use her blood to trick Erik into believing she had murdered the two of you in payment for her immortality. Your mother knew she was going to die but instead of fighting it, she demanded Odin's protection for her sons. She took her own blade to her throat in sacrifice."

Silence reigned between us as the weight of that fact fell upon my brother and I. Julius shook his head as if he wanted to deny what she was saying, but I could feel the truth of her words in my heart.

Our family was all our mother had ever cared about in this forsaken world. She had loved my father fiercely and his death had destroyed a major part of her soul. After his passing, she had lived and breathed for the two of us.

Leaving her behind to rest in slumber had been as hard for me as driving that blade through my father's heart.

I knew she would have had nothing left with us gone, but she had been adamant that we do it. She craved vengeance for the death of my father above all else. When Valentina came to murder her, she had already sacrificed the last things she had to live for by laying us to rest. And it wasn't at all hard to imagine her giving her own life to preserve ours.

"She loved you both so much," Callie breathed.

"Before I slept, she begged me to take revenge for Father's death," Julius growled. "And yet now we find ourselves living among the very monsters who caused it."

"No, brother," I said in refusal, the truth of my words as clear to me as the light of day. "Erik and his siblings were not behind our father's fate. It's the gods who owe us that debt."

Julius's eyes lit with fire as he moved to grab his sword from the grass where we'd left them while we sparred. He drew Menace from its sheath and held it before me, pointing out the glimmering rune which was newly emblazoned on the blade.

"Odin told us that these weapons can kill a god," he snarled. "They were forged by the gods themselves and hold the power required to end the existence of a deity."

I reached out and pressed my fingers against the rune. A deep power thrummed through my veins as it met with my skin and a new solution occurred to me.

"If it's vengeance we seek, then we know who owes us it," I growled. "Idun and Andvari have toyed with our lives for far too long. I think it's time we focused on our true enemies at last."

I lay still in the soft bed with Callie in my arms as the rising sun claimed the sky outside. Her breaths came deeply and I trailed my fingers through her hair as she rested her head over my beating heart. I wondered if she was visiting anyone's dreams. She seemed so peaceful that it was hard to imagine her consciousness could be fully engaged in someone else's psyche, but the gifts of her kind were subtle enough that it was entirely possible.

Her left hand rested on my stomach and I could just make out the silver cross on her palm which bound her to Fabian. I hadn't exchanged any civil words with that particular Belvedere yet and I wasn't entirely sure if I would. He hungered for this woman in my arms and I found it hard to think of anything else when I was presented with him.

My jaw ticked as I imagined her crossing over into his dreams as I knew she'd done before, but it wasn't out of any mistrust on her part. It was more that I didn't trust *him*. In my absence, he'd convinced her to let him feed from her and I shuddered to imagine what other perverse desires he might have aimed her way.

Callie had told me that he was willing to give her a divorce, but I wasn't going to hold my breath until he did it. It was easy enough for him to promise her the moon while he was away from his castle without any way of delivering it. If he truly set her free, then maybe I'd try to alter my opinion on him as I'd been forced to do with his brother, but until then, I was happy to hold on to my animosity against at least one of the Belvederes.

Callie mumbled something incoherent and rolled off of me, turning her back on me as she rearranged herself in her sleep.

I missed the warmth of her body against mine as soon as it left and I shifted towards her, pressing my chest to her back as I draped my arm over her. I'd been wearing a black t-shirt before we came to bed and she'd pulled it on alongside some underwear to sleep in. Though it had been a little small on me, it grazed her thighs when she wore it and the soft material tickled my skin as I moved my body closer to hers.

I didn't bother to try and get back to sleep. Ever since I'd woken from the slumber that my mother had put me in for a thousand years, I'd noticed I didn't need as much sleep as I used to. I guessed I'd banked some extra for myself in all of that un-waking time. But I didn't want to risk rousing Callie by getting up, so I stayed in the bed. Besides, there were worse places I could be than lying beside the woman I loved.

I thought about what she'd revealed to me of my mother's death. Though it had opened up a lot of painful truths, it felt a little like cutting into an old scar. I'd known that she was dead the moment I'd awoken from my slumber and I'd carried my grief with me from that moment.

Finding out about Valentina's involvement in it didn't change the fact that she was gone. It only gave me an answer I'd never sought to have. And yet another reason to hate my betrothed.

"You're frowning so hard that I can hear it," Callie murmured and I chuckled, dipping my mouth to brush a line of kisses over the back of her neck.

"I'm sure you could cheer me up if you want to give it a try?" I offered.

She rolled in my arms, looking up at me as I propped my head on my fist so I could admire her properly. I didn't think there had ever been a time when I was just content to sit and stare at a woman. But Callie was no normal woman. She was the one that I'd been waiting for and if hers was the only face I could ever look upon for the rest of my life, then I would die happy.

"What are you thinking?" she asked.

My gaze slid from her face, skimming over the baggy t-shirt which concealed her figure and she hit my chest playfully.

"Forget I asked," she said with a laugh.

"You didn't let me answer yet," I protested, catching her chin in my grip so I could kiss her.

Before my lips could meet hers, she snatched my hand and propelled herself on top of me, pinning my wrist to the pillow beside my head. I tried to reach for her with my other hand, but she caught that wrist too, pressing it to the bed and using the strength of her gifts to hold me there.

My heart pounded with desire as she leaned down until her lips almost met mine and her golden hair fell around us, blocking out the world.

"Magnar?" she breathed seductively and my cock hardened at the sound of my name on her lips. I'd never tire of hearing her say it; something about it just had me undone. It was like she claimed me with it, marking me as her own and I never wanted to be anything but hers.

"Yes?" I asked with a smile as she pressed me down even harder and I found I quite liked relinquishing control to her.

"I'm going for a shower," she whispered.

"What?"

Callie laughed as she sprung from the bed and she raced across the room before I could fully comprehend what had just happened. The door banged shut between us and her laughter carried down the hall as she ran for the bathroom.

I got up swiftly, hounding after her as I tried to decide whether to curse or laugh.

But as I pulled open the door to our bedroom, I found Chickoa walking down the hall.

I stilled, unsure if it would be too rude of me to ignore her in favour of continuing my chase. I glanced along the hallway and Callie laughed at me again as she headed into the bathroom, closing the door behind her. The sound of the lock turning made me bite my tongue with frustration.

"You're Magnar, right?" Chickoa asked with a faint smile and I was forced to accept defeat as I looked at the vampire before me. "I was just bringing you these." She held out a bundle of clothes and I accepted them with a word of thanks.

"Finding things to fit Callie was easy enough but you're a bit harder to cater for," she said apologetically. "My husband was a big man but you're…"

I laughed as her eyes travelled over my muscular body. "I'm sure I'll make do. Thank you."

"There's another bathroom at the far end of the hall," she added. "If you don't want to queue for the shower - I'll get you a towel."

I gazed towards the door that Callie had closed between us and sighed in defeat as I let Chickoa lead me in the opposite direction. The next time I got that girl to myself, I wasn't going to let her go so easily.

I emerged from a hot shower, begrudgingly accepting the fact that *some* of these modern ideas weren't all terrible. I wrapped a towel around myself as I looked in the mirror at the bite wounds I'd received while in Valentina's clutches. I was pleased to find that the ones on my neck had healed over and my gifts had made a lot of progress with the two I'd received in her bedroom just before our escape. I wanted every mark she'd inflicted on me banished from my flesh as soon as possible.

I grazed my thumb over the tattoo above my heart, the old habit finding me again as I imagined it carved from my flesh. Valentina's death would remove the stain of the ink from my skin and I couldn't wait for that day to come. I wanted no part of me to be tied to her and I would celebrate wildly when my body was free of that mark.

I pushed the bathroom door open and found Fabian waiting for me in the corridor. I had very little to say to the parasite who wished to steal Callie from me, but I wasn't going to turn away from him if he wanted to cause some conflict over it.

"Did you want something?" I asked as he failed to move aside.

His eyes dropped to take in the tattoos which marked my flesh and I folded my arms as I waited for him to halt his assessment of me.

"I want many things, savage, but it would appear that just wanting something isn't always enough to mean I can have it."

"I think Callie has made her feelings about you and I clear enough, if you think that you might convince me to give her up, then you're deluded-"

"I'm not foolish enough to believe you would do any such thing for my sake," he replied irritably. "I just came to warn you."

"Warn me?" I laughed. "I'd have to fear you for any warning you

299

gave to cause me a moment to pause."

"You'd do well to fear me," he replied darkly. "I would have killed you in our battle if it wasn't for my brother pulling me back."

"Well if it's a rematch you're after, then I'd be happy to oblige," I growled.

"It's not," he replied icily. "As much as I might like that, I don't think Callie would appreciate it."

"Since when have you cared what she wanted in all of this? You weren't so bothered about her feelings on it when you dragged her down the aisle. And I'm sure if she hadn't escaped you that night, you wouldn't have been interested in her views on being taken to your bed either," I snarled.

Fabian's gaze darkened and I could tell he was fighting the urge to bite back at me.

"You presume much about me while knowing nothing of me at all," he growled. "And things have changed since I married her. Our understanding of the prophecy is different now. I only wish for her to be happy."

"Then stay away from her and I'm sure she will be," I replied. "Every foul thing that has befallen her has come down to your actions or was a result of your rule. So take yourself out of the equation if you wish for her happiness."

I made to walk past him but he shifted to block my path. Adrenaline tingled through my veins as I looked down at him. He was tall but I'd never met a man I didn't have to look down on and I could tell the fact irritated him as he raised his eyes to meet mine.

"I don't know what she sees in you, barbarian," he hissed. "But if you're what she wants then I won't stand in your way-"

"It would make no difference if you tried. Which you should have figured out by now. Or do you want to send her another poem to be sure?" I taunted.

Fabian bared his fangs at me, and I laughed in his face.

"If you ever do anything to hurt her then your death will follow swiftly," he swore. "And if she ever wants a real man-"

"Then I'm sure she'll look for one with a heartbeat." I shoved my

300

way past him, slamming my shoulder into his and he was forced to let me by or resort to violence to stop me.

I headed back into the bedroom I'd shared with Callie and pulled on a pair of jeans before moving back out into the corridor and making my way downstairs. Fabian had disappeared and I hoped it might be a permanent deal, but I guessed that was just wishful thinking.

The smell of food led me to the kitchen and I found Julius devouring a huge plate of eggs at the breakfast bar while Chickoa cooked some more. Callie was sitting at the long dining table on the far side of the room with an empty plate before her and she smiled at me as I entered the room. She was still wearing the black t-shirt she'd stolen from me and had tied a knot in it revealing her naval. She'd paired it with black jeans which hugged her legs and I eyed her appreciatively for several seconds. She bit her full bottom lip as I continued to stare at her and my heart rate picked up a little.

My stomach flipped over as she looked at me like that and I wondered if I'd ever get past the thrill of the feelings she roused in me.

"Are you hungry?" Chickoa asked warmly as she noticed my arrival.

"Always," I replied with a smile, forcing my attention away from the woman I loved.

Callie had told me what Fabian had done to Chickoa and I actually found myself feeling comfortable in the presence of this vampire. She'd never chosen this life but her beliefs had trapped her in it after she was turned. I could respect that even if my own beliefs would have demanded a different path from me in her position. I was also warmed to her by the knowledge that she'd shot Fabian upon his arrival at her house.

"Here you go." She passed me a heaped plate and I accepted it as my stomach growled.

"You didn't have to cook for us," I said. "I'm sure it's not something you're used to doing often."

"It was," she replied. "I used to love cooking for my husband and my human friends... at least I did until most of them were killed in the Final War and the rest were gathered up and forced into the Realms," she muttered.

I glanced at Julius awkwardly and he shrugged as if the mood hadn't just darkened considerably.

"And I'm just glad to have use for the eggs again after so many years," she added.

"Can't argue with that logic," Julius said brightly as he shovelled a forkful into his mouth.

The back door opened suddenly and I looked up as Fabian, Miles and Clarice all stumbled in. The sight of the Belvederes still sent the hairs raising along the back of my neck and I stiffened as I tried to shrug off the desire to defend myself. The situation we found ourselves in was anything but natural for me and as hard as I was trying to adapt to it, I was still struggling with the world-altering fact that I was no longer aiming to kill these creatures with every decision I made.

"Sorry," Clarice muttered as she slid into a chair opposite Callie. "We were going to let you eat in peace but the sun came out so..."

"So your undead flesh began to wither under the light of the truth of what you are," Julius supplied.

"Yes. And I'm forced to endure the torture of your company again in place of the sunlight. Which may mean I'm actually worse off in here," she replied but her tone was more teasing than irritable.

Fabian quickly dropped down beside Callie and I took a seat at the breakfast bar with my brother rather than entering into any petty competition with him for her attention. I knew her heart and I wasn't about to give in to the bitter taste of jealousy over some parasite who didn't know how to take no for an answer.

I started on my food, sighing in satisfaction as I filled my stomach. My night with Callie hadn't been entirely restful and I felt like I needed more nourishment after my so-called rest than I had done before it. Not that I had any complaints about that fact.

The stool beside mine slid back and Miles dropped into it silently. I didn't look up at him but I could feel his eyes on me and it sent a prickle running over my skin.

"I've been thinking," he said when I made no effort to address him.

I glanced at my brother but all I got in return for my efforts was a raised eyebrow as Julius maintained his devotion to his meal.

"Did it cause you some difficulty?" I asked as I turned towards the vampire I'd dedicated my youth to hunting.

"Not as much as usual," he replied with a smirk. I wondered if his boyish demeanour was put on or if there really was some level of childish naivety to this creature who had walked the Earth for over a thousand years.

"And?" I asked, wondering why he'd felt the need to single me out for the discussion of these thoughts he'd been having.

"And a long, long time ago, I almost faced you at the top of a mountain," he said, smiling as if that was some kind of fond memory between friends instead of the brutal hunt I remembered.

"I recall you running away like a babe in need of his mother's teat," I replied flatly.

"Well that's my point," he said enthusiastically. "We never did face each other and now that we're all friends-"

"We're not friends," I replied and my voice was echoed by Julius, Clarice and Fabian at once.

Miles laughed as he looked between all of us.

"Well now that we're all united against Valentina and the gods then," he said. "I thought it might be time that we find out how a match between the two of us would have gone."

"I was there too," Julius said before I could respond. "So it would have been Magnar and I against you alone. I'm sure you would be dust now if that battle had occurred."

"Well you weren't Blessed Crusaders then," Miles countered dismissively. "So I highly doubt it. But maybe releasing some of this pent-up tension is just what we all need."

"What are you suggesting?" I asked with a frown, though I had a feeling I knew and I was doubtful that it was a good idea.

"Spar with me," Miles said. "Spar with all of us. We can find out once and for all which breed of the gods' creations are the strongest."

I glanced at Julius as I wondered if I should even entertain his offer and I could see that my brother wasn't entirely opposed to the idea.

"The whole point of us resting here a few days is so that we can heal," Callie reminded us. "What good will kicking the crap out of each other do us?"

"She has a point," I said and Miles's shoulders sagged in disappointment but I smirked as I continued. "So we'll need rules."

Miles looked up at me with a huge grin and bounced in his chair with excitement. "Okay. No blades," he said.

"No teeth," I replied.

"No broken bones," Julius added.

"And no ripping off limbs," Clarice said.

I turned to look at her in surprise, a wild kind of excitement building in my chest at the idea of testing my skills against these creatures.

"And no dick punches," Julius added, pointing at Callie accusingly.

"I didn't know I was playing," she replied but I could see that same hunger in her eyes as I was feeling. Playing at fighting was part and parcel of being a slayer and my blood sang with the prospect of it.

"You're not," Fabian replied tersely. "I'm not going to stand by while you attempt to take on-"

"You don't tell her what to do," I growled. "But feel free to sit this one out yourself; I doubt I'd be able to hold back on killing you anyway."

"The clouds are back!" Miles said excitedly before he could respond. "Let's do it now."

I released a dark laugh as I pushed myself to my feet and followed him outside. "Well don't forget you asked for it."

MONTANA

CHAPTER THIRTY

"I could take you any day, Clarice," Julius's voice carried to me from outside.

I jolted upright in bed and Erik rolled over beside me with a groan. I hurried to the window, pulling back the curtains to reveal a cloudy sky hanging above the lawn below. The slayers were flexing their limbs, sizing up Miles and Clarice before them.

"Oh shit," I gasped, throwing on some jeans and a white t-shirt before running from the room.

I darted downstairs with a flicker of panic inside me, skipping steps as I propelled myself faster.

I threw the front door open and all eyes swung to me on the porch. "Please tell me you're not fighting again," I begged, though the looks on their faces didn't hold any of the anger I'd expected to find there.

"No, we're sparring," Miles announced excitedly.

"Which I think is bullshit," Fabian grumbled. He was sitting on the porch steps below me with a miserable expression.

"No one's going to get hurt," Callie promised me, a smile lighting her features. "Well, the vampires might meet the wrath of my fists, but that's all." She laughed and I gazed between the two groups with a bubble of excitement growing in my chest.

The tension ran out of my limbs and I sighed my relief as I dropped down to watch them on the step beside Fabian.

Erik appeared in a pair of baggy sweatpants and nothing else, drawing my gaze to the firm lines of his abs.

"Did I hear right? You're sparring?" he asked eagerly.

"Yeah, come join our team," Clarice said with a grin. "Let's show these slayers who would win in a real battle."

Erik padded out to join his family on bare feet, a bright smile on his face. Fabian watched him go with a forlorn look.

"Ooh, this is going to be good." Warren appeared, dropping down beside me with a bottle of blood in his grip.

"You don't wanna play?" I asked.

"Nah, I like to watch." He grinned, his eyes wheeling to Miles as he pulled his shirt off and tossed it onto the dusty ground. "I *really* like to watch."

My own gaze flipped to my husband's sculpted chest and I fell into stifled laughter with Warren.

Fabian grumbled something inaudible and I glanced at him as my amusement fell away.

"What's up?"

"Nothing," he muttered, clearly in a mood.

"Don't destroy my yard," Chickoa called as she stepped onto the porch behind us, resting her shoulder against a wooden beam.

Miles saluted her. "Yes, ma'am."

Erik set his feet and shot a glance over at me with a sideways grin. "Are you watching, rebel? I'm about to show you how to win a fight."

I laughed. "Are you absolutely sure about that?" I glanced at Magnar as he rolled his shoulders, setting his sights on the Belvederes.

Erik clutched his heart. "You wound me, wife."

"You need your ego kept in check sometimes," I said lightly and he chuckled, turning to face the slayers again.

"Warren, referee us!" Miles called.

Warren nodded, gaining his feet and leaving the half-drunk bottle of blood on the steps. My eyes slid to it as the delicious scent washed over

308

me and I pushed it away from me to escape it.

Warren stood before the group, raising a hand. "Three, two, one – fight!"

The slayers and the Belvederes crashed together with fists swinging. Clarice immediately cut Julius off from the others, throwing a feral punch into his gut. He stumbled back, blocking her next attack and catching her by the throat.

Magnar went for Miles, trying to sweep out his legs with heavy kicks, but Miles danced back, using his speed to his advantage as he avoided Magnar's ferocious attacks.

Callie and Erik clashed together and I got to my feet as the two people I loved most in the world started kicking and punching each other. My heart squeezed as Erik knocked Callie to the ground, but she darted upright in seconds, smashing her fist into Erik's ribs.

I relaxed as I realised none of their attacks were powerful enough to break bones and a smile took over my face as I absorbed the sight, wishing I could join in. But I wasn't well trained. And mostly I'd had to rely on Nightmare and my vampire instincts in the fights I'd faced. The way the six of them fought was with skills I longed to learn.

Magnar brought Miles to the ground with a punch to the head and Miles aimed a kick between his legs.

"Foul!" Warren said. "No dirty play, Miles. Magnar gets a free strike."

Miles opened his mouth to complain and Magnar punched his face so hard he hit the ground again.

I hissed between my teeth at the sight, but Miles just laughed, scrambling backwards in the dirt to get up, his golden hair dusty and wayward.

My gaze swung to Julius as Clarice leapt into the air, so high she rose above his head. She fell on top of him and he slammed to the ground as she released a scream of victory. Her thighs were locked around his head.

"You're always trying to get me between your legs," Julius wheezed from beneath her.

She slapped him across the face and he aimed a punch at her chest.

She fell backwards, clutching her breasts.

"Hey – no tit punching!" she gasped.

"Foul!" Warren barked at Julius.

"Oh but her vagina head-lock *wasn't* a foul?" Julius demanded as he regained his feet.

Clarice started laughing and Julius cracked a grin.

"Free strike," Warren offered Clarice and Julius fell stock still, waiting for her to approach.

She moved up into his personal space, cupping his cheek softly, then whipped her hand back and smashed it into the same spot. Julius barely reacted, throwing himself at her in a wild tackle as he rammed his shoulder into her stomach.

She crashed to the ground and Julius straddled her, pinning her arms above her head as a lock of hair fell over her face.

Julius beamed at her as she struggled beneath him.

"You're dead," Warren announced and Clarice huffed, making the tendrils of golden hair flutter above her mouth.

"You can get off of me now," she said to Julius, but he didn't let go, leaning down instead, so close I almost thought they were going to kiss.

"Just let that sink in, Clarice," he breathed in her face. "Really feel it."

Her lips pursed. "Oh I feel it, Julius. It's digging into my thigh."

Julius released a breath of laughter, gaining his feet and pulling her up after him.

Erik suddenly uprooted Callie, holding her to the ground by her throat. She kicked and thrashed, but he held her down until she started spluttering for air.

"You're dead," Warren announced and Erik released her in an instant, pulling her upright.

Callie smiled, clearly not bothered by her defeat as she brushed the dirt from her backside.

All eyes turned to Magnar and Miles as they battled to get the upper hand. Their attacks were growing more brutal and Warren edged closer as if readying to step in.

"Go on, brother!" Julius called.

Miles grabbed hold of Magnar's arm, trying to throw him over his shoulder. Magnar dug his heels in, locking an arm around Miles's neck instead. He fell backwards, taking Miles with him to the earth, then rolled and shoved Miles's face into the dirt. The Belvedere fought valiantly but Warren finally said, "You're dead," with a sigh.

Magnar released a booming laugh, jumping upright. "I told you I would have won that fight."

"You weren't a Blessed Crusader then!" Miles complained, rolling to his knees.

Surprisingly, Magnar offered him his hand and silence fell over the group as Miles took it. Magnar released him the second he was up, but the message was clear. Magnar was starting to show respect to the vampires he'd hunted for a thousand years. And I couldn't have been happier to witness it.

Erik ran toward me, grabbing my hand and pulling me up from the step. "Your turn, princess."

"Oh, I don't think-"

"You need to learn," Erik pressed, nudging me toward the group.

"Yes, come on Monty!" Callie cried, raising her hands into the air.

"I'll tap out," Miles said, nursing his wounds as he moved to join Fabian on the steps.

The slayers, Erik and Clarice gazed at me excitedly.

"Are you going to join in, Fabian?" Callie called to him, but he shook his head and she gave him a confused look.

"Let's teach Montana how to use a blade." Julius scooped up a stick from the ground, passing it to me.

"No, her fangs are her best weapon," Clarice countered, snatching the stick from my hand and snapping it.

I gazed between the two groups with a frown. "Maybe you could teach me both ways?"

Erik took hold of my shoulders, angling me toward Callie and beckoning my sister closer. He raised my arms and I curled my fists on instinct.

"That's it," he encouraged. "Now plant your feet like this."

He showed me and I mimicked him, aware of everyone's eyes on me.

"Callie, just block her attacks for now," Erik instructed.

"Sure," she said, but Magnar moved up behind her, folding his arms.

"I learned by facing my attacks," he said. "Callie should fight properly and Montana should get used to taking the blows."

"If she doesn't learn the basics first, she won't be able to defend herself," Erik pushed.

Callie looked to me, rolling her eyes. "Just let Montana show us what she can do and we'll go from there. She's already fought against the biters, she can handle herself."

I nodded my agreement and Erik and Magnar backed up to give us room to fight. I didn't much like the idea of hitting my sister, but I knew we wouldn't really hurt each other.

Julius moved next to us excitedly. "I'll be referee. Three, two, one – fight!"

Neither Callie or I moved.

I bit into my lip and she released a laugh. "Ready?" she asked and I nodded.

She sprang at me, throwing a punch to my jaw. I deflected it at the last second, catching her wrist, but she wrenched her hand free from my grip. Her next punch came toward my stomach and I didn't react fast enough, stumbling back from the hit.

"Kick her!" Julius instructed me.

"Use your speed," Erik urged.

"Ignore them!" Callie insisted.

My mind spun and I narrowly avoided another blow from my sister, both trying to run and punch her at once, confused by the instructions.

As I ducked Callie's next blow, she slammed her elbow into my back and I stumbled forward.

"Roll to avoid her," Clarice called.

I hit the ground, rolling as Magnar shouted, "Take out her legs!"

I swung my feet mid-roll and Callie jumped them easily then planted a kick into my side.

"Get up!" Erik barked.

"Stay down!" Julius contradicted.

I held up my hands as I knelt before them, frustration spilling through me. "Enough!" I cried. "I can't think straight with you all shouting at me."

"You're even putting me off," Callie agreed firmly.

I got to my feet and glanced between Erik and the others.

"I'll tell you what," Erik offered. "Spend some time learning with us, then spend time learning with the slayers. Then fight how you want in the next spar."

I smiled, nodding my agreement and the slayers huddled together as if they were colluding.

I headed away to the edge of the yard with Clarice and Erik, feeling like I was about to get my ass kicked.

"Let's show the slayers how it's done," Erik said with a wicked grin and Clarice squealed her excitement.

With a long afternoon of training behind me, I felt better prepared for the next fight. I lined up with Erik and Clarice as we faced the slayers, curling my hands into fists and planting my feet the way Erik had shown me.

Julius stood ahead of me and nerves flooded me as I sensed he was going to come straight for me. How the hell was I going to win against him?

Fabian had headed inside and I felt a pang of pity for him, sure he was feeling left out. But he could have joined in if he wanted to.

Chickoa and Warren had fought a few rounds with the slayers and everyone was looking riled up from the excitement.

"Go on Montana!" Miles called from the porch. "I'm betting on you."

Warren took his place beside us, his shirt now removed and tucked into the back of his waistband. He had a row of scars lining his arms which made him look more fierce than I'd thought before. Especially now he was caked in dust and his hair had fallen out of place into a mess of raven locks.

"Three, two, one – fight!" he cried and I ran forward, trusting my newly learned skills to guide me.

Julius tried to ram me into me - which seemed to be his signature move. I darted aside, using my momentum to spin around behind him and grab his bare shoulder. His skin was slick with sweat and I lost my grip as he rounded on me, throwing a punch into my stomach. I stumbled backwards from the blow, jumping aside to avoid another hit.

He came at me with a hungry grin and I dropped to the ground, swinging my legs and smashing them into the backs of his knees. He fell forward and I leapt onto his back, taking hold of his hair as I tried to force him to the ground. He jerked his shoulder back to bring his arm out from beneath him, then caught hold of my thigh and forced me to the earth beside him.

I lurched upwards to gain my feet but he fell on top of me, wrestling to pin my hands down. I slammed a palm into his face, shoving him back as hard as I could. He forced his knees between my thighs then flattened himself on top of me with all his strength.

I groaned as he caught my wrists at last and pinned them to the ground above my head.

"You're dead," Warren announced and I dropped my head back onto the earth with a breath of defeat.

Erik appeared over Julius's shoulder with a dark frown. "Get off of my wife."

Julius rolled off of me with a laugh and Erik caught my hand, dragging me into his arms.

"Did you win?" I asked him and Erik scowled.

"No, Magnar beat me." He pushed a hand in to his hair and dust cascaded from it. "Callie beat Clarice." He pointed to them and I realised they'd been watching the remainder of Julius's and I's fight.

"I failed," I sighed, leaning against Erik with a groan.

"You did amazing," Julius said from behind me and Erik nodded his agreement, cupping my chin to make me look up at him.

"He's a Blessed Crusader, rebel. You did fucking brilliant to last so long."

I beamed, a lightness filling me as my disappointment faded away.

With Erik looking at me like that, how could I possibly care about failing?

"Who fancies a drink?" Chickoa called to us. "I've got a whole wine cellar that's been neglected for years."

"Fuck yes!" Julius cried, running up the porch as Clarice chased after him into the house.

"Shower first?" Erik asked me with a devilish smile that sent a heated wave coursing through me.

"Shower first," I echoed keenly as we headed back inside.

When everyone was washed and gathered in the large lounge indoors, Chickoa appeared with several bottles of wine, planting them on the wooden coffee table before us. Miles helped her retrieve enough glasses for everyone then poured out the drinks.

I sat between Callie and Erik on one of the couches, taking a glass as Miles offered me it. Callie and I had changed into more of Chickoa's floaty dresses and we'd accidently picked two black ones that looked almost exactly the same.

Erik raised his glass into the air. "To allies."

"And friends," I added and he smirked at me.

"And that," he agreed.

Everyone drank just as Fabian walked in and a pang of guilt hit me that I hadn't realised he'd been missing. The alcohol fizzled down into my chest as I shot him a smile.

"This looks cosy," he muttered, his eyes flitting to Magnar next to Callie on the other end of the couch.

Miles poured him a glass of red and handed it to him. "Where've you been, brother? You've missed all the fun."

"Sleeping," Fabian murmured, taking the glass and downing the alcohol in one long gulp.

Chickoa put some music on, turning her back on him as she fiddled with the stereo.

Fabian refilled his glass then searched around for a seat before

315

settling for sitting on the floor with his back to the wall.

"Let's play a game," Julius announced, shifting forward on the other couch opposite us.

Clarice was sitting beside him and turned to him with a curious look. "Like?"

"Whoever gives the best description of killing Valentina wins," Julius said.

"What do we win?" I asked.

Julius glanced at Magnar conspiratorially. "How about we play by the old rules, Magnar, remember?"

Magnar started laughing, nodding his agreement.

"Which are?" Callie pressed, eyeing the brothers eagerly.

"The winner picks someone to do the Drikk Eller Drukne challenge," Julius announced and I frowned.

Erik barked a laugh. "We used to do that in our village too."

"What is it?" I asked, resting my hand on his thigh as I turned to him.

"It means drink or drown," Erik explained and I frowned as I wondered what exactly that entailed.

Julius grinned. "So I'll go first-"

"Wait, how do we pick the winner?" Miles asked, patting his knees excitedly. He was sitting in a large blue chair with Warren perched on the arm, looking ready to dive into the chaos of a party.

"Whoever gets the biggest laugh." Julius shrugged.

"Go on then," Magnar encouraged.

Julius took a breath. "First, I'd seduce her-"

"Unlikely," Clarice sang.

"That's not true and you know it," Julius said with a smirk.

She gave him a sideways smile. "I'll suspend disbelief, go on."

"Once I'd seduced her and she was begging me to take her – oh, Julius, please ravish me with your ten inch-"

"We get it," Callie cut him off, laughing.

Julius grinned wider. "And then I'd force her into a wooden box with lots of pointy objects inside it, lock her in it and roll her down a hill."

Everyone chuckled and I could feel the alcohol making my head swim as I joined in.

"So what did the seducing have to do with it?" Clarice asked.

"There isn't a worse fate than dying horny, Clarice," he said seriously and she shook her head at him, but there was a hint of amusement in her eyes.

"I'll go next," Miles said, sitting up straighter. "Mine's simple. I'd tie her to the pole at the very top of the New Empire State Building and tickle her until she farts a lightning strike into existence and fries herself alive."

Warren high-fived him as laughter broke out again. The game continued on and Clarice described drowning Valentina in a bath of angry crabs, whilst Warren went into way too much detail about chopping her into pieces and feeding her to a flock of crows. Fabian seemed cheerier as he explained how he'd use a pack of wolf familiars to tear her limb from limb too.

Chickoa cracked a smile at Fabian's story, but decided not to play the game herself.

Erik took his turn next, his mouth hooking up at the corner. "I don't think I'd waste my time torturing her. The sooner her heart was ripped out of her chest, the better. But I'd happily gather up her remains and flush them down the toilet afterwards."

"I actually did that once," Callie said and I sat up straighter, needing that story right now.

Magnar patted her back, sipping on his third – or was it fourth? - glass of wine. "That's my girl."

Fabian scowled. "I hope that wasn't one of my men."

Callie shrugged innocently. "His name was Benjamin."

"Oh hell, I had people searching for him for days," Fabian huffed.

"Your turn, rebel." Erik nudged me, obviously hoping to move the subject on before everyone's murderous pasts ruined the mood.

I bit my lip as I thought on it. "Umm...I'd bake her in a pie. And then not eat it," I offered with a weak smile.

"No one would want to eat your cooking anyway, Monty. You'd burn that pie." Callie fell into laughter, clutching my shoulder.

317

"You bitch." I shoved her, grinning as her laughter increased.

"To be fair, it's a pretty shit fate to end up in a pie no one eats," Erik mused.

"Exactly," I said, turning to him with a wide smile before rounding on Callie again. "What's yours then?" I demanded, pushing her playfully again.

"Hm..." She brushed her fingers through her hair. "I'd drive Fury up her ass."

"Callie!" I snorted, falling into laughter once more which was echoed around the room.

"My turn," Magnar announced and I looked over at him. His face fell into a stony expression as he waited for everyone to grow silent. When he had their attention, he drew his shoulders back and said, "I would dash her head on a rock. One thousand, one hundred and thirteen times. One for every year she has tormented me, and a hundred and thirteen more for luck."

The frankness of his tone sent me over the edge again and everyone laughed even louder than before.

"She'd still wanna marry you, brother. She'd bandage that shit up with her wedding veil," Julius said and Magnar cracked up.

"I win," he insisted when he'd reined in his mirth.

"I don't know if we're laughing at what you said or if we're all too wasted to *stop* laughing," Julius pointed out.

"Let him win." Callie waved a hand and Julius shrugged.

"Who faces the challenge then, Magnar?" Miles asked excitedly.

"One fucking guess," Fabian drawled and Magnar nodded at him.

"On the table, Fabian," Magnar instructed, plucking a bottle of red from the floor.

Surprisingly, Fabian didn't fight it as Chickoa cleared the coffee table for him.

"Thanks," he said dryly.

"Oh it's really no bother," she said airily, watching keenly as Fabian laid down on the table and Magnar plucked the cork from the bottle with his teeth.

"Drink it or drown in it," Magnar warned.

"I can't drown," Fabian said with a smirk.

"No, but if you spill one drop, I start punching," Magnar growled.

"Holy shit," I said, moving to the edge of my seat.

Erik caught my hand with a wild glint in his eye. "It's a Viking game."

"You guys are insane," Clarice groaned. "I always hated this game."

Magnar tipped the bottle up and it poured into Fabian's mouth in a furious flow. "Funny, I always loved it."

CALLIE

CHAPTER THIRTY ONE

The alcohol set a fire burning in my throat as it went down, but I found myself enjoying the fuzzy feeling in my head that accompanied it.

I couldn't help but laugh as Fabian valiantly swallowed the entire contents of the bottle of wine as Magnar tipped it down his throat and he grinned in triumph as he sat back up again.

Miles whooped in celebration and I joined in with the others as Magnar tossed the empty bottle on the floor.

"You should never underestimate me, slayer," Fabian said victoriously, and Magnar clucked his tongue in dismissal.

"Perhaps you're a bit more of a man than I expected," he admitted as he landed beside me on the couch once more and pulled me under his arm, his fingertips drawing patterns across my shoulder. I glanced up at him with a smile and he pressed his lips to mine for a moment, surprising me as butterflies writhed in my stomach.

"Do you have to do that in front of me?" Fabian asked irritably and heat crawled across my skin as everyone in the room looked our way.

"Do I have to kiss the woman I love?" Magnar asked, cocking an eyebrow at him tauntingly. "Yes, I'd say I do. But if it makes you uncomfortable then you don't have to stay."

Fabian scowled at him and I shifted my hand onto Magnar's thigh, squeezing it gently in an attempt to get him to back off.

"Cut my brother a little slack," Miles said placatingly. "He didn't ask Idun to give him that mark."

"I'm blocking the bond right now," I muttered. "So it's not that."

"No, it's not the bond," Fabian agreed, stumbling a little as he pushed himself to his feet. "It's this whole fucked up situation that's got me on edge. And the rest of you are just acting like it's normal. Like we aren't all sitting in a room with the very men who made our lives hell-"

"Enough," Erik said firmly. "We all know what we were. It's what we are now that matters. Why don't you suggest the next game seeing as you lost the last one? You need to lighten up a little."

Fabian scanned the room as if he were looking for an ally, but he didn't find one. He sighed in defeat as he moved to sit against the wall again, slumping down heavily.

"Let's try a more modern game then," he said. "Spin the bottle?"

"As half of the members of this room are related to you in some way and most of the other half hate you, I'd suggest that's not the best game to attempt," Miles said.

"You have a point there, I suppose," Fabian muttered, glancing at Chickoa. "How about never have I ever then?"

"What are the rules?" Julius asked from the couch opposite.

Clarice was beside him and as he leaned forward, his leg pushed against hers but she didn't move away.

"We take it in turns to say something we've never done. But if anyone in the room *has* done it then they have to drink," Fabian explained.

"Got it," Julius said, raising a glass in anticipation. "But I'll do a practice round to make sure: I've never had a threesome with two men involved." His eyes stayed fixed on Clarice and she rolled her eyes as she drained her glass. "Yeah, I thought so," Julius said with a smirk.

"Well it takes a lot to handle me in the bedroom. There aren't many men who can satisfy me alone," she replied suggestively and Julius raised a brow.

Miles and Warren drained their glasses and Chickoa did too,

shrugging dismissively as Fabian stared at her in shock.

Erik looked towards Magnar, half raising his glass to his mouth.

"That doesn't count," Magnar growled irritably and Erik nodded in agreement as he set his glass back down on the table.

Miles noticed their interaction and his eyes lit with excitement. "Did Valentina make the two of you-"

"No," Magnar snapped as Erik said, "It was only kissing-"

"Which we agreed never to mention again," Magnar added firmly.

Clarice bit her lip in amusement and I decided to move the game along before anything else was said on the subject.

"I've never seen a sandy beach," I said, thinking of one of the things my dad had told us about. "I don't even know what sand is, really."

Everyone but Montana drank, and the Belvederes exchanged guilty looks as I felt Magnar's posture stiffening beside me instead of relaxing. I'd only been trying to think of something random but it seemed like my confession had just reminded everyone of the things the vampires had done to the humans and none of them were entirely happy about that.

"I've never wrestled a wolf with my bare hands and survived," Julius said loudly, cutting the tension as Magnar released a chuckle and emptied his glass.

"I have to hear that story," Miles said enthusiastically.

"It's not as glamorous as my brother makes it sound," Magnar said dismissively. "It just thought it'd found an easy meal when we were camping in the wilderness one night." He brushed his fingers over the line of scars on his bicep and I looked up at him in surprise.

"I thought they were fingernail marks from a vampire," I said.

"There are still plenty of things you don't know about me," he replied darkly.

"I woke up to the sound of a wolf howling in panic as it was launched over my head," Julius said, snorting a laugh.

"I only kicked it off of me. Besides, *you* had fallen asleep on watch," Magnar accused.

"Fabian had a run-in with a bear once, didn't you?" Clarice said, looking at her brother.

"Yes," Fabian replied without elaborating.

"Tell us," I begged and his eyes softened a little as they fell on me.

"I was looking for a new hiding place from your *friends,*" he said, eyeing Magnar and Julius. "And I tried to take shelter in a cave. I was tired and more than a little thirsty. I failed to note the odour of the beast before I stumbled upon it. It tore my arm from my body before I managed to escape. That was the first time I ever had a limb detached."

I smiled at his story and Magnar shifted uncomfortably beside me. I glanced between them, wondering if they'd ever figure out a way to get along but it seemed like a fairly tall order. It might have been because of my involvement, but I wondered if it was also because they were just too different. It seemed to me like their personalities simply grated against each other's regardless of the history they shared.

"Well, *I've* never forgotten a lover's name by the next morning," Clarice said, raising an eyebrow at Julius, her intention clearly to get revenge for his dig at her.

"Does it still count if I didn't know her name in the first place?" Julius clarified.

"Ew," Montana said, scrunching her nose and Julius laughed as he swallowed his drink.

Magnar, Warren, Fabian and Chickoa followed suit and I glanced at Fabian's ex-fiancée in surprise.

"Before I met Terry, I was always afraid of forming close connections with humans," she explained. "So I went for meaningless physical interactions instead."

I nodded in understanding. In the Realm I'd never wanted to form any close connections either. The lovers I'd taken had always been kept at a distance and I'd ended things with them if they'd seemed too keen for anything more emotional from me. I'd been afraid to love anyone outside of my family in case they'd ended up getting taken away to the Blood Bank. And I'd never been tempted to change my mind on that decision until I met Magnar.

"Never have I ever fucked Valentina," Fabian said, smirking at Magnar as he tipped his own drink down his throat.

I raised an eyebrow as Erik drank then Clarice followed suit.

"Seriously?" Montana asked Clarice in surprise.

Clarice shrugged. "I'm a thousand years old, I like to enjoy women for a change every now and then and she was always very..."

"Available," Miles supplied with a snigger.

"You didn't drink," Fabian said, pointing at Magnar. "You can't seriously expect us to believe you never had her; she was your fiancée!"

"I had plenty of opportunity and no motivation to take her up on it." Magnar shrugged and I couldn't keep the smile off of my face as the vampires gaped at him. I was just glad that Odin had come through for him before she'd managed to change his answer.

"Oh shit, I love this song!" Miles announced loudly, jumping out of his seat and speeding across the room to up the volume on the stereo.

He sped to the other side of the room and dimmed the overhead lights so we were left in the orange glow of several lamps and then leapt up onto the coffee table. He started dancing without any care for the fact that he was the only one in the room doing it, and I smiled as I watched him gyrating for us like we were his own personal audience.

He turned towards Warren, smiling widely as he beckoned him up too and they started moving together to the beat of the music.

"Come on!" Miles shouted, trying to urge everyone into joining them and I bit my lip as I was tempted. But we'd never really done anything like that in the Realm and I wasn't entirely sure I would have known where to begin.

Clarice laughed as she got to her feet and she kicked off her shoes before climbing up on to the table too. She was wearing one of Chickoa's long dresses and she accidentally stood on the hem of it as she moved, tearing it straight up the back.

"Sorry," she laughed before ripping more of the skirt off so that she could move more freely. The result was that her ass was half hanging out of the bottom of it, but she didn't seem to care about that. "I'll pay for a new one!"

Chickoa waved off her apology as she started dancing too and I noticed Fabian's eyes following her as she moved.

Miles jumped from the table and landed right in front of me, reaching for my hand with a devilish smile.

"Come on," he begged as he tried to pull me out of my chair. "I've never danced with a slayer before."

I glanced at Magnar and he shrugged, clearly not intending to join me but voicing no protest at the idea of me getting up.

"Okay," I said, draining my glass and placing it on the floor. Miles hoisted me to my feet so quickly that my head spun.

As I tried to right myself, Miles caught the edge of my dress and tore the skirt from it just as Clarice had done to her own, though thankfully my ass was still covered by mine. I cursed in surprise and he laughed as he dragged me against him, holding my back to his chest as he started moving to the music.

I laughed as I tried to follow what he was doing, finding it surprisingly easy with him guiding me.

Warren had dragged Montana up too and I noticed Erik watching her hungrily over the rim of his glass, his free arm slung over the back of the couch.

Julius grabbed two bottles of wine from the floor and moved to take my seat beside Magnar as he handed him one. The two of them started talking in low voices as they drank but Magnar's eyes kept travelling to my bare legs and the heat in his gaze made warmth pool in my core.

Miles twisted me in his arms, laughing as he pulled me closer before lifting me up.

I shrieked as he spun me around and some of the others had to scramble aside to avoid us colliding with them.

He placed me back on my feet and I staggered a few steps as my head swam. Warren wrapped his arms around Miles and drew him away again, leaving me stumbling back towards Magnar.

He looked up at me with a dark smile as I approached and I dropped onto the arm of the couch beside him with a sigh.

"You're drunk," he noted as he looked up at me and I swivelled my legs to place them in his lap.

"You've had four times as much as I have," I protested, bopping him on the nose with my finger.

"Mmm, but I think I can handle my alcohol better than you can." He placed one hand on my knee and caught my ankle in the other, his thumb skimming up and down my skin.

"I dunno, you don't look like you're having much fun here in the corner," I teased.

"We're just enjoying the show," Julius piped up and I followed his gaze back to where the others continued to dance.

Clarice was moving in a way that was so sexual I wasn't actually sure if I was doing something wrong by looking at her. Julius had definitely noticed too and I couldn't help but smirk as his eyes followed every move she made.

"You look like you're *really* enjoying some parts of it," I teased.

Magnar chuckled and he shifted his hand from my ankle up to my thigh, slowly inching it towards the hem of my now-ruined dress.

"You might want to watch yourself around that parasite, brother," Magnar teased. "I think she's working damn hard to get your attention."

"Pfft. I'd never be interested in a woman whose blood runs cold," Julius said dismissively and he tore his eyes away from Clarice as he pushed himself to his feet. "I'm hungry. Do either of you want anything?"

"Nothing you can give me," Magnar replied, his eyes falling on me again as his hand shifted beneath the hem of my dress and my heart leapt excitedly.

Julius rolled his eyes then headed out of the room, and Magnar tugged me down into his lap so I was straddling him. His hands moved to my waist, skimming lower until they found their place above my hips. I dipped my mouth towards his and he drew me in, kissing me passionately as I pressed myself onto his lap, feeling his arousal beneath me with a sigh of longing.

"By the gods, I love you, Callie," he growled, his grip on me tightening and he pushed me down more firmly, making my body ache with desire at the feeling of his solid dick beneath me.

I caught his bottom lip between my teeth, biting down just enough to make him curse.

Magnar groaned with desire and pushed me to my feet abruptly, snaring my hand in his as he dragged me from the room.

As soon as we made it beyond the door, he propelled me around, slamming my back against the wall as he took my lips hostage once again.

He pressed his tongue into my mouth and I trembled with the need to feel it on the rest of my body too.

His hand moved to my thigh, pushing beneath the material of my ruined dress until his thumb found the edge of my underwear. My breathing turned ragged as I willed him on, not caring that we hadn't even made it upstairs.

I gripped the material of the flannel shirt which hung open over his chest, dragging him closer to me as his thumb pushed my underwear aside and my heart juddered with anticipation.

"Oops, sorry," Clarice gasped as she stumbled out into the corridor. "I'm just looking for the kitchen. I saw nothing."

I laughed breathily as Magnar withdrew his hand from beneath my skirt.

"Come on," he said. "Let's find somewhere more private."

He stepped back and I made a move to follow him, but he grabbed me instead, tossing me over his shoulder as I cried out with excited laughter and he carried me further into the house.

"Callie?" Montana called and Magnar stilled with his hand on a door at the end of the corridor.

He dropped me to my feet with a sigh of disappointment as my sister spilled out of the front room, stumbling towards us in a very un-vampire like way.

"There you are!" she exclaimed. "Erik says he's going to show us how to play with his little balls." She burst into a fit of giggles and Erik sped out into the corridor, snaring her in his arms.

"That is *not* the way I phrased it," he said, nipping at her neck.

"What are you talking about?" I asked in confusion, a smile pulling at my lips even though I didn't understand the joke.

"Chickoa has a pool table and I thought we could play," Erik explained, pointing at the door Magnar and I were blocking.

I looked up at Magnar pleadingly. Though I ached for his body, I couldn't resist the offer to spend some time with my sister and Erik together. I'd hardly had any time to see the two of them interacting as a couple and the wide smile on her face set my heart singing with joy. Happiness had always been something we'd had to work hard for and the idea of us having this one night to simply have fun together was something I couldn't say no to.

"Fine," Magnar growled, penning me in against the door as he gripped the door handle. He leaned down so that his lips were brushing my ear before continuing in a low tone. "But when I do get you to myself, I'm going to torment you just as you're doing to me right now."

He pressed a kiss to my lips as the door fell open behind me and only my grip on his shirt stopped me from falling back into the room.

We moved inside, finding a huge green table waiting for us with a bunch of brightly coloured balls arranged on top of it inside a plastic triangle.

"I'll show you how to play," Erik said as he grabbed a wooden pole from a rack next to the door.

We watched as he removed the plastic triangle then used the long stick to knock the balls into little pockets hidden around the edges of the table.

"What is the point of this?" Magnar asked with a frown as he scooped a red ball into his grasp and turned it over with interest.

"No point. It's just meant to be fun," Erik admitted. "But we could make it a little more interesting if you want?"

"How?" I asked.

"For each ball one of us pockets we can give a forfeit to the opposing team."

"Agreed." Magnar moved to grab one of the wooden poles and I followed him to claim my own.

I turned back to find Erik draped around my sister as she leaned over the table and he tried to show her how to pocket the balls.

"I have an idea," I said as I headed towards them. "Girls versus guys. You two can see what you're up against when me and my sister team up."

Erik sniggered. "That hardly seems fair; we'll beat you too easily."

"Hey!" Montana exclaimed indignantly as she nudged him away from her with her hip. "You're not going to beat us."

She moved to my side and I grinned at her as I twisted the stick in my hand.

"That's not a baton," Erik pointed out and I could tell he thought he had us beaten already.

"Oh, you're going down, Belvedere," I threatened, and Magnar laughed as he headed around the table to join Erik.

"You asked for it," Erik growled. He rearranged the balls and stepped back with a mocking smile. "Ladies first."

"Go on, Callie," Montana said with a hiccup and I wondered just how much wine she'd consumed. My own head was still fuzzy with the intoxicating beverage and the more I thought about it, the more I wanted another drink.

I stepped forward, bending over the table before I slammed the stick into the white ball. It crashed into the others way too hard and bounced up into the air then flew over the edge of the table, rolling away on the wooden floor while Erik and Magnar laughed behind me.

I turned to scowl at them as Montana cheered.

"We win!" she announced excitedly, pointing at the green ball which had somehow ended up in one of the pockets.

Erik shook his head in denial. "You don't just win by pocketing any old-"

Montana planted her hands on her hips and frowned at him. "Are you too chicken to face the forfeit?"

"Never," he laughed. "But you're supposed to-"

"I got your little ball in the pocket," I said adamantly, and he sighed in defeat.

"Fine, I guess this will just be a free for all then. But stop calling them my little balls."

"Why are you so touchy about your little balls?" Magnar mocked and I couldn't help but snigger.

"I'm not," Erik protested. "And they're not - rebel, tell them-"

"You want me to tell them about your little balls?" Montana teased and I laughed harder.

Erik's eyes lit with mischief and he gave in. "Fine. What's the forfeit?"

I glanced at Montana conspiratorially.

"We should make it harder for them to beat us," she suggested. "Drink another bottle of wine each."

"I see fighting dirty runs in the family," Magnar teased as Erik shot out of the room to retrieve the wine.

He returned in a flash of motion, knocking into a side table as he re-entered the room and sending a lamp smashing to the ground.

"Whoops, sorry Chickoa," he muttered as he handed Magnar a bottle of wine.

Magnar pulled the cork out of it with his teeth and the two of them clinked the bottles together before tipping the contents down their throats.

Magnar nudged Erik's arm, making him spill some of the wine down his chin as Magnar raced to finish his bottle first.

Erik batted him off, guzzling his own wine as he drove his elbow into Magnar's ribs, forcing him to pull the bottle out of his mouth with a laugh before he could continue drinking it. Erik finished his first and Magnar cursed at him half-heartedly before tossing his empty bottle into the corner where it smashed.

"Oh, shit," he said, noticing the mess he'd made.

"Ever the savage," Erik mocked, and Magnar laughed as if he thought that was a compliment.

I crossed the room to retrieve the white ball and pressed it into Magnar's hand. His eyes were alight with the heat of the beverage as he accepted it.

Magnar moved to the pool table next, lining up his shot before making the same mistake as me and using too much force behind the strike. The balls scattered across the table and Montana and I cheered as he failed to send any of them into the pockets.

"This game requires subtlety," Erik chided as Montana moved forward to take her shot.

"That's not really my strong suit," Magnar replied, and my heart lifted a little as Erik smiled in reply. They were acting *almost* like friends. And if there was even the slightest hope of them becoming something like that then it would make everything so much easier for me and my sister.

Montana lined up a shot and managed to pocket the pink ball, causing me to whoop in response.

"This is not turning out the way I expected," Erik grumbled.

"Arm wrestle!" I announced excitedly for their forfeit.

Magnar smiled wickedly as he placed his elbow on the table and Erik reluctantly followed suit, clasping his hand.

"This isn't exactly an even match," Erik grumbled. "The Blessed Crusaders were designed by Idun to be stronger than us-"

"Stop pouting about it," I replied with a laugh. "Be a good sport and the two of you can race next time we win so you have the advantage instead."

Magnar chuckled and his grip on Erik's fingers tightened as Montana reached forward, placing her hand on top of theirs.

"Three, two, one-" She removed her hand and the two of them locked their muscles in place as they fought to win the contest.

I eyed Magnar's bulging bicep with heat rising in my veins as the seconds dragged on, the two of them straining to beat the other. Then Magnar slammed Erik's hand down onto the table and a huge crash sounded as the strength of his blow made the leg buckle beneath it.

I sprang back as the pool table collapsed to the wooden floor and the balls rolled in every direction.

"My little balls!" Erik exclaimed and I fell about laughing as we all ran from the room like a bunch of naughty children.

I guessed Chickoa was going to be wondering why the hell she'd invited us all to stay come morning and my laughter doubled as the effects of the wine warmed my heart with amusement.

ERIK

CHAPTER THIRTY TWO

I dropped down onto the couch and pulled Montana into my lap with a slanted grin, my head fuzzy with alcohol. I'd always been able to handle my drink even back when I was human, but I was definitely drunk right now and I suspected my rebel was too.

"Enjoying the party?" I asked, tilting my chin up to brush my mouth over hers.

"Feels good to let loose," she sighed, pressing her forehead to mine.

"I think I want to eat you." I kissed her neck and she shifted back from me with a laugh. "I want a rebel sandwich."

"That sounds like a snack," she pointed out, her eyes dancing with light. "I can be more than a snack."

"You'd be a whole meal. Five courses. Mostly I'll focus on dessert." I glanced around her with a smirk, finding the others perfectly busy drinking and playing more games. "Let's go somewhere else...I'll sneak a knife and fork out of the kitchen," I suggested, sliding my hands up her thighs.

She caught my wrists with a mischievous smile and I groaned, resting my head back on the sofa. There was nothing in this world like this girl, and she was mine. All mine. Gods be damned, I didn't deserve her, but there was no chance I would ever let her go.

"No...I've decided it's not acceptable," she teased, dropping her head against my shoulder. "You can't eat me."

"You know I don't really want to eat you, I want to f-"

"Heeeeey, Erik! Come dance!" Miles shouted at me from across the room.

Montana rose from my lap, pulling me up after her. "Go join them, I'm gonna talk to Callie." Her hand slid out of mine and she headed across the room to join the slayers. My eyes followed the curve of her hips and a carnal need filled me as she left me behind.

I glanced around the room, searching for Fabian but I couldn't spot him.

I headed toward Miles, knocking into the coffee table as I went and swearing between my teeth. My brother was dancing with Warren, his eyes glazed as he turned to me and slung an arm around my shoulder.

"Have you seen Fabian?" I asked.

"Yeah, he walked out of the room a minute ago," Miles slurred.

I frowned. "Did he say anything to you before he left?"

"Nah." He shrugged. "Oh actually, he said...um...he said something like he's sick of everyone hating him, he's tired of everyone thinking he's a selfish prick and er...something about Chickoa never forgiving him." Miles grinned, swaying slightly and I braced him.

"Shit," I muttered, pulling away from him but Miles caught my arm, turning me back to him with wide eyes.

"Oh wait a second...do you think that's why he left?"

"Yes Miles. I think that's why he left." I shook my head at him, looking to Warren. "Get him to drink some water."

Warren nodded, but half closed his eyes as he started waving his arms in the air to the beat of the music. I scanned the room and spotted Clarice dancing near Julius while he perched on the edge of an armchair. I beckoned her over and she joined us, dancing all the way to close the gap.

"Do you mind getting these two to drink some water? I need to find Fabian."

"Sure, is everything okay?" she asked.

"Fine, Fabian's just upset. I'll go talk to him."

She tip-toed up to peck me on the cheek. "You're a good brother. And you're so tall. Look how tall you are," she cooed and I had the feeling she was pretty inebriated herself.

I headed back across the room, knocking into the coffee table again with a curse. I headed into the hallway, trying to listen for any sounds of him but the music was too loud to hear anything.

"Fabian?" I called, then spotted the front door open a crack. I pulled it wide, finding my brother sitting on the porch with a bottle of whiskey in his hand.

"Where'd you get that?" I dropped down beside him, eyeing the label. That bottle was worth a lot of money.

"Found it in the kitchen at the back of a cupboard," he said with a shrug.

Considering he looked miserable as fuck, I decided not to point out that Chickoa might not have wanted him to take it. Instead, I snatched it and took a sip, delicious notes of oak and honey rolling over my tongue.

Fabian grinned and it was possibly the first time I'd seen him smile since we'd arrived here. I knocked my shoulder into his playfully. "You're missing all the fun."

He sighed heavily. "I just can't see eye to eye with the slayers. Magnar and I have nothing in common. Except the fact we're both in love with the same woman."

I frowned. "You love her?"

"Well...I think so. I don't know, my head's fucked since I got here. Seeing Chickoa makes me want to rip my heart out and give it to her just so I can make up for what I did to her. And now I'm confused because I thought my heart wanted Callie, but with my ex here..." He shook his head.

"You don't really know Callie, she's only started opening up to you recently," I said with a frown.

"I know," Fabian sighed, a war contained within his eyes. "Sometimes I think I just want to love someone so much, that when she showed up I felt like the gods had chosen her for me. I didn't have a courtier for the wedding ceremony. And there she was, beautiful and feisty and mine for the taking. She looks the complete opposite to Chickoa and I guess that became my type so I could forget about her. I just wanted to make it work so badly..."

My brow furrowed as I gazed at his pained expression. "And what about now? You feel different now you've seen Chickoa again, right? I know how much you loved her, brother. It was as clear as day to me when I saw you together all those years ago."

Fabian nodded weakly. "That was love. I know that. And I think... after I turned her and she cast me aside, I lost that part of myself. I stopped treating women with respect. Maybe I was always a heartless shit because I did the same thing to the only woman I'd ever loved in the end. I turned her against her will, Erik." He gazed at me intently. "What kind of person does that?"

My chest hollowed out as I stared at him. "I know it didn't come from a bad place, Fabian. As much as you want to see the darkness in yourself, there's so much good in you if only you'd let it out more often."

"Do you think Chickoa can ever forgive me?" he whispered, his eyes burning with desperation.

"I think you need to try and right the wrong you did to her. But her forgiveness depends on her own feelings."

"I'm so fucking screwed." He tipped the bottle into his mouth and started downing it.

When he reached halfway, I tried to grab it from him, but he jumped to his feet and headed down into the yard. I ran after him, missing the final step as I moved toward him and crashing into him.

He dropped the bottle and it smashed to pieces.

"Oh fuck...sorry," I said.

Fabian awkwardly kicked some dirt over the shards. "No, I'm sorry." He hung his head.

I caught his shoulders, shaking him a little too violently. "You need to get your shit together. Go sort it out. I know you can." I gripped his face with both hands and his lips puckered as I held him too hard.

"But what if I can't?" he said through his pursed lips.

I released him, a laugh rolling from my throat and he tentatively joined in.

"You can," I urged. "You're a Belvedere. You fuck up shit and then you make it right. That's what we're great at."

"That's true," he said hopefully. "Montana hated you at first, didn't she? How did you make her love you?"

"It's not about making anyone do anything, Fabian," I said, my mirth dying away as I remembered how she had once looked at me. Like I was a plague on the Earth. "But...I let her in, bit by bit, I tried to show her that I wasn't the asshole she thought I was. And to be honest, I *was* an asshole. But somehow she made me a better man. She brought out a side to me I'd long forgotten."

"That's what Chickoa did to me once," Fabian sighed. "And Callie helped me remember it now too. In a fucked up way, the bond the gods put on us made me realise how much I'd been missing. How much I'd given up by burying my emotions so deep for all these years. I want to love again, Erik."

"You will." I gazed at him with my heart softening in my chest. Fabian usually opened up to me more than our other siblings. We'd always had each other's backs, even though we hadn't always seen eye to eye. For the past few months, I'd been so convinced he was my enemy, but now I felt sure we were finally getting back to normal. I wanted him to make peace with the slayers and find someone to love again one day. He deserved to be happy.

I pulled him into a fierce hug. "I miss being like we used to."

"Me too." He clung to me. "When I saw you sparring with the slayers earlier...I got so jealous. It was stupid. But you're my best friend, Erik. And they're taking you away from me."

"Never." I shook my head, jabbing my finger into his chest and he staggered back a few steps. "We'll always be brothers. But Fabian, they're not so bad. We spent all those years hating each other, but we never exchanged any words besides threats up until now. And after being forced to spend time with Magnar, I came to realise that we all did bad shit to each other, but we aren't bad people."

Fabian nodded as my words slid over him. "Magnar and I can't see eye to eye. Not after what's happened with Callie."

"Well...I know you have your issues with him, but why not try talking to Julius then?"

"I could do that," he agreed, a glimmer of hope shining in his eyes.

I clapped my hand on his back, steering him toward the house.

We headed indoors and returned to the lounge where the music was thumping louder than before. Clarice was grinding against Montana, and I smirked at the sight of them moving in time to the beat. Magnar and Callie seemed to have forgotten they had an audience as she straddled him in a chair.

I shoved Fabian toward Julius who was staring at Clarice, taking huge bites out of a sandwich. I followed Fabian across the room and it took Julius a second to notice we'd approached.

"Hey," Fabian said stiffly.

Julius swallowed the last bite of his sandwich, his brows raising as he looked at Fabian. "What?"

"I was thinking we could do some shots," Fabian offered and a tiny part of my brain told me that was a bad idea. Another, wilder part of me which had been unleashed in the past few hours brought my next words to my lips. "Hell yes."

I sped to the kitchen, knocking a stool flying into a wall and shattering it into a hundred pieces.

"I will pay you back," I murmured to the chair, but my words were really meant for Chickoa. I spotted a bottle of tequila by the sink and snatched it up, taking three egg cups from a cupboard before speeding back to the lounge.

Julius and Fabian had moved to kneel before the coffee table and I dropped down next to them, placing the bottle on the table beside the egg cups.

"Ooh are we doing shots?" Chickoa fell to her knees beside me, gazing eagerly at the tequila.

I grinned, happy she wasn't bothered I'd taken the bottle without asking, but I decided not to mention the chair I'd murdered.

"Hang on." Chickoa shot out of the room, returning a second later with another egg cup and kneeling back down beside me.

"Okay let's play most likely," Julius slurred.

"What's that?" Chickoa asked.

"We make a statement and whoever the group votes most likely to do it has to do a shot," Julius explained.

"I'll go first," Fabian said and I hoped this wasn't going to descend into dangerous territory again. "Who's most likely to get laid tonight?"

"Erik," Julius announced and I shrugged, smirking.

"Agreed," Chickoa said, glancing at Fabian coolly.

I poured a shot into an egg cup and downed it, the sharp bite of the alcohol fizzing through my chest.

"Who's most likely to make up with Fabian?" I looked between Chickoa and Julius with a slanted grin.

Chickoa shook her head, though she laughed as she did so.

Fabian looked to Julius with hope in his gaze and the slayer rolled his eyes.

"I suppose that's me then," Julius said, slapping the back of Fabian's head so he jerked forward, his forehead smashing into the coffee table and sending a crack up it.

"Oh shit, I don't know my own strength," Julius said and I sensed it had been a genuine accident.

Fabian started laughing and laughing until we all joined in.

"Fuck the game." Julius poured out shots for us all and I'd soon had more to drink than I'd had in a hundred years.

My eyes slid to Montana again and a hungry smile took over my face. Julius got up, stumbling over to her and Clarice, draping his arms around their shoulders.

I rose to my feet, half aware I was leaving Fabian with Chickoa as I followed the slayer.

I extracted Montana from his arms, tugging her against my chest and claiming her for myself. Julius kept his arm around my sister and she placed a hand on his chest, her fingers toying with the buttons of his shirt.

"Wanna go do some exploring?" Julius murmured to Clarice and she nodded keenly.

"Monty!" Callie called suddenly, springing out of Magnar's lap. "I just had an idea. Remember when we used to do handstands in our apartment? Let's see who can do one the longest."

"Yes!" Montana sprang out of my arms and the two of them pushed an armchair out of the way.

Both of them flipped themselves upside down on their hands and their dresses immediately fell down to their necks.

"Rebel!" I barked, darting forward as she bared her body to the room in her underwear. Desire unfolded inside me as I caught her waist, flipping her back upright, and she leaned against me, laughing wildly.

Callie still had her legs in the air and Magnar dragged her back into his lap again with a demanding groan.

I ran my hand down Montana's spine, my cock thickening as I pulled her closer to me so she could feel it.

Her mouth parted and she grinned mischievously as she ground against me.

I released a grunt of pleasure, dropping my mouth to her ear as she continued her teasing. "Let's go somewhere I can fuck the living daylights out of you."

Her eyes widened with lust and she bit into her lip as she nodded.

I towed her through the room, spotting Miles and Warren on the floor making out. Julius and Clarice had vanished, but I didn't have much brainpower to wonder where they might be as my jeans grew tighter.

We headed into the hallway and I turned toward the front door, an idea sparking in me. Montana laughed as she followed me onto the porch.

"Are you going to show me your little balls?" she asked airily.

I pushed her back against the edge of the porch, forcing my knee between her thighs.

"Maybe your memory's failing you," I growled, taking her hand and pushing it beneath my waistband.

She gasped and I groaned deeply as her fingers curled around my cock, crushing my mouth to hers as she stroked the length of me.

A moan caught my ear that definitely hadn't come from my wife and she tugged her hand free from my boxers as we turned to investigate. The moaning sounded again and I leaned forward over the railing of the porch.

My mouth fell open as I spotted Clarice pinned against the wall by Julius, the two of them kissing like there was no tomorrow. His hand was sliding beneath the top of her dress and her leg was wrapped around his waist. I jerked my head back so I didn't have to see any more of my sister dry-humping a slayer, a grimace gripping my features.

Montana slammed a hand to her mouth and I tugged her down the porch steps with a grin as we rounded the corner to face them. I folded my arms and Montana shook her head desperately, trying to tug me away. But fuck that.

I cleared my throat and Julius threw a glance over his shoulder, his eyes hooded and his mouth set in a stupid grin. His amusement fell away as he spotted us.

"Don't tell Magnar," he blurted and a wide smile took over my face.

"Oh, I won't. I'm just making you aware of how much I'm going to torment you over this tomorrow," I promised and Montana slapped me on the shoulder.

"Don't be an asshole," she said, nudging me again to try and get me moving.

"This never happened," Julius growled and Clarice nodded her agreement.

"Okay." I shrugged. "I'm sure you'll stop kissing the second we leave then."

"We will," Julius agreed.

"Bye, bye, Erik." Clarice started giggling then grabbed Julius by the back of the neck and forced his lips onto hers again. He groaned eagerly, seeming to have forgotten about his declaration already.

Montana raised a brow at me and we both smirked. I caught her hand, stumbling a little as I tugged her through the yard.

We headed away from them down a dusty track that looped around the back of the house. Beside the path, a red tractor sat beneath a large oak tree and I had half a mind to stop here and fuck my wife against it. But it was a bit too close to the house for my liking.

A meadow sprawled up a hill before us and we walked into the long

343

grass, forging a path through the flowers which had closed their petals for the night.

We crested the hill and the sight before us was breath-taking. A stream carved through the valley, sparkling under the moonlight as it passed through a cluster of trees.

I swept Montana's legs from under her and dropped to the ground on top of her. The grass bent around us, making a cocoon within it.

I gave her a dark smile, snaring her waist and tugging her closer. She slid her fingers around my neck and into my hair, her full lips grazing mine and the taste of her possessing me. She tugged hard and I groaned, my hips pressing her down into the earth. It was always like this between us, rough and sweet at once.

She pushed her hand beneath my waistband and I inhaled sharply, biting into her neck at the same moment. My heart was seized by her along with every other vital organ in my body, this little rebel of mine. Her hand slid down the length of my cock to caress my balls, making me so hard I was losing my mind.

I extracted her hand from my pants with a wry grin, even though it pained me to do so as my cock swelled against my boxers. But I wanted her first. I wanted her begging and wet and aching for me inside her.

I knelt up between her legs and slid my hand beneath her dress, tugging her panties roughly aside. She gasped my name as I pushed two fingers into her and brushed my thumb across her clit, staking my claim on her.

A feral growl escaped my throat as I felt how much she wanted me, her pussy so tight and soaked for me, it was a miracle I was able to hold back on fucking her immediately.

She was my new empire. One I wanted to conquer and claim again and again.

I was wasted and she was too, but it didn't matter. I wanted her with a primal intensity and her expression told me she wanted that too, drunk or not.

I stroked and teased her, prolonging this for as long as possible. She rocked her hips to meet the rhythm of my hand and her moans were carried away on the wind. She tried to move closer but I kept her in

344

this desperate place, devouring the way she looked at me like I held the whole world inside my eyes.

"Erik, please," she sighed and I released a breathy grunt, my willpower chipping away one piece at a time.

She was mine right in this moment, mine to rule, mine to please. I'd always enjoyed the power sex gave me, but this was something else. Having this particular woman at my disposal was nothing short of divine. I didn't just respect her, admire her and adore her. I fucking worshipped her. She could have me in any form, vampire or mortal. Monster or man. Absurdly drunk or blindingly sober.

She released a noise of frustration and pushed me into the dirt beside her. I rolled drunkenly onto my back and she swung a leg over me, sitting across my hips.

I released a throaty chuckle, taking hold of her waist and preparing to roll us over again.

She placed a firm hand on my chest, her inky hair falling around her shoulders and brushing against my neck. "You rarely let me go on top."

I grinned darkly, sliding my hands under her dress and skating them over the velvet flesh of her thighs. "I like being in control. Maybe I have issues."

Montana flicked my forehead with a smile. "Let's work through those issues." She rocked her hips and I groaned deeply, taking hold of her waist again to try and move her under me.

"Erik," she laughed. "Even your hands are bossy. Stay down there for once."

I chewed on the inside of my cheek, giving in to her as I dropped my arms to my sides.

"I'm not sure I like this," I admitted and she lowered down, pushing my shirt up and pressing her mouth to my stomach, crawling backwards as she ran her tongue down to my waistband. Kissing, sucking, biting until my thoughts were flung to the wind. "Alright...I may be changing my mind."

She laughed, fumbling with my belt and stroking my cock through my pants, sending fire rippling across my body. She pulled them down and crashed forward onto me.

"Clumsy," I scolded.

She tried again and was far less clumsy this time as she licked the solid length of me, making me curse between my teeth. Her lips closed around the tip of my cock and she swirled her tongue over me, making me want her so fucking bad.

I fisted her hair in my hand, dragging her over me, my lips clashing with hers.

"I think I'm drunk, Prince Belvedere." She tossed her hair over her shoulder as she righted herself, straddling me once more and grinding her hips down so my cock rubbed over her panties.

"Well I wouldn't want to take advantage of you." I pushed her dress up to her waist and tore her underwear away.

"Your hands say otherwise," she said, then gasped as I slid my fingers between her thighs.

My hand circled slowly as I made her wait for this, holding her on the edge of climax, teasing her clit, pinching then caressing. Her hips bucked, her head tipped back and I observed her, getting a kick out of how well she fell to ruin for me.

When she was about to come, her pussy so wet and ready for me, I shoved my pants down and pushed deep inside her. Ecstasy darted through me as she took the whole length of my cock like a good girl and I tugged her closer, sitting up and yanking her hands behind her back.

"This doesn't count as me taking control," she moaned, but I couldn't stop myself. I grazed my fangs over her neck, breathing in the inviting scent of soap that laced her skin. I brushed my teeth across her collarbone and her back arched, pushing her breasts against me.

I released her wrists and dragged her dress over her head, tossing it into the grass, desperate to revel in every inch of her flesh. I tugged her bra down and slid my tongue onto her nipple, sucking and biting while she moaned for me. Her hips rose and fell in time with the movements of my tongue, my hips driving up hard and making her bounce on my lap as I fucked her. I pushed my hand beneath her bra to continue my torment as I leant up to bite her neck, leaning into the monster in me.

She gasped in pleasure as my fangs dug in and I took hold of her waist, driving her hips down as an urgency grew in me, her pussy tightening and making me curse. A desperate agony, a furious need. I would never get enough of this girl. My rebel.

A breeze sent the grass rippling around us and the stalks tickled Montana's side, raising goosebumps where they touched. I ran my nails down her back in feather light strokes as her body responded to the tiny amounts of pressure. We became nothing but a single being moving in perfect harmony, her body meeting every thrust, every tug and pull of my desire to get closer.

I slowed my pace, brushing my mouth up to her ear, her muscles constricting and tightening telling me she was so damn close. But I refused to let it end as I contained her pleasure, holding it in my grip.

"Please," she begged, her nails raking down my arms.

I guided her hips into a deliciously slow speed that brought her ever closer. Moving a hand between us, I brushed my thumb in soft circles against her clit.

"Fuck," she gasped which made me grin darkly.

Her lips crashed clumsily against mine and I laughed as she found her release, her hips grinding against me as she bit down on a moan.

I needed more and she knew it, going limp in my arms so I could flip her beneath me. "My turn." I smirked, thrusting into her again and barely giving her a second to prepare.

In response, she reared up and bit deep into my shoulder, making me hiss through my teeth as the pain simmered away, turning to pleasure. It spurred me on and I leant up to look at her, spying my blood smeared across her mouth.

I kissed her, tasting my own body on her lips as our tongues met, our feral natures meeting in this frantic moment.

She clawed at my shoulder blades, her hips rising to meet my fervent thrusts. My fingers dug hard into her thighs as pleasure invaded every cell in my body, taking me over, all-consuming. I braced myself against the ground beside her head as I found my release with a roar, her pussy clutching my solid cock and giving me the most perfect ending.

"You. Are. Fucking. Everything," I said through my teeth.

I pulled out of her slowly, then fell beside her with a sense of satisfaction that resounded through to my core. I turned toward her,

347

finding her watching me with a dreamy smile.

I dragged a thumb across her cheek. "What are you thinking?" I growled, wishing I could hear her thoughts at that moment.

"I'm thinking...that I'm so in love with you I can't believe there was a time you weren't in my life," she said and I smiled, weakened by her words as I tugged her toward me in a fierce kiss.

Her fingers slid into my hair as I jerked her even nearer, needing all that pretty skin against mine. We smelled the same, our scents combined. Montana was my mate and I was hers. I was flawed and tainted and cursed, but she still loved me with all her heart, and I loved her more profoundly than I'd ever thought I was able to love someone.

She gazed up at the sky while I gazed at her, because she was the centre of my universe. The sky didn't begin to compare, no matter how bright, how clear.

"Do you want to go back inside?" I asked her.

"No," she whispered. "I want to stay here forever."

CALLiE

CHAPTER THIRTY THREE

W e'd never really had any music in the Realm beyond the kind that people made themselves with their voices and drums - which were really just trash cans or kitchen pans.

The wild rhythm of the songs Miles had selected to play for us set my soul alight with a hunger for movement. It was like they demanded that my body submit to the rhythm of the beat and I was a slave to their desire.

Clarice had claimed me for her dance partner as soon as she'd reappeared from getting some fresh air and she moved her body in time with mine as we both gave in to the music. Chickoa, Miles and Warren were still dancing too and between the five of us, the squat coffee table was pushing the limits of full. The cool touch of their bodies against mine didn't even frighten me anymore and I wondered what the Callie who had grown up in Realm G would think seeing me now, dancing with my enemies.

Magnar and Julius were standing together watching us with amusement as they continued to drink. I was sure the two of them had consumed as much wine as everyone else put together and their raucous laughter kept drawing my attention back to them as they joked with each other.

Despite most of his attention being on his brother, Magnar's eyes kept finding me, his gaze trailing over my exposed skin in a way that made a fire build in my blood. I hadn't forgotten the promise he'd made me earlier and I couldn't wait for him to fulfil it.

My mouth was growing dry as I moved between Miles and Clarice and when the song ended, I hopped down from the table, going in search of a drink.

Magnar laughed loudly at something Julius said and I left him to it as I moved away into the kitchen.

I snagged a glass from the cupboard and filled it with water before draining the whole thing and repeating the process.

My thoughts started to realign a little better and I pushed open a window to let the cool air wash over my heated skin.

"Having fun?" Fabian's voice came from behind me and I turned to look at him with a smile.

"Where have you been hiding?" I asked.

I hopped up onto the counter and let the winter air wash over my skin as I took another long drink.

"I guess I'm finding it a little harder than my siblings to accept the slayers among us," he replied with a faint shrug, moving closer to me. "But I did make some effort with Julius so maybe it's not entirely hopeless."

He leaned against the counter on my right and I offered him a small smile in thanks for him staying out of my personal space for once.

"Well, *I'm* a slayer," I pointed out. "And you don't seem so offended by my company." I pulled my hair over my shoulder and started twisting it into a braid.

"No. But you're not really the same," he countered. "You didn't spend years hunting me-"

"I came to New York with the full intention of hurting you if I could," I pointed out.

"I suppose so," he agreed. "Maybe I can overlook your crimes because of how dearly I'd like to get in your pants."

"Perhaps you should just fuck Julius then?" I suggested, refusing to respond to that comment. "And then you could stop hating him too."

"I'll leave kissing the slayers to Erik for now," he replied with a smile.

I rolled my eyes as I finished braiding my hair and we fell into silence.

Chickoa entered the room, moving straight towards the refrigerator as her eyes trailed over Fabian irritably.

"Sorry for all the mess we're making," I said, wondering if she'd discovered the pool table yet.

"It's alright," she replied dismissively. "My guests can afford to pay for the damages. And in all honesty, it's nice to *have* guests again. I've been pretty lonely since *someone* rounded up the last of my human friends and locked them away." She lifted a bottle of blood to her lips and Fabian inhaled sharply beside me.

I glanced at him and found him eyeing my neck hungrily before he quickly turned away again.

"The alcohol lowers our inhibitions," he muttered apologetically. "But I won't bite you again - unless you offer."

"Which I won't," I replied firmly.

Chickoa tossed him a bottle of blood and he fumbled as he caught it, nearly dropping it to the floor. I bit my lip against the laugh which tried to find its way out of my throat; seeing the vampires stripped of their grace was ridiculously amusing.

"Best you sate your thirst now," Chickoa growled. "Before you decide to ignore her wishes and bite her anyway."

Fabian stayed silent as she swept from the room and I pursed my lips awkwardly.

"Have you tried talking to her about what happened?" I asked as I could tell how miserable her continued hatred was making him.

"I'm not convinced there's anything I can say. She's held this grudge for a thousand years. There was a time I hoped that eventually she would see what I'd given her as the gift I'd intended it to be, but a hundred years passed, two hundred...she never forgave me. And I don't see how she ever will."

"But you were still thinking about doing the same thing to me," I said flatly.

Fabian eyed me carefully. "Well, I'm a selfish creature," he said eventually. "And after I felt the love that Idun gave me for you, I thought perhaps eternity didn't seem like such a long time if I just had someone to share it with."

"Don't you think that choice would have to be made by the person you were asking to share it with you?" I arched an eyebrow at him, unable to believe that what had happened to Chickoa hadn't made him see things differently.

"I intended to convince you," he assured me. "I wasn't really planning to turn you against your will. At least not after Idun got her claws into me."

"Well I guess fake love is good for one thing then. But I think you owe Chickoa an apology. Even if she still hates you after it. It's the least you can offer her."

Fabian's lips parted but he didn't seem entirely sure of what to say in response to that. I downed the last of my water and dropped off of the counter, leaving him in the kitchen to think about it.

I almost walked right into Magnar as I made it back to the hallway and he smiled predatorily as he spotted me.

"I was looking for you," he said, the tone of his voice making my heart skitter.

"And what are you going to do with me now you've found me?" I asked, backing up a step.

"You're about to find out," he growled, hounding after me.

I backed away again with a teasing smile as I made it to the stairs. "You'll have to catch me first," I breathed.

Desire flared in his eyes and I turned and fled.

His footsteps pounded up the stairs behind me and my heart thundered in my chest as I raced to get away.

I made it onto the wide landing and sprinted down the corridor, my hair falling out of the braid as I went.

I grabbed the door at the end of the hallway which led into the room we'd claimed last night and I dragged it open. I slammed the door behind me again and raced across the room, throwing the window wide before ducking behind the heavy wardrobe out of sight of the door.

Magnar threw the door open and he laughed as he found the room empty.

I bit down on my lip so hard that it almost split open again.

"The longer you keep me in suspense, the longer I'll do the same to you," he promised and I clenched my thighs together as his rumbling tone sent an ache of yearning right down to my toes. Magnar closed the door behind him with a sharp snap, the noise sending a wave of desire through me. We were finally alone and I intended to spend the whole night caught in his arms.

Magnar moved to look through the open window and I shifted out of hiding behind him. The bed sat waiting for us, full of promises, and I headed towards it with a feral grin, moving to perch on the edge of it.

"I hope you mean that," I breathed and he turned towards me swiftly.

"You want me to make you beg for me?" he asked seductively as he took a step closer, shrugging out of the red flannel shirt and letting it fall to the floor.

"Yes," I agreed, practically begging already as I eyed his broad chest.

"You may regret that request." He grinned as he dropped to his knees before me, his hands catching my ankles as I looked down at him.

I eyed the strong lines of his features, reaching out to brush my fingers along his jaw tenderly and drawing his golden eyes up to meet mine.

"I love you, Magnar," I breathed.

The desire in his gaze deepened as I coaxed a smile from his lips and I brushed my thumb across them gently.

He caught my thumb in his mouth, biting down just hard enough to send a shiver racing through me. I could tell he had no intention of being gentle with me and an ache began to build between my thighs as he slowly drew his hands up from my ankles until he reached my knees.

He held my eye for a moment then pushed my legs apart so swiftly that my breath caught in my throat.

He dropped his mouth to my inner thigh, kissing me slowly, his stubble grazing against my sensitive skin as he carved a line higher inch by inch.

I released a moan of longing, fisting my hands in his hair as he closed in on exactly where I wanted him to be, my pussy throbbing with need.

He made it to the apex of my thighs and pressed his mouth down on precisely the right place through the barrier of my panties, his teeth dragging over my clit and making me suck in a sharp breath. I groaned hungrily but he left me wanting as he shifted back again and started his ascent along my right leg next.

"Magnar," I breathed, as he moved closer to that spot again, urging him not to leave me hanging in suspense a second time.

As his mouth pressed down on top of my underwear once more, I bucked my hips beneath him, demanding he stay there this time. He laughed in response, the rumbling tone of his voice sending a vibration right through my clit and drawing another moan from me.

He shifted higher, and I groaned desperately as his fingers caught the hem of my torn dress. He tugged at the material, causing it to tear straight up the middle and freeing my breasts as he pushed the tattered remains of it off of me.

He growled appreciatively as he surveyed my naked flesh, shifting up onto his knees as his mouth claimed my nipple instead. His hand grabbed my other breast, the roughness of his flesh sweeping across mine sending butterflies dancing in my stomach.

His teeth grazed my nipple as he tugged on it just enough to send a spark of heat racing straight to that spot where I wanted his mouth.

I reached for him, pushing my palm beneath his waistband for a moment and feeling the considerable length of him waiting for me, hard as stone.

Magnar sucked in a breath as my fingers swept around his cock then he pulled back, removing my hold before I could do anything more.

He smiled wickedly at me, tugging me to sit upright then turning me around. "I think you need to be restrained, drakaina hjarta, your self-restraint is severely lacking," he growled, taking the torn remains of my dress and quickly binding my hands at the base of my spine.

"Okay," I agreed breathily as he turned me back to face him then pushed me down onto the bed again, my bound hands beneath the small

356

of my back, tilting my hips upward.

"Good."

Magnar dripped his mouth to my nipple, sucking it between his teeth and groaning softly while I moaned for him. His fingers bit into my hips as he held me still and his mouth shifted lower, abandoning my breast and leaving it aching for more of him while his mouth painted a line down to my navel. But I knew where he was going and I wasn't about to call him back again.

He made it to the line of my underwear at last and his fingers shifted from my thighs as he caught the edge of my panties and tugged them down. I lifted my ass so he could remove the final layer of my clothes as he leaned back for a moment, eyeing every inch of my naked flesh with unconcealed lust.

"Don't stop," I moaned as he held me in suspense once again.

Magnar took hold of my ankles and lifted them one at a time, placing my feet on the edge of the bed, pushing my legs further apart and baring me to him completely.

He ran his hands from my knees down the insides of my thighs, circling the backs of them until he was gripping my ass, pinning me in place like a feast for him to devour. I cursed as he looked down at me like that, laid out before him, legs wide and he slowly moved closer once more.

"Fuck," I cursed, desire consuming me as his breath skimmed over my skin, heating my core as he dipped his head between my thighs and I moaned, twisting my fingers into the sheets beneath me desperately, bucking my hips in a plea for him to end this torture.

"I'm going to fuck you with my mouth, drakaina hjarta, I'm going to taste you as you come then claim you with my cock and listen to you screaming my name. Tell me how much you want that."

"Stop taunting me and do it," I growled, my core so wet that it was a torture of its own.

I needed him to release this rampant energy inside me and I needed him to stop wasting time about it.

The first stroke of his tongue against me almost had me undone.

I tried to grind my hips into the motion, but his hands held me still, keeping me in place as his mouth moved against me again in exactly the way he wanted to devour me.

I moaned so loudly that I was sure everyone in the house must have heard me but I couldn't help it. He pushed his tongue down harder, his stubble grazing the inside of my thighs as he feasted on me, lapping from my opening to my clit, drawing me closer and closer to the edge.

I groaned, my muscles tightening as he buried his face deeper, his tongue sweeping around the tight walls of my entrance before riding my clit again, pressing down firmly and I knew I was about to free fall off of the cliff - but his tongue didn't come for me again. I arched my back in desperation as he shifted back to look up at me.

"Don't stop," I begged as he left me there, teetering on the edge.

"Say please," he teased and my skin flared as he offered me that one chance at release.

"*Please,*" I moaned and he dipped his head low, his tongue pressing against my clit again, sucking and lapping until I was crying out with the rush of my release. He drove two fingers inside me at that exact moment and my climax tore through my body like wildfire.

I cried out, calling his name as I came apart around him and he kept licking and sucking, pumping his fingers in and out of me as I writhed on the bed beneath him, his tongue worshipping me as his fingers filled me. He didn't release me and I writhed beneath him as I felt my body tightening again.

His tongue circled me, driving down again as he groaned his own arousal and praised the taste of me, the vibrations of his voice against my core making me cry out even louder.

I couldn't take any more of it. I was an empty vessel, shuddering in the throes of his control as he forced me into yet another climax.

My body shook as a tide of pleasure passed through me and he growled my name, his voice heady with desire for me.

He finally released me, withdrawing his fingers with a deep laugh as he unbuckled his belt.

The sound of his pants hitting the floor filled the dark space within my mind as I lay lost in the aftermath of what he'd done to me with my eyes firmly shut.

My whole body was alight with it. Every inch of my skin so sensitive that I wasn't sure I'd ever be able to move again.

He climbed on top of me, shifting between my legs as I felt him pressing against me, demanding more of my body.

I gave way to him, wanting to feel the fullness of him inside me as my heart pounded.

"Look at me," he breathed and I opened my eyes at his command, gazing up at this man I loved so dearly.

He held my eye, his hand moving to my throat, grasping me possessively as he held me still.

My breathing grew more ragged as I clenched my fists in the sheets, the awkward angle they were tied in keeping my hips angled up so that his cock drove against my clit where he held me in suspense. He was everything to me. All I ever could have dreamed of and more. And he was mine.

Magnar's mouth lifted in a teasing smile and I pushed my hips up off of the bed, urging him to take me as he watched me writhe in desperation.

"Fuck me," I panted. "You promised."

More. I need more of him, right now.

Magnar grinned wickedly then drove his cock into me with a violent thrust and I gasped as he filled every inch of me, my legs curling around his broad back as he pulled out a little then slammed into me again. He groaned in deep satisfaction as he claimed me for his own, our souls merging alongside our bodies.

I cried out with each thrust, unable to quiet myself as a different kind of pleasure built in me.

He pushed himself all the way inside me, then drew back all the way to the tip until I was whimpering, begging and panting his name.

Again.

And again.

He didn't stop and I never wanted him to. His mouth seized mine and I was lost to him as he drove me on and on, my selfish body aching for more as he built me up all over again.

He reared back, hoisting me into his arms and standing, his cock still deep inside me as he moved me to the wall and drove me up against it, my bound hands driving into the base of my spine.

His hands were in my hair, on my breasts, my thighs, everywhere at once, setting my skin on fire as he wrung every inch of pleasure from my flesh. I was forced to take all of it in my bound position, completely at his mercy, a willing prisoner for his sinful desires.

He fucked me harder, deeper, a growl riding in the back of his throat when I came for him, my pussy clamping tight around his cock, urging him to follow me into release but he held out, gritting his teeth and pulling out of me.

"Don't stop," I gasped, but he only chuckled darkly.

"As if I could finish this without coming all over your pretty flesh," he growled, flipping me around and shoving me face first against the wall, my nipples grazing the cold stone as he tilted my ass back and took me again.

I swore as he fucked me savagely, my name and countless praises falling from his lips while he chased his release and I approached another of my own.

I didn't want it to ever stop but I could feel that pit of ecstasy waiting to swallow me whole again and his breaths came faster as he moved towards his own ending too.

I knew that no other feeling in the world could compare to this. His skin on my skin. His breath mixing with mine. Our hearts beating in their own flawless harmony. And our souls combined as one perfect being for those few immeasurable seconds before we came crashing to an end.

But just as I was about to explode, he pulled out of me, ignoring my whimpered protests as he shoved me down onto the bed face first, wrapping his hand around my throat and drawing my spine into an arch.

His cock sank into me again and he groaned as he began to fuck me like a heathen, the friction driving my clit down onto the mattress with enough force to have me coming all over his dick within moments. I called his name and he swore violently as he came too, pulling out almost entirely before driving down again one final time and groaning my name as he filled me with his cum.

I cried out, my limbs trembling beneath him, my whole body going tight then limp and burning, burning, burning up until I wasn't sure there was anything left aside from the frantic pounding of my heart and his.

I tried to pull the scattered pieces of my body back together as we rode out the final throes of it and he gripped me tightly in his strong arms, his fingers flexing around my throat before falling away.

Magnar finally withdrew, rolling over to lay beside me as we caught our breath, his fingers deftly releasing my wrists from their bonds and I fell onto my back, breathing hard and blinking through the fog of pleasure which had ensnared me.

He twisted his fingers between mine, lifting my hand so that he could place a kiss on the back of it, his golden eyes drinking me in like he could never get enough.

"I've never known anything like you, Callie," he sighed, a deep satisfaction lacing his tone. "And I know I'll never want for anything ever again now that I've found you."

"This is it," I agreed, my heart lifting at the truth of the words. "You and me."

"Forever," he murmured, pulling me beneath his arm.

I laid my head on his chest, lingering in the beautiful rawness of my tender flesh and listening to the deep thudding of his heart as my eyes fell closed and rest called to me.

A smile held my lips captive as I drifted into sleep, knowing I wouldn't be wandering off into any dreams tonight. I was exactly where I wanted to be and I was going to stay here for as long as I could.

MONTANA

CHAPTER THIRTY FOUR

Voices carried to me on the breeze, waking me from a deep and restful sleep where I lay in the grass. I sat upright, my body already recovered from our night of drinking thanks to my vampire abilities and I had to admit that I liked this part of the curse. I grabbed my dress, tugging it on before a gruff voice reached me again. A shudder of fear fled through me. That wasn't one of my friends.

I nudged Erik and he blinked awake, sitting up beside me. I pressed a finger to my lips, pointing at the house and his brow furrowed heavily.

I knelt up to look across the sweeping meadow, gesturing for Erik to do the same.

He remained quiet, sensing my concern. Panic warred inside me as I spotted shadows moving closer to the house. They crept around each corner, checking the windows for a way in.

Biters.

I looked to Erik, swallowing the sharp lump in my throat, the danger in the air crackling against my skin.

He pointed to where a tractor lay at the base of the meadow and moved forward through the grass on his hands and knees. I followed, anxiety winding its way through my body as I hurried after him.

I increased my pace, moving after Erik as we met the edge of the grass. He darted across the path and crouched behind the tractor, holding his hand up to stop me from following. I took in a slow breath, ducking lower as a male biter's legs came into view. He was a step away from spotting Erik and I readied myself to leap into a fight to protect him, curling my hands into fists, wishing I hadn't left Nightmare in the house.

"Andrew, we're gonna check around the side, you coming?" someone whispered and the male turned back, heading away again.

Erik gestured for me to move and I laid my life in his hands as I rushed across the path and ducked down beside him. He rose to his feet, his back bent as he gazed over the hood of the tractor toward the house.

I peered around the large wheel in front of me, spotting the biters heading into the shadows on the other side of the building. A large male with a huge scar across his nose had stayed behind, inspecting the windows as he moved. His finger hooked into the kitchen window and he started grinning as it opened.

Fury clawed at my heart as I watched, half tempted to shout out to alert our friends as he crawled inside, but I couldn't give up our advantage. As he disappeared into the kitchen, Erik caught my arm and tugged me into a run toward the back wall of the house.

Faint footfalls sounded further around the building and I feared how many of them were lurking on the farm.

I gazed up at the window on the second floor, unsure which of our friends were sleeping in there but needing to alert them. Erik lunged upwards, catching hold of the window ledge and tapping gently on the glass as he swung his legs up to perch on the sill.

The window opened and Clarice looked out at him, her golden hair falling around her. "What the fuck? Did you get locked out?" she asked.

Erik pressed a finger to his lips to quiet her.

"Biters," I hissed, pointing at the window the male had gotten in through. "One of them is inside."

Clarice's mouth parted and horror slid into her eyes. "I'll wake everyone else."

"We'll check the front," Erik said in a low tone before dropping to the ground beside me.

Clarice disappeared and Erik squeezed my hand, catching me in his gaze.

"Let's see how many we can take out before they realise we're onto them."

"But the others," I pressed.

"They can handle themselves," Erik insisted and I nodded, sure he was right.

He led the way to the corner of the house, leaning around it then mouthing, "One here."

I nodded, my instincts sharp and my fangs tingling as he inched forward on silent feet. I followed, spying the biter on the path up ahead, a knife in his grip. Hatred curled through me and I had no hesitation in killing him before he could attempt to do the same to one of us.

Erik crept toward him like a predator stalking its prey and I curled my hands into fists, ready to step in the second he needed me. Erik lunged, slamming his hand down on the male's mouth and wrenching his head backwards with a violent tug. The biter slashed his blade down Erik's arm and I shot forward to help, grabbing the knife and prising it from his grip. Erik wrenched the male's head back further, his screams muffled as my husband twisted his head sideways.

A sharp crack sounded and the biter fell dead to the ground between us. I dropped down fast, finishing him with his own blade and his body turned to dust.

Erik grabbed the handful of clothes left behind, tossing them into the bushes lining the path. He gave me a nod then padded further down the track, keeping in the shadow of the wall.

Erik rubbed the wound on his arm as it slowly healed and my lip peeled back in a snarl at seeing him hurt.

In a flash of movement, he pulled me down, dragging me behind a lawnmower as five biters darted along the path toward the back of the house.

"Andrew texted to say he got in a window back here," a female whispered as they darted past us.

"Good. All the exits are covered," a male hissed back. "They won't get away this time. Our queen will let us bathe in human blood for weeks after this."

I shared a tense look with Erik and he clutched my hand. "We need to clear a path to the truck," he breathed as quiet as the wind.

I nodded firmly, prepared to do whatever it took to protect our family and friends.

I will not let them down.

367

CALLIE

CHAPTER THIRTY FIVE

I woke with goosebumps lining my flesh and I shuddered as the cool breeze blew in through the open window.

I pushed myself upright, glancing down at Magnar's achingly perfect body as he lay sleeping on top of the covers. We'd fallen asleep still tangled in each other's arms, fully naked and I guessed I could thank the wine for the fact that I hadn't noticed the winter air sweeping over us from outside.

I shook my head to clear it of the last dregs of the alcohol as a thumping headache started up in my forehead. My tongue was thick with a desire for water and I swallowed against the heavy lump in my throat.

I crawled out of the bed, wrapping my arms around myself as I hurried to shut out the cold wind.

I glanced up at the starlit sky for a moment before closing the window and drawing the curtains.

A faint noise sounded downstairs and I strained to listen for it again, wondering who was still awake. I didn't want to risk waking Magnar so I didn't turn on any lights but I could just make out the clock on the wall saying it was four fifteen.

I pulled open the drawer where I'd stored the clothes Chickoa had lent me and pulled out some clean underwear and thick socks. I pulled them on before locating a pair of black yoga pants and a soft green sweater. I kicked my boots on too, seeking to banish the cold from my limbs while I went in search of a drink.

I smiled down at Magnar before I headed for the door. He was spread-eagled across the bed exactly where we'd ended up after he'd finished destroying me. I managed to roll a little of the duvet across to offer him some warmth but he was on top of most of it so I soon gave up, not wanting to wake him.

I slipped out into the dark corridor just as the sound of breaking glass reached me. I sniggered, wondering who else had managed to break something and was somewhat impressed with them for still being awake. Though I guessed as the vampires didn't need as much sleep as us, I shouldn't have been that surprised.

I hurried along the corridor, aching to satisfy my need for water as quickly as possible.

I left the lights off as I went, not wanting to disturb anyone.

A faint scraping sounded downstairs and I vaguely wondered if someone was trying to rearrange the furniture. I frowned, making it to the top of the stairs and slowing my pace as I headed down them and a shiver ran along my spine, my instincts making me slow.

I paused, listening more carefully, gripped by the sense that something was wrong.

"Hello?" I called uncertainly. "Is someone still awake?"

The silence stretched and a prickle ran along the back of my neck, my fingers curling with the desire for Fury.

I glanced back up the stairs, wondering if I should go and wake Magnar, but was there any real reason for me to be considering that? I shook my head, dismissing the creeping feeling as paranoia. It was a big, unfamiliar house and I was just jumping at shadows. I'd grown up in an apartment where my bedroom opened right onto the living space and kitchen; it was no wonder I found this place so weird in the dead of the night.

Suck it up Callie, you don't need help getting a glass of water.

I jogged down the rest of the stairs, determined to get my drink and head back up for some more sleep as quickly as possible.

I took three steps towards the kitchen before a huge shape collided with me from the darkness.

I let out an oomph of pain as I was slammed back into the wall and the male vampire hissed as he lunged for my throat.

My head spun, my reflexes kicking in before my mind had fully comprehended what was happening and I threw my fist into his temple, knocking him aside before his teeth could find their mark. He came at me again but I landed my boot in his chest, launching him backwards and he skidded past the bottom of the stairs on his ass.

I staggered away, racing into the kitchen and crossing the tiled floor as quickly as I could, needing a weapon. I grabbed the edge of the island and propelled myself around it, snatching a huge knife from the block on the counter.

I whirled to face my assailant but as my gaze fell on the door to the hall, there was no one there.

My heart pounded as I pushed my tongue into my cheek, tasting blood.

I was frozen by indecision, unsure if I should call out to wake the others or whether doing so would alert my attacker to my position.

I shifted towards the door again, my heart pounding as I made it into the corridor. I hunted for a light switch but the walls either side of the doorway were bare.

I glanced up at the stairs then along the hallway, not knowing which route to take. The shadows were thick with the promise of hidden figures and my fingers trembled slightly as I searched for any sign of the vampire.

A faint rattle sounded at the end of the hallway and I made up my mind to face this opponent. I refused to lead them towards anyone who was sleeping unaware upstairs and I couldn't risk calling out.

I placed my feet carefully as I went, drawing on my gifts as I gave in to the call of the hunt my people had been born for. I wished I hadn't left Fury upstairs; the blade's guidance was precisely what I needed in the dark. But there was no point in worrying about it, I had to get through

371

this with the kitchen knife. Which should be more than good enough to take on one vampire.

So I just had to hope that was all there was because my heart was pounding warnings through my veins which made me doubt the likelihood of that. If there was one vampire here crazy enough to break into a house filled with Belvederes, then I could bet there were more. And the chances were that Valentina had sent them. I fought off the fear that raised in me, determined to finish this monster before I dealt with the possibility of others.

I continued down the corridor, moving slowly.

A floorboard creaked and I spun to my left, raising my knife just before the vampire barrelled into me again. I wasn't fast enough to pierce his heart and I was slammed back, crying out as I collided with a door before crashing through it.

My arms cartwheeled as I fell, sailing through air instead of landing on the floor. The kitchen knife was knocked from my grip as I screamed and I tumbled down, down-

My back crashed into concrete and I cried out as pain sliced through me. My head swum dizzily and I was sure I'd hit it too somewhere along the way to the ground.

I coughed, squinting up at the wooden staircase I'd fallen down and the huge silhouette which was framed in the doorway above me. A little light spilled in from the window at the end of the hallway behind him and I noticed a red scar across the bridge of his nose.

I clenched my fist, willing my body to do as I commanded while the pain from my fall paralysed me and my limbs refused to cooperate.

Something wet trickled down my forehead and I sucked a breath in through my teeth as the vampire who had attacked me moved onto the top step.

"Mmm," he moaned, inhaling deeply. "You smell *good.*"

MONTANA

CHAPTER THIRTY SIX

Erik stole a glance around the lawnmower and I followed suit, tightening my grip on the knife I'd taken from the biter we'd killed. I spotted three vampires blocking the track that led out of the farm. They were armed with guns and swords, but they were lessers so if we could get close enough, I knew we could take them.

"I'll distract them," Erik whispered to me and my throat constricted as I nodded. "The second they shoot at me, close the gap and take out who you can."

I nodded firmly, and his jaw tightened as he ran out from our hiding place.

"Hey fuckers!" he shouted, sprinting toward them then launching himself behind a tree at the edge of the track.

The lessers turned, firing their guns at him and relief filled me as I realised the noise would wake the whole house up. Erik took cover behind the tree trunk and bullets ripped the bark to shreds. While they were distracted, I sped out of the shadows and powered toward them with my teeth gritted. I barely felt any fear as I barrelled into the three of them, willing to do anything for the sake of those I loved.

I dove on top of a female, bringing her to the ground with such force that the earth trembled from the impact. She snatched the knife from my hand, tossing it away, but I lunged for the gun in her grip at the same moment. I seized it and turned it back on her, firing quickly at her chest, sending her bursting into ash.

The final two lessers rounded on me with cries of alarm, unleashing more gunfire. I rolled, but didn't move fast enough as a bullet ripped across my cheek. I snarled, righting myself as fast as I could and firing my gun with the aid of my vampire abilities. A male turned to ash and the remaining lesser faced the wrath of my husband as he launched an attack, ripping off limbs and tearing flesh from his bones. The biter fell to dust around Erik and he hurried to meet me, his hands coated in blood before it turned to ash too.

"Holy shit," I breathed, my body trembling with adrenaline.

Erik ran his thumb across the graze on my cheek, but it had almost healed already, the sting of it long gone. Gun shots were fired inside the house and we didn't waste another second as we sprinted toward the front door.

I ran up the porch steps, reaching for the door handle just as the entire door flew off its hinges and knocked me and Erik back into the dirt. A weight crushed me down beneath the door but with mine and Erik's combined might, we managed to shove it off of us.

Julius rolled off of the door onto the earth, clutching his side as he righted himself and raised Menace. An Elite stood in the doorway with an axe in his hand and as he bared his fangs, drool slid down his chin. He pointed his weapon at me, a dark savagery flaring in his eyes.

"Valentina has sent me for you and your sister," he snarled, stepping out onto the porch and the wood groaned beneath his weight.

"You'll have to get through a Belvedere and a slayer first," Julius snarled, cracking his neck as he awaited the Elite's attack. Two dark figures appeared behind him, stepping into the light of the porch. A male and a female, both lessers, but with high-powered rifles in their hands. They took aim at Julius and Erik. My husband moved like the wind to avoid the fire, and I threw myself at Julius, knocking him to the ground to avoid the second gunshot.

We gained our feet fast and started running away from the house.

Bullets tore up the dirt around us and I weaved left and right, keeping behind Julius to shield him. Erik ran at my side, but I knew we were slowing him down.

Erik gasped as a bullet ripped through his shirt, skimming his hip and fear pounded through me.

"Fuck this." Erik scooped Julius into his arms and charged forward. I kept pace as we ran into the darkness toward the large red barn on the other side of the valley.

The onslaught of gunfire stopped abruptly and I heard a shout behind us. I threw a glance over my shoulder, spotting Warren and Miles beating the Elite to death, the lessers reduced to dust around them. More biters appeared around the side of the house and started shooting at us, forcing us to keep fleeing.

We increased our pace and raced across the valley toward the barn. As we arrived outside it, I wrenched the door open and Erik carried Julius inside. The slayer shoved his way out of his arms with a grunt.

"I didn't need your help," Julius snapped.

Erik shook his head at him in exasperation, moving to lock the door with a heavy wooden beam. "You'd have been shot to shit out there, asshole."

Julius glowered but nodded reluctantly, then he turned, eyeing the large space filled with hay. "Callie told me there's tunnels running under this farm. There must be a hatch in here somewhere." He jogged forward, hunting the area and I joined him, searching the edges of the room.

"Here!" Erik called and we ran to his side as he yanked open a metal door and a gust of cool air floated over us.

"We have to get to the truck," Erik said. "But the keys are in the house. And we need to round up the others."

"Let's head back there then," Julius agreed, diving into the passage out of sight.

I followed and Erik shut the door as he moved after us. Motion-censored lights sprung to life on the walls, the dim orange glow spreading away ahead of us. As I hurried along, Julius's breaths filled my ears alongside the frantic beat of his heart.

We came to a fork in the passage and I could see a bright light at the end of one of the tunnels. "Which way?" I whispered.

"It must be this way," Julius chose the darker path lit by only a few bulbs and neither Erik or I questioned him as we followed.

MAGNAR

CHAPTER THIRTY SEVEN

"**G**et up!" The door flew open as Clarice sprang into our room.

I was on my feet with Venom in hand and pointed at her before I remembered I was naked.

She raised her eyebrows as her gaze travelled over my body. "Holy shit, it runs in the family," she muttered.

"Why are you here?" I demanded, looking behind me and failing to spot Callie anywhere.

Gunshots carried to me from outside and adrenaline licked down my spine.

"We're under attack," Clarice said, remembering herself. "Miles, Warren and Julius are already downstairs. Erik and Montana are outside. We've gotta get out of here; Valentina's found us. So get dressed and get ready to leave."

"Where's Callie?" I demanded.

"She's not here?" Clarice tore her eyes from my exposed flesh and looked around the room with a confused frown. "I haven't seen her."

Fear burrowed into my heart as I glanced around the room as if I might spot her hiding somewhere, but she wasn't there. I quickly pulled on the clothes I'd been wearing last night, leaving the ill-fitting flannel shirt unbuttoned before tossing my sheathes over my back.

Clarice left while I was dressing and I heard her banging on Fabian's door next.

I noticed Fury laying on the nightstand and tucked Callie's blade into my waistband with a snarl of frustration that she didn't have it with her.

Where the hell are you?

I kept my swords in hand and headed out onto the landing as gunfire rattled outside once more.

I ground my teeth at the sound of the firearms going off. No matter my skill with a sword, any well-placed bullet could allow a much lesser opponent to end me. Those modern weapons were a curse.

Fabian called my name and I slowed so that he could catch up to me at the top of the stairs.

"How many are there?" he asked me tersely.

I focused on my blades, urging them to give me an answer. "Hard to say. At least eight Elite. Twice as many lessers," I replied eventually. They were too spread out for me to be certain on precise numbers.

Clarice sped toward us, stilling in the shadows out of sight as I peered around the staircase, making sure it was clear to head down.

"What's the plan?" she breathed and I looked around to find her hand on her brother's arm as if she were afraid. Fabian gripped her fingers reassuringly before releasing her as he turned to me for an answer.

"We secure the entrances and find everyone else before making a run for the trucks," I said, giving them no time to voice objections as I stepped out of our hiding place and ran down the stairs two at a time.

A lesser leapt over the banister at me and I swung Tempest around, carving through his chest before he could reach me. I turned my face aside as ash washed over me and Fabian shot past me in a blur of motion.

He slammed into another vampire at the foot of the stairs and she shrieked as he wrestled to claw her heart from her body with his bare hands.

"Callie?!" I bellowed, vaulting the banister and landing heavily on the floor below.

Chickoa shot past me towards the front door where the sounds of gunfire boomed through the air. Clarice followed her but I wasn't going outside until I knew that Callie wasn't in the house.

I kicked open the door to the living room then a dining room and an office, finding nothing inside. I cursed as I strode towards the room at the end of the hallway where the pool table was, but the door burst open before I could get there.

I snarled in outrage as I raised my blades and six vampires swarmed at me. Two of them were Elite and they smiled darkly, sniffing the air and baring their fangs as they came for my blood.

I released a battle cry as I stabbed out with Tempest but the vampires were well trained and they managed to duck aside. One of them leapt below my strike and collided with me before I could follow the blow with Venom.

The corridor was too confined for me to move freely and I was forced back as the vampire tried to bite my arm. I slammed Tempest's hilt down on his skull but the moment it cost me gave three more vampires the chance to get close.

I kicked and punched, slamming my fists into faces and my elbows down on backs.

"The queen wants you home, Magnar," one of the Elite purred and I realised I knew him from my time under Valentina's command.

"The *queen* can suck my ass," I replied viciously, driving Venom down so that one of the lessers was carved in half, turning to dust as my blade met his heart.

I was still struggling though, my back pressed to the wall as I fought them away with a fierce desperation. Valentina would never get her claws in me again. I refused to be parted from Callie.

As I thought of the woman I loved, I could have sworn I heard her screaming. My heart plummeted and my rage increased. If any of these monsters had laid a hand on her then their death would be anything but swift. It would be an artistry of pain and suffering. I would make them bleed before the end and beg for death.

A great cry met my ears and my blades burned hungrily in my palms as Fabian crashed into the fight.

He knocked my opponents back, barrelling into them and he took one to the ground, grappling with him as he pounded on the flesh above his heart. The lesser exploded into dust and I swung Venom over Fabian's head, meeting the blow as one of the Elite aimed a sword for his back.

Fabian leapt up, grabbing the Elite's arm and breaking bone.

While he screamed, I slammed Venom through his heart with a snarl of rage.

The final vampires came at us at once, but with the Belvedere by my side, we cut through them like they were stalks of grass.

Fabian smirked at me in a moment of camaraderie and I returned the gesture with a snort of laughter. It seemed that despite our differences, we had each other's backs when it mattered and I guessed that was all that really counted.

I heard Callie screaming again and fear licked down my spine as I hunted around for any sign of her.

Fabian inhaled deeply beside me and headed away at a fierce pace. "This way," he growled and I ran to keep up. "She's bleeding."

ERIK

CHAPTER THIRTY EIGHT

We were going around in circles in the tunnels and I was starting to get pissed off with Julius leading the way.

"I'll go ahead," I demanded, running forward, but he elbowed me as I tried to get past him.

"I'm doing just fine," Julius snarled, squaring his shoulders.

"Stop it," Montana sighed. "Don't fight."

Julius nodded to me in agreement and we set the pace together, speeding up to the next junction.

"Left must lead to the house," I insisted, gazing that way.

"No, we already took a left, it must be right," Julius pushed back, making me snarl in anger.

Montana pushed between us, gazing down the two long tunnels.

"What do you think?" I asked her and her lips pursed in thought.

"Left. That way curves right at the end anyway. Look." She pointed and I grinned smugly as I got my way, heading off down the tunnel at a quick pace.

We moved in silence and I sensed we must have been nearing the house at last. It couldn't be far. And these tunnels were starting to feel suffocating. I needed to find my family and then we had to get the fuck off of this farm.

What if Valentina is here?

The thought circled in my mind and fear crushed my chest at the idea. What if she'd found another way to control us? A magical bracelet...or maybe a mystical dildo was more her style. She was hell-bent on getting Magnar and I in her bed, and that woman needed to learn a thing or two about boundaries.

"-think we're lost, Pete," a male voice carried to me from afar and I froze, gesturing for the others to do the same.

"Yeah, Pete. Why'd you bring us down here?" a girl hissed.

"Because they didn't teleport out of the barn, did they Melissa? They came down here," answered a male who I guessed was Pete.

"Great, so now we're lost. We've definitely passed this wall several times," Melissa said.

"How do you know it's the same wall?" Pete snapped.

"Because it had that same slime on it shaped like your big nose," Melissa laughed.

I edged toward the end of the tunnel, making sure every one of my footfalls was silent. Julius lifted his sword and I gave him a nod as he moved along behind me. As we reached the entrance to another tunnel, Montana readied her fists and I mimicked her.

The biters moved quietly, but their voices continued to ring out, drawing closer and closer.

"Perfect, another T-junct-" Pete didn't finish that sentence as I slammed my fist into his face. He stumbled back into the man and woman behind him with a yelp of fright. I aimed a sharp kick to his chest, knocking them all down like dominoes.

Julius came at them from my left and Montana ran forward on my right. I leapt onto the group, pummelling my fists into every pound of flesh I could find, rage setting my most vicious instincts alight.

Pete grabbed my arm, digging his fangs into my skin and I headbutted him to get him off.

Melissa gained her feet, diving at Montana and they crashed into the wall, smashing a light so glass showered everywhere. Anxiety darted through me as I slammed Pete's head down on the ground to try and disable him.

Julius swiped his blade at the other male, skewering him with a grunt of effort. Dust exploded around us and I screwed up my eyes as it floated over me. Pete kicked and bit me, not letting me near his chest as I tried to rip his heart out.

Julius released a roar, kicking me in the side and I hit the ground with a hiss of anger. I realised why a second later as he drove his sword through Pete's chest and cast him to ash.

I turned to help Montana, but my wife had already snapped the female's neck, and I gave her a grin as Julius strode forward to finish the biter off.

I hurried to Montana, checking her over for wounds, finding a bite mark on her hand. I frowned, running my thumb around it gently and Julius cleared his throat.

"Any time today," he sang. "I don't wanna stand here watching you make out for an hour."

"Oh, but you enjoyed doing just that with my sister last night," I taunted.

Julius raised his sword at me with a dark glare. "I did no such thing."

"Guys," Montana hissed. "We have to move."

I nodded, clapping Julius on the shoulder as we headed along the tunnel. "Don't worry, your secret is safe with me."

"There's no secret to hide, bloodsucker. Nothing happened," Julius growled.

"Can we just focus on the task at hand?" Montana pressed. "We can talk about how Julius kissed Clarice later."

Julius glowered at her back.

"I did no such thing," he reiterated.

"Sure," I said lightly. "Keep telling yourself that."

"Even if I did kiss that parasite – which I didn't – I was wasted last night. Clarice took advantage of me," Julius said.

"Don't start throwing accusations around about my sister," I warned, rage daggering through me. "You were all over her and I don't care how much you had to drink."

Julius opened his mouth to retort but a weight collided with me from behind and fangs buried into my neck.

"Fuck!" I slammed myself back against the wall to crush my attacker, spotting Montana and Julius darting forward to help.

This is place is swarming with these assholes.

I slammed the vampire against the wall again, my attacks ferocious and unforgiving. My assailant fell off of me and I turned, kicking her in the face. Between the three of us, the biter met a swift and brutal end. Her remains scattered around us and the tension ran out of my muscles.

"We better be quiet from now on," Montana whispered.

"Okay," Julius breathed. "But one more thing...I didn't kiss a parasite and I never will."

CALLIE

CHAPTER THIRTY NINE

I scrambled away from the stairs on my hands and knees, diving into the pitch black confines of the wine cellar as I struggled to locate something I could use as a weapon.

The Elite's footsteps pounded heavily down the stairs as he came for me, not bothering to hurry.

I could hear the fight that had broken out upstairs and my heart raced with anxiety for my friends.

I wiped my sleeve over the cut in my hairline and hissed as the pain of it found me. It hadn't stopped bleeding and I bit my tongue against the burning sensation as I moved on.

My hands met with something big and metal and I clutched at it, heaving myself upright and realising it was a washing machine.

I moved on from it quickly as the Elite's footsteps drew closer.

Come on, Callie. Anything you can lift into your arms. Now!

I cursed internally as I fumbled my way past a dryer next. I found the wall, grabbing hold of a wooden shelf and ripping it off of its bracket as the vampire drew closer.

The Elite chuckled as he closed in on me and I snarled angrily, knowing he could see better than I could in this infernal darkness.

The air in the room shifted as he lunged at me and I swung the shelf around, shattering the wood over his head with a furious cry.

The vampire flinched aside and I ripped a second shelf from the wall, slamming it into his face and knocking him to the ground. I smashed it down over his head again, releasing it as it broke too and the wooden pieces clattered to the floor.

I turned and fled but his icy hand curled around my ankle and he yanked me off of my feet with a violent wrench.

I hit the ground hard, pain flaring through my chin as it collided with the concrete floor, my head spinning at the contact.

The vampire crawled on top of me and I flipped beneath him, punching him as hard as I could.

He reared back as the full force of my gifted muscles slammed into his cheek and his scarred nose, but he didn't stop coming.

The Elite threw his own punches into my gut so forcefully that all the breath was knocked from my lungs.

I wheezed in pain, kicking and thrashing as I tried to buck him off of me.

"The one true queen wants your head, girl," the vampire snarled.

He caught my throat and panic gripped me as he yanked upwards and tried to rip my fucking head off.

I drove my knees up, ramming them into him and knocking him off balance before I managed to drive a punch into his chest, then another and another. Ribs cracked and his fingernails cut into my neck as he fought to maintain his hold on me. But I refused to let this asshole kill me. Not now. I had too damn much to live for and I fucking refused to die.

The Elite reared back, dragging me with him before slamming me to the ground again, the back of my head colliding with the concrete.

My vision darkened and my arms fell limp at my sides as I tumbled towards oblivion.

The Elite growled in satisfaction and pain speared through my neck as he bit me. He dragged my limp body up into his arms as I tried to fight against the urge to black out. If I succumbed to the darkness, I knew I'd never wake from it.

A fearsome cry rang out from somewhere behind me and my heart leapt with relief as I recognised Magnar's voice.

The Elite dropped me and I managed to shield myself with my arms so that my head didn't hit the floor again.

I rolled onto my hands and knees, blinking the stars from my eyes as Magnar swung Venom straight at the Elite's head, but he ducked aside to avoid the blow.

"Your death has come for you, Andrew," Magnar spat. "Your whore queen won't save you now."

Fabian leapt from the stairs too, blocking Andrew's retreat as he tried to dance away from Magnar's rage.

The Elite sprang back from Fabian and Tempest severed his left arm at the elbow as he got too close to Magnar.

Andrew howled in pain and Fabian jumped on his back, knocking him to the ground before catching his remaining hand in his grasp.

"No, no - please!" the Elite begged as Fabian jammed his boot down on the vampire's chest and heaved until he'd torn that arm free too.

Magnar bellowed in rage as he slammed Venom down, removing the vampire's legs as well.

Andrew was screaming, wailing in pain and begging for mercy from the men who'd come to rescue me. But there was no pity in either of their eyes.

I grabbed the wall and heaved myself upright, shaking my head to clear the last of the darkness from my vision as I approached them, blood pooling beneath my boots.

The pain of the Elite's venom still burned in my neck and I rubbed my hand against it in an attempt to get it out.

Fabian looked at me with relief filling his eyes as he stepped aside to let me approach the doomed vampire.

Andrew was crying out for someone to save him, but anyone who could hear him either couldn't help or didn't care.

Magnar's eyes raked over me with concern and I held my hand out as I spied my blade tucked into his waistband.

He drew it, turning it in his grasp as he offered me its hilt.

Let's end him, Sun Child, Fury purred.

My lip pulled back as I looked down at the vampire who had tried to take my life and his eyes widened with a dawning comprehension just before I slammed Fury down between his ribs and he was cast to dust.

MONTANA

CHAPTER FORTY

The pounding of soft footfalls sounded somewhere off in the tunnels and I stiffened. There were a lot of them. Erik laid a hand on my shoulder, glancing back the way we'd come.

"Hurry," he urged and we quickened our pace to a sprint, moving as quietly as we could along the tunnel.

The passage rose upwards and we finally arrived at a metal door. Julius turned the handle excitedly but it didn't open.

"Shit," he breathed. "It's locked." He rammed his shoulder against it and a loud gong rang out.

"This way!" a female voice called to us from somewhere back in the tunnels.

Erik snarled, moving past me and slamming his foot to the door. He and Julius started battering it and I turned, raising my fists.

Two biters lunged out of the darkness and I screamed as nails slashed across my throat. One of them caught my hair, the females battling to kill me together. Erik roared as he intercepted them, bringing one to her knees as he tore her head from her shoulders.

I kicked the other female in the chest and she hit the far wall with a loud crack. Erik grabbed her by the throat and threw her to the ground.

She rolled upright, darting back into the tunnel, hissing furiously at us.

"Rachel!" she called and several Biters poured out of the gloom one after the other. A tall female led the swarm and I backed up with Erik by my side, terror rattling through me.

Julius started banging on the door. "Open up!" he yelled then spun around and lifted Menace before drawing Vicious from his hip too, ready for the fight.

There were so many of them, packed into the space wall to wall with guns in most of their hands. There was no way we could win.

Rachel rolled up her sleeves as the lesser female joined her side with a wicked grin. "Three green bottles standing on the wall." She smiled widely, stepping forward, raising a huge machine gun. "Let's smash them all."

Erik grabbed me, turning sharply around as he shielded me with his body.

"No!" I screamed, slamming my eyes shut as gunfire exploded through the air.

Someone shoved me forward.

Hands were on me. Erik's hands, Julius's.

I stumbled through the door and Erik fell on top of me with a groan.

Chickoa stood there with a shotgun. "Fuck you!" she yelled, lifting a grenade to her mouth and pulling out the pin with her teeth before throwing it into the passage. She kicked the door shut, twisting a lock and catching Julius by the arm. "Run!" she bellowed and I willed my legs to move as I clung to Erik, forcing him along as he staggered from his injuries.

The explosion shook the foundations of the house and fire burst through the room. We hit the floor again, scrambling to our feet.

"There's another passage, the others have already gone ahead," Chickoa said as she leapt upright.

I nodded, relief spilling through me to know they were alright. My gut dropped as I turned to Erik to inspect his wounds. His shirt was torn to ribbons at the back and several bullets were deep in his flesh.

Anger and pain tore through me as I supported him, unable to believe what he'd done for me.

"Is anyone upstairs?" Erik gritted out at Chickoa.

"No, it's all clear," she confirmed. "But there's vampires all over the farm. I saw them from my room."

Erik turned to me with a wince. "Go upstairs, rebel, get the truck keys from my pants' pocket."

I nodded, my hands shaking and coated in blood as I released him.

"Get to the tunnel," I urged the others.

"I'm not going anywhere without you," Erik breathed, resting his hand against a wall as he turned to Julius with a wheeze. "Go with her."

Julius nodded and we ran into the hallway, finding the house riddled with bullet holes as we sprinted upstairs. I charged along the landing to my bedroom, kicking the door open and grabbing Erik's pants from a chair. The keys jingled in his pocket and I snatched them out before running to the nightstand and retrieving Nightmare.

"All good?" Julius asked as he guarded the doorway.

I nodded, my throat constricting as we darted back onto the landing. Every step I took was more urgent. Erik was wounded and I needed to be by his side. I had to get him out of here.

I hurried down the corridor to where he was waiting, cupping his neck and pressing my forehead to his. "Let's go."

He nodded and dropped an arm over my shoulders as he let me support him.

Chickoa led the way into the kitchen and I heard footsteps pounding into the entrance hall. Panic filled me as Chickoa tugged open a door beside the fridge which was concealed as a cupboard. She gestured for us to head into it and Julius helped me guide Erik into the passage.

"Go on," Chickoa encouraged.

"Are you coming?" I asked as she stood before the tunnel.

"I've got a rodent problem I need to take care of first. See you at the trucks." She slammed the door behind us and my heart twisted as we were left in darkness. A second later, orange lights flickered on along the walls. We hurried down the passage and I kept my arm around Erik as we followed Julius.

"You okay?" I whispered frantically as he moved at my side.

My hand slid through blood and tears pricked my eyes at the agony he must have been in.

"Perfect, rebel. Don't worry about me," he said firmly, but my stomach twisted with concern. We needed to get those bullets out so he could heal.

A loud boom sounded from the house above and sediment cascaded down on us.

I drew in a breath to quiet my nerves, praying my sister and the others were okay. And that they'd be waiting for us when we resurfaced above ground.

Erik stumbled and swore through his teeth.

"Wait," I begged Julius, coming to a halt and moving behind Erik. "We have to get the bullets out."

"We don't have time," Julius objected.

"We're one man down right now," Erik groaned. "Rebel's right. The quicker they're out, the quicker I'll heal. I'm only slowing you down like this."

"Fine. But let's make it quick." Julius took a small knife from his hip, tossing it to me as a loud bang sounded against the door we'd come from.

I glanced back, but the door didn't budge.

I can do this.

"Sorry," I breathed as I eased the blade into the first hole. Erik released a low groan but didn't flinch. I wiggled the bullet free and it dropped to the floor with a ping.

"Six more," I whispered, digging the knife into the next hole.

Another bang sounded behind me and I winced, accidentally digging the knife in too deep.

"Argh," Erik groaned.

"Sorry, sorry," I said, frowning heavily. I continued as fast as I could, the bullets falling to the floor one at a time. The first holes in his skin were already stitching over and I released a sigh as I extracted the final bullet.

"There," I said resting my palm to his back.

"Thanks," he said heavily.

"No, thank you," I said thickly. "You saved my life. You shouldn't have put yourself between me and danger."

He caught my hand, tugging me around to face him. "I'll always do that," he murmured, his iron eyes glinting like molten silver. "I owe you everything."

I squeezed his fingers, my heart clenching. "If you die, I'd rather go out at your side."

"I would never let-" Erik started but Julius cut him off.

"We get it, you'd both die for each other and it's all very fucking romantic. Now can you get moving please, lovebirds, or you might end up actually fulfilling that promise."

I released a small laugh as Erik and I started running side by side behind the slayer.

His movements were already smoother and relief ran through me to know he was going to be okay. Julius raced on in front us, raising Menace ahead of him as he returned Vicious to its sheath.

I took Nightmare from my hip, releasing Erik's hand as I mentally prepared myself to face any enemy who found us. We had to reach the others and get the hell out of here. That was all that mattered.

The lights flickered overhead and a shiver raced across my skin.

"There's a way out here," Julius whispered, pausing next to a ladder that ran up to a hatch.

"Let's see where we are," Erik encouraged, his back straightening as his wounds healed at last.

Julius headed up the ladder, quietly pushing the hatch open and peering out.

"What can you see?" I whispered.

"I think I'm in a chicken shed," Julius said then a surprised *ca-caw!* sounded from above and a flutter of feathers fell onto Julius's shoulders. "Yep, definitely a chicken shed. Hello ladies."

"Get up," Erik ordered, stepping onto the ladder below him.

Julius climbed out and Erik swiftly followed. I darted after them, hauling myself into a large shed full of hay. A row of wooden nests ran along one wall and several chickens were gazing at us indignantly.

Erik ran to the door of the shed, tugging it open a crack and peering outside. He quickly closed it again, turning to us with a dark expression.

"The truck is three hundred yards away up the hill. But there's twenty biters out there and no sign of the others."

"Shit," I breathed, my grip tightening on Nightmare. "What do we do?"

A yell of defiance tore through the air outside and Erik tugged the door open again in alarm. "Fuck, Clarice is running at them alone." He darted outside, but Julius shouldered his way past him, tearing off across the field.

I gasped, chasing after them both, my chest tightening with alarm. Ahead of me, Julius released a battle cry, slamming his sword through a biter and sending her to ash.

I raised Nightmare at the ready, determination racing through me as I ran into battle with my mind set one thing: survival.

CALLIE

CHAPTER FORTY ONE

We'd almost made it to the top of the cellar stairs when Chickoa burst through the door, slamming it behind her again. Her eyes widened as she spotted us but she didn't slow her descent.

"Take cover!" she cried as she charged towards us.

I had no time to figure out what she meant before an explosion rang out in the space above us and the blast threw me from my feet.

I cried out as I was propelled backwards into Magnar and Fabian and we all fell in a heap at the bottom of the stairs.

Magnar groaned as I scrambled off of him and I offered him my hand so that I could drag him upright.

"Are you okay?" I breathed.

"You're heavier than you look," he teased and I scoffed.

Fabian lay unmoving at the bottom of our heap and Chickoa tutted irritably as she realigned his broken spine, leaving him to heal on the floor. She shot across the room, flicking on a flashlight before yanking a hidden door open.

"This leads to the stables," Chickoa said. "Everyone else is outside already. I need to make sure the horses are okay and the rest of my animals too. You'll have to come this way as well."

"Why the hell do you have so many grenades?" I asked, eying the cluster of them strapped to her belt.

"There was a military base not too far from here during the Final War but the bombs dropped so suddenly that the soldiers based there never even got deployed. During the mayhem that followed, I decided to head there and arm myself just in case the war ended up at my door. Of course I never could have guessed that the Belvederes would seize power. And after they had, I just put the weapons I'd gathered aside in case Fabian ever came knocking on my door." Chickoa shrugged.

The sound of coughing started up at the top of the stairs and I stilled as a second vampire groaned.

"Which way did she go?" a female asked.

"Through one of those doors," a male replied roughly.

Footsteps sounded on the landing above and I focused on Fury as I assessed what was coming for us. Six Elite and nine lessers were close by. If they all came for us armed with guns then I wasn't convinced we could stand against them.

"We need to move," Magnar breathed, propelling me towards the hidden door.

"I'm not leaving him behind," I protested, pointing at Fabian.

His fingers twitched as he shifted towards consciousness again but he still hadn't woken.

"I'll wait for him and we'll catch up," Chickoa replied, though she didn't seem overly thrilled at the prospect. "We're faster than you."

"You swear?" I clarified, unsure if that was really the best idea. Fabian was vulnerable in that state and the vampires hunting us were moving closer with each second.

"Yes, I'll deliver your husband back to you safely," Chickoa agreed.

"He's not my husband," I hissed.

More footsteps moved across the landing, heading straight towards our hiding place. Chickoa raised her shotgun as I hesitated, not wanting to split our group up.

Magnar sighed as he realised I wasn't going to leave and moved past Chickoa to pick Fabian up. He tossed him over his shoulder and hurried towards me.

Chickoa raised an eyebrow in surprise just as the door above us burst open. I turned my back on her and raced into the dark tunnel behind Magnar.

Chickoa followed quickly, pulling the door closed behind us so that we were left in the dark. After a beat, orange lights flared to life and I stared at the long tunnel ahead of me in surprise. They flickered a few times then died, plunging us into darkness once more. Chickoa cursed, quickly turning on a flashlight. She raised her shotgun, tossing Magnar the flashlight as she aimed at the door where the biters were sure to appear at any second.

Fury hungered for me to stay and fight, longing for the blood of the creatures who chased us and I had to push my will against the blade's to quiet its persistent nagging.

Feed me their blood, Sun Child!

Magnar started moving, passing the flashlight to me and looking vaguely disgusted by it. Fabian groaned softly as he shifted towards consciousness.

"Go," Chickoa breathed as I hesitated. "I'll hold them off and catch up."

I eyed the shotgun in her grasp, nodding my acceptance as I turned away. My blade was no match for those weapons and she could move faster than me when it came time for her to abandon her post. I started running, the flashlight's beam bouncing back and forth along the corrugated metal walls in time with my steps.

"Is everyone else okay?" I asked Magnar as we ran.

"I hope so," he replied darkly and I tightened my grip on Fury as concern spiralled through my chest.

The tunnel angled left then suddenly swept right again. We raced on and Fury started to grow warmer in my palm once more.

Gunshots rang out behind us and I ducked my head instinctively as the sound echoed through the tunnel and sent panic skittering through me.

Behind you! Fury screamed and I hesitated, pointing the flashlight over my shoulder to make sure we knew who was chasing us.

Chickoa appeared and I gave her a brief smile as relief filled my chest. More gunshots rang out and I doubled my speed as I charged towards the far end of the tunnel.

"We've got 'em on the run!" a biter hollered behind me and raucous laughter followed his words as the group sped after us.

Adrenaline surged through my veins as I raced on, my legs trembling with the effort of moving me ever faster. My slayer gifts made me really damn fast but there was no way I could outrun a horde of vampires for long.

"I'm awake - let me down!" Fabian snarled in Magnar's arms and I almost tripped over him as Magnar let him fall to the floor.

Fabian regained his feet almost instantly, hissing his disapproval as he took up position at the rear of our group. I wondered why he didn't just run on ahead of me and Magnar, then realised he was using his immortal body to shield me from harm.

"I'm glad you're okay," I panted.

"There are certainly better ways to die than to be crushed beneath a slayer's ass," Fabian growled and I couldn't help but laugh.

Magnar chuckled darkly, catching my hand as he propelled me to move faster.

I ran flat out but Chickoa outpaced me easily, her black hair billowing behind her as she sprinted on ahead.

More gunshots fired behind us and I flinched, imagining them tearing through us just as soon as the biters managed to get a straight shot in our direction.

Every twist in the tunnel gave us an extra reprieve. Each left turn was another few seconds before they could aim at us. Every right was a few more moments that we would remain breathing.

"Here!" Chickoa called urgently and my grip on Magnar's fingers tightened in anticipation of us escaping the infernal tunnel.

Magnar and Fabian kept close to me and my heart pounded unevenly with fear for my sister. I hadn't seen her since all of this had started and I had no idea if she was okay.

We charged on as we approached the end of the tunnel and I flicked the flashlight off. It was one long, straight run to the exit but I could

410

feel the vampires gaining on us with each second. They'd turn that final corner before we'd make it out, I just knew it.

Chickoa threw the door open and my lungs felt fit to burst as we raced towards it.

Gunfire started up behind us and the air was knocked from my lungs as I was propelled through the door by Fabian as he collided with me and Magnar, giving us the final spurt of speed we needed to make it outside.

Chickoa scrambled out of our way and I tumbled aside, wheezing for breath on the straw-covered floor of the stable.

MONTANA

CHAPTER FORTY TWO

Nightmare guided my hand, but I used the skills my friends had taught me just yesterday too. It seemed like a dream now, but my muscles seemed to remember the moves. I cut through a male's heart and ran through his cascading remains as I hunted for Erik.

He was alive. And the biters he was attacking had more to worry about than he did.

I turned away from him, facing down my next opponent. I felt strong, powerful, impossibly able to take on this group of psychos.

I lunged sideways to avoid the slash of the female's nails, rolling to the ground and sweeping out her legs just like the slayers and vampires had taught me. She tumbled across the grass and I launched myself on top of her with a wolfish snarl.

End her, Nightmare urged and I gave the blade what it wanted, finishing the girl with a sharp stab.

Miles and Warren joined the fight, crying out their rage as they tore guns from the hands of lessers and turned them back on them. In seconds, the remaining five biters were overwhelmed, their bodies guided away on the wind.

I glanced over at Erik then turned to search the yard, the fields, desperate to find Callie.

Where is she?

We ran toward the armoured truck as a unit and I tossed Erik the keys as we slowed to a halt in front of it.

"Get in," Erik ordered everyone. "It's fitted with high-powered weapons, we can take out any biters who come for us from inside."

Clarice, Julius, Warren and Miles clambered into the back and I got into the passenger's seat beside Erik. A loud clunking noise sounded the truck locking and I sucked in a breath, resting my head back against the seat and soaking in the small moment of calm.

"Did anyone see Callie?" I asked, turning to face the others in the back as my anxiety found me again.

They all shook their heads and Erik reached across the space parting us, laying a hand on my knee. "She's probably with Magnar. She'll be fine," he said and I nodded, but the knot in my chest didn't unfurl.

"Sound the horn, the others might hear it and come running," Miles called from the back.

"Is that a good idea?" Clarice hissed. "We don't know how many biters are out there."

"This baby can handle it," Warren said, knocking his knuckles on the metal wall beside him. "Titanium alloy with enough firepower to destroy an army."

"I love when you talk truck," Miles purred and tense laughter broke out between us.

I glanced over my shoulder, spying Julius and Clarice side by side, angled away from each other as they worked hard not to touch.

Clarice's eyes suddenly lit up and she snatched a phone out of her jeans' pocket. "I can call Fabian!"

"By the gods, Clarice," Erik growled. "Do it now."

She dialled a number, holding the phone to her ear. It rang on and on and finally, I heard Fabian's voice down the line.

"Hey, you alright? Did everyone get out?" Fabian asked.

"Yes, we're all alive." Clarice listed off our names. "Who's with you?"

"Callie, Magnar and Chickoa," he answered and the tension ran out

414

of my body. Erik gave me a comforting smile and I had the urge to crawl into his lap and die of relief in his arms.

"That's everyone," Clarice sighed. "Where are you? We made it to one of the trucks. Can we come pick you up?"

Fabian murmured something I couldn't hear then replied, "Chickoa said there's no road out here. We're at the stables. We'll come to you."

"Okay, be careful," Clarice breathed then hung up.

A loud bang made me jump and I turned to find a biter on the windshield with a rock in his hand. He smashed it against the window with a feral snarl.

"I'm coming in," he said in an eerie tone.

"No you're not." Julius lunged forward between Erik and I, jamming his hand against buttons on the screen embedded in the dashboard.

Erik shoved him, trying to push his hands away. "Stop it, you don't know what you're doing."

The wipers turned on and the biter's face was swatted with them.

"There's another one here!" Miles yelled as a biter slammed into the side door, trying to wrench it open.

"I have the gift of technology," Julius insisted, tapping on the screen, his elbow nearly catching me in the face.

"I can manage," Erik snapped, trying to push him aside again and a gun started firing randomly at the back of the truck.

"We need the front guns," Julius muttered then a huge bang sounded as the truck fired some sort of missile into a tree and it exploded.

"Julius!" Erik barked, trying to wrestle him back.

"Aha!" Julius announced triumphantly, slamming his palm down on the screen. The truck nearly left the ground as another missile fired over the head over the vampire on the windscreen. I gasped as I spotted it taking out a group of biters running down the road.

"Oops, not that one," Julius muttered. "But that was a lucky shot, right?"

The vampire on the windshield snarled, bashing his rock on the glass again.

"For fuck's sake." Erik forced Julius into the back of the truck then tapped several buttons on the screen. A mechanical noise sounded and the biter looked up as a gun bent down from the top of the windshield.

"Oh f-" the biter's head exploded and his body swiftly followed as bullets threw the remains of him from the hood and turned him into a cloud of ash. Julius flicked on the wipers to clear the last of it away, sniggering at the sight.

Erik fired more shots from the guns and the other biters trying to get in were destroyed under the onslaught.

Silence rang out and I uncurled my clenched fist.

I ran my thumb over Nightmare's hilt, letting its reassuring vibes roll through me.

I turned to gaze out of the windows, hoping to spot Callie running toward us but all was still.

A clunking noise sounded as the doors unlocked and I turned to Erik in alarm. "Why did you unlock it?"

"I didn't." He jammed his thumb on a button but the locks didn't respond. "Shit."

"What's wrong with it?" Julius called.

"I don't know," Erik said anxiously, pressing the button again to no avail.

"There's no biters close at least," Warren said with a note of relief in his voice.

A heavy presence washed over me and fear stung my heart as I sensed a deity drawing near.

"Oh fuck," Erik gasped, gazing left and right beyond the truck as he sensed it too. "We're outside the boundaries of the ring's power."

"Drive the truck! Get closer to Callie!" Julius demanded.

Erik turned the key in the ignition but the engine didn't start. All four doors burst open and I felt the grip of Idun pulling my arm. With a jolt of fear, I was hauled from the vehicle, tossed into the dirt. Julius and Clarice were thrown out too and I heard the others hit the ground on the far side of the truck.

I sprang to my feet, but Idun's power dripped through me and I winced as she held my limbs in place. I spotted Erik over the hood of the truck, rigid as he fell under her control too.

Panic crashed through me as my legs started moving of their own accord. Clarice and Julius marched forward ahead of me and we met with Erik, Miles and Warren at the back of the vehicle.

I trembled as my feet guided me to the piles of clothes on the ground which had belonged to the biters. My fingers rooted through them under Idun's will and I gathered up six guns before being forced to face my friends.

"Hand them out, good girl," Idun purred through the air and a shudder seized me. Fear tore through my chest as I strode forward and handed everyone a gun, keeping one for myself.

No, this can't be happening. We have to stop her.

My finger slid onto the trigger and I bit down on my lip as I tried to fight the compulsion taking me hostage.

"No need to struggle," Idun whispered in my ear and her will butted up against mine, forcing me to raise the gun and point it at Erik's heart.

"No," I snarled through my teeth, a tear of rage escaping my eye as it tracked down my cheek.

Erik raised his own gun to point at my chest and I felt a hand push into my back until we stood a foot apart, the barrels of our guns digging into each other's flesh.

I spied Clarice and Julius aiming their own weapons at each other and Miles and Warren promptly did the same.

"What do you want?" Erik snarled, his jaw ticking with his fury at the situation.

The air swirled beside us and Idun stepped out of it, her golden skin gleaming beneath a silvery dress of leaves that was near-transparent. Her feet were bare as she silently approached us, the press of her power pounding through me like blood in my veins.

She ignored Erik, sliding her finger under Julius's chin and angling him to face her. "My slayer, how close you are to killing a Belvedere. You must hunger for her death greatly," she purred but there was a mocking edge to her tone that racked my heart with fear.

"Don't do this," Julius hissed through his teeth. "Take me if you must, but leave Clarice."

Idun's upper lip peeled back and her canines grew to sharp points. "Is this what you desire, traitor? Fangs on the women you covet?"

"No." Julius shook his head, but his brows were pinched together as he battled with some emotion inside him.

"Then you won't mind pulling that trigger," Idun said lightly, her fangs disappearing and her lips pulling into a warm smile. "Go ahead, prove yourself to me, slayer. I have gifted you everything you need to kill vampires and now I lay one at the end of your weapon. Why haven't you fired yet?"

"Julius," Clarice begged as if she feared he was going to shoot her. But he wouldn't. I was certain he wouldn't. Though Idun could force him if she wanted to.

A tense moment passed and Julius made no move to pull the trigger on Clarice. Idun turned sharply away from him and fear blossomed through me as she approached Erik and I instead.

"Lovers in sinful bodies," she whispered, her nose wrinkling. "Montana Ford...where is your twin? She holds a very precious item of mine. A stolen trinket. A ring that doesn't belong in the hands of mortals." She slid her fingers into my hair and as her beautiful, dark eyes locked with mine, I fell under her spell, my mouth moving with the words I didn't want to give. "She's in the stable."

"Well let's hope she comes here soon." She smiled widely then lifted her hand before my chest. Fire burst along my veins like poison coursing through every inch of me. I screamed and screamed, lost to the agony as she drove a thousand needles into me at once.

The attack stopped abruptly and I found myself exactly where I'd been before, still holding the gun to my husband's chest. Erik's face was contorted with abject rage. I could see him struggling with the binds that held him, but it was no good. We were trapped.

I gazed into Erik's eyes, desperate to make a plan, but what could we do? His hand trembled around the gun that pressed to my heart and I wished I could soothe the fear I could sense in him.

Two terrible fates were all I could see ahead of us. One where Callie returned the ring to Idun and she killed us all anyway. And one where Callie didn't get here in time and Idun made us pull our triggers. Either way, I couldn't see a way forward that didn't end up with us dead.

CALLIE

CHAPTER FORTY THREE

Chickoa leapt between us, pulling a grenade from her pocket and hurling it into the passageway just as the gunfire started up. She screamed as bullets tore through her and Fabian ran forward, knocking her aside before a bullet could find her heart.

Magnar kicked the heavy, metal door shut and a mighty blast exploded through the tunnel beyond. Fabian's phone was ringing and ringing but he ignored it as he held Chickoa's unmoving body in his arms.

I rolled upright, my heart pounding as I tried to catch my breath. I gripped Fury's hilt, reaching out to sense for any vampires close by and relief spilled through me as I failed to locate any besides Fabian and Chickoa. The grenade had ended them all.

Chickoa took a shuddering breath, her eyes snapping open as she came around, healing from her wounds. She stared up at Fabian for half a heartbeat in confusion then shoved out of his arms, hissing angrily.

Fabian's face dropped and he pulled the cellphone from his pocket, finally answering it.

Magnar offered me his hand and I let him pull me up as Fabian had a brief conversation with Clarice.

I moved closer to Fabian, trying to listen in, and sighed with relief as I heard her confirming that everyone else was with her at the truck.

"Sounds like we might have dealt with all of them for now," Fabian muttered as he ended the call and replaced the phone in his pocket. "Let's go and meet the others before reinforcements arrive."

I allowed myself a smile and headed after Chickoa as she moved through the stables.

"I've never been so relieved that my horses are all out to pasture," she muttered as we moved between the empty stalls towards the exit.

The moon hung in the starlit sky outside and the faintest hint of blue lit the horizon as the sunrise approached.

I could just make out the truck on the far side of the valley where all of our friends waiting for us. A desperate need to reunite with my sister spilled through me at the sight.

We started to run for it but I stumbled, cursing as a heavy presence washed over me. I stumbled to a halt as the ring's power flared and I drove my will into it, struggling as the deity searched for us.

Magnar caught my arm, tugging on my chin to make me look at him as I struggled for breath. The ring drew on my own strength as the powerful entity threw all of their efforts into finding us.

"Stay close," I gasped and Fabian and Chickoa moved nearer to me with fearful looks in their eyes.

"Who is it?" Magnar asked, his gaze filled with fury as the gods tried to involve themselves in our lives once more.

"I don't know," I breathed.

I gritted my teeth, slamming every ounce of my strength into the ring until I forced the deity back. The writhing power was pushed away and I sucked in a breath as I sagged against Magnar.

Tinkling laughter floated across the valley and I noticed a glimmer of light spiralling away from us towards the truck.

"Idun," Magnar growled and my heart plummeted as I realised where she was going.

Our escape had driven us away from the others and the ring's protection no longer covered them.

"Montana!" I cried, tearing out of Magnar's hold and racing down into the valley.

Fabian swore as I sped away from them and they were forced to chase after me or be left vulnerable too.

The sloping hill leant me extra speed as I tore back towards the farm house which was beginning to burn in the centre of the valley.

My boots splashed through the stream and freezing water sprayed over my legs. I waded through it, the water climbing to my thighs before I clambered back out the other side again.

We raced between a flock of startled sheep who wheeled away from us in terror, bleating their objections to our passage as we started up the other side of the valley towards the farmhouse.

"Wait!" Magnar called but I couldn't slow. My sister was out there and Idun was well ahead of us already. I felt his fingers brushing against my elbow as he attempted to grab me and I wrenched my arm away as I upped my speed.

"Stop her," Magnar snarled and a rush of footsteps came for me just before I was tackled to the ground.

Fabian flipped me over beneath him, catching my arms and pinning them above my head. I tried to knee him in the balls and he grunted, forcing his leg between my thighs so that he could keep me in place.

"Get off," I growled. "I have to help them!"

"It's too late," he replied darkly and my heart plummeted in defiance of his words though I knew the truth of them.

"Let her up," Magnar said firmly and I looked beyond Fabian as he moved to stand over us.

Fabian grunted before heaving me to my feet but he kept my wrists locked in his grasp.

"We have to be smart about this," Magnar breathed.

"How?" I asked desperately. The fight went out of me and Fabian slowly let me go.

Magnar beckoned us forward and we followed him towards the house.

Chickoa's eyes glimmered with emotion as more smoke spiralled from the windows on the far side of it and a few hungry flames began to lick along the wooden beams.

Fabian gazed at her for a moment then shot away from us. I gasped as he moved beyond the safety I could offer with the ring but Magnar caught my arm to stop me from following.

"What the hell is he doing?" I hissed.

"Probably saving his own ass," Chickoa replied in disgust as Fabian wheeled around the side of the house and out of sight.

"Whatever it is, we don't have time for it," Magnar growled as he moved along the wall of the farmhouse, heading for the far end so that he could look out.

Fabian shot back towards us. His clothes were singed and his face was smeared with soot but he held something firmly in his hand.

"Sorry," he muttered, passing the picture frame to Chickoa and I spied the wedding photo which had been sitting on the shelf in her front room.

Chickoa opened her mouth, seeming at a loss for words. But before she could say anything, Magnar cursed and snared my attention again.

His back was to the wall at the end of the house as he peered up towards the drive. I slipped under his arm so that I could look as well and my heart leapt in horror at the sight before me.

My sister and all of our friends stood in a line before the truck, their eyes lit with fear as each of them held a weapon trained on each other's hearts.

As my eyes widened in terror, Idun slipped out of the wind and looked down into the valley.

She was clothed in rustling silver leaves which swirled about her flesh in a tumbling breeze, revealing her nudity and concealing it again endlessly.

"I want that ring!" she called and her voice echoed throughout the valley, making my bones vibrate with the force of her desire. "And if I don't hold it in my hand within the next five minutes, your friends will start killing each other!"

My heartbeat thundered in my ears and panic washed through me as I turned to Magnar desperately.

"We have to give it to her," I said, not caring that it would give her power over us again or that it would stop us from ending the curse. The

424

only thing I could think about was my sister standing up on that hill with Erik's pistol aimed at her heart.

"Wait," Magnar said, catching my arm and pulling me back behind the house. "I have another idea."

"What is it?" I hissed. Time was running out and I couldn't see how we could possibly do anything other than bow to Idun's demands.

"We're going to need your husband's wedding ring," Magnar said fiercely and I turned to look at Fabian in surprise.

He glanced down at the band of platinum which he hadn't taken off since I'd placed it on his finger at our wedding.

"Why?" Fabian asked reluctantly and the glimmer in Magnar's eyes made me dare to hope.

MONTANA

CHAPTER FORTY FOUR

"I love you," I whispered to Erik and his brow furrowed heavily. "Don't do that," he growled. "Don't give up."

"I'm not, but...just in case," I breathed and a tear rolled down my cheek, dripping uselessly to the ground and soaking into the dry earth.

"No one needs to die today," Idun said, moving closer, her bare feet seeming to glide across the ground. She brushed away another tear on my cheek and I tried to recoil, but my body was fused in place. "If your sister gives me the ring, you can all go back to your pathetic little lives."

I didn't trust the word of this beast. She'd done nothing but manipulate us since I'd learned of her existence. And probably long before then too.

I glowered at her, mustering my strength as I felt my finger curling tighter around the trigger. "You're taking away our one chance at breaking the curse. Andvari needs the ring to pay his debt. Don't you want the vampires gone? Isn't that why you created the slayers?" I demanded.

She tilted her head and her golden hair slid over her shoulder like a living stream. "What could a mortal mind ever do with such information?" she tittered.

"At least tell us," Julius called. "We're dying for some entertainment here, baby."

Idun's endlessly dark eyes swung to Julius and a smile crept onto her face which was so hauntingly beautiful I couldn't stop staring at it. "The ring can hide gods from other gods too. And it also allows passage into the holy mountain."

"You want the treasure," Erik snarled in realisation.

"Yes," she breathed and warm air gusted around us, carrying the feeling of her joy at the idea. "The treasure is much more than gold, Erik Belvedere. And with it and the ring, I will rule the entire world."

"Odin won't be too happy about that," Warren said, his arms tensing as he strained against his grip on the gun pointed at Miles.

"Even Odin won't be able to defeat me once I have the gods' treasures." Idun smiled wider, her gaze wheeling to the valley. "Two minutes left, then we start pulling triggers. Let's hope Callie Ford isn't late." She grazed her fingers over my hand and slid her palm along the barrel of my gun onto Erik's chest. Hatred spewed through me as she caressed him. "He won't be so pretty when he's turned to dust, Montana. Your sister will be responsible for your husband's demise. How terrible it will be."

Fear clawed at my heart, but I made sure none of it spilled into my expression. "I know exactly who's responsible for all of this," I hissed, and her eyes flashed with a raging storm, more powerful than anything ever conjured by Valentina. "And if you take Erik from me, I won't go out of this world without taking you with me."

"An idle threat," she said as her features twisted into amusement.

Idun turned away from me and her hair whipped across my face, burning my flesh where it touched. I hissed, trying to jerk backwards, but I was rooted in place.

Erik frowned at me, looking so desperate that I longed to tell him it would be okay. But how could it be? We were caught in a trap so powerful the only way out of it was Callie giving up that ring.

Idun sighed as she approached Warren and Miles, gazing between them. "How long have you two loved each other?"

Warren clamped his lips together but Idun drew the answer from his tongue as she curled her fingers into a fist, her power resounding through the air like the beating of wings.

"Three hundred and seventy-three years," he croaked, his eyes straying to Miles with a fierce love in his gaze.

My heart twitched as I saw how deeply devoted they were to each other.

"I've adored every day," Miles breathed, and fear scraped through my chest as I sensed he was saying goodbye. "I remember the first day I saw you, working in the fields of some old asshole's plantation. I thought, I wanna give that man a real life."

"You did," Warren whispered, his brows drawing together as he gazed at his husband with emotion pouring from his eyes. "Every day was more beautiful than the last."

"Two minutes," Idun purred, running her hand down Miles's arm.

"I've loved you every moment of every hour we have spent together," Miles said with a sad smile.

"I'll love you all the days after this. Wherever you go, I will be there," Warren said, his voice cracking.

"Well you've had many lifetimes together. And I always was impatient," Idun said with a deadly smile.

She raised a hand and my heart splintered and cracked with terror.

Erik roared and Clarice screamed, the noise nothing in comparison to the sound of two bullets exploding from the barrels of Miles and Warren's guns.

The weapons fell, their fingers brushing for an eternal moment before they turned to dust, their remains coiling together in one final embrace.

"No!" Erik bellowed, his face contorted in agony.

The earth stopped turning. My ears rang. My mind couldn't process what I'd just witnessed.

Idun started laughing and hatred spewed through my veins like venom.

They were gone. Dead. Cast to the wind. Their bodies scattered around us on a fierce breeze.

I released a guttural sob as tears poured from my eyes. The world was falling to ruin around us. Erik's agony at their loss cut into me, and I bore the weight of it too.

Clarice's screams were all I could hear as I closed my eyes and prayed to Odin with all my heart, with everything I had left, that he would help us.

MAGNAR

CHAPTER FORTY FIVE

Callie and the others raced up the hill ahead of me and I gripped my blades tightly as the girl I loved moved to stand before the goddess who was determined to rip us apart.

I concentrated on the power of the ring she'd given me, wrapping it around her securely until the moment I had to pull it back.

Idun was pacing back and forth before the line of our allies as their eyes widened upon seeing us approaching. They were locked in place but unlike the goddess, they could see us.

Julius's eyes burned with fear and he glared at me, trying to warn me away from here despite the fact that Clarice held a gun to his chest.

I gave him the barest hint of a smile, reassuring him as best I could given our predicament. I'd never imagined that I'd mourn the loss of a Belvedere but what Idun had just done was beyond cruel. I could see the haunted look in Erik and Clarice's eyes and I would do everything in my power to save my own brother from that fate.

Fabian's cries of horror had hardened into a desperate desire for revenge and I knew that only his faith in our plan was stopping him from leaping at the deity himself.

Callie looked over her shoulder at me one last time as she prepared to remove Fabian's wedding ring from her finger.

"I'm here!" she called loudly as she pulled it off.

Idun's gaze snapped around as I withdrew the protection the ring offered and revealed her presence.

Idun's eyes widened with lust as she trailed her gaze across Callie, Fabian and Chickoa, noticing them for the first time though they stood right before her. The goddess stepped towards Callie hungrily, reaching out to take the decoy ring as the leaves which formed her dress spiralled around her in a storm of her own desire.

Callie moved the ring close to her finger again, warning the goddess back. "Release my friends from your hold," she demanded. "Then you can have it."

"Do you think I am a fool?" Idun asked with a dark laugh which drew black clouds across the sky.

I shifted closer to her, Venom and Tempest held ready as I took each silent step.

The force which surrounded Idun swept over me as I moved within it and it felt as if my very bones were trembling under the influence of so much power. I drew closer still, a wolf stalking its prey, though I feared her teeth were far sharper than mine.

"How do I know you'll release them once you have it?" Callie demanded.

"You'll have to trust me," Idun purred, her gaze fixed on the ring in Callie's hand as if it was the answer to all of her prayers.

"Then swear it," Callie said as the goddess drew closer to her. "Swear that once you have it, you'll leave us be."

"It's so beautiful," Idun sighed, moving towards Callie again. "I never thought it would look so..." Her brow pinched as she suddenly realised she shouldn't be able to see it at all.

I wasn't as close as I'd hoped to be but I leapt forward all the same, releasing a cry of rage as I swung Venom for her head. The goddess twisted aside just before I could land the blow and my blade carved a line across her shoulder instead.

She still couldn't see me but she sure as hell felt that.

Idun screamed and the ground trembled beneath me as if it felt her pain too and golden blood poured from the wound.

The goddess's power slammed into Callie and she was thrown from her feet, tumbling over the ground then crashing into Fabian and Chickoa.

"Magnar!" Idun bellowed, realising what we'd done. Her gaze flickered around as she hunted for me but the true ring still hid me from her detection.

I ground my teeth, leaping at her again as lightning flared from the sky. Another wave of power slammed out from her and Julius and all the others were thrown back too, but she couldn't touch me. I felt the energy of her attack washing around me like a tide breaking on the prow of a ship.

Callie and the others were on their feet again, running to help me bring down this monster but she drove them back as easily as breathing. I was the only one she couldn't see coming and who couldn't be touched by her power.

I threw my will into the ring, sweeping its protection out in a wide arc and hiding all of my allies, releasing them from her hold before she could hurt them or use them against me. Her mouth parted in horror as she lost sight of them, finding herself facing eight invisible enemies.

Idun turned sharply, trying to disappear into the ether but she stumbled, her power failing her as a rumbling laugh filled the heavens and the sound of two great blades colliding set the air vibrating all around us.

"I think it's time you faced your creations, Idun." Odin's voice spilled through the sky, making the hairs rise along the back of my neck.

Idun spewed curses at the king of the gods as he stopped her from leaving this place, fear filling her beautiful eyes as she turned back and forth, searching for us. She couldn't see us anymore with the ring concealing our presence, though she knew we were all coming.

I grinned savagely as I ran for her again and she shrieked in pained outrage at my betrayal. But I didn't care. She had betrayed me first. I'd dedicated my life to this goddess and her cause only to be rewarded with pain and misery, to be used as a pawn in her sick games. But no more. The ring shielded me from her and I was determined to end her

435

reign of terror once and for all.

I twisted behind her, slicing Tempest across her thigh and she screamed in agony, making the valley tremble, reaching for me but missing by inches.

I was a ghost. The ring hid me and she couldn't see me coming.

She threw the leaves from her dress out in every direction at once and I ducked low, using my swords to shield me as they cut my exposed skin like razor blades. My arms were torn and bloody but I avoided the worst of the blows as my blades deflected them.

As the maelstrom dropped away, I spun to look for Callie, finding her safe, shielded behind Fabian and Chickoa while their own injuries slowly healed. The others were closing in again too from the top of the hill and before long we would have her surrounded.

Idun was left naked and bleeding golden blood before me, each drop sizzling as it hit the dirt by her bare feet, the goddess facing away down the hill as she braced for the next attack.

I sprinted at her, noticing my comrades doing the same in my periphery. Clarice was screaming for vengeance and Erik ran alongside my brother with matching snarls of rage filling their features.

Idun slammed her hands to the dirt, digging her fingers into it as her power flooded through the land. The ground beneath my feet turned to thick mud which sucked and pulled at me, halting my advance. The hands of the dead reached up to grab at my limbs and I slashed through them, hacking and cutting as they fought to drag me down to join them.

Montana screamed as one of the dead and blackened hands tore her down into the earth and Erik grabbed her arms, heaving her backwards as she sank in up to her hips.

I hurled Tempest at the goddess and the blade sliced across her cheek as she lurched away from it. But the moment her hands left the soil, the ground returned to normal and I raced forwards, aiming for her neck with Venom held ready.

My father's blade was overdue a bath in the blood of one of the gods who had caused his death. And Venom would drink well tonight.

ERIK

CHAPTER FORTY SIX

I pulled Montana to her feet as the withered hands retracted from the soil. Revenge burned through me like a wildfire; it devoured me from the inside out.

Idun had taken my brother from this world, his husband too. Their love was pure and abhorrence coursed through me that they had been robbed of their lives for no other reason than power.

I ground my teeth, tearing away from my wife toward the deity who'd taken them from me. From each other.

The world faded to black as my gaze trained on her.

I grabbed hold of her throat, rearing forward and sinking my fangs into the flesh of her neck. It was like biting through bark and her blood tasted as vile as acid. I ripped and tore her flesh apart, desperate to finish her as I swallowed mouthfuls of her disgusting life force. She wheeled around in my arms with a shriek as her golden blood coated me. She was so strong I had to let go, but nothing matched my rage as I came at her again.

For Miles, for Warren, I will destroy you.

I darted forward as she retreated, sensing Magnar closing in on my right, wielding his huge swords. I kicked her in the spine, forcing her towards him, but it wasn't like fighting anything that walked on earth. She spun through the air on a rolling wind, avoiding his ferocious strikes by sheer luck.

Callie darted forward to stab her with her blade, but Idun kept moving in a blur of motion to avoid any attack that came her way. Adrenaline tangled with the desperation in my veins. I couldn't leave this place without Idun's body destroyed for good. No one hurt my family and got away with it.

Clarice joined the battle, miraculously catching Idun's hair in her grip but it turned to liquid in her hand and my sister hissed as the touch of it scalded her.

The ground quaked beneath my feet, so violently that chunks of stone burst up from the soil, making me stumble as I tried to close in on the goddess again.

Idun wailed her anger and the ground split apart, a great fissure opening between us and her. Clarice took a running leap, catching the ledge on the far side and trying to clamber up. Idun sent another violent tremor through the ground and my sister screamed as she almost lost her grip.

Panic spilled through me and I backed up to take a running jump toward her, but a shadow flew past me and I spotted Julius landing on the other side of the ravine. He caught Clarice's hand but the chasm started closing and the earth shook so much that he was forced to his knees. As the gap continued to close and threatened to crush my sister to death, I sprinted across the ground, my eyes locked on Idun as a snarl peeled back my upper lip.

Julius yanked Clarice out of the hole just as it shut and she fell against him as she righted herself, her body trembling in his arms.

Callie darted forward, her eyes locked on Idun who continued to retreat, her gaze flipping left and right as she tried to spot her invisible assailants. The goddess's hands raised and a golden vine shot out from her palms in two thorny whips. Someone tackled me and I hit the floor before the smoke could touch me, finding Montana above me.

Her cheeks were stained with tears, but her jaw was set in anger. She'd saved me from Idun's wrath and a swell of love filled my heart for my wife.

One of the vines hit Clarice and Julius and they yelled in pain as the gold tendril coiled around them, crushing them in its grip. Callie was caught too, but Magnar ripped her from the ethereal vine, falling to the ground with her to avoid another whip of the vicious weapons. Idun slashed them blindly at us and that was our only advantage.

Fabian released a battle cry, diving at Idun and catching hold of her arm. He wrenched with all his might, but she tugged it free and backhanded him, sending him tumbling over the earth with a hundred cracks as his bones broke. The vines rippled out of existence and Clarice and Julius crashed to the ground, nursing their wounds before gaining their feet again.

Chickoa fired her shotgun over and over, but she realised her mistake as Idun cast the pellets back at her. She hit the ground in a pool of blood, disabled and groaning in agony.

Magnar and Callie ran at the deity from separate sides and I charged forward to help, hearing Montana taking chase after me.

With the taste of Idun's blood in my mouth, energy pounced into my veins. I'd drink every drop before this fight was done.

CALLIE

CHAPTER FORTY SEVEN

My heart lurched with horror and pain at what had happened. Clarice was screaming. Fabian was bellowing his rage to the sky and Erik was fighting like a demon released from the gates of hell. The four Belvederes had been together for over a thousand years. I couldn't even begin to imagine the agony they were feeling after the scattered remains of their brother and his husband had swept across the valley and into the sky.

My own chest felt like it was caving in two. Grief slammed into me like a wrecking ball, but I had no time to feel it as the fight raged around us.

Idun started running, her bare feet pounding into the ground with such force that the whole hill trembled beneath my boots.

Each step she took was marked by a shimmering footprint and as my attention snared on them, bright green vines burst from the ground. Her path carved a line between our group. Fabian, Chickoa and I were cut off from the rest of our friends by the vines which whipped towards us like a horde of angry snakes.

I backed up quickly, my heart pounding with fear at the thought of what those vines would do if they managed to make contact with us.

Julius had made it to Magnar's side and the two of them charged forward with their swords raised to intercept the goddess as she tried to flee.

The vines spread across the soil, gaining speed as they shot straight towards us. It was almost as if they could see us and I knew without doubt that I didn't want them getting anywhere near me. They kept coming, writhing like worms as they sought us out and I stumbled back as one of them shot towards my legs.

I sliced Fury into the vine before it could make contact, cutting it in two. But the severed pieces just split again, creating more of the demonic plant which moved towards me even faster.

I gasped as I leapt over one vine, then threw myself beneath another.

Idun screamed in pain and I turned toward the sound, my heart lifting with hope as golden blood flew and Julius bellowed victoriously. Magnar was several paces behind him, scrambling to avoid huge holes in the ground which were appearing all around him.

Idun kicked out, aiming for the place where the attack on her had come from and Julius wasn't quick enough to move aside. Her foot collided with his chest and she sent him flying away from her.

He tumbled through the air, slamming to the ground halfway down the valley and crashing to the floor with enough force to carve a crater into the earth.

Magnar roared a challenge as his brother failed to rise and my heart thundered with panic.

We can't do this. How could we have thought that we could? Who were we to try and stand against a deity?

I shook my head against the negative thoughts, banishing them with the memories of all that Idun had done to us. She'd murdered Miles and Warren. She needed to pay. And it was time she did.

My moment of inaction cost me and I screamed as I was yanked off of my feet by one of the vines.

It snaked up my leg, tightening painfully as it moved further along my body like it had a mind of its own.

I hacked at it, severing golden tendrils again and again with the force of my blade. Each piece I cut split in two and grew twice as fast

444

but the grip it had on me was loosening.

Fury hissed encouragements through my mind, screaming at me to keep fighting no matter what. The blade seemed more desperate to taste Idun's blood than I had ever known it to feel for a vampire.

Feed me her heart!

I could hear Magnar bellowing a battle cry and Idun screaming, but I couldn't look up to see what was happening.

I cut again and again, kicking at the grasping vines until finally, I was free of them. I scrambled upright, panting my relief as I turned and fled, racing towards my sister and away from the demonic flora.

Fabian and Chickoa were caught in its grasp too and I hesitated as I spotted them trying to fight their way free of it.

"Just kill that bitch!" Fabian snarled as he noticed my hesitation. He didn't want me to help him - he wanted me to go after Idun.

I nodded, continuing my desperate bid to reach Montana. If I could just get to her and the others then maybe we could work together to bring that malicious deity down for good. It was time that Idun learned the price of playing with our lives.

ERIK

CHAPTER FORTY EIGHT

Vines seized my arms and I battled to get up as I fought against their painful grip. I spotted Magnar swinging his sword viciously at those holding his legs and he managed to break free. Beside me, Montana used her fangs to escape those holding her down and I mimicked her, lifting the vine around my arm and ripping through it with my canines. Another immediately snared my leg and I shouted my fury as I struggled to tear every one of them from my body.

Idun's laughter rang through the air and the vines fell to the ground around us, coiling up into tight balls and shifting into golden snakes instead. I sprang to my feet, snatching Montana's arm in the brief seconds we had to escape, pulling her up beside me.

We started kicking and crushing the skulls of every viper that got near. Their tongues flicked out as their heads lunged towards us. A snake bit into Montana's leg and she screamed in agony. I dragged her closer, killing the snake who'd bitten her with a harsh stamp of my heel.

"Erik, kill her," she murmured, then her eyes turned blank and she fell limp in my arms. I gasped, kicking out at the tide of snakes which tried to get their fangs in me too, stamping and stamping as I retreated.

I lifted Montana into my arms to keep her out of their way, leaping over a group of them and charging away from the battle to lay her in the grass a hundred feet from the fight. My heart clenched as I gazed at her still form. But she was safe here and I couldn't leave the others to battle Idun alone. I squeezed her fingers, my throat tight with emotion.

"I'll come back." I turned and sped away into the battle with my heart tearing in half. I needed to protect her with every ounce of my being, but the only way I could do that was by bringing this bitch to her knees.

Callie, Magnar and Clarice were the only ones still standing and I sprinted toward my sister as four snakes struck at her at once. She kicked them, desperate to keep them away, but before I reached her, their fangs found her skin and she collapsed to the ground. I crushed the creatures beneath my heel with a grunt of anger. When I'd killed them all, I tugged Clarice away from the mass writhing toward us, laying her down and stepping in front of her, ready to take on the vipers.

They surged toward me like a tide, so many of them that I knew it was only a matter of time before I got bitten. As the first one reached me, I smashed my foot down on its skull.

A scream caught my attention and my eyes whipped to Callie several paces away. Three vipers bit into her leg at once and she tumbled to the ground unconscious. The snakes moved away and I noticed the fallen were safe from more attacks. Idun was taking us out of the fight one by one.

My gut knotted as I realised how close we were to losing. We could die here. But it couldn't end like this. Not after everything we'd been through. After all that had been taken from us.

Magnar yelled in anger as he cut the snakes to ribbons at his feet. As he killed those surrounding him, he set his sights on Idun and sprinted forward, swinging his sword in a fierce arc as he finally closed the space between them.

My heart lifted as his sword hit its mark and Idun's stomach ripped open. She wailed and the heavens boomed with thunder as she stumbled back. Gold blood poured from the wound, but I could tell it was beginning to heal already. She whipped her hand through the air and struck Magnar by chance. He slammed into the ground and fear

448

coursed through my veins.

Magnar rose to his feet as Idun's wound started to heal, but the injury had cost her sorely. The snakes dissolved to nothing, giving me a clear path to the goddess.

I started running, eating up the ground parting us with my fangs bared. Holes opened up in the dirt and I leapt over them, determined not to fall as Idun regained enough strength to wield her powers once more.

My foot caught in a fissure and I stumbled, my knees crashing into the ground. I swore, leaping up again and powering on, my body filled with the need for revenge. My brother and his husband were gone because of this beast. Everything that had ever happened to us came down to her and Andvari. But the other god wasn't here. She was alone. And she was now my prey. The next victim of the vampire curse.

Her immortal fruit had led us here, and she was going to find out what it felt like to fall victim to her own powers. My fangs would bury deep into her throat before I tore her body apart. I'd destroy every inch of her perfect flesh just like she'd done to my brother and Warren.

My eyes locked with Magnar's as he tried to get close again and a silent promise passed between us.

We'd kill this goddess. Come hell or high water. And we would fucking well do it together.

The ground ripped apart at Magnar's feet and I released a shout of fear as he teetered on the edge of it, about to fall into the dark abyss opening up behind him.

"Magnar!" I yelled, pushing my legs to their limits in a desperate bid to reach him.

MAGNAR

CHAPTER FORTY NINE

I stumbled back, my boot slipping on the top of the crevice Idun had carved into the hill. The rocks at the edge of it crumbled beneath me and I cried out as I fell.

I slammed Venom into the ground as I tipped over the edge of the hole and grunted with the effort it took to cling onto the blade as my weight hung suspended beneath it.

My boots scrambled against the crumbling earth and I glanced down at the unending chasm below. If I fell, there would be no coming back from it. No vengeance for my father. No death for this deity who toyed with our souls. No life with the woman I loved.

I snarled as I heaved myself higher and my blade juddered as its purchase in the soil started to give way.

My heart crashed into my throat as the sword slipped again and I released my left hand from it, clawing at the soil in a desperate attempt to pull myself up before it gave way.

My heart shuddered with realisation as Venom split through the soil. My hands flailed, my gut soared. The chasm was going to swallow me whole and everything I'd ever hoped for would be lost.

A hand grasped mine and I grabbed hold of it with a harsh breath, my life hanging in their arms.

My blade swung uselessly at my side as I gripped my saviour's hand with a savage determination to survive. Erik hoisted me skyward and I managed to hook my leg over the edge of the fissure as he dragged me back onto solid ground.

"Let's end this," Erik snarled as he yanked me to my feet and I could see the grief of his loss deep within his eyes.

I scanned the battlefield anxiously. We were the last two standing against the goddess and somehow that felt right. Like it always should have been that way.

"Let her see me," Erik said, tightening his grip on my hand. "I'll draw her to you."

"And I'll gut her," I growled in agreement before releasing him.

Erik nodded determinedly and he turned from me, running towards Idun as I pulled the ring's protection away from him.

Idun shrieked triumphantly as she spotted him and a line of fire burst from the ground beneath his feet. Erik leapt away, catching a rock in his grasp and hurling it at her with his inhuman strength.

I lifted Venom high and sprinted towards her, dodging the fire which flared close enough to harm me.

Flames blossomed again and Erik danced away, turning and running towards me over the destroyed earth as I tightened my grip on Venom between both of my hands, aiming it straight at the deity's heart.

Idun snarled, her lip curling back to reveal a row of sharpened teeth as she sprinted after Erik. Predator turned prey. She was charging straight towards my blade and she had no idea of the death which raced to meet her.

She caught him just before he reached me, her hand closing around the back of his neck before she lifted him clean off of his feet and hurled him into the air.

A sharpened spear appeared in her hand and she rotated her arm back as he fell towards the ground again, ready to impale him and destroy his undead heart. I ground my teeth in fierce denial of that act; this Belvedere had become a part of my life in ways that were so convoluted it was hard to align my true feelings for him. But I knew in my heart that his death would pain me now and I had no intention of letting that happen.

I pushed the ring's influence back over Erik before she could take aim and he crashed to the ground, missing the spear as she hurled it in his general direction.

Erik lay unmoving in the dirt and I was left alone to face her, but he'd done what he'd promised and she was well within range of my long sword.

With a bellow of rage, I charged forward, closing the final gap between us and slamming Venom straight through her chest.

Idun's eyes widened with shock and I withdrew the ring's influence from myself so that she could look into my eyes before she died. I wanted her to know who had ended her eternal existence.

Our faces were inches apart, her eyes glowing with the fading embers of her power as the life fled from her body. The world was alive with the pain of this divine being coming to her demise. The air shuddered, the grass rippled in an unnatural breeze, the ground beneath my feet moaned a lament at her loss.

"You swore an oath to me," Idun murmured, her final breaths washing over my face.

"This is me breaking it," I snarled.

"You've broken your vow. Your life is forfeit." Idun's power snared me in its hold one final time as she leaned forward and pressed a kiss to my lips.

I was frozen in place, unable to pull back as her golden blood flowed into my mouth.

My heart thundered in my chest as her lips fell cold and hard against mine. She released a soft sigh and a warm wind shifted around us, pulling her away from me.

Her beautiful flesh slowly dissolved into a host of writhing maggots which tumbled across her bones, feasting on the remains of her soul. The pieces of her broken body crumbled to the ground and the grasping hands of the dead reappeared, claiming each and every part of her, dragging her beneath the soil and removing her immortal existence from the world.

Her power fell to nothing at the moment of her death, but still, I couldn't move.

I dropped to my knees, driving Venom into the ground before me.

Something was crawling beneath my skin, pooling in my blood and burning within my flesh.

My heart slammed against my ribs so hard that it hurt. It was a desperate, pleading thing, thrumming in a hopeless effort to stop whatever poison the goddess had given me.

I lifted my eyes, searching for the face of the woman I loved, aching to see her one last time as a torturous fire simmered through my veins, drawing me closer to death.

I started shaking, tremors raking through my body as my grip on Venom's hilt tightened, and I was fairly certain it was the only thing keeping me upright.

There was movement all around me but I couldn't see anything beyond my hands as they clenched the sword. My slayer's mark burned more fiercely than anything else, the pain driving right down to the bone of my forearm. If I could draw breath, I'd have been screaming from the agony of it.

I was dying. I knew it. I could feel it in the depths of my soul. Something was horribly wrong with my body and the thundering pace of my heart was so loud that I could hear it resounding inside my skull.

"Magnar?"

I dragged my eyes up as Callie dropped to her knees in front of me, her golden hair glinting as the sun crested the hill behind her.

"What's happening to him?" She looked beyond me, behind me, all around as the rest of them drew closer too.

The shaking was getting worse and my heart was racing towards a conclusion which I knew I couldn't avoid.

This was the price of taking a life from the gods. I should have known that doing such a thing could not be done freely. My life to pay for hers.

Idun had told me that I would find love but she'd never intended for me to have it. It had been a fleeting thing, never meant for the likes of me. But whilst it had been mine, I was happy. Truly happy in all the ways I'd ever hoped to be and more. And if this was all I got to have of it then it was more than I'd deserved.

Callie reached out to touch my face but I couldn't feel the brush of her fingers on my skin.

I met her blue eyes and I was glad that they were the last thing that I would see.

Her lips moved. She was saying something. I couldn't hear her anymore. But I could see what it was. I wished I could say it back. Three little words that had changed my whole world and made my life worth living again.

I love you.

And I love you more. More than you could ever know.

My heart pounded.

Once.

Twice.

And then it stopped.

I hung suspended in that moment of my death as my grip on my father's sword loosened and I tipped backwards.

Darkness came for me, swallowing me whole before I even hit the ground.

If I'd known that this was how it was going to end then I wasn't sure if I would have done anything differently. But I knew what I would have done the same.

The pain in my flesh fizzled to nothing. I was empty. Unfeeling. Lost.

I thought of Callie and of the life we should have had together as I drifted away from her. We should have had so much longer. But the gods had been trying to keep us apart from the very beginning. We'd even been born in different ages, destined never to know of the other's existence, let alone find the love we had. And while it had been mine, I had cherished it. So I could part this life knowing I'd made the most of what little we'd had. Even if I still dreamed of taking just a bit more...

"Please don't leave me." Her voice was raw, begging, desperate.

Her tears fell against my skin and they were burning hot.

She pressed her lips to mine and though I couldn't move, I could feel the soft fullness of them unlike I'd ever felt anything before.

Her fingers grazed along my jaw and my skin was alight with the movement in a way that should have made my heart race, but it remained still in my chest.

"Magnar," she begged again and the sound of my name on her lips pulled me back to her. But I wasn't sure I *was* me anymore.

My eyes opened and there she was, her hand on my cheek and her golden hair falling around us like a curtain against the world.

Her eyes were the most stunning shade of blue. But I'd never noticed the darker line around the edge of her irises before. I could see every long eyelash which shone wetly with the tears which pooled amongst them. She blinked at me, inhaling sharply as she saw that I was awake.

"You're alive?" she asked in astonishment and I could tell she knew that I hadn't been.

She kissed me again and my whole body lit with the feeling of her flesh against mine. Every inch of skin sparked and reacted in a way which was at once familiar and totally alien. I ached for her in all the ways I always had and more besides. Her closeness built a clawing desperation in the back of my throat and her scent sailed through me like the promise of my salvation. How had I never noticed the way she smelled before? It was the most delicious temptation of her alluring body and I breathed it in recklessly, longing for more.

I pushed myself up and I moved so quickly I almost knocked her off of me, but I caught her before she could fall. I wasn't going to let her go. She was mine. And I was hers.

She pulled back and her relief turned to concern as she cupped my cheek in her hand and the warmth of her skin almost burned against the chill of my own. A tingling itch crept along my skin as every injury I'd gained in this battle and those I'd held before it knitted over, healing until my flesh was made new once more.

My throat rasped and tightened in a way I had no words for and the most beautiful noise filled my ears. I lifted my hand and placed it above her heart, enraptured by the sound of her pulse reaching me.

Her lips parted but no words came out. My gaze slid down to the soft bobbing of her throat as she swallowed back whatever she'd been going to say. The sun-kissed skin of her neck called to me and I leaned closer, inhaling the most intoxicating scent.

"Holy shit," Erik murmured, wrenching Callie back but she fought to stay with me and I caught her hand to keep her close.

"Get away from him, Callie. He's not safe," Fabian warned and rage built in my veins as they spoke to her that way.

She shifted a little, her eyes widening as they raked over me. Seeing every small change and every similarity. I was the man she loved and I was something else too.

Hands pulled her away and she got to her feet, leaving me beneath her on the floor. I rolled upright so swiftly that I almost beat her to it and all of them shifted back in alarm.

"Callie," Montana breathed fearfully as she gripped her sister's arm. "He's one of *us*."

Callie shrugged out of her hold and approached me again as that delicious scent rolled off of her skin, drawing me closer, building on the ache in the back of my throat. And with a comprehension that hit me like a wave crashing against a cliff, I realised what it was that called to me so forcefully.

The one thing I needed above all else.

What I'd live for.

And die for.

Blood.

AUTHOR NOTE

Well, well, well, what a twisty tale we wander. I think this is actually one of my favourite cliff hangers we have written. Not that I enjoy ruining our characters' lives or making them face their worst nightmares, but come on, Vampy Magnar is a particularly fucked-up little nugget of reality for them. Ah, what sweet torture we weave.

But worry not – this is indeed the final cliff hanger of this series! Book 7 winks at you from the horizon, beckoning you home into its safe embrace with a promise of an ending which will delight and horrify in equal measure.

As always, this series, these words, this crazy reality we live in would all be for nothing if it wasn't for you, our dear readers, and our thanks to you for relishing our words and devouring our frequent doses of heartache are endless. But stick with us, because we won't stop here and we have many more tales of fractured souls and twisted lovers to tell and we want you along for every gut wrenching moment of the ride.

Love, Susanne and Caroline X

WANT MORE?

To find out more, grab yourself some freebies and to join our reader group, scan the QR code below.